ONE FOR
THE ROAD

A Novel

* * *

DAVID J MATHER

A PEACE CORPS WRITERS BOOK

A Peace Corps Writers Book

An imprint of Peace Corps Worldwide

FIRST PEACE CORPS WRITERS EDITION, September 2011

One For The Road.
Coypright © 2011 by David J. Mather

For more information, contact peacecorpsworldwide@gmail.com

ISBN: 1935925059
ISBN-13: 9781935925057

Library of Congress Control Number: 2011940476

TO THE MEMORY OF
DON RAUL CORONADO,
MENTOR AND FRIEND

Acknowledgments

One For The Road is a mix of fact and fiction. The Chilean colony of Cufeo is real, and many of the book's characters are based on its people. However, with the exception of Oso, all names have been changed and many events altered for the sake of the story. There is absolutely no intent to malign anyone—I have only the deepest respect for the small farmers of Cufeo.

My first thank you is to Bruce Burwell, who graciously allowed me to use his nickname Oso and to build on his interesting and entertaining persona. I also chose *The History of Chile* by John L. Rector (one of my Peace Corps Trainers) as a reference from Amazon.com. As a traveler, I have always relied on good guidebooks. Writing *One For The Road* was certainly a journey and several times I referred to both the 1969 *The South American Handbook* and The Lonely Planet's 2006 *Chile y la isla de Pascua*. I also Googled much of my anecdotal information: emedicinehealth.com for info on a collapsed lung, Wikipedia for the *copihue* and for the game of *tejo*, centralconnector.com for the game of *cacho*, the USGS for the Chilean earthquake of 1960, and clemezoo.com and peregrinefund.org for the Andean Condor. I used Claudio Zegers' *Arboles Nativos de Chile* as a tree reference.

A big thank you to members of my tightly-knit Peace Corps group, who answered many questions about Chile when my memory failed. Thanks to Lisa Howell, my stepsister, who expertly explained how to prepare a horse to race. Thanks to Judy Barker, Allie Farrar, Alex Sawyer, and Nini Meyer who read and re-read several versions of this book, and to my copyeditor Jan Williams. Thank you to my friend Jennifer Brown for all the artwork, and a huge thank you to Don Metz for his expertise, advice, and unceasing encouragement.

I would also like to thank both the Montoya and Coronado families of Cufeo, with whom I lived during my two years there. Their input as well as their friendship were invaluable. Finally I would like to thank my wife Lindy, who has wholeheartedly supported me in this and everything else I have ever tried to do.

ONE FOR THE ROAD

Road to Reumen

firewood
clearing

Lote Once

copihue
clearing

don
manuel

don eulogio

La Palo

School
house

Casa Blanca

don
pedro

School
house —

don ramo

gomez

widow
carlota

Central Ca

school
house

don ju
maria

worker
shack

don ricardo

←Valdivia ════════════ Pan American highway

Los Guindo

don luis

don en

La Colonia
de Cufeo

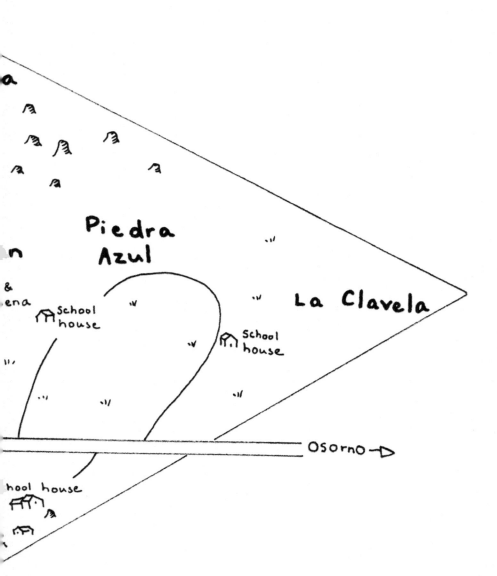

a

Piedra
Azul

n

La Clavela

&
ena

School
house

School
house

hool house

Osorno →

CHAPTER ONE

La Llegada (The Arrival)

"So when do you want to get married?"

"Tomorrow," he answered.

He knew she was smiling even though he couldn't see her face.

"No really, Tomás. When?"

He was leaning back against their stump with Maria Elena sitting between his legs and leaning back against him.

"I know one thing," he said. "I want to get married before winter. There is no way that I am not going to have you in my bed by then keeping me nice and warm."

He slid his hands around her waist. She sighed and shifted her head so they could be cheek to cheek.

"How about mid fall?" she asked. "If the rains do not come early, the weather will be cool but still nice."

"Sounds good to me."

He pulled away from her and fiddled with her braid. They sat there thinking about the wedding.

"But Maria Elena, just what kind of wedding do you want? I mean, in Valdivia in a church or what?"

He dreaded that she might want a big Catholic ceremony. She folded her forearms across her knees and gazed out towards the hills.

"What I would like is a small, private ceremony at the *copihue* clearing. I cannot think of a more beautiful spot. Then I would like to have a very big *asado* here at the farm and invite all our friends to celebrate."

He moved her braid out of the way so he could kiss her neck. He thought, was this girl something or what?

"Perfect. I have to confess that I really did not want a big church wedding."

"Do you think I do not know you, *mi querido*? I know you would have hated that. And I also know you would have done it for me without a word. But you can relax now. I swear you are such a worrier. What about your parents? Do you think they will come all the way down here?"

"I don't know. Even though they can afford it, I have a feeling they might not come. It is such a long way. I have written to them about our engagement and said I would let them know the date as soon as we decided."

He did not tell her that he had received a letter back from his father, who thought he was out of his mind. What was he thinking? Marry a poor uneducated peasant girl who couldn't speak English? And live out in the boondocks of a third-world country without electricity or even indoor plumbing? Had Tom gone nuts!? She must be very good in bed because he was obviously thinking with the wrong part of his body. He hoped that when Tom had his pants back on, he would come to his senses and reconsider.

He tried to clear his mind of the letter.

"What about our honeymoon, Maria Elena? I was thinking of hiring the captain of a fishing boat to take us through the fjords. I have heard that's possible in Puerto Chacabuco and maybe we could go as far as the Glacier San Rafael. But the weather is so unpredictable down there. Maybe we should go to Brazil—it is nice there that time of year."

He loved the Spanish for honeymoon—*luna de miel*—literally 'moon of honey.'

"I don't know Tomás. That is not so important to me now. We have plenty of time to decide."

As they sat there gazing out at the volcanoes, he thought of all the changes in his life—not the least of which was becoming engaged to this beautiful young woman. He vividly recalled when he walked up into these hills with Bob for the first time. Had it really been over two years ago? He laughed and shook his head.

"What is so funny, *mi amor?*"

"Oh, I was just thinking about when I first arrived in Cufeo. My Spanish was so terrible and I was so dumb about everything. And I guess I was scared too."

"I cannot imagine doing what you did. It must have been very difficult. And lonely too."

He nodded. Boy, was that ever the truth. He put his hands behind his head and leaned back against the stump. He looked out again at the volcanoes. They looked just like they did that first day. So much had happened since then—both good and bad. But still, it seemed like only yesterday when he and Bob stepped off that bus.

* * *

The bus let them off at the Los Guindos trailhead and they watched it slowly pull away. It gained speed rapidly as it headed downhill towards checkered farmland with snow-capped volcanoes beyond. It was a clear, fine day and the volcanoes stood out against the deep blue sky.

"It's about an hour's walk from here, Tom," Bob said. "All up hill. Find a good stick because we'll pass close to some farms and the dogs there can be vicious. But if they see you have a stick, they usually won't attack. If you're ever caught without a stick, bend down like you're picking up a stone."

After Tom found a stick and adjusted the shoulder straps of his heavy backpack, Bob led the way up a steep narrow path no better than a goat trail. The packed red clay was slippery from the morning dew and Tom had to hang on to bushes to keep from sliding backwards. He was breathing hard by the time the trail widened and leveled off.

The pair walked in silence and soon came alongside a crude fence of thick wooden slabs sticking out of the ground. The long fence line had settled and the slabs leaned away from each other like crooked teeth in need of braces. Beyond the fence, charred stumps dotted a pasture, and a large silver-gray dog was dozing near a flock of sheep. The dog sprang to his feet barking, and the sheep started running around, bumping into each other. Bob gave the dog a wide berth.

"Dogs guard the sheep here and, believe me, they mean business. They are called *pastor,* like pastor in English."

The path followed the crooked fence and went uphill again. Tom had a hard time keeping up with Bob's long strides. His shoulders began to ache and the sweat ran into his eyes. As he fell behind, he rationalized that Bob wasn't lugging a pack, and that he had been walking these trails for two years.

Bob had just completed his Peace Corps stint in Chile and would be returning to the States. Tom was his replacement. Bob had arranged for him to live with a family up in these hills, and that's where they were headed. Tom wasn't sure what to expect exactly, but he certainly knew it would be a far cry from his home in a well-to-do suburb of Boston. He wished he could speak Spanish better. On a scale of zero to five, his Peace Corps instructors had graded him a one-minus.

He got a second wind and caught up with Bob. They passed a couple of small shacks with even smaller out-buildings. Bob called them farms. Quite a change, Tom thought, from the dairy farms back in New Hampshire where he had graduated from college. Six months ago, when he had told his roommates about wanting to join the Peace Corps, they thought he was just trying to stay out of Vietnam. The truth was, war or no war, he had wanted to join ever since Kennedy and Shriver had gotten things going. What a concept—get paid to travel abroad, live in some exotic place, learn another language, help those not as fortunate, and boost America's reputation for a change. He was gung ho and ready to save the world. Of course, receiving an occupational deferment for being in the Peace Corps was a plus—he certainly didn't want to go to Vietnam—which totally pissed off his father.

His father was a WWII vet and had been shot in the leg during the Battle of the Bulge. The war in Europe had been the most important period of his life and he never let Tom forget it. He said the duty of every young man was to fight for his country—right or wrong. It made a real MAN out of you. They had several arguments about Vietnam and his father would limp heavily around while lecturing him. Tom believed the limp was always worse when he talked about manly duty—he certainly never limped like that on the Country Club golf course. His father accused him of being a draft dodger. Well, in a way, Tom guessed he was. But he didn't agree with the war, and figured he could do a lot more for his country by helping someone rather than shooting at him.

Bob stopped so Tom could rest. He took off his pack, leaned it up against a thick bush, and sat down on a stump. The back of his shirt was soaked with sweat.

"Now in the *campo* the one thing you always have to remember is to show respect," Bob said. "When you address anybody but a child here, always use *usted*—the formal you—rather than the personal *tu*. It's not that way in Valdivia, but it is here. You also always address the men by *Don,* which is like sir, before their first name and you never call the *señoras* by their first name. Address them as Señora."

Bob paced around. He was antsy. After a short while he looked over at Tom.

"All set?"

Tom got up and shouldered his pack. The trail continued uphill. They flushed some green parrots out of a tall tree, and Tom wondered what these birds were doing here in a climate like Seattle's. The trail leveled off again and Bob said they were close. They came to a small wooden gate that swung on hinges made out of pieces of old tire.

"Here we are."

They passed through, and Tom carefully shut the gate and looked at the house he would be living in for the next two years. It wasn't much. The small cape had a patchwork roof of rusty tin sheets that overlapped like a puzzle without a pattern. Jutting through the roof was a skinny stovepipe with white smoke shooting straight up. The wooden siding was weathered-gray, and there was only one window facing them. It was to the left of the plank front door and was missing a pane of glass—a piece of cardboard was tacked in its place.

Five gray and white geese with bright orange beaks, quietly grazing, began honking when they saw them.

Hearing the geese, a brown mongrel dog tore out from underneath the house, barking and showing its teeth. Bob ignored it and kept walking. The dog circled Tom, and Tom didn't dare turn his back. He nervously poked at it with his stick and the dog went crazy. Tom thought it was going to attack.

The door opened and a dark haired, heavy-set man with a thick mustache stepped out. He was followed by a younger, thinner man and a broad woman with a big smile on her face. The first man yelled at the dog and it slunk away.

The men wore patched pants, heavy sweaters, and tall black rubber boots. Both could use a shave. By contrast, the woman was dressed up, wearing leather shoes and a green floral dress. Her hair looked damp and recently combed.

"Tomás," Bob said, "This is Don Emilio Martinez, his son Don Jaime, and, of course, the Señora."

Tom smiled and shook hands all around. His stomach was churning—he wanted so badly to make a good impression. The men followed the Señora into the house and took turns wiping their boots on a flattened cardboard box on the plank floor. The floor was spotless and the Señora was watching them. Tom wiped his boots a second time. They passed through the kitchen, where three young girls stood around a big wood-fired kitchen range. The youngest was dressed in a simple white dress with red polka dots. The other two were in skirts and sweaters and were older—teenagers, he guessed. They were tending large, bubbling pots on the stove and did not look up. It was dim and smoky. A simple wooden table with several chairs around it was in front of the window with the tacked-on cardboard.

Entering a more formal room with two windows and a rear door leading to a garden, the Señora motioned for them to sit at a large table and hurried back to the kitchen. Emilio said something to Tom, but he didn't understand and looked to Bob for help. Emilio addressed Bob as Don Roberto, and they started talking nonstop. It was the first time Tom had heard Bob speak Spanish at length and he was impressed. Bob spoke smoothly and quickly.

In the middle of the table was a round loaf of sliced bread fresh out of the oven. It smelled delicious. The two elder daughters entered carrying steaming bowls of soup. Emilio introduced them—Rosa and Ana. They were very shy. They made only brief eye contact and quickly left the room. The soup was hearty with vegetables and a chunk of lamb in the middle of each bowl. Bob explained in English that the meat was in honor of Tom's arrival, and that to show appreciation, he should eat it only after he had finished the rest of his soup. When Tom ate the lamb, he nodded to Emilio. Bob smiled.

Tom tried hard to understand the Spanish. He could follow some of what Bob said, but when Emilio spoke, he was lost in a heartbeat. The youngest daughter came in to clear the dishes and Emilio introduced her—Lilia. She stared at Tom so much that she nearly walked into a wall on her way back out to the kitchen. But, unlike her sisters, when he thanked her for taking his empty bowl, her face lit up in a smile.

The Señora came in after the meal and sat down next to Tom. She asked if he missed his home. He thought she had asked how he liked her house, so he said it was very beautiful. The Señora looked at him strangely as Bob laughed. When Bob translated, Tom was mortified, but the Señora saw his embarrassment and patted his hand.

As she returned to the kitchen, the men stood up. Emilio pointed to a cot-like couch against the far wall.

"That is your bed, Don Tomás."

The cot looked hard and Tom resisted the urge to go over and sit on it. He thanked Emilio. Emilio beckoned him to come outside. Bob, Emilio, and Tom walked to the corral behind the house. Emilio explained that the sheep were put there every night to protect them from mountain lions and thieves. He showed Tom the outhouse and also a wide wooden shelf nailed to the side of the house, under the shade of a Eucalyptus tree. Emilio walked up and put his hand on it.

"This is the place to wash. We use it now during the good weather. If it storms, then we wash up in the kitchen."

On the shelf was a tin can holding some well-used toothbrushes, a bar of yellow soap on a little plate, a beat-up razor, and a tin wash basin turned upside-down. Emilio demonstrated by gesture that the used water was flung out into the yard. A small hand towel hung on a nail hammered into the edge of the shelf, and two buckets of clear water were underneath.

Emilio pointed down the hill.

"We bring the water up from a spring over there."

Bob looked at his watch and said he should leave if he was going to catch the last bus back to Valdivia. Tom's stomach began to churn again—the cord was about to be cut and he would be on his own.

"Let me tell the Señora," Emilio said and went inside.

Tom thanked Bob for bringing him up, and told him he'd try his best not to screw up.

"Don't worry, Tom. You'll do just fine. These are good people and they'll gladly work with you if you treat them with respect. But if you don't treat them with respect, then as far as getting anything done, it will be like pissing up a rope."

Emilio, the Señora, and the three daughters came out. Jaime came over from the corral. Bob thanked the family for the meal and said goodbye.

He shook hands with Tom and spoke in Spanish.

"Good luck, Tomás. You are in good hands here with the Martinez family."

With that he turned and walked towards the gate. Passing through, he waved one last time and headed down the hill. Once he was out of sight, no one knew quite what to say or where to look. Everything had gone smoothly when Bob was around, but now it was all rough edges. Everyone stood looking around and shuffling their feet until the Señora finally broke the silence.

"Come on girls. We still have work to do in the kitchen. *Con permiso*, Don Tomás," and they headed back towards the house.

Jaime quickly excused himself.

"I have my work too. *Con permiso*, Don Tomás."

He returned to the corral where he was replacing a post, leaving Emilio and Tomás. Emilio smiled at Tomás, but didn't say anything. He started to fidget. Several times he looked over towards his son. He wanted to join him, but he didn't want to insult Tomás by leaving him alone. So they stood there in uncomfortable silence. Emilio cleared his throat but still didn't say anything. Tomás looked out towards the gate. Emilio rubbed his neck and scratched his face. Tomás put his hands in his back pockets and looked over at the house. It was a ridiculous situation and Tomás felt he had to do something. Finally, stumbling badly over the words, Tomás said maybe he should return to the house and arrange his things.

Emilio nodded emphatically.

"Si, si! Un muy buen idea!" Emilio made a beeline to the corral while Tomás went up to the house and sat down on the cot. It was hard. He sat there a long time because he didn't want to get in anyone's way and didn't know what else to do. He thought about Bob's work.

Bob had convinced the members of a small cooperative to plant pine trees, and helped them get a loan to make it possible. Emilio was one of the members. Tomás was supposed to take over Bob's job as supervisor even though he had no forestry experience. He hadn't even planted a single tree. How the hell was he supposed to run a forestry cooperative?

The sound of kitchen bustle and the rattling of pots and pans stopped, and the front door opened and shut. The house was quiet. Bob had said Emilio would take him to the next co-op meeting to introduce him to all the *socios*—members. But that wasn't until next month. There were a couple of Ministry of Agriculture meetings to attend in Valdivia before then; but that was it. What else was he supposed to do? At some point it started to get dark and he looked around the room. There were no pictures on the walls—only a few faded calendars from past years.

He went outside and looked for a private place to pee, hoping the girls weren't somewhere around. When he returned, Jaime was standing by the corral gate, which was made with sapling bars that slid in and out of two stout wooden posts. Tomás walked over, passing the outside wall of the kitchen where a pipe spewed soapy water onto the ground. The dog came out from under the house and growled at him until Jaime told it to shut up. Lilia approached, driving the sheep with a long skinny stick. She smiled and waved, and he happily waved back. As the sheep bunched up in front of the gate, Jaime pulled the three upper bars part way back and the sheep jostled each other until singles or pairs squirted out and jumped over the lower two bars. After Jaime finished counting them and Lilia slid the bars back into place, the three of them went up to the house.

The Señora entered his room with a smile, lit the lamp, and carried it over to the dining table. She motioned him over as she set the table. Emilio entered the room and sat down. Tomás joined him and the Señora brought them each a bowl of soup and some bread. Emilio tried to strike up a conversation.

"*Bueno,* Don Tomás. *Echaremos de menos de* Don Roberto. *Es muy guapo y un gran caballero, no es cierto? Y a el le gusta tanto a andar! Parece que tiene 'patas' de hierro, no eh?"*

He knew Emilio had said something about Bob, but other than that, he didn't have a clue.

"I am sorry, Don Emilio. *No comprendo."*

Emilio's smile faded and he spoke louder. Tomás repeated he didn't understand and asked him to speak more slowly. But Emilio only spoke louder. Tomás still didn't get it and held his hands out to the side. Emilio asked him something else. He didn't get that either. Emilio began shaking his head in exasperation and asked yet another question which he repeated several times, louder and louder, until he was almost yelling. Tomás felt his face flush. The Señora came in.

"Emilio!" Not so loud, she motioned with her hands, and left the room.

Emilio gave up and they lapsed into a helpless silence. When Emilio finished his meal, he bolted from the room. Tomás felt like an idiot. He got up and walked over to his pack where he pulled out his Spanish books. He had originally promised himself that he'd do a grammar and vocabulary lesson each night—but now he felt like he needed to do five. He could hear the family in the kitchen. They were talking in hushed tones because they didn't want to disturb him. Some time later they took turns going out to the wash station. He waited until they were finished and then, by the light of the kerosene lamp, took his turn. The dog growled while he brushed his teeth. It was somewhere close, but he couldn't see it outside the lamp's circle of light. He hoped it wouldn't suddenly jump out and bite him.

Jaime yelled at the dog from the kitchen window and it stopped growling.

He returned to the table and after awhile heard the creaking of the stairway and the floorboards above his head as the family went to bed. Soon the house was silent and he started to nod over his grammar book. He was utterly exhausted from trying to pay such close attention to everything, from tuning in every second. He didn't want to do the wrong thing. His mind was numb from trying so fiercely to understand the Spanish. And being nervous took its toll. He was drained. He stood up from the table and walked as quietly as he could over to the cot. He pulled the cover back and there was a wool blanket and thick sheets that he guessed were muslin. They felt damp and cold.

His mind was full of the day. He thought of the long walk up the hill and of jackal dogs. He thought of not understanding anyone and making Emilio uncomfortable. He wondered how he was going to take Bob's place. And he wondered what he would do tomorrow. And the day after. And the day after that. Finally— thankfully—he dozed off.

Some time later he was awakened by what he thought was the dog scratching at the door. But that didn't make sense.

"Dogs in the *campo* aren't pets," he remembered Bob saying. "They are watch-dogs."

The noise got louder and he realized it wasn't coming from the door. It sounded like gnawing, and like it was coming from the wall right behind his head. His eyes popped open. It was gnawing! And he knew exactly what it was. Oh my sweet Jesus, he thought. A rat. No. Rats! They gnawed and gnawed. He wondered if they were going to chew through the wall and run across his face—or worse—start chewing on him if he fell asleep. He wanted to pound the wall and scare them away. But he didn't want to wake the family. So he did nothing. He lay awake listening to the rats for what seemed like forever, sure that he would never fall asleep. He finally did—but not before he realized just how alone he really was.

CHAPTER TWO

El Torneo (The Tournament)

"Don Tomás, look at this one. It is the *chupone* and has little fruit inside!"

He saw a cactus-like plant about five feet high with intimidating spears for leaves. He touched one of the points and it pricked him. Lilia giggled.

"Yes, Don Tomás, it is very prickly. But look… "

She showed him how to use a stick to push the prickly leaves aside to get at the tear-shaped fruit within.

"If they are yellow like this they are not ready. But later, when the summer is almost over, they are a more red-brown color. Then they are ready—then they are very sweet and very good."

Lilia was a godsend. The first few days had gone by so slowly. He had followed Emilio around like a puppy dog, studied at the table, taken long walks about the *campo*, and avoided the dog the family called Tobi as much as possible. Although he had been told in training that it could take months before he'd feel comfortable with his new job and living situation, he was impatient and ready to get on with it. But being here in the boonies, where there wasn't even a village, what exactly was he supposed to do? There was no office to go to. He didn't have a boss or anyone to direct him. It was only when Lilia started sitting with him at the table after the evening meal that he felt he was making some real progress. With the patience of a ten-year-old angel, she asked him what he had done that day and corrected his mistakes when he told her. At first she was shy and, out of respect, covered her mouth when he said something stupid. But as they grew more accustomed to each other, she felt comfortable enough to laugh with her whole face one big smile. He would sometimes make a mistake on purpose or play the fool just to see her laugh.

He watched Rosa and Ana wash the clothes. They would start a fire a little ways from the house and heat water in a big smoke-blackened cauldron. Sleeves rolled up and kerchiefs on their heads, they bent over two galvanized tubs and rhythmically rubbed the clothes up and down on large scrub-boards. After wringing them out by hand, the sisters spread the clothes out on the fence and nearby bushes to dry, creating a palette of colors around the pasture.

He and Lilia brought pails of water up from the spring, and he thought of Jack and Jill. They went out in the evenings to bring in the sheep. Sometimes the sheep wandered down into the *quebradas* where there were tall trees and bamboo-like thickets called *quila*. Lilia said this was a bad place for the sheep because of mountain lions. Oftentimes a very loud bird cried out, adding to the jungle-like atmosphere, but he could never spot it in the dense undergrowth. One day when he heard one close by, he asked Lilia what it looked like. She took his hand and made him stop walking.

"It is the *chucao*," she whispered. "He is always very curious."

In a few seconds a little gray bird with a dark orange breast hopped out of the thicket and looked at them. It held its tail upright like a wren and didn't seem afraid. Then it hopped back into the thicket and perched on a branch. He watched as it swelled up its tiny chest and let loose with its bold song. Every trip with Lilia was an education.

"Come on, Don Tomás. Let's go look at the *chuchos*."

They walked side by side as Lilia swung her stick and whacked the bushes. They passed some black and white pigeon-sized birds she called *treles* that were looking for bugs in the close-cropped pasture. The birds spooked and took off, shrieking down at them.

"These are like the geese at home. They make a lot of noise when someone comes near and they give you warning."

When they came to a wooden fence, Lilia stopped. She pointed to a level section of pasture where he saw a colony of little brown owls with white bellies. They were tiny, maybe ten inches tall, and they stood in front of their burrows like big-eyed, feathered prairie dogs. Lilia said she didn't know why but the *chuchos* lined their burrows with the dung of the oxen and horses.

Tomás loved these outings with Lilia; everything was so different. Back home, being outdoors meant playing sports or watching a game at Fenway or trying to pick up girls at the Cape. But learning about the flora and fauna here seemed so healthy and clean, and he was beginning to enjoy the *campo's* simplicity and silence.

They returned to the farm and when Lilia joined him after dinner, he told her how much he had enjoyed the day.

"And the best part Lilia was the *chuchas*—they were so small and cute. I would love to have one here now and pet it."

Lilia's eyes widened in surprise and she covered her mouth with both hands. She quickly turned towards the kitchen door and watched it like a hawk. Finally, taking her hands from her mouth, she turned back to him.

"Oh no, Don Tomás," she whispered. "The birds are called *chuchos*...you have to say *chuchOS*...not...not the other word." She was blushing furiously.

Tomás pulled the notebook from his front pocket where he had logged the day's new words. He looked at his notes and of course she was right—it was *chuchos*. But what was the big deal?

"Yes, Lilia, you are right. But then what are *chuchas?*"

Lilia flushed even more deeply and quickly held her finger to her lips. She turned and looked towards the kitchen again.

"Don Tomás, you must not say that. What you say is a part of a woman's body—the part between her legs."

"Lilia, I didn't know! Excuse me, please!"

No wonder she had turned towards the kitchen, he thought. Had anyone heard him? Good God—talking about cute little *chuchas* with a ten year old girl! Wanting to pet it here at the table! Oh Lord, Emilio and the Señora would think him a pervert! No one came out of the kitchen and he apologized again. Lilia nodded and they quickly changed the subject.

The next morning he was relieved when Emilio gave no sign that he had heard anything improper. Emilio and Jaime had started building a wagon, and it was like stepping back in time. He watched as they cut down polesized trees with long-handled, heavy axes. The wood was brought back by oxen and peeled with a drawknife. With axe, adze, and handsaw, father and son cut and shaped all the parts, and then fastened them with hand-whittled pegs. The work area was soon covered by a carpet of bright white chips, and after a week a new cart emerged from the jumble. Tomás ran an appreciative hand over the cart.

"What type of wood is this, Don Emilio?"

Emilio walked over to the cart.

"Many different ones. But all of them are hard and strong."

Emilio put a hand on a wheel.

"It is not so important which is used for the body of the cart as long as you can work with it. But the wheels, they must always be *laurel*. This wood will not part."

The weather was turning warmer each day, and Emilio and Jaime began to shear the sheep. They worked side by side with hand clippers, peeling away whole fleeces. A few days later the sheep were dipped. Emilio and Jaime filled a large hand-hewn log trough with many buckets of water, mixing in a chemical solution for parasites that turned the clear water milky. Tomás helped Jaime bring the sheep over from the corral, and Emilio lifted each one up and dunked it in the trough. Emilio stood on two pieces of wood, trying to keep his feet dry as the panicked sheep thrashed around, spraying water everywhere.

Tomás would need a horse for his work and Emilio located one for him. It was brown with a white spot on its forehead and a white stocking above its rear right hoof. Like most Chilean horses, it was small. Emilio also brought up Tomás's trunk and a Peace Corps-issue saddle from the highway in his oxcart. The saddle had a sturdy wooden frame, covered with two thick sheep pelts and a layer of suede leather. Unlike American western saddles, there was no horn. The pointed stirrups were hand-carved out of wood, and looked like the front halves of large Dutch wooden shoes. Tomás had never ridden before, so Emilio showed him how to saddle the horse and gave him a few pointers. When Tomás finally rode out alone he could not help but feel excited.

One afternoon Jaime came into his room wearing shorts and soccer shoes and had a string net bag holding two soccer balls draped over his shoulder. He was the local soccer team's captain and guardian of the jerseys, soccer balls, and pump.

"Don Tomás, do you play *futbol*? I know it is not as popular as your *beisbol*. But do you play?"

Tomás told him he had played for four years on both his high school and university teams.

"Truly? Then come over to the school and kick the ball with us. It is a beautiful afternoon and there should be several players at the field."

Tomás jumped at the chance. Jaime waited while he put on some sneakers.

"Don Tomás, those are not very good shoes for *futbol*."

"Yes, I know, but it is all that I have."

They left the house and followed the much-used wagon path that weaved its way between stumps until it came to a large gate.

Climbing over, Jaime asked, "What position do you play?"

"In the front...usually center."

"I play in the midfield."

Not surprising, since Jaime had a halfback's build. He was tall for a Chilean and lanky, and had a spring in his step. He looked like he could run forever.

They followed the dirt road to the soccer field next to the school. Two horses were tied to a hitching rail and a small group of players lay on the grass in a circle, talking quietly. They stood up and Jaime introduced Tomás before rolling the balls out onto the field. One of the players wore soccer shorts like Jaime, but the others were in work clothes and looked like they had just laid down their axes. But they all wore soccer shoes.

The young men began passing a ball around, and Tomás could see that they were very good. Each could flip the ball up into the air and keep it there by deftly bouncing it off feet, thighs, and head, before passing it off again. One of the players, Miguel, had incredible ball handling skills. Tomás didn't dare to try and match them. When the ball was passed to him, he controlled it and dribbled it a few steps before passing it off again. Jaime suggested they play half-field and divided them into two teams.

It felt good to be out on the field where there was only one language—*futbol*—and the only constraints were those of the game itself. He may not have had the individual skills of the Chileans, but he was quick and understood the game. It soon became apparent that, as good as the Chileans were, they tended to dribble the ball too much and pass too little. Jamie and he started working the ball with give and go passes. Jaime was fast and Tomás took advantage of that. He would chip the ball over the defending players while Jaime streaked past them. Jaime would take the ball on the run and usually get off a shot on goal. They played well together.

A few more players arrived and one, Jorge, was built like a bull. He played aggressively even though this was just a fun game between teammates. Jorge reminded Tomás of those rough 'hatchet-man' players back in the States—usually some big jock who had quit football and had minimal soccer skills. But, Jorge had all the skills and still tried to knock players down or trip them up. Jorge was on his team, so Tomás didn't have a run-in with him. But Miguel did.

Jorge was playing defense when Miguel faked him out and dribbled past him towards the goal. Jorge's face contorted in rage, and he raced after Miguel and viciously tripped him from behind.

Miguel sprang to his feet.

"*Huevón,* what are you doing? This is just a practice game, you idiot!"

Jorge smiled smugly.

"What is the matter, Miguelito? Maybe you cannot play with the big boys, eh? Maybe you are too much of a baby..."

"And maybe you would play better, Jorge, if you had any brains."

Jorge's smirk vanished and he cocked a fist. He looked ready to charge just as Jaime stepped between them.

"Enough, you two! What are you? Two dogs ready to fight over nothing? This is only a game and we are on the same team. Settle down! We have tournaments to play and we have to play together."

In a few minutes the game continued, although anger was still plain on Miguel's face. Jorge acted as if nothing had happened. But the confrontation put a damper on things and they didn't play much longer.

Walking back to the house Jaime said, "You play well, Don Tomás."

"I enjoyed it...except maybe not so much playing with Don Jorge."

Jaime nodded and was silent for a few steps.

"Yes, he plays *muy duro.* He gets called for many penalties in the tournaments and it can be a problem. I think he knows he is not so smart and maybe because of this he uses his strong body to try to make up for it. But he is also a very good player and we have no one with equal skills to replace him. But yes, Don Tomás, he is not much fun to play with."

Wherever there was a school in Cufeo, there was a soccer field. And wherever there was a soccer field, there was a team. When the winter rains stopped, players of all ages started kicking the ball around, and meetings were held to schedule the summer tournaments. The tournaments were what it was all about, and during the dry season there was hardly a weekend when there wasn't one somewhere. They were like the rural round robin softball tournaments in the States where everybody traveled for miles to play—except here people traveled by horse or on foot.

Over the next couple of weeks, Tomás played a lot of *futbol* and became comfortable with his teammates. Jaime put together the tournament team, with Miguel and Tomás playing together in the front line, Jaime at center half, and Jorge at fullback. The first tournament of the season would be Sunday at Piedra Azul, which was about a two hour ride from their community of Los Guindos. With play slated to begin at ten-thirty, the team planned to meet at the school at eight and head over.

Miguel did not own a horse and on the day of the tournament he mounted up behind Jaime. Tomás rode along side. He couldn't imagine riding for two hours like Miguel, without a saddle, but Miguel chatted away as if he were sitting in a living room chair. As they went up and down the hills, Jaime pointed out the farms where cooperative members lived. There were barking dogs at every gate. When they passed a small colony of *chuchos,* Tomás thought of his conversation with Lilia. So did Jaime.

"Don Tomás, do you know what those are?"

He answered matter of factly.

"Of course. *Chuchos.*"

Both Jaime and Miguel were smiling.

"Are you sure? Are you sure they are not 'cute little *chuchAS?*'" Jaime asked.

Tomás blushed. The family HAD heard him. Or maybe Lilia had told them.

"Yes, Don Jaime. I'm sure," he muttered.

Miguel put his two cents in.

"Don Tomás, if you would like to 'pet' some 'cute little *chuchas*,' you must come with me to Valdivia sometime. I know some places where this is possible, but you'll have to bring your wallet."

Miguel and Jaime burst out laughing. Tomás looked away and shook his head.

They rode on, passing more farms and caught up with some soccer players on foot. Jaime turned to him.

"This is the first tournament of the season, so there will be a lot of people at Piedra Azul. They have the best field in Cufeo and there may even be one or two teams from Valdivia and Paillaco, although their players always say they do not like to play here because our fields are too rough. I think the real reason is that they do not want to get cow shit on their shoes."

Tomás laughed.

"There are good prizes too. And, Don Tomás, word has gotten around that you are playing, and many will come to watch you. People are curious. They have never seen a *gringo* play."

Tomás was already nervous about his soccer debut and hearing this didn't help any.

"What are the prizes?" he asked.

"First place is a lamb. Second is a leather soccer ball. And third is a case of canned peaches."

Good grief, he thought. Canned peaches?

As they crested one last hill, the soccer field lay below them. There was quite a crowd, with different teams bunched together in their bright jerseys. There were horses everywhere. There was also what looked like a small three-sided shed made out of sticks with an oxcart parked nearby. As they descended, Jaime explained that the stick building was called a *ramada* and was built for the home team to sell food and drink. They would build one later in the summer for their tournament.

People lined up in front of the *ramada,* while inside women cooked over charcoal. Like their field in Los Guindos, no nets were attached to the goals. An official-looking table was on the sideline with a clipboard, a new soccer ball, and a case of canned peaches on top. Tethered nearby was a bleating lamb. People were eating, drinking, and talking everywhere. Many were sitting on blankets and *mantas* spread along the sidelines. Children, some barefoot, were running around chasing each other.

Tomás and his teammates tied off their horses and put on green and white jerseys. Jaime went over to the scorer's table to meet with the referees and other captains. When he returned he said there were eight teams playing and the first game would begin right away. Theirs would follow. They walked over to the field to stretch and loosen up on the sidelines while a team from Valdivia won their game 2-0.

As he stretched, Tomás looked around the crowded sidelines. He was very nervous, much more than his customary 'butterflies' before a game. He thought about what Jaime had said—about people coming to watch the *gringo.* The referee called the two captains over for the coin toss; the other team won and chose to defend the end near the *ramada.* Tomás's team would kick off. As he walked up to the center circle with Miguel, Tomás felt everyone's eyes on him. Miguel was playing center forward and he was right-inside. Their standard opening move was for Miguel to touch the ball to him and he would put it out to the left wing. The referee blew the whistle and Miguel passed him the ball. When he went to kick it he missed completely. Instead, his momentum spun him around, and he fell down to sounds of the crowd erupting in laughter. Never, ever, had he done anything like that. Not even close. Jaime ran by and gave him a look like "What was that all about?" Tomás was totally embarrassed.

He got up and ran towards the player with the ball. He vented his frustration by intentionally bumping him hard, and the referee called a penalty. But the physical contact calmed him down and he was better able to concentrate on the game. He began to play as hard and as smart as he could.

The two teams turned out to be evenly matched with few scoring opportunities. Late in the first half, with the score knotted at zero, Jaime passed the ball to Tomás and he took it out towards the sideline. A defender angled up perfectly, squeezing him against the sideline and leaving no room to get by. He kicked the ball hard against the other player so it bounced out of bounds with Tomás awarded the throw in. Tomás followed the ball into the crowd where it was picked up by a tall, slender young woman. When she turned around and threw the ball back, he almost dropped it, he was so startled. She was absolutely the most beautiful woman he had ever seen; regal, with high cheekbones, smooth skin, and olive-shaped eyes. A thick black braid hung down past her waist. She was a cross between a young Spanish *doña* and an Indian princess.

Tomás managed to nod his thanks to the young woman as he turned back to the game. He took a deep breath, threw the ball in to Miguel, and followed him up field. Two fullbacks quickly converged on Miguel and battled him for the ball. Legs flailing and bodies bumping, somehow Miguel came away with it and dribbled towards the goal. There was only the third fullback between him and the goalie. When the fullback challenged Miguel, Tomás ran past, calling for the ball. Miguel passed it but Tomás didn't control it well, so it ricocheted off his shin and bounced toward the goalie. As he sprinted after it, the goalie came out. Both quickly realized that, unless someone backed down, it was a do-or-die play.

Tomás had been high scorer on every team he played, but it was not because he was the best player. It was because he had very quick feet which enabled him to almost always get a foot on the ball during a scramble in front of the goal. He also didn't panic. When an opportunity presented itself, he stayed calm and took advantage of it.

At the last second, the goalie realized Tomás would get to the ball first, so he planted himself, arms and legs outstretched, trying to cut off all angles. As Tomás reached the ball, he saw there was only one place to put it— the gap between the goalie's wide-spread legs. He flicked the ball through, a split second before they collided. The goalie was bowled over, and Tomás went airborne landing hard and getting the wind knocked out. As he lay there trying to breathe, Tomás knew he had scored because of the crowd noise; but he never saw it go in. Suddenly his teammates were all around him, helping him up. Miguel was all smiles and pounded Tomás on the back. Jaime had an ear-to-ear grin. When everything settled down, Tomás thought, even if it had not been pretty, it was a good goal. He looked over to the sidelines and no one was laughing now. A couple of fans from Los Guindos yelled, "Well done, Don Tomás," and he felt pretty darn good.

The goal stood and Los Guindos won 1-0. After the game Tomás and his teammates went to the *ramada* to get something to eat and drink. Jaime spoke to them while they waited in line.

"Remember, no wine. Not until we have finished playing."

The women were frying *empanadas* and Tomás ordered three along with a soda. *Empanadas* were as classic to Chile as hamburgers were to the States.

Today they were making *empanadas de pino,* spicy tarts filled with hamburger meat, onions, ripe olives, egg, green peppers, and raisins.

Taking his *empanadas* and soda back over to the sidelines, Tomás watched Central Caman beat Paillaco. The Central Caman team had a crippled young man in the goal and Tomás was amazed at how athletic the man was with his bum leg. He made a pair of really fine saves that was the difference in the game. Tomás's team played next, beating Valdivia which put them in the finals. Central Caman was the other finalist.

The players from Los Guindos and Central Caman knew each other's strengths and weaknesses well because they had played each other for years. They were also friends, sometimes family, and there was a lot of joking and bantering on the sidelines. But when the teams took the field it was all business. It was obvious that Central Caman respected Miguel's skill, as one of their best players shadowed him the entire game. Whenever Miguel was near the goal he was double-teamed, and outside the penalty area he received more than his share of bumps and pushes. Jaime had his best game of the tournament. He was all over the field and won every challenge on head balls. One of his headers just missed being a goal when it hit the crossbar. During a corner kick for Central Caman, they brought up their bearded and very tall fullback to try to head the ball in. He and Jorge bumped and jockeyed for position. When the ball was kicked into play, Jorge pushed the taller player from behind and he fell down. When he jumped up to his feet, he went at Jorge. It took several players from both teams to separate them and both were thrown out of the game which ended tied at zero. Jaime selected Miguel, Tomás, himself, and two others for the shoot-out that followed.

Jaime and Tomás both scored, and Miguel was
the last shooter. It was 4-3 in favor of Central Caman
and if Miguel scored there would be another shoot-
out. If not, the game and tournament were over.
Miguel kicked the ball to the right side, but the crippled goalie guessed correctly and launched himself
early. He got his fingertips on the ball just enough to
deflect it into the post, and it bounced away. Central
Caman's fans cheered and the goalie, grinning like a
school kid, was mobbed by his teammates. The fans
came on to the field, and Tomás again felt a jolt when
he saw the beautiful young woman with the long braid
among them. She ran smiling up to the goalie and
gave him a big hug. When the players from both teams
lined up to shake hands, Tomás congratulated the
goalie.

"Señor 'Goalie,' that was a great save. Well done."

Still grinning from ear to ear, the goalie shook
Tomás's hand.

"My name is Juan Montoya, Don Tomás... and I
think sometimes a dog is lucky and is thrown a bone,
eh?"

Tomás shook his head.

"That was not luck, Don Juan. And you played well
in every game."

The prizes were awarded and Jaime, holding the
second place soccer ball above his head, congratulated
his team.

"Well done teammates! Now it is time to celebrate.
I will buy the first cup of wine!"

The team cheerfully went to the *ramada*, drank
wine, ate *empanadas,* and drank more wine. They
rehashed this play and that over their *copas de vino.*
Tomás's teammates joked with him about his goal.
They laughed, saying he looked like a big bird flying
over the goalie—but they also congratulated him.

Tomás was thankful they did not bring up his early mis-play. A few players from Central Caman came up to the *ramada,* ordered a pile of *empanadas* and refilled several liter bottles of wine. They good-naturedly kid-ded the Los Guindos players while they waited for their food. When they returned to their teammates near the tethered lamb, Tomás again noticed the goalie's pretty young wife—definitely a knock-out. She was taller than all the other *señoras* he had seen and certainly much thinner. Her braid hung down over the front of her light green sweater and she had a beautiful figure. The goalie Juan was sitting on the ground and she had her hands on his shoulders.

Tomás turned back to Jaime.

"Don Juan Montoya is certainly a very lucky man. He not only wins the tournament, but he also has a beautiful *señora.*"

They looked over to the Central Caman team.

"Oh no, Don Tomás. She is not Don Juan's wife. She is his sister Maria Elena. But you are right. She is very beautiful."

As he spoke, the young woman looked their way, causing Tomás and Jaime to quickly turn back to their teammates. A few moments later Tomás looked over again. Maria Elena was looking at him. Flustered, he turned away.

It was getting late. The crowd had thinned and the women at the *ramada* dumped out their coals and began to pack up. There were no more *empanadas,* but the wine kept flowing. As the players and fans drank, the women loaded the oxcart next to the *ramada* with their cooking gear and the empty bottles of wine and soda. A man approached the cart leading a pair of yoked black and white oxen. He walked in front of the oxen, holding one end of a long skinny pole—called a *garrocha*—which he used to steer them. The other end of the pole rested on the middle of the yoke. As long as the pole rested on the yoke, the driver could walk left or right and the oxen would follow. The man led the pair past the cart, and then backed them up to it by holding the pole horizontally and gently tapping their noses. When he had them where he wanted, he lowered his end of the pole to the ground and left it leaning against the yoke. The oxen did not budge as he began to hook up the cart. They would sit there patiently until he picked up the *garrocha* again. Tomás thought it was like putting the pole in 'park.'

It was almost dark when the Los Guindos team finally got around to changing back into their regular clothes and preparing to leave. Only the hard core drinkers remained, and they were talking loudly and slurring their words. Some were hanging on to the counter to keep from falling down. One man staggered off to relieve himself, and he pissed all over his clothes as he swayed back and forth. He returned half-buttoned, and then tried to talk a buddy into buying him another *copa*.

Tomás and his teammates mounted their horses, doubling up on several so no one would have to walk. The team was in a festive mood as they headed up the hill, and when the road leveled out, things got a little wild. It was too dark to see who was in the lead, but whoever it was let out a sharp yell and took off at a gallop. They all followed him, flying down the road. Tomás's horse stumbled, and he lost a stirrup that clobbered him repeatedly in the shin. He wondered if it drew blood. Several riders were 'yipping' and laughing as they tried to pass each other. Tomás hung on for dear life, wondering if he should have had more wine or less. He thought these guys were like teenagers in the States, driving home after a party. They finally slowed down when they began to go down a hill.

He couldn't believe that none of the doubled-up riders had fallen off.

They eased their mounts down the steeper sections, and, with spurs just touching their flanks, picked up the pace as they climbed the hills. When they came to a level area again, off they went. This time he locked his stirrups hard against his horse and grabbed anything he could get a death grip on, including its mane. They galloped and galloped, with the same 'yip-yips' and occasional sparks flying as the shod horses clipped stone. He prayed that his horse wouldn't stumble and fall, and that he wouldn't fall off either, and get trampled. They passed a farm at a full gallop and some dogs came out. His horse tried to kick at them with his rear hooves, which translated in more jerkiness up in the saddle. But he did not fall off and his horse did not let him get left behind.

It was very late when they finally re-crossed the highway and entered Los Guindos. As they climbed that last long hill, one by one the players said their good nights and split off to their homes. When Jaime and Tomás reached their gate they bid the final riders good night and went up to the house where they were greeted by the barking of Tobi. By the light of a kerosene lantern left sitting out on a stump near the corral, they put their saddles, and the burlap grain sacks that served as saddle blankets, in the outbuilding. After wiping down the horses and pouring two little piles of grain on the ground, they took off the bridles and set the horses free. The horses ambled over to the grain as Jaime picked up the lantern and led the way to the house.

It had been quite a day. Jaime and Tomás smiled wearily at each other as they shook hands and said good night. As Tomás undressed and climbed into bed he heard Jaime slowly climb up the stairs. It would not take either of them long to fall asleep, but Tomás wanted to stay awake long enough to savor the day. He put his hands behind his head and thought about the ride home. Jesus, he was lucky to be alive and in one piece. He thought of his successful debut with the soccer team and relived every good play he had made. He flashed on his do-or-die goal. He thought of Juan's save that won the tournament. He thought of Juan's sister running out on the field and giving Juan a big hug, and how beautiful she was. And he thought of her looking at him and his turning away. Tomás punched his pillow and turned over. Just before sleep, he also thought how pleased he was that Maria Elena had seen him score his goal, and that she was Juan's sister, and not his wife.

CHAPTER THREE

La Reunion (The Meeting)

The night before Bob brought Tomás up to the Martinez farm, they had had dinner in a small restaurant in Valdivia. Bob talked about the Cooperative and explained why planting trees in Cufeo was crucial.

"The soil in those hills, Tom, is too damn poor for more than subsistence farming and the *campesinos* can only eke out a living from selling firewood and *carbón*—charcoal. The sad thing is that when Cufeo was settled back in 1929, it was all virgin forest. But that didn't last long. Trees were cut down to build houses and corrals and outbuildings. Then they were cut down for the bark, which was the first cash crop because it was light enough to haul to tanneries here in Valdivia. When the land was cleared for animals, the brush and slash were burned during the dry summer season. Sometimes the fires got out of control and large areas of forest were torched. The good quality trees that remained were cut down and sawed up by steam sawmills that were hauled in by oxen. And as these trees disappeared, the sale of firewood and charcoal was about all that was left."

A pretty waitress came over and cleared their plates. Bob smiled at her and thanked her by name. She returned the smile and swung her hips as she walked away. Tomás wondered if they had something going on. Bob winked at Tomás before continuing.

"Now most of the trees left are in steep ravines called *quebradas.* It is incredibly difficult to work there and the oxen can only pull out a small amount of firewood at a time. The wood is handled several times until a full oxcart load is put together. Then the *campesinos* take the wood down terrible roads to the highway, where the wood is unloaded and stacked yet again. Finally it is sold for a pittance to the wood merchants who come out with their trucks from Valdivia. There's not much of a future for the people of Cufeo if something isn't done. But, luckily, pine grows like a weed there and I figure it's their only chance. That's why I helped them get the forestry loan. Your job, Tom, will be to supervise the clearing and fencing, and deliver next winter's trees."

"How long before they can begin harvesting the pine?"

"Twenty—twenty-five years."

"Then what'll they do between now and then—I mean, if they're already running out of wood."

Bob shrugged.

"Try to hang on," he said.

Thanks to Lilia, Tomás's Spanish was improving every day. But he also knew that outside of the Martinez family, people had a hard time understanding him and he worried about how he would do at the upcoming Cooperative meeting. When the day of the meeting finally arrived, he had his speech ready. He had gone over it at least a hundred times on paper and in his head. Emilio came into his room.

"Dress warmly, Don Tomás. It might rain, too. Do you need a *manta*? You can use Jaime's."

Tomás shook his head, and pulled a plastic rain poncho from his trunk. They went outside where Jaime was hitching Tomás's horse to a post. The whole family had agreed on the name Lobo for the horse. In the dictionary *lobo* meant wolf, but Lilia had told him it was also the name for any animal that was wild and hard to catch. Lobo was gentle and easy to ride. Tomás could turn the horse left and right and stop him with the reins curled around one finger, which was probably why Emilio had selected him. But Lobo was miserable to catch in the pasture. Without another horse, it took two men a lot of running and swearing to corner him where he could be lassoed.

Spurs jingling, Emilio walked over to his horse. He was wearing a dark jacket and a white shirt buttoned at the collar. For a change there were no patches on his pants. His hat looked like it was out of the forties—the sort a gumshoe private-eye wore in the movies. He also wore a *manta*, but it was folded up so that it looked like he had a blanket draped over each shoulder. The Señora gave him a little bundle wrapped in old newspaper tied off with string. Emilio explained that this was their lunch.

They passed through the big gate and wound down and around towards the highway. They came to a barbed wire fence. On the other side were thousands of pine seedlings planted in neat rows. A short way further they turned into an open gate and rode up to a house not much more than a shack. A saddled horse was tied to a tree. The front door opened and a little man hurried out, all in a fluster. With his gray stubble it looked like he had not shaved for a couple of days. Wearing a white shirt rolled up at the sleeves and carrying spurs, jacket, hat, and *manta,* he looked to be at least sixty years old. Yet his body was trim and fit—muscles bulged in his forearms.

Emilio introduced Tomás. The man's name was Luis, and he immediately apologized for not being ready.

"It is the fault of my damn sow," he said sitting down on a bench and putting on his spurs. "She entered the Señora Marta's garden this morning and I had to go get her. I have her shut up again, but she'll probably figure out a new way to get out. She is very smart."

He untied his horse and mounted.

"The Señora Marta was very angry. I must bring her some lettuce tomorrow."

The trio set off and soon arrived at the paved Pan American highway. Although most horses in Cufeo were not shod, theirs were, and they made a sharp clip clop on the pavement as they crossed over to a steep path on the other side. The path turned out to be a short-cut to another dirt road leading up into the hills. Tomás hung on to the front edge of the saddle as Lobo, legs flailing and back humping, followed the other horses up the path. Emilio and Luis laughed when he said he couldn't believe a horse could climb such a trail.

The road was much easier going, but it was all up hill and the farther they went the steeper it got. Ruts two feet deep were all over the road. One area would get bad and the oxcarts would go around it. Then that spot would get bad and they would go around it, until the whole road was a mess. The road had eroded down to packed clay and the horses' hooves barely left a track.

"In the winter with the rains," Emilio said, "this road is very dangerous. It can be like a river and is very slippery. Animals can break a leg in these ruts."

At places the erosion was so bad that the pasture was above their heads. The road on the Los Guindos side of the Pan American was a superhighway compared to this. About an hour from the highway, the road leveled out. It was a cool, cloudy day, which muted the colors of the countryside, but the view was still striking. The rolling terrain of light green pasture was dotted with dark stumps. To the east the pasture fell away to distant hills which were also green, posed against a gunmetal gray sky. After passing several farms they came to a junction where the road branched off to the left and passed a schoolhouse and a soccer field before continuing up a long hill. Straight ahead the road continued up another hill and to their right was the gate for a two-story farmhouse set back off the road.

"This is Central Caman," Emilio told Tomás. "We are well over halfway now, so we might as well go over to the school to rest the horses and eat."

They tied the horses up to the front porch of the school and loosened the cinches. Tomás's butt was sore, so he walked around before gingerly sitting down on the edge of the deck. Emilio handed him a portion of bread and some crude, rubbery white cheese that tasted like salty Feta. There wasn't much conversation while the three ate, but they were soon interrupted by the shrill cries of *trele* somewhere behind the school. Food in hand, they went around the corner to look. Near the crest of the long hill they could see two riders descending.

Luis said, "It must be Don Pedro and Don Claudio."

Emilio agreed.

"You are right. It is certain that is the big mare of Don Pedro."

He turned to Tomás.

"Don Pedro and his son Claudio are members of the Cooperative. They live in the section of Cufeo called Casa Blanca. Don Pedro is the oldest *socio* of the Cooperative and is much respected."

They finished their lunch before riding out to meet them. Don Pedro was on a beautiful and very tall roan mare. He was wearing a smart black brimmed hat and a gray *manta* with a subtle red and black geometric pattern around the neck. His spurs were large and polished. Like Luis, he was unshaven and covered in gray stubble. His face, etched by weather, crinkled into a hundred wrinkles when he smiled. He looked like an old Indian with whiskers.

Don Pedro and Emilio gave Tomás a geography lesson while they rode. They told him there were seven general districts in the 18,000 hectares of Cufeo. Except for the very remote Lote Once, Tomás recognized all the names. The names were the same as the soccer teams —Piedra Azul, Casa Blanca, La Clavela, Los Guindos, Central Caman, and, finally, La Paloma, where they were headed. Emilio said that there were forty-two farmers planting trees all around Cufeo.

Don Pedro grinned and looked at Tomás.

"I hope your backside is tough, Don Tomás, because you are going to be doing a lot of riding." Tomás shifted in his saddle and inwardly grimaced.

When they arrived at the La Paloma schoolhouse, there were horses tied up everywhere. The school did not look much different from the farmhouses they had been passing all day. Emilio explained that the government had thought this area too wild and remote for a school, but if the *campesinos* built one, the government would provide a teacher. There were no more schools farther up in the hills because no teacher would live there.

Emilio showed him how to tie his reins with a slipknot so Lobo would not injure himself if he shied. But it was hard for Tomás to pay attention. He had that queasy, nervous feeling in his stomach again. He felt awkward and very young, so he stuck close to Emilio. The *campesinos* were wearing dark hats and jackets, wool *mantas*, and spurs. Everyone was waiting for Manuel Vargas, the *gerente*—manager—of the Coop to arrive. But it was getting late, and many, like Emilio and Tomás, had a long ride home. And the weather was not improving. Emilio, Don Pedro, and a few of the other older members decided to start the meeting, and the men crowded into the dimly-lit schoolroom.

The ceiling was very low. There was the sound of spurs jingling and the floor creaking, as the chairs were pulled out. The older men, still wearing their hats and *mantas*, sat down on little student chairs in front of little desks that faced the blackboard in the front of the room. The chairs were so small that the men's knees were above their waists, and the bottom folds of their *mantas* lay bunched up on the floor. The younger men leaned against the rear and side walls. Tomás recognized the crippled goalie Juan Montoya, and walked over to him and shook his hand.

Don Pedro went up to the front of the room and stood behind the teacher's desk. Holding his hands up for silence, he called the meeting to order.

"As you all can see, Don Manuel is absent. With your pleasure, I would like to take his place for today."

He paused while there was a collective murmur of assent.

"We have several things to discuss and it is already late. But first of all, I would like to say that Don Roberto has finished his work with the Cooperative. I am sure you agree that we were very fortunate to have had such a man help us, and we will persevere and go forward in life thanks to his efforts. You also know that he had requested to have another member of his organization take over his work, and he is here today."

He looked at Tomás.

"I would like to present Don Tomás Young, who will be working with us for the next two years."

All heads turned towards him and he nodded at the room, his stomach churning.

"Don Tomás has asked that, if it is agreeable with you, he would like to speak after we finish our business."

As all heads nodded seriously, Don Pedro began to conduct Coop business. After he finished and sat down, individuals took turns coming up to the front of the room and reporting on what was happening in their area. Tomás tuned in and out as the meeting droned on. He looked around at all the weathered and mostly unshaven faces, and tried to guess how old each man was. He tried to go over what he was going to say. But his mind kept going blank, so he soon gave that up. The last person to speak was Emilio for Los Guindos.

When he sat down, Don Pedro said, "Don Tomás?"

He walked up and stood behind the teacher's desk. Facing these middle-aged and older men, he wondered just what the hell he was doing here. Don Pedro and Emilio were the only ones who smiled encouragingly from their little chairs. He took a deep breath.

"Thank you, Don Pedro."

He thought of speech class at college—eye contact, good eye contact.

"As Don Pedro told you, my name is Tomás Young and I am the replacement for Don Roberto. I hope to work as well with you as he did."

Heads nodded and he thought, all right—good start!

"I know that my last name is difficult for you to pronounce, but it means *joven*...so if you cannot say 'Young,' I know you can say *joven*."

He thought he might get a chuckle or a couple of smiles with that; but nope, just blank stares. Shit! He quickly continued and told everyone that he would visit their farms soon to see how their work was going. Bob had told him this should be a pep talk, so he encouraged the men to do their work promptly and well, saying that it was the only way that they would be able to pay off the loan in the future. That got some more nods. He also warned them not to let their animals into the fenced-off plantations.

"I know that as time passes the grass will grow long between the trees. But do not let your animals in. An ox will kill two or three trees each time he lies down."

Don Pedro was nodding emphatically, and Tomás began to feel good about how his speech was going. Heads were bobbing all over the room. At least, he thought, everyone was understanding him.

"Finally, I want to say that I will enjoy getting to know each of you. I will try hard to continue the work of Don Roberto, and if there is something I can do to help, please let me know. Thank you very much."

He thanked Don Pedro and returned to his spot at the rear of the room.

He felt about thirty pounds lighter and, by God, he thought it had gone ok. Don Pedro returned to the front of the room and adjourned the meeting. Spurs jingling again, they went outside. The weather had deteriorated—the clouds were lower and there were a couple of spits in the air. Some of the men went to their horses and pulled on heavy black *mantas* that had been left covering their saddles. These *mantas* were extra long, with high collars that could be buttoned. Tomás asked Emilio about them.

"They are called *mantas de Castilla*. They have very thick and tightly woven wool. They are usually worn in the wintertime. But these men were smart to bring them today. The weather is turning bad."

Everyone quickly mounted and said their goodbyes. Tomás set off in a large group and headed down toward Central Caman. Riders peeled off at this gate or that trail. Juan, who rode with his bad leg extended way out—like Matt Dillon's sidekick Chester in the early "Gunsmoke" series – traded stories with Don Pedro all the way down to Central Caman. Tomás couldn't understand them, but smiled at the merriment as the others laughed hard and often. Now that the speech was over, he enjoyed the ride. He patted Lobo's neck. Although his butt was tender, the shifting of the saddle lulled him. The smell of the horses, the wind in his face, and the jokes and laughter of these older men made him feel like he was somewhere in the old west. Every now and then he would shift his weight to get more comfortable, or kick off a stirrup and stretch a leg. His thoughts shifted to the States. Being south of the equator, he was still trying to get his seasons straight. It was spring here, but at home brightly colored leaves would be falling. He thought of riding his motorcycle down sunny country lanes, and playing soccer in the afternoons.

They said goodbye to Don Pedro and his son Claudio at Central Caman, and continued on until they arrived at Juan's farm, about a kilometer or so below the school. His house was set back a little ways from the road. Maria Elena heard them and came around the corner of the porch. She leaned against a post and folded her arms, glancing from one of them to the other. Tomás followed his companions' lead and tipped his hat to the young woman. She coolly nodded back. Then they turned their horses and continued on down the hill.

It began to rain lightly and they stopped so he could put on his plastic poncho. At the heavily eroded, steep area, the horses tiptoed their way down. It was getting dark by the time they crossed the highway and it was raining and blowing in earnest when they said good-night to Luis at his gate. A little farther up the road, a gust of wind caught Tomás's poncho and it flared up like a sail, spooking Emilio's horse. It shied violently to the side and into the barbed wire fence, rearing up as Emilio let out a cry of pain. Emilio swore at his horse and slapped its neck with the flat of his hand as he pulled it under control.

"Don Emilio, I am sorry. The wind..."

"It is nothing. These things happen."

Emilio grimaced as he looked down at his leg, and he pulled a white handkerchief out from under his *manta*.

"But I think, Don Tomás, that you should buy yourself a wool *manta*. It is not so light."

Emilio's *manta* had been rock solid in the wind. Mortified, Tomás pulled in the corners of his poncho and sat on them the rest of the way home.

Tobi announced their arrival. Jaime came out with a kerosene lantern and took care of the horses and saddles while he and Emilio went around the corner of the corral to relieve themselves.

Jaime called over, "Papa, what happened to your horse?"

Emilio limped up to his son.

"Here, hand me the lantern."

Emilio passed the lantern slowly along the side of his horse. There were several shallow cuts, which he examined closely.

"My horse spooked and ran into Don Luis's barbed wire fence. But it is good that the cuts are not so deep. Son, go get soap and water and some of the purple salve."

"Papa! You are hurt too!"

Tomás looked down at Emilio's leg. The pants were torn just above his boot and he had stuffed his handkerchief there. It was soaked with blood and had slipped down, revealing a wicked slice.

"*Sí.*" Emilio smiled thinly. "I think I may need some of that salve too."

"Papa, come! Come into the house for my Mother to take care of this. It looks deep. I will tend to the horses later."

Tomás wished he could disappear as he followed them inside. Jaime called upstairs for his mother, and lit every lantern he could find and brought them in the kitchen. The Señora came down dressed but wearing a nightcap.

"*Por Dios*, Emilio. What happened? Aii! And your best pants too!"

She carefully rolled up his trouser leg and examined the wound.

"Jaime, go get my medical things."

Jaime hurried off.

She turned to Emilio and asked him again what happened.

Before he could answer, Tomás said, "It was my fault, Señora. The wind blew my poncho and it scared Don Emilio's horse and it jumped into Don Luis's fence."

"Ahh, that explains it then."

Jaime entered with a small wooden box from which the Señora pulled out a needle and thread, and little vials of disinfectant. Tomás wondered if Emilio had ever had a tetanus shot. The Señora carefully washed out the wound and sterilized everything before she went to work. As Tomás watched her skillfully sew him up, he wondered what his mother would have done in a similar situation. Probably fainted. Emilio, whose face was usually so expressive, showed nothing. It must have hurt like hell, but other than an occasional flicker of his eyes, he calmly drank a cup of Nescafe while talking to Jaime about the horse's cuts. When the Señora finished, Tomás apologized again. Emilio said it was a small thing—that his pants would need more stitches than him.

He gave him a pat on the back before asking his wife, "Is there no soup, Señora? Don Tomás and I are hungry after such a long ride."

CHAPTER FOUR

Tobi (Toby)

Two weeks had passed since the Coop meeting and
Tomás thought it high time to meet Manuel Vargas, the
gerente of the Cooperative. He set off early one morning with a map Emilio had drawn for him on a piece
of torn paper bag. The map was perfect. About a mile
above the La Paloma schoolhouse he found the steep
downhill trail to Manuel's farm. The trail was lined with
impenetrable walls of *quila*, but occasionally he caught
a glimpse of the rugged, snow-covered volcano aptly
named Puntiagudo—sharp point. He hoped the *gerente*
would be at home, but there was no way to be sure. At
least, since he had visited another *socio* along the way,
today's trip would not be totally wasted if Manuel were
not around.

It hadn't taken long to realize that Los Guindos was
not central and that there were only three *socios* on his
side of the highway. This meant long trips almost every
time he set out to visit the farms and it was taking a toll

on Lobo. He guessed Bob had not considered that—
or maybe the Martinez family was the only one Bob
could find who would take Tomás in.

He approached an area which had been recently
cleared. There were several piles of *quila* and brush
ready to burn. About two hundred yards down the slope
was a barbed wire fence with pasture beyond, and below
that was a farmhouse with the ubiquitous smoking stovepipe. Two dogs rushed up barking, while a man holding
a long handled axe appeared from around a large brush
pile. Hushing the dogs, he looked at Tomás for a second or two before he laid down his axe and approached,
smiling.

"You must be Don Tomás."

"Yes, and you must be Don Manuel."

Manuel was about his height but stocky and heavily muscled. He was hatless with short cropped dark
hair and small, very dark eyes. His face, although tan,
looked fleshy, and his nose had the swarthy and pitted
look of a heavy drinker. Just visible sticking out over
the top of his pants was the red edge of a *faja*—a six
inch wide strip of tightly woven cloth that the *campesinos* wrapped around their waist for lower back support. Tomás had been told that a *faja* was good for the
kidneys and good for the health because it was red, the
color of blood. He thought that a little far-fetched but
imagined it would help if someone had to chop and
stack heavy cordwood all day.

"Come," Manuel said. "I will get my jacket and hat
and then you can meet the Señora and have *onces*."

They walked down the hill, with Tomás leading
Lobo and the two dogs following. He could see a
woman had come out of the house and stood waiting,
hands on hips, at the front door. After hitching Lobo,
he walked up to the woman. She had gray-brown hair
pulled severely back, which made her high forehead

all the more noticeable. Although she smiled at him, her eyes did not, and she looked like a hard, tough woman. When Manuel introduced her, she welcomed him and invited him in. Tomás hung his hat and new brown *manta* on hand-whittled pegs in the hallway. He was wearing spurs for the first time and he loved the jingle they made.

They entered the kitchen, and he and Manuel sat down at a small table. There were two big windows that helped to brighten the smoke-darkened wood interior, and braids of garlic and a garland of dried red peppers hung from nails in the ceiling. A round white cheese was curing on a slatted wooden shelf near one of the windows, and the light from the afternoon sun glistened on its sweat. Like all *campo* kitchens, the room was dominated by a cast iron cook stove.

The Señora looked over from the stove.

"Don Tomás, would you like tea or *mate* with your *onces?*"

"I am sorry Señora but I have never had *mate*. I do not know it."

The Señora looked at Manuel and chuckled.

"You live in the *campo* but have not drunk *mate!?*"

She laughed again. She had the raspy voice of a smoker and a tone that he had not heard before. It may not have been disrespectful, but bordered on it.

"As I say, Señora, I do not 'know' *mate*. I have only had tea or Nescafe in the Martinez home."

"Well, it is like a strong tea and you drink it from a cup with a metal *bombilla*. Some people like it bitter, but most like it sweet. It gives a lot of energy—more than tea or Nescafe. Would you like to try it?"

He said he would. His Spanish had improved a lot. He was competent with subjects like food, reforestation, and farm goings-on—but he still had a long way to go with just about everything else. He would often have to repeat himself and continually asked others to repeat what they had said. Even simple conversations could take some time to complete.

The Señora opened the firebox door and inspected her fire. She removed two of the cast iron rings on top and slid a large kettle over the opening for quick heat. Unfolding a small red-and-white paper bag, she shook a coarse tea that looked like chopped marijuana into a coffee mug, and stuck the bulbous, perforated end of a metal straw into it. After filling the cup with water, she sucked on the straw and spit green-tinted water into the sink. She looked over at him.

"It has to be cleaned first to get rid of the very small pieces of *yerba* that come through the straw."

She cleaned it twice, each time sucking and spitting into the sink. The *yerba* swelled with the water and filled the cup. Finally, after wiping the end of the *bombilla* with a small towel, she put in some sugar, filled the cup with boiling water, and set it down in front of Tomás.

"Careful. Take small sips. It is very hot and the *bombilla* is too."

Indeed it was. Even though he let it cool for a few minutes, he burned his tongue on the first sip. He jerked his head away. The Señora chuckled.

"I told you."

The *mate* was bitter, but with the undercurrent of sweetness from the sugar, it was good. Definitely a distinctive taste. He sipped until the empty straw signaled he had finished. The Señora came over and took the cup away. She put in more sugar, re-filled it with steaming water, and wiped the straw again. This time she put it down in front of Manuel who took his turn. Neat, Tomás thought, sort of like passing a peace pipe. They were served fresh bread and blackberry preserves, along with a fried egg served separately in the little frying pans they were cooked in. The Señora replenished their *mate* several times.

Manuel said, "It is about time we finally met."

"I agree, but I thought I would see you at the Cooperative meeting."

Manuel and the Señora exchanged a quick look. Manuel put an elbow on the table and slowly stroked his chin before he answered.

"We have a small house in Valdivia and when I am in town I am very busy with politics. I am involved with the Allesandri party. I had important meetings to attend."

On an earlier trip to Casa Blanca, Tomás had visited the plantations of Don Pedro and his son Claudio. He had asked Claudio why the *gerente* had not made the meeting. Claudio had replied, "I was told that Don Manuel was seen very late the night before drinking wine in a bar in Valdivia and talking politics to anyone who would listen. I think that maybe he drank too much and did not get up in time to catch the bus."

"Have you heard anything from Don Roberto?" the Señora asked, obviously changing the subject.

She sat down and took her turn with the *mate* and ate some bread with blackberry preserves.

Tomás said he hadn't seen Bob since Bob had brought him up to the Martinez home. He thought he had left Chile by now.

"Don Roberto is 'much man,'" Manuel said while folding his cloth napkin and putting it on the table. "He can walk forever and is very strong."

He paused and then grinned.

"Did you ever hear about Don Roberto eating raw eggs?"

Tomás shook his head.

In training he had been told all about *machismo* and how being 'manly' was mandatory in the Chilean culture—like Emilio not flinching when the Señora stitched him up. Because of his height and rugged build, the *campesinos* thought Bob *muy macho,* and Tomás knew that physically he could never match up. Bob had also occasionally enhanced his image by doing something outrageous. He was a hard act to follow.

Manuel leaned back in his chair.

"Don Roberto went into a bar in Paillaco during a rainy day last winter. The room was full of people because the weather was so bad. Almost everyone noticed him because of his great height and the noise made by his heavy boots as he walked up to the bar. He did not speak or look at anyone.

The barmaid came up to him and asked what he would like and he answered, 'Bring me an Escudo beer and two eggs.'

'*Si,* Señor, and how would you like the eggs?'

'*Crudos* with the shells washed.'

The barmaid thought she had not heard him correctly and asked, 'I am sorry but did you say 'raw' with the shells washed?'

It became very quiet in the bar and everyone looked at Don Roberto.

'Yes Señorita, I would like two raw eggs and I would like you to wash the shells before you bring them to me.'

The barmaid looked at him for a second. Then she took two eggs from a wire basket and went out back to the kitchen to wash them. After a time, she returned with the bottle of beer and the two eggs rolling around on a plate. She put them all down on the counter in front of him. Don Roberto picked up an egg and bit a hole in one end. He sucked the egg out and ate the empty shell. It was so quiet you could hear the sound of him chewing the shell all the way across the room. He drank half the beer with the first egg and finished it with the second. Then he paid the barmaid, who had stayed close by to watch.

Her eyes were very big when he said, 'Thank you, Señorita, that was delicious.'

Still not looking at anyone, he left the bar."

Both Manuel and the Señora laughed, and Tomás wondered how he could ever measure up to Bob.

He asked, "How is the clearing and fencing going?"

"Too slow. I need help. But I have two workers coming in a week or so, once they are finished making *carbón* for my brother. Then it will go much faster. Come," he said, standing up from the table. "Let us walk around and I will show you."

After thanking the Señora for the *onces*, he followed Manuel out the front door. They walked up the hill with the dogs. Manuel pointed out the thousands of pines that had been planted last winter. They looked healthy, which Manuel proudly pointed out.

"The *pino* really like it here. Almost all survived last winter's planting and I will have to re-plant very few."

Nearby, a pair of oxen looked longingly across the new barbed wire fence at the tall grass in the plantation. Manuel noticed Tomás watching them.

"Don't worry, Don Tomás. It is tempting to let them in, but I know it would be stupid to do so."

They talked a little more before Tomás thanked Manuel for his hospitality and mounted Lobo. Manuel pointed out the best way back to the trail and he started back. He was soon lost in thought, and before he knew it he was back at the main road and passing the school in La Paloma. Lobo had correctly turned left at the trail junction and was heading down towards Central Caman. He thought it amazing that he could just let Lobo go and the horse always knew the way home. About the only thing he ever had to do was occasionally spur Lobo on when he took advantage of Tomás's day-dreaming and slowed down to a plod.

It was late afternoon when he approached the quiet Central Caman schoolhouse. He saw the teacher locking the door and begin walking down towards the highway. Tomás had introduced himself on an earlier trip to Casa Blanca. The teacher was young—maybe in his early thirties—which was a good thing because he commuted from Valdivia five days a week. Tomás spurred Lobo and quickly caught up with the teacher. They greeted each other and amiably walked down the hill. They passed the Montoya farm and soon approached the heavily eroded section of the road. As they carefully picked their way down, the teacher said, "This horrible road. It is bad enough during good weather, but during winter…"

He skirted a deep rut.

"During winter," he continued, "when the wind is blowing, the rain feels like bullets and it is so slippery and dangerous. It is such a hardship for the farmers."

Tomás pictured the men bent against the rain, holding their *garrochas* while leading their oxen, and slipping and sliding as they inched their way along. When they reached the better section of road the teacher asked how his work was going.

"Okay, *Profesor*, except that I spend most of my time on my poor horse here. I really need to live in a more central location. It is impossible for me to visit more than one or two farmers in a day when I have to ride all the way from across the highway."

The teacher didn't say anything, and the pair continued in silence until the highway came into view. There was a small group of *campesinos* waiting for the bus. The teacher suddenly stopped and looked up at him.

"Don Tomás, I have an idea that might solve your problem—at least temporarily. Summer vacation will begin in a few weeks and there will be no classes again until early March. The school is locked and is not used for almost three months. There is a large storeroom which is nearly empty and it has a big window. It could make a nice room to live in for the summer, and if living in the Caman area works out for you, then you will have time to locate another place nearby before school opens again. If you like, I can ask the school board and let you know next week."

Tomás told him that sounded like a great idea and would look forward to hearing what the board said. They arrived at the highway where they greeted the *campesinos*, and after shaking hands with the teacher, he crossed the highway and rode up to the farm. It was almost dark when he arrived at the corral. As he wearily dismounted, Tobi rushed out to bark at him. What was that damn dog's problem? He should know him by now. As he led Lobo over to the hitching post, Tobi nipped at the horse. Lobo shied away and nearly yanked Tomás's arm out of its socket. He tried to calm Lobo down and waited for someone to call Tobi off. Usually it was Lilia who came out and said, "*Sali, pero!*" and he would meekly go off to lie down somewhere.

The problem was that Tomás was scared of Tobi, and the dog knew it. He thought of Chilean *machismo*, and that the Martinez family must think him a pansy. But they did not know why he was so scared. When he was six years old he was severely bitten in the face by a Great Dane. The dog had missed his eye by a terrifying fraction of an inch. Ever since then, whenever a dog growled or barked at him, the hair on his arms and on the back of his neck would rise up. Also, he was told by the Peace Corps health officer in Santiago that very few dogs in Chile received rabies shots, so that if he were bitten in the *campo*, he had to do one of two things—cut off the head of the animal and bring it in to be tested, or undergo the Pasteur series of fourteen shots in the stomach. Now if there was one thing Tomás hated, it was shots—the thought of fourteen of them in his stomach would put him in a cold sweat.

So, what was he supposed to do? How would he explain that to the Martinez family? "Excuse me Don Emilio, but may I borrow your axe. Tobi just bit me and I have to chop his head off and take it to Valdivia to be examined. Speaking of taking it to Valdivia, Señora, would you lend me one of your string shopping bags? It would make it much easier to carry Tobi's head down to the bus."

Chopping off Tobi's head was out of the question, and that was why he was so scared of him and, for that matter, all of the *campo* dogs. But he was especially scared of Tobi because the dog had so many opportunities to bite him. He supposed the best thing to do would be to grab a stout stick and have a one-on-one session with him. But he never got the chance, because there was always someone around and he did not want to be seen bludgeoning their dog. And so, Tobi continued to terrify him.

The worst times were when he went out to the wash station before bed. Every night, he held the kerosene lantern while brushing his teeth, and it cast an orange-yellow circle of light on the ground around him like a spotlight. Outside of that circle it was pitch black and somewhere in the dark would be Tobi, softly growling. Tobi was very, very close, but he was invisible. Tomás knew that at some point the dog would make his move, but he never knew when Tobi would thrust himself into his circle of light with a terrorizing growl and teeth bared. The lantern light would highlight his teeth and eyes, and make him look like a jackal as he lunged. Knowing the attack was coming made it worse. Each time, Tomás would jump a foot and vainly try to kick the dog and hang on to the lantern at the same time. But Tobi was too fast and he never connected, and the dog disappeared into the dark where he would continue to circle and growl. By the time Tomás entered the house again he was a nervous wreck. The most embarrassing moments, though, were when the dog attacked and he inadvertently let out a little scream. The kitchen was the closest room to the wash station and sometimes when the family was still up sitting at their table by the window, he could hear their muffled laughter. They could not understand how anyone could be so terrified of a small dog.

Lilia came out of the house and called Tobi off. Tomás grained Lobo and put the saddle and bridle away. When he entered the house, the Señora had the table set and told him to wash up for dinner. After he ate, Lilia came in to visit for awhile and then he studied Spanish. He went to bed early because the next day he would accompany the family, except for Jaime who would stay and watch the house, to Valdivia, where they would attend the funeral for a family of four.

The Valdivia family had been poor and slept in a single room heated by charcoal. One night they brought a *brasero* into their bedroom without letting the charcoal burn down to coals first, and they tragically died in their sleep from carbon monoxide poisoning. Emilio, the Señora, and the girls would attend the funeral and would stay overnight in town. Tomás was going in for a meeting at the Ministry of Agriculture but would not stay over. He wanted to return in time for a soccer practice in the late afternoon.

When he got off the bus at the Los Guindos trailhead the next day, he went over to the bushes where he always hid his walking stick. Because the bus had been crowded and had made a lot of stops, he needed to hustle to make it to practice. He set off at a brisk pace and arrived at the house in record time. When he opened the gate, the first thing he noticed was that there was no smoke coming out of the stovepipe and that the sheep were already in the corral. Jaime had put them in and was most likely at the soccer field. As he approached the house, the geese sounded the alarm and, true to form, Tobi streaked out from under the house. The dog barked and growled, occasionally looking back at the house. But no one came out, and Tomás realized this was his chance.

"Okay motherfucker, it's just you and me now. Come and get me. Come on, nice and close, you little fuck."

Tobi wisely kept his distance, but Tomás knew that if he turned his back, the little shit would try to bite him for sure. Tobi circled around as Tomás started to walk towards the house. The dog lunged and Tomás never moved more quickly in his life. He turned and swung the stick hard, hitting Tobi smack dab on one of his canine teeth. He was amazed the tooth did not break, and if he had not been so pissed at the animal, he might have laughed at the look of total surprise on Tobi's face. The dog immediately backed off, tucking his tail between his legs. Tomás gleefully looked at him and hoped he would try again. He held the stick up in anticipation, but the dog knew that things had changed.

"Come on you little motherfucker. Come on. One more time. Come on!"

But Tobi slunk away, and Tomás turned and walked to the house. He still kept his eye on the dog, but now Tobi followed at a very respectful distance. He leaned the stick up against the side of the house and went inside to change into sweatpants and soccer shoes. When he came out, Tobi was lying silently out in the barnyard, head on his paws, looking up at him.

"What do you think now, Tobi? Huh?"

The dog did not move. Tomás turned and hurried towards the soccer field, confidently leaving the stick leaning against the house.

CHAPTER FIVE

El Incendio (The Fire)

Jorge, who lived with his *abuelos*—grandparents—on the adjoining farm, began showing up at the Martinez home in the late afternoons before soccer practice. He would sit around and wait for Jaime to finish his chores before he, Jaime, and Tomás went over to the field together. To his credit, when Jaime showed up with an oxcart full of firewood, Jorge would cheerfully pitch in to help unload. Tomás couldn't believe how strong he was; Jorge could easily carry twice what he could. He had the build of a short, explosive college running back, with no neck and legs like tree trunks, and who was so fast and low to the ground that it was like trying to tackle a cannonball.

But Tomás thought that Jorge didn't come over to help Jaime with his chores or to be sociable. He came over to ogle the Martinez sisters. One afternoon when Jaime was still down in a *quebrada* cutting firewood, Tomás took advantage of the empty wash station to shave. Jorge was sitting at the table under the eucalyptus tree, and Tomás watched him in the mirror. Ana and Rosa were bent over, doing the washing in the pasture. Their butts were bobbing up and down, and Jorge was transfixed. He had one hand on top of the table, but the other was in his lap. Tomás saw that he was playing with himself.

A few days later, Tomás crossed the highway to visit some *socios* in Casa Blanca, and to learn what the teacher had found out in Valdivia. It was a cool, misty morning, and to keep his hands warm he held the reins underneath his *manta*. He was chilled, and couldn't wait for the sun to come out and burn everything off. As Lobo clip-clopped across the pavement, he thought of the teacher's idea. He hoped it would work out because he really had to do something. These trips were just too long and they were killing his poor horse. Time-wise, riding to Casa Blanca was like commuting to New York from Boston. Jaime kept telling Tomás that Lobo was too *flaco*—thin—and that Tomás was wearing him out.

"It is not like in your movies, Don Tomás, where the cowboys gallop everywhere all the time. You have to let your horse rest."

As he approached the Montoya farm, he saw Maria Elena out in front of the house wearing a man's hat, *manta*, and a long dark skirt. She was scattering scraps for the chickens. Her back was to him and she had her hair in that single braid again. She heard him pass by and turned. He waved, and she smiled and waved back before continuing to feed the chickens. Even all bundled up, he thought she was gorgeous.

Soon the soccer field and the school came into view. The thick dark smoke of a fire just lit came out of the chimney, and there were only a few children in front of the school. He could see others walking down the Casa Blanca and La Paloma roads. He rode up and, tying Lobo to a post, stepped onto the covered deck. Walking over to the schoolroom door, his spurs jingled. He wore spurs all the time now.

He knocked on the door and the teacher said, "*Pase adelante.*"

Standing at his desk, dressed in his usual pressed slacks and long-sleeved white shirt, the teacher was taking books and his lunch out of the green daypack he used every day.

"You are here early, Don Tomás."

"Yes. I hope to visit two farms in Casa Blanca today."

The teacher hung the daypack on the back of his chair.

"I have good news for you. The Committee said you can stay in the storeroom if you want. They thought it might even be a good idea to have someone keeping an eye on things. Come," he said heading towards the door. "Take a look at the room and see what you think."

There were actually two rooms. The front, smaller room wasn't much more than an entryway. There were shelves partially filled with cleaning utensils, and a mop and a bucket in a corner. An open doorway led into the other room, which was empty and had a large window that looked out to the Casa Blanca road, winding its way up the long hill behind the school. There was plenty of room for all his stuff. He told the teacher it was perfect.

The teacher smiled.

"I thought you would like it. I also went over and talked to Don Ramon Rodriguez yesterday," the teacher said, pointing towards the house set back from the road junction. "He said you could keep your horse there. You should talk to him."

Damn, he thought. He hadn't even thought about Lobo. Tomás and the teacher returned to the front deck. The children were congregating near the school-room door. The teacher looked at his watch.

"I should call the children in now. I will have a key made for you and you can start bringing your things over whenever you want."

He thanked the teacher several times before mounting Lobo and riding over to the Rodriguez farmhouse. The gate was one of the very few he had seen made from sawn lumber and real hinges. It swung open easily. A big gray dog heard him and rushed up barking. He was glad he was on Lobo.

He rode up to the two-story house and thought that whoever had built it had been ambitious. The first story had several windows, and was sheathed with horizontal boards that had a single bead running along the lower edge. A small, enclosed porch faced the road, and the vertical boards above it were scalloped on the bottom. Thick shakes covered the roof. Although the house was severely weathered, and there were a few missing or cracked panes in the downstairs windows, it was by far the fanciest structure he had seen in Cufeo.

A solid-looking middle aged man came out of a side door and down the steps from a small landing. He called out to the dog, which immediately stopped barking and ran up to him wagging his tail. As the man reached down to pet it, the dog flopped down and rolled onto its back. The man laughed and scratched its belly a moment before looking up, smiling. He was wearing a sweat-stained cowboy hat and a thick, cream-colored wool sweater-vest over a white shirt with the sleeves rolled up. His forearms were massive. Tomás had not met a *campesino* yet who did not look rugged, which made total sense considering all the wood they chopped with those big heavy axes. Although the man's pants were haphazardly patched, he did not appear ragged in the least—just weathered like the house behind him.

"Good morning," Tomás said. "Are you Don Ramon Rodriguez?"

"Yes, Don Tomás. It is good to finally meet you. I have seen you ride by many times."

"You must see many people passing by here."

"Yes. Sometimes too many. I like to visit—but then I do not get my work done."

He had a genuine and gentle smile. His eyes were warm and they smiled too.

"Then it is a good thing you talk now with a *gringo* like me, because I do not know how to say much. That means you can get your work done."

Ramon chuckled.

"No, this only makes it possible for me to do most of the talking."

Tomás laughed, instantly liking the man.

"Don Ramon, the *Profesor* said I might be able to keep my horse here during the school vacation."

"Yes. It would be a pleasure to have your horse here."

Tomás explained how Lobo got his name, and that he almost always needed help to catch him. Ramon said that wasn't a problem.

"My brother's two sons will be here for the summer and, believe me, they would much rather help catch your Lobo than help with the firewood. It truly is not a problem."

When he asked how much it would cost to keep Lobo there, Ramon refused any money.

"But, Don Ramon..."

"No. With your permission, it is settled. As I say, it is our pleasure. My family will not accept any money. Besides," he said looking at Lobo, "I do not think he is big enough to eat much of our pasture."

The dog came over and rubbed up against Ramon's leg. Ramon absently scratched his ears.

"Come. I will show you where you can put your saddle and other things."

After the barnyard tour and some *mate*, Tomás left for Casa Blanca. As he rode up the hill, he thought how *simpatico*—likable—Ramon was. He also thought that he had better tell the Martinez family about his moving plans right away. It was amazing how fast news traveled in the *campo* and he wanted them to hear about it from him first. It was not going to be easy, and he didn't want to insult them in any way. There was also the fact that he was settled in. Lilia was like a little sister, and Jaime had become a friend. He was even getting along so well with Tobi that he pet him the other day. The only part of living there that he didn't like was eating alone at the big table, waited on at every meal as if he were royalty. He yearned to be more part of the family.

Tomás crested the Casa Blanca hill. It would be his first visit to these two farms, and he knew they were somewhere past Don Pedro's on the main road. Time passed quickly as he thought about moving to the school. He was just passing the gate and trail that led down to Don Pedro's when he saw black smoke ahead. The smoke soon thickened and, in the clear weather, shot straight up in the sky. He watched it for a few minutes before he suddenly heard a horse galloping up from behind. He turned and saw Don Pedro flying up the road on his large mare. He held his hat with his free hand, and his gray hair and unbuttoned coat flew out behind him. He didn't slow down as he approached.

When he passed he yelled, "Fire, Don Tomás! It must be Don Eulogio's. He will need help. Hurry!"

Tomás spurred Lobo into a gallop. Don Eulogio was one of the two *socios* he had planned to visit.

He didn't gain on Don Pedro—not even close.
Man alive, he thought, that old man can ride! Don
Pedro disappeared around a bend in the road. The
smoke was much closer, and once he followed Don
Pedro around the bend he could see the fire. There
was a huge fireball on the backside of what was left of
a small barn. Don Eulogio's house was maybe fifty or
sixty feet from the burning barn and people were running in and out. They were dumping furniture and
other household items in a pile away from the house.
Two men ran up the road from the other direction,
and behind them someone approached by horse at a
full gallop. Tomás tied Lobo next to Don Pedro's mare
and ran as fast as he could to the house. He got there
just behind Don Pedro.

It was chaos. People were running in different
directions and screaming at each other. The heat
from the fire was brutal, and the eaves of the house
had begun to steam. When Don Pedro bellowed for
attention, everybody stopped and turned towards him.
He took control.

Don Pedro called Eulogio over.

"Ladders, Don Eulogio. And buckets and shovels.
Get them quickly! It is your only chance to save the
house."

Others arrived and formed a circle around Don
Pedro. Eulogio and his sons returned with everything.
They had a total of six buckets.

"*Niño*," Don Pedro said calmly to one of Eulogio's
sons, "show Don Tomás and Don Guillermo where
your spring is."

He turned to Tomás and a tall bearded man, whom
Tomás recognized as the fullback who had been thrown
out of the soccer tournament with Jorge.

"You two follow that boy and keep bringing us buckets of water."

He turned to two men who had just arrived. "You two start digging and fill the other buckets with dirt. Eulogio, do you have any more buckets?"

Eulogio shook his head. He was sweaty and soot covered, and he looked like he was about to cry.

"Then your largest soup pots—chamber pots—anything that can hold dirt."

Eulogio took off. Don Pedro turned back to Guillermo and Tomás. "What are you waiting for? Go!"

Guillermo and Tomás flew down the hill behind the boy. The spring was about two hundred feet from the house. They fast-walked and jogged back, trying not to spill water. When they got back to the house, two ladders were leaning against the building. Eulogio and another man were on the roof. People continued to carry out furniture. Someone was dumping clothes and bedding out of an upstairs window. Smoke was coming from several places on the roof, and Eulogio and the other man beat those areas with small rugs. Don Pedro yelled at Tomás and Guillermo to hand up the buckets, and men with containers of soil were ready to quickly follow.

Don Pedro yelled to the men on the roof, "Any place that is steaming, throw the water and then the soil on top of that spot so it will stick. Then it won't burn."

The heat was almost unbearable and the ladder very hot. Tomás handed a bucket up. It was three quarters full. He flew back down the ladder and a man followed with dirt. Tomás climbed back up with the other bucket and handed that up.

Don Pedro shouted, "Wet the edges and the corners—they catch first!"

The barn collapsed behind them, and a million sparks showered through the sky toward the shake roof. Eulogio and his neighbor scrambled around the ɔof like mad men, slapping at sparks with their little rugs.

Tomás had no idea how many trips he and Guillermo had made, but his arms soon ached and his thighs began to quiver. Running up and down stadium stairs back at college, when he was trying to get in shape for soccer, was nowhere near as intense as this. And the ladder was slippery from all the spilled water and soot. He was dog tired and he began to spill more water with each trip. But he and Guillermo kept hauling bucket after bucket.

It was late afternoon when they all agreed that the house was out of danger. Thank God and Don Pedro, Tomás thought. He collapsed with Guillermo next to the other men under a shade tree. Guillermo's soot-covered face matched his black beard.

"Don Guillermo, how did the fire start?"

Although they had worked side by side for hours, it was the first time Tomás had spoken to him. Guillermo pointed towards the huge pile of glowing coals on the other side of the burned down shed.

"*Carbón.* They had just harvested a cartload and there must have been a few smoldering pieces in one of the sacks."

He shook his head in dismay.

"It is a terrific loss for Don Eulogio and his family— the building and all the income from the charcoal. But at least they got his saddle and many of the tools out before it burned. And, *gracias a Dios*, he still has his house."

They saw Don Pedro bustling about, bringing things back inside the house. Tomás sighed and looked at Guillermo. They got up stiffly and went over to help.

After returning the large and heavy items to the house, the neighbors began to disband. They left a very grateful Eulogio and his family to sort through the rest. Tomás walked over to the horses with Don Pedro. Lobo's nostrils flared and he was skittish when Tomás untied the reins. Don Pedro laughed.

"He does not like the way you smell, Don Tomás. You must stop at my house to clean up—and for some refreshment."

Even though it was late and it would be dark soon, he accepted. He was famished.

The trail to the house wound down between pastures dotted with thousands of young pine. Don Pedro was planting more trees than any other *socio,* and this year he and his workers would plant a whopping twenty hectares. They dismounted in front of the house and Don Pedro led him around to the wash area. They both stripped off their shirts, and lathered up and rinsed with buckets of water. He couldn't help noticing Don Pedro's sinewy, hard muscles. For a man well into his sixties, he was in incredible shape.

Don Pedro offered to loan him a clean shirt and went off to get it. He returned with the shirt thrown over an arm and two glasses of an amber-colored drink with thick sediment in the bottom third of the glass. A spoon stuck out of each glass.

"Have you ever had *chicha con harina?*"

Tomás shook his head.

"It is apple cider with toasted wheat. Stir it up and then drink it. It is very nutritious."

He handed Tomás a glass and stirred his.

Tomás was about to take a drink when Don Pedro smiled and said, "Of course, this is last year's cider, so it is not *dulce.*"

They took long pulls of the cider. Tomás thought Don Pedro was right—the cider was certainly not 'sweet.' So this was what hard cider tasted like.

They sat on a bench as they finished their drinks.

"It is late and you need to return to Los Guindos. My Señora is making you something to eat for along the way. Do you want more *chicha*, Don Tomás?"

"Please."

Tomás thought about how the fire started, and realized he had no idea how charcoal was made. When Don Pedro returned, he asked him. Don Pedro took a large slug of cider and wiped his mouth with a sleeve before answering.

"It is a very difficult and very dirty job. Only the poorest farmer who cannot afford to hire a worker does it himself. There are big operations and small ones and everything in between. Each has its own special name, but the technique for all of them is the same. It is like a big kitchen cookstove. By opening and closing different vents, the fire is controlled and made to burn very slow. The *carboneros* carefully stack firewood and cover it with branches and then earth. By leaving small air tunnels in the mound, they can control how quickly the fire burns."

He stirred the sediment in his glass again and took another long drink.

"Because wood is no longer plentiful and because it is so difficult to bring up out of the *quebradas*, most charcoal operations here are small now. They are called *monos*. A *mono* is round and about four meters in diameter on the ground and smaller towards the top. It is about two-and-a-half to three meters tall."

His description matched a smoking and squat, dirt covered mound Tomás had seen on one of his rides.

"It burns for about eight days and yields about sixty sacks. Every *mono* has a little tunnel called *la mecha* that is built out of thin dry sticks and is set on fire. It burns into the pile and ignites the mass. The *carbonero* has a long stick with a piece of tire on the end which he lights and then sticks in the *mecha*. But it is all very tricky. You have to watch where the smoke is coming from and how much smoke, and then make sure it is burning thoroughly. If one side is not burning, you have to make new holes or tunnels to draw the fire over. But maybe the most important thing of all is the harvest."

Don Pedro's Señora came out with a little newspaper-wrapped bundle. She waited for Don Pedro to finish.

"The *carbonero* has to be very careful when he uncovers the charcoal and breaks it apart to put into sacks. He has to make absolutely sure that there is not a single ember. It only takes one smoldering piece to set the whole sack on fire, which is what happened today. I don't know what Don Eulogio was thinking, when he parked that cart so close to the buildings. He knows better. But one thing is for sure," he said standing up. "He will never do that again."

The Señora stepped forward and handed Tomás the little bundle.

"It is not much, Don Tomás. Only some bread with some marmalade and cheese. But it is at least something to tide you over during your return."

They escorted Tomás to his horse and wished him a safe journey home. He set off, and it was dark by the time he passed the Central Caman schoolhouse. There was some moonlight, but that really didn't matter because Lobo knew where they were headed. Once they crossed the Pan American, Lobo picked up his pace. When they arrived home, the Señora hustled him inside and sat him down at the table. In minutes she set a bowl of hot soup in front of him and asked why he was so late. As he told her about the fire, the whole family crowded around the table to hear the news. Emilio looked stunned and sat down heavily next to Tomás. The Señora shook her head slowly from side to side.

The next morning, he wanted to tell the family right away about moving into the school. But he slept through breakfast, and Emilio lunched down in the *quebrada* where he was cutting firewood. That evening before dinner, Tomás went over to the kitchen doorway and asked the family permission to enter.

"*Con permiso?*"

"Yes, Don Tomás," the Señora said. "Come in, come in."

The kitchen was lit by simple kerosene lamps made out of old Nescafe coffee cans. The wicks, encased in small metal tubes, had been driven down through the tops of the cans and they gave off a soft yellowish-orange, slightly sooty light. The evening was chilly and the cookstove made the kitchen warm and cozy. The floor was swept and the kitchen very tidy and organized. There were pots and pans on the walls, and different dried food hung from nails driven into the upstairs floor joists. Emilio looked very comfortable in a chair close to the stove. His hands were folded in his lap and he looked like he had been dozing. Jaime, Ana, and Lilia were sitting around the table in front of the window while Rosa, kerchief on head, was moving pots around the stove and stirring things. The Señora sat in a straight-backed chair, working a spinning wheel set in front of her. With her thumbs and index fingers she pinched and picked and pulled at the bunch of wool in her lap to feed the simple machine, while pumping the pedal beneath it. She kept spinning even as she looked over at him expectantly. There were a couple large balls of yarn at her feet. The Señora must have noticed the serious expression on his face because she stopped spinning. Everyone looked at him. He cleared his throat and began.

"I do not know how to say this, but I hope I say it well. First, I want all of you to know that I am very happy here. It is very comfortable, and I think I have even made friends with Tobi."

"It seems that maybe one day," the Señora said smiling, "you and Tobi came to an understanding."

He wondered if they knew he had belted their dog; but whether they did or not, it was obviously okay.

"You have seen the map that I have been making and you know how far your farm is from all of the other *socios*. Every time I go on my visits it means many hours of riding and I can only go to one or two farms in a day. There are still several farms, like in Lote Once, that I have not even been to yet. And, as Don Jaime has told me many times, Lobo is getting thin from all these long trips. For these reasons I have been thinking that I should be in a more central location to do my work."

Lilia's eyes were suddenly dark and serious.

"Believe me, I am very happy here. But I think it is important to live closer to the other *socios*."

No one said anything.

"I have talked to the *Profesor* in Central Caman and he has given me permission to live at the school during the summer vacation. I thought that maybe I should try this and see how it goes."

The Señora was the first to speak.

"Don Tomás, please sit down. Lilia, would you pull up a chair for Don Tomás?"

He sat down and folded his hands on the table.

"We suspected for some time that you have been thinking this way and, yes, your map and horse are proof that maybe this is the wrong location for you. We want you to know that if you decide to go to Caman, we realize it is because of your work. We believe you are happy here, do not worry. But we also want you to know that we too are happy to have you here. If you go to Caman and it does not go well, you always have a home here."

Emilio nodded in agreement with his wife.

"It is the truth, Don Tomás."

With a lump in his throat, Tomás said, "Thank you. It was not easy for me to say these things—but now you make me feel much better."

As he started to get up, the Señora asked, "Don Tomás, would you like to eat dinner with us here tonight?"

He quickly sat back down.

"Yes Señora. Very much."

"Lilia," the Señora said, "Go and bring in Don Tomás's dinner things and set a place at our table for him."

When Lilia returned and set the table, the Señora went back to her spinning, and it suddenly seemed the most natural thing in the world for him to be in the kitchen. Suddenly Jaime turned to him with a startled look on his face.

"What is it, Don Jaime?"

"What about *futbol?*"

"What about it?"

"Does this mean you will be playing now for Caman this summer?"

"Of course not. You have my hand on it."

He reached across the table. Jaime visibly relaxed as they shook, and Tomás could see the Señora smiling out of the corner of his eye. After a moment or two, Ana got up to help Rosa at the stove while he and Jaime talked soccer. The Señora continued to spin, Lilia reached for her schoolbooks, and Emilio started to snooze. It was family business as usual and he was loving it.

When dinner was ready and on the table, the Señora and Emilio came over and sat down and they began to eat. Later, when Lilia cleared his dishes, the Señora said, "Lilia, when those are clean, I do not think they need to go into the other room. Put them with ours. I think Don Tomás will be eating with us from now on."

Over the next two weeks, anything he could lash to the saddle or fit in saddlebags he dropped off at the storeroom of the school when he passed by. The teacher gave him the key and said he would leave a charcoal brazier to heat water. He would also leave the school's water buckets and would move his desk and chair into the storeroom. Ramon lined up a nearby family to cook him two meals a day and to wash his clothes.

Tomás was excited about the move, although it was going to be hard to leave the Martinez home. Things there were more comfortable than ever, except for Lilia, who seemed angry with him. One evening the Señora explained to him, while he watched her spin, that usually the big dining table in his room was only used on holidays or when relatives and friends visited. But she had thought he would feel more comfortable eating there because it was their prettiest room. He told her that he much preferred to eat with them, and they agreed that if he returned after the summer, he would always eat in the kitchen. He decided he would leave on the Sunday that there was a tournament at La Paloma. Jaime would help him take the last of his things on the way. His trunk, which was mostly empty now, would remain at the house until the end of school vacation, when he would decide what he would do next.

So, with everything arranged, the final day came and he said his goodbyes. He shook hands with Ana and Rosa, and thanked them for the excellent meals and for his clean clothes. He started to shake the Señora's hand, but she would have none of that and instead she hugged him and kissed his cheek.

"Remember, Don Tomás, our home is your home."

Don Emilio, smiling as always, gave him an *abrazo*—he shook Tomás's hand, hugged him while thumping his back, and shook his hand again. Lilia had hung back, not saying anything, and he was not sure what to say to her. He knelt down so he was about her height. Her big dark eyes looked sad.

"Lilia, I want you to know that you were my first and best teacher. I have learned so much from you—the words for all the things around us, and all about the *campo*. I want to thank you. I will miss you very much."

As he stood up, Lilia ran forward and hugged his waist hard. She was shaking and silent as tears streamed down her face. He stroked her head, trying to keep his own emotions in check, and then gently freed her arms so he could kneel in front of her again.

"Lilia, the Los Guindos tournament is at the end of the summer. If I come over early, would you take me to find some *chupones*? They should be red-brown by then and I hear they are 'very sweet and very good.'"

Lilia looked at him, smiling through her tears.

"*Sí*, Don Tomás. *Con mucho gusto*"

He stroked her head a few more times before he stood up and went over to mount Lobo. As Jaime and he headed out towards the road, Tomás turned in his saddle to wave at everyone. And they all waved back.

CHAPTER SIX

La Carrera (The Horserace)

For the first week, Tomás was excited by the move to the schoolhouse. He enjoyed his new privacy. He could change his clothes or bathe without the Señora or one of the daughters walking in. There was more than enough room for his things, which were neatly arranged on the shelves in the entry. He hung his *manta* as a curtain over the window at night. He bought a bag of charcoal and placed it and the *brasero* in one corner of the entry. In another he placed the two buckets of water, which he had filled from a nearby spring. In the big room, his sleeping bag lay on a thin foam pad on the floor, and the *Profesor's* desk and chair were in front of the window. It was comfortable enough. It was his cozy little home.

His mornings were leisurely and he loved them. He would take the *brasero* out to the deck and start a charcoal fire to heat some water. While he waited for the water to boil, he sliced up some bread and cheese and prepared his *mate*. When everything was ready, he ate out on the deck and watched life go by. He looked straight across the soccer field to Ramon's farm and occasionally he saw movement there—Ramon walking in the pasture or letting the sheep out of the corral, the oxen grazing, the large gray dog patrolling his territory. An old rooster crowed weakly every now and then. Hearing its feeble salute added to the bucolic setting and made him smile. On a clear day, Volcán Osorno was visible in the distance. Occasionally he would hear the *trele* birds sound the alarm somewhere, and eventually a rider or an oxcart would pass by. It was all very pleasant. But, as much as he enjoyed these mornings, they also seemed unreal. Could he really be here? It was like he was sitting at a theater watching a movie about a different time.

The newness and excitement of living in the storeroom quickly wore off. He began to miss the Martinez family and the comfort and warmth of their home. Their routine had been reassuring. He missed going out with Lilia to bring in the sheep in the late afternoon, and the exercise and camaraderie of kicking a soccer ball around with his team. A couple of times when he wasn't off visiting farms, Juan invited him to join the Caman players in front of the school, but it wasn't the same.

He took his meals nearby with the Gomez family. They were nice, but overly respectful, which made things stiff and formal. And there were long periods of silence that were all too familiar, like he was starting all over again.

Sergio Gomez was the head of the family. He and his much younger Señora, from a second marriage, were the parents of a cute five-year old named Margarita. There was also Flor, the daughter from Sergio's first marriage who was about Tomás's age. The routine never varied. Sergio would sit at the end of the table and whenever Tomás spoke to him, he would nod seriously as if Tomás was expounding on Einstein's theory of relativity. Sergio would say, "Yes, 'Meester.' That is so, 'Meester,'" nodding his head up and down like a bobble-head doll. He would beam at Tomás throughout the meal, while telling his daughters to pass this or that to 'Meester.' They never had a conversation of any length.

Tomás did not say much to the young Señora. He thought she seemed a little too friendly. He didn't know if she was actually flirting, but she made him uncomfortable. And the older daughter, Flor, was terribly shy. She was not a beauty, but did have beautiful, very dark and sensitive eyes. He thought that if it was true that eyes mirrored the soul, then Flor was probably a very good person. But she was so shy. Every time he spoke with her—even if only to ask her to pass the butter—she would blush furiously and avert her eyes. So, he did not say much to her either. And poor little Margarita was hushed by Sergio every time she tried to say anything.

The family had a dog that made Tobi look like a Chihuahua. Whenever Tomás arrived it went berserk, and he had to hold it off with his stick until Flor and the Señora came out to pull the struggling, snarling beast off to a corner and chain it. He could not figure out why they didn't chain the dog before he came over, since he always arrived at the same time. It was not long before he began to dread taking his meals with the Gomez family.

One evening he came over for dinner and Sergio wasn't there. The Señora explained that he was working late cutting firewood in the *quebrada*. She said he wanted to finish a load before going to Valdivia early tomorrow with Flor. Tomás sat down and they ate dinner in customary silence. When the plates were being

cleared, the Señora came up from behind and put a
hand softly on his shoulder as she leaned over to take
his plate. A breast grazed his head and he looked up.
There was no mistaking the look in the Señora's eyes.
He quickly glanced over to Flor in the kitchen, but her
back was turned. The Señora's fingers lingered as she
took his plate away.

Sergio arrived a short time later. He sat down at the
head of the table and his wife brought him his soup.
He apologized for being so late.

"And 'Meester,' just because Flor and I are going
to Valdivia tomorrow does not mean my Señora will
not have the mid-day meal ready for you at the usual
time."

Sergio reached for a piece of bread and dipped it
into his soup. Flor was watching Tomás closely. The
Señora smiled at him from the kitchen. Warning flags
popped up in Tomás's head. No way should he be
alone with the Señora.

"Thank you, Don Sergio, but please do not worry
about lunch for me tomorrow. I have to go to Casa
Blanca in the morning and will not return until late in
the afternoon."

He stood up and bid them goodnight. As he walked
back to the school, he thought about the Señora and
the look in her eyes. He hadn't been with a girl for a
long time, and she was young and pretty enough. He
started to fantasize.

The next morning he was taking a sponge bath
when there was a knock at his door. It startled him
because he had never had a visitor. He thought it must
be Ramon wanting to tell him something.

"*Un momento.*"

He quickly dried off and threw on his pants.
Grabbing a shirt, he opened the door. Sergio's Señora
stood there with a basket on her arm. Tomás didn't

know who was more surprised—him to have her standing there or her to see him half naked.

"Señora," he exclaimed and quickly put his shirt on. Her eyes swept over his naked chest and navel. She said, "I have brought you some *empanadas* for your trip today."

Stumbling over the words he said, "You shouldn't have. But thank you. But I was just leaving and I..."

Tomás hoped no one came up the road. This did not look so good. She leaned around him and peered into the storeroom.

"So this is how you live. You are very organized."

She leaned in a little more and glanced towards his sleeping bag. "Is that where you sleep... on the floor?"

He finished buttoning his shirt and squeezed past her to get his socks and boots. She smelled like fresh bread. She really wasn't bad looking, he thought. Hard to tell about her body though, with all those clothes on.

"That cannot be very comfortable, sleeping on the floor and," she said looking directly into his eyes, "it must be very lonely." She moved closer.

Tomás hesitated in the doorway, not sure what to do. And he couldn't help it—he started to get an erection. Wait a minute, he thought. Try to think, Tomás! If you mess around with her, you could get killed by an angry husband. At the very least, there will be a scandal and you'll be kicked out of the Peace Corps. And you'll lose your occupational deferment and be drafted the moment you set foot back in the States. Want to go to 'Nam,' Tomás? Was that worth a quick roll in the hay? He quickly made up his mind.

"Excuse me, Señora," he said and squeezed by again, shutting the door behind him.

He sat down on the edge of the deck. If he could just get his boots on before anyone came by, then

everything would at least look respectable. He watched
the road like a hawk. There. One on and one to go.
He reached for the other boot when—shit!—a horse
and rider came around the bend. Damn! It was Maria
Elena. She saw them on the deck. He thought she
pointedly looked at them as she came up the road. He
finished putting on the boot and, out of the corner of
his eye, saw the Señora move away from him. When he
stood up she was all business, and made quite a show
of bestowing the *empanadas*. When she turned towards
the road, she pretended to have just seen Maria Elena.
The Señora smiled and waved to her, then turned back
to him and formally shook his hand goodbye as if that
was all there had been to it. She stepped off the deck
and began walking back towards her house.

Tomás wondered if maybe he was mistaken about the
Señora's intentions. But he'd never known his body to lie
to him before. As he watched her walk away, he thought
he had passed a test. What was that joke? God gave man
a heart, but he did not make it strong enough to pump
blood to his penis and his brain at the same time.

About a week later he was out on the deck drinking
mate when the Rodriguez gate opened and Ramon's
two nephews, Javier and Alex, rode out on their father's
big tan-colored horse. Ramon's brother Pablo and his
family had moved up from Valdivia for the summer.
The two boys rode bareback with Alex, behind, carrying an axe that was about as long as he was tall. They
returned a little while later, as Tomás was throwing out
dirty dishwater. Javier was on the horse and had a small
evergreen tree over his shoulder while Alex walked
next to him, still carrying the axe. Alex opened the
gate and the pair continued on up to the house where
the big gray dog greeted them, its tail wagging. They
had gone out to cut a Christmas tree. Tomás had for-

gotten about Christmas, but now he realized that it was less than a week away. How could that possibly be— everything was green, it was warm, and it was summer.

What should he do to celebrate the day? He knew he didn't want to eat with the Gomez family on Christmas—anything but that! Maybe he would hear from the Martinez family; but there had been no word from them since he had moved. What to do? There was a volunteer he had hung out with in Valdivia, but Tomás knew he planned to spend the holiday with a volunteer couple up north. He waited a couple days, but when there was still no word from the Martinez family, he decided to go at the last minute to Valdivia to buy some special treats for Christmas day. Things like smoked meats and fine cheeses, ripe olives, and a good bottle of wine. Maybe a pastry or two for dessert. He would have his own smorgasbord.

On Christmas day he arranged everything on the teacher's desk, surveyed his little feast, and tried to get excited. But it was hard. As he munched on some cheese, he began thinking of all the things he missed from home: listening to Lionel Barrymore as Scrooge in "A Christmas Carol"; going to the local pageant with his parents; secretly singing along to carols on the car radio. It also seemed strange to not be going to parties with his friends, who would be home from school now. And where was his stocking anyway? He drank half of the bottle of wine, hoping the alcohol would perk him up. It did, but not for long. He wished he had someone to talk to, someone with whom he could share his thoughts. But he probably couldn't speak Spanish well enough to communicate them, plus who here would care about a *gringo's* take on things anyway? The thought depressed him. He sat at the desk and stared out at the hill for a long time. What was he doing here?

For the first time since arriving in the *campo* he decided to skip his studies. The Peace Corps office in Valdivia had a good paperback library, and he had brought several novels up the hill with his Christmas goodies. He took one over to his desk. At least, he thought, reading a book would pass the time.

As the days passed after Christmas, he became more and more depressed. He read more and studied less. He stayed in bed a little longer each day. He would read and read. When he tired of that, he would stare at the ceiling. When he finally got up, his breakfast and *mate* would last until late morning. Afterwards he would walk over to tell the Gomez family that he would skip the mid-day meal. He just didn't have the energy to sit at that table and suffer through the silence. Everything, for that matter, seemed to require a lot of effort— except reading the novels. His Spanish suffered and so did his housekeeping. He began to rinse his plate and silverware in cold water rather than wash them in hot. He stopped sweeping the storeroom. He hoped the *Profesor* would not make a surprise visit because he wasn't taking very good care of the place. He knew he should get up off his ass and clean up his act. But he couldn't— he had never felt so down before.

He made fewer trips out to the farms. Occasionally he inspected the *roce a fuego* work being done by the *socios* as they prepared their land for the planting season. What a joke, he thought. A degree in history hadn't prepared him for this. What did he know about clearing land, planting trees, and stringing fence? He couldn't even tell if a clearing was five hectares or ten. When he inspected their work, he tried to look like he knew what he was doing. But he felt like an impostor.

He thought he had been adjusting pretty well to *campo* life, and that he was over the culture shock of living with people who were poor and whose way of

life was so different from his. Sure they had very little
money—and what they had, they worked very hard for.
Yet, they had clothes on their backs and food on the
table. Their homes were functional and well-kept, and
mostly cheerful. And they had gardens and animals,
plus the tools that they needed to take care of it all.

But when he rode farther up into the hills, he discovered the *socios* there were desperately poor. The
land was steep and extremely hard to work. Most of
the houses were two and three room shacks with dirt
floors and few if any windows. None of the windows
had glass. If the weather was bad, rough wooden shut-
ters were pulled in and latched, making it dark inside.
Simple benches, tables, and beds, made from the same
rough slabs that sided the exterior, were the only furniture. Two or three beds, their lumpy mattresses stuffed
with wool, were shared by a whole family. During the
good weather when the windows and doors were open,
chickens or a pig often wandered into the houses, sul-
lying the floor as they poked around. The children
looked wild, with runny noses and dirty faces. Their
thick and unruly black hair looked like they had just
gotten out of bed and their clothes were threadbare.
Few wore shoes. Girls who must have been Lilia's
age had sores and pale scars on their bare legs. They
helped their mothers with chores while holding a snot-
nosed baby brother or sister on a cocked hip.

He was always invited to share their food, which was
the last thing he wanted to do because he knew how
little they had. And, of course, he was the guest of
honor and was always given the largest portion. One
day he sat down to share the midday meal with a family
of seven. The only light came through the open
doorway and a small window near where the food was
prepared. There wasn't even a sink in the kitchen—
only a dish pan and a bucket. From his place at the

table, he could see some molting chickens outside scratching around the yard. They were half bald with skinny red necks. The Señora had severely wiped the faces of the children with a damp cloth before they were allowed to sit down, and their cheeks had a raw, flushed look. They could not take their eyes off him. The Señora nervously apologized for the humble meal. The watery soup had some cabbage and potatoes in it, and he noticed that he had twice the cabbage and potatoes of anyone else. He also had the only piece of meat, a chicken's foot. He looked outside again at the molting chickens, scratching around in the muck of discarded potato peels and dirty dishwater. He looked back at his soup and wondered how he was supposed to eat a chicken's foot. At the same time, he felt terrible for the family—for their poverty and for their embarrassment at having so little to offer. Following custom, he left the meat until he had finished the rest of his soup. When he began to eat the chicken's foot, he quickly realized that his knife and fork were useless. He picked it up with his hands, and forced himself to smile in between attempts to pull the rubbery skin away from the gristly cartilage with his teeth. He had never noticed before how long the toenails of a chicken were.

Riding back to the school, he wondered if he could really make a difference in these people's lives, or if he was just wasting everybody's time and eating the food—including chickens' feet—that they needed for themselves. He visited a few more families in that area that week. He did not have to eat any more chickens' feet, but the farms were all the same—very poor land, small shacks, large families with shared beds, no shoes, runny noses, and dirt floors. He did not enjoy these trips. And he was not enjoying his life. He hid more and more in the storeroom, reading his books and sleeping a lot.

At the end of the week, as he returned late down the Casa Blanca road, he saw an oxcart piled high with fresh-cut saplings and branches parked near the school. Men were hammering and sawing and had some poles laid out on the ground. He saw Juan pulling branches from the cart, and rode up to him.

"Don Juan, what is all this? What is happening?"

Juan put his bundle of branches down near the poles.

"We are building a *ramada* for the *carrera* this Sunday."

Tomás hadn't heard anything about it and he didn't even know what a *carrera* was. He thought the word meant highway.

"What is a *carrera?*"

Lobo was tugging at the reins, impatient to get to his grain and pasture.

"A horserace. A horse will be brought out from Valdivia to race against one from Casa Blanca."

Tomás looked around. Other than the piles of branches, everything looked the same.

"Where do they race?"

"They start near the road junction and race along the cut-in section alongside the road here. Come with me. I will show you."

Juan sort of skipped with his bad leg as they walked over to what Tomás had always thought was an old section of road that wasn't used anymore. At the far end of it, near the La Paloma and Casa Blanca junction, he saw that a horizontal pole thirty feet long, made out of two saplings lashed together, was nailed to the tops of four short posts. As they walked up to it, Juan explained.

"The race will start here. This track was scraped into the pasture many years ago when the Caman road was built and it is where we always have our *carreras*. The riders line up on either side of this pole up at that end. They do a running start and have to pass this end at exactly the same moment. There is a judge, the *griton*, who makes sure the riders are *a la pareja* when they pass here, and if they are he yells and the race is on. If they are not even, he will not yell and they will have to start over."

Juan looked down the track.

"The distance has to be agreed on by both horse owners—but it will probably be two hundred and fifty meters. After that, the track begins to go up hill. Ours is a short track. Most are longer."

They began to walk back.

"There will be other races later in the day, but those will be between the horses from around here."

Juan grinned.

"After drinking some wine and watching the big race, many will want to prove that their horse is faster than their neighbor's. There will be a lot of betting."

As they returned to the oxcart, Juan told him that the race would be an all day event and that *empanadas* and wine would be sold at the *ramada*. Tomás said he wouldn't miss it for anything.

"Good. But you'd better not drink too much wine, Don Tomás, or you may end up racing yourself."

"You do not have to worry about that. I will leave Lobo over at Don Ramon's. Until Sunday, Don Juan."

He turned Lobo towards the Rodriguez farm. It was the first time all day the horse wanted to trot.

Sunday turned out to be gray and cool, and it looked like it might rain. But still, Tomás was excited, and he felt perkier than he had for some time. Maybe this would get him out of his rut. He rose early, lit a charcoal fire, heated some water, and shaved. He cleaned the storeroom and his dishes. With all the people around, he thought, he might even have a guest today. Maybe Emilio and Jaime would come and he could show off his little abode. Except for Sergio's Señora, he still hadn't had a single visitor. He sat on the deck and drank *mate* while several women arrived with their cookware and supplies, and began to set up in the *ramada*. Maria Elena was one of them. Her hair was in that long thick braid again and she was all business as she bustled around. A man brought a burlap bag of charcoal and the women immediately started a fire. Early-bird spectators began to arrive. As the morning went on, more and more people came—most were men on horseback. By midday there must have been close to a hundred people. The *ramada* was busy and a lot of wine had been drunk even though the race would not start for some time. Anticipation built as the men drank, ate, and made their bets.

Tomás walked over to look at the two horses kept by their handlers in separate areas of the pasture. There was a small circle of spectators around each. Both horses were saddled with a single sheep pelt with the cinch passing over it and around the horse's belly. There were no stirrups. The horse from Valdivia was an impressive, glossy jet black, with muscles that were bulked up and well defined. The other horse was gray and very large—but, other than that, Tomás thought, it looked nondescript. Although he was told that the big gray had never been beaten, he picked the horse from Valdivia to win easily.

He went over to the *ramada* and ordered some *empanadas* and a cup of red wine. Maria Elena brought him his *empanadas*.

"*Muchas gracias*, Señorita Maria Elena."

There was a flicker of surprise in her eyes when he said her name.

"*De nada*, Don Tomás," she said with a beautiful smile.

Of course she would know his name, he thought. Who didn't by now? God, she was pretty. Such deep dark brown eyes. She turned back to her cooking. The *empanadas* were delicious and so juicy he had to wipe his chin on his sleeve. Pretty, and she could cook too, he mused.

Tomás wandered around looking for someone he knew. He did not see Juan or Ramon anywhere. Or Emilio and Jaime. A lot of the men were still on horseback. Everyone was having a good time—laughing and joking, making their bets, and drinking their wine. He saw the two racehorses being led up to the starting area and he walked over to the track and crowded in near the finish line. Everyone's head was turned towards the starting area as they waited. Suddenly the horses were off, but they didn't go far before they slowed down and stopped. They returned to the starting area. A short time later they were off again and the same thing happened—they stopped and returned to the starting area. The crowd began to buzz. Someone next to him was shaking his head. The horses lined up again and the crowd quieted. The horses took off and this time there was a shout from the *griton,* and a roar went up from the crowd as the horses kept on running. They were flying down the track. The black horse was off to a quick lead. From his vantage point he could only guess, but he thought the black horse was at least a couple of lengths ahead. That quickly changed. The big gray was incredible. Once he got up to full speed and extended those long legs, he was beautiful to watch. With long powerful strides, he caught up and thundered past the black stallion. Such raw power. The big grey was at least three lengths ahead when he passed the finish line to the cheers of the locals. There was a lot of laughter and backslapping. *Escudo* bills were changing hands everywhere.

Tomás returned to the crowded *ramada* for another cup of wine, and was surrounded by lively bar conversation. He tried to join in, but failed miserably. It was as if he were invisible. People were talking all around him and sometimes across him. A couple of times he said "That was a good race, wasn't it?" and he would maybe get a nod of agreement before the person would turn away and continue his conversation with someone else. He recognized a *socio* and thought he caught his eye. But the *socio* pretended not to see him. Tomás felt like a duck out of water. And what would he say to them anyway? Comment on the weather? Talk about reforestation? Ask how the work was going? No. Today was a boys' day out and it was about drinking and horseracing. And the only thing he knew about horseracing was that mint juleps were drunk at the Kentucky Derby. This was a day for the *campesinos* to do their own thing— take the day off and enjoy themselves—and he did not fit into the picture. He finished his wine, and, as he ordered another, he noticed that Maria Elena was looking at him. Was that a look of pity? Their eyes met and held for an instant before she turned away and started poking the *empanadas*.

He wandered through the crowd. Several *campesinos* stood around two young men on horses that were saddled with simple sheep pelts. Money was exchanging hands. Nearby was another small group and he recognized a *socio.* He walked up and greeted him. The *socio* smiled stiffly and politely introduced Tomás to the others. Suddenly no one had anything to say. The men looked around and fidgeted; it reminded him of when Bob had left to catch the bus and he was alone with the Martinez family for the first time. He said it looked like it might rain and they all nodded. Then silence. They stood there looking around. Finally he said that it was nice to have met them and that he wanted to head over towards the track. He saw relief surface in their eyes, and he wasn't more than a few steps away when they were deep in conversation again.

A crowd was beginning to form along the track, and he walked over to the finish line. This race was fairly close, but he felt like he was watching it from a distance. Even the noise seemed muffled, as if he was not really there. After the race he bought another *copa* and went off by himself to observe the crowd. He wondered how many races there would be. Some of the men were very drunk. Many had mounted their horses, and when they rode up to the *ramada* their friends passed wine up to them. He saw a man purposely nudge his horse up against another man, making him stumble forward a couple of steps and spill his wine. The man on horseback laughed. The other man looked up at him and angrily said something. Heads turned, and the man on the horse went ballistic. He leaped off the horse, and soon the two men were rolling around in the dirt trying to do as much damage to each other as possible. A circle closed in around them. Finally someone pulled them apart and they went to separate corners of the *ramada* and resumed their drinking. It was late afternoon now, and more and more men were stumbling around. One *campesino* that Tomás didn't know came up with a big smile and greeted him as if he were a long lost friend. But he knew the *campesino* only wanted him to buy him a cup of wine. It looked like another race was about to be run, but he couldn't care less. It was time to leave. As the men crowded around the track, he bought a liter bottle of wine and went to the schoolhouse.

He entered the storeroom and shut the scene behind him with relief. He set the bottle down on the *Profesor's* desk in front of the window. Some of the race fans had begun to leave and he watched them as they went up the hill towards Casa Blanca. He went to the entryway and returned with a glass. It looked like it would rain.

He drank almost half the bottle before he realized it was time for dinner at the Gomez home. Reluctantly he washed up. When he looked in the mirror to brush his hair, he saw that his lips were stained from the wine and his tongue was purple. He quickly brushed his teeth and even scrubbed his tongue with his toothbrush. Finally, when he thought he was half way presentable, he put on his *manta* and grabbed his stick for the dog. He hoped that all the wine he had drunk would at least make dinner more tolerable.

When he arrived at the house, he didn't even mind the dog's stupid barking. During the meal he surprised everyone, including himself, when he became downright chatty. Sergio had not been at the race so Tomás told him all about it. Sergio nodded enthusiastically. Tomás talked to the Señora for a change and she was all smiles. Flor, of course, blushed furiously when he spoke to her. But, at least there wasn't the usual silence. Maybe this was a break-through, he thought. When the dishes were being cleared and he was talking about the race again with Sergio, little Margarita interrupted him.

She blurted out, "Listen to 'Meester' tonight. He is talking like a parrot."

Sergio immediately scolded her because he thought she was being disrespectful. She began bawling, and Tomás was totally embarrassed. He knew Margarita had just been telling it like it was—he HAD been talking like a parrot. He was a regular chatterbox. A heavy silence fell and he didn't say another word at the table. And no one else did either.

It was almost dark when he returned to the school, and a small but noisy crowd was still at the *ramada*.

Four or five men in *mantas de Castilla,* with hats pulled low, were on horseback, swigging wine from a bottle that they passed around. Some ragged looking men were leaning against the bar and were very drunk. He guessed they were *trabajadores*—workers—who did not own land and who cut firewood and made charcoal for a living. They were usually paid little more than a cot to sleep on and food. They were too poor to own even a horse and, sadly, many spent their meager wages on drink. In the *campo* hierarchy, they were only a step above the dogs.

Tomás entered his room and lit the kerosene lantern. He took off his *manta* and hung it over the window, and then sat down heavily at the desk. Today had been terrible. He felt more than ever that he didn't fit in. He pulled out his novel, but he couldn't concentrate and soon put it down. He filled up his glass with wine and thought about the families he had visited recently. Something bumped hard into the side of the schoolhouse. Tomás started to investigate, but sat back down when he heard someone begin to vomit. What a cheery night, he thought as he finished the bottle of wine.

After awhile he heard a few rain drops on the metal roof. Then it began to rain in earnest. It was raw in the room. He mustered the energy to stand up and get the brazier out of the corner of the entryway. He took it outside to the deck, bumping his shoulder hard on the doorframe on his way out. There was no noise from the *ramada.* The bad weather had shut it down and there was only the sound of the rain. Water poured off the deck roof. There were no lights anywhere and it was pitch black. With paper and kindling, he soon had a good fire going and the firelight danced on the schoolhouse wall. He brought his chair out by the brazier and added charcoal to the fire as it burned down.

So how's life, Tomás? he pondered. Having fun yet? Yeah, right. Face it. What you've been doing here hasn't amounted to a pee-hole in the snow. What have you accomplished—other than eating a lot of poor people's food? Let's see. You scored a few soccer goals. Whoop-dee-do. Now that's really made a difference in these people's lives. And how many friends have you made? How many have knocked on your door? You haven't had a single visitor since you've been here. And how was your 'day at the races' for God's sake? Great. You made everybody around you uncomfortable. Everybody!

Hell, you don't even have a life back in the States. How many friends have written since you have been here? Zilch. And your parents? What a joke. A cursory letter once a month if you're lucky. So, what's the problem? Well, that's pretty easy to see. You. You just don't fit—anywhere.

He got up and went in to get some more charcoal for the fire. He glanced over at the empty bottle and wished he had some more wine. He added the charcoal to the fire and sat down, thinking again.

Hell, Father says I should be in Vietnam. Thinks the Peace Corps is for draft dodgers and sissies.

"But this isn't the Second World War, Dad. This isn't your Battle of the Bulge. This war is wrong."

"Hogwash! Your generation is just scared and spoiled. Going to war will make an instant man out of you."

Maybe he should scram. Go back to the States and get drafted. Now there's a great solution—get drafted and go fight in a senseless war. Maybe a bullet would end it then. Put this fucking misfit out of his misery. Yeah, and Dad could have his instant man—his instant dead man. Shit, he didn't have to go to Vietnam for that. He could put a bullet in his head anywhere.

Except he didn't have a gun. And it would be messy. And probably hurt a lot too. He watched the charcoal smoking. Now there's a peaceful way to go. Carbon monoxide. Like that family in Valdivia. Die in your sleep. No blood. No pain. No mess.

He stared at the fire. He had no idea what time it was when he finally stood back up. He didn't care either. What difference would it make? He brought the brazier inside and put it next to his sleeping bag. He stumbled when he went over to the sack of charcoal and realized he was quite drunk. So fucking what! He scooped up handfuls of charcoal and walked back over to the brazier. As carefully as he could, he loaded up the brazier to the max. It became a little game trying to balance all the different shaped pieces into a pyramid. Pieces kept falling off the top and he replaced them until he had it just right. His hands were filthy but he didn't care. He stepped back and admired his little structure. He brought the chair in from the deck and sat down to watch the charcoal ignite. He could see a cloud of soot rise with the heat. It soon became very warm and he became sleepy. He stood up and blew out the kerosene lamp and laid down on his sleeping bag fully dressed. He watched the orange glow of the fire pulsate on the ceiling for awhile until he fell asleep.

If he hadn't needed to take a piss, he would have died. It was as simple as that. A bodily function saved his life. He woke up disoriented and groggy, with the worst headache of his life. He opened his eyes and tried to get his bearings. When he saw the orange glow still on the ceiling he remembered what he had done. You stupid idiot, Tomás! What were you thinking? That was really fucking dumb! He struggled up off the floor and had to hang on to the chair a second or two to get his balance. God, you idiot! It must have been at least ninety-five degrees in the room and the air was so thick and soft it felt like a warm cloud against his hands and face. He walked over to the door and opened it wide. Using his towel as a potholder, he grabbed the *brasero* and dumped the coals off the deck, where they hissed on the wet ground. It had stopped raining, but it was still dark. He left the door open and stood on the porch breathing in the fresh air. He hung on to a post as he peed off the edge. His balance was not great. He could not believe what he had done and, man-oh-man, did he have one hell of a headache. Whether it was from the wine, the charcoal fumes, or both, it was definitely head-splitting.

Once the air had cleared he shut the door again, lay back down, and went to sleep. When he woke, it was light and his head still throbbed. He got up and went over to the bucket of water to wash up. His hands were so filthy that he had a tough time washing them in the cold water. He had to change the water several times and clean the basin out with a rag before he refilled it to wash his face. He propped up his mirror behind the basin and, as he bent over to wash, he couldn't believe what he saw. His eyes were blood shot and his face was totally grungy from the soot. He looked like a coal miner. His nostrils were jet black inside and there was a black ring around each. He reached for his roll of toilet paper and blew his nose. Gobs of black snot were on the tissue. He blew his nose again and again, and reamed out each nostril as best he could. He scrubbed his face twice, thinking all the time, you stupid idiot.

He spent the morning regrouping. He started a fire and the scent of the charcoal made him nauseous. He had to walk away and only returned when the fire was down to a hundred percent coals. He heated water for tea, and then a lot more for washing the ceiling and the walls that were made filthy by the smoke. Finally, he sat at the desk with a second cup of tea and forced himself to eat some bread and cheese. He thought, okay, he had been very, very stupid. And also very lucky. Obviously he was taking all this Peace Corps 'save the world' stuff way too seriously. What he was trying to do here was, yes, very important to him—but it certainly was not worth taking his own life. If he failed, then he failed. If he never fit in, then he didn't fit in. That was all there was to it. All he could do was try—give it his best shot—nothing more. Time to lighten up. So, okay Tomás, just what are you going to do about this?

It did not take long for him to decide that he had to get out of Cufeo for some R&R. There was nothing pressing with his inspections and there was no soccer commitment for another week. He decided to go to Valdivia for as much time as he needed. If the Peace Corps or the Ministry of Agriculture had a problem with that, then too bad, because that was what he was going to do. He would hang out with his friend, who should be back from his Christmas visit up north. He would take nice hot showers at his place, catch up with him, read the newspaper, and get back into studying Spanish. He would eat a big steak with French fries. He would have two eggs over easy for breakfast and brewed coffee. When he felt like it, he would check in with the Ministry of Agriculture—not before. And when he was ready, he would return to the *campo*.

By the end of the morning the storeroom was spotless, and he told the Gomez family at the mid-day meal that he would be going to Valdivia. He would let them know when he returned. He told Ramon he would be gone for a few days and offered him the use of Lobo. Ramon said Lobo could use a rest. Finally, with his backpack loaded, he set off to catch the early afternoon bus. All the way down he thought about what he had tried to do. He couldn't believe it. He thought he was stronger than that. Whatever was he thinking?

CHAPTER SEVEN

La Casa de Putas (The Whorehouse)

As Tomás waited for the bus, he could see the large lake down in the valley outside Valdivia. It was bright blue and sparkled in the early afternoon sun. Eight years ago that lake was not there. It was formed when the 1960 earthquake, one of the largest ever recorded, caused thousands of acres of farmland to sink below the water table. Roads had been ripped up, buildings destroyed, and hundreds of people had died.

Tomás heard the bus from Paillaco long before it crested the hill. For a change there were hardly any passengers and he chose a seat a couple rows behind the driver. It was almost all downhill to Valdivia. Tomás thought that if the driver had nerves of steel he could put the bus into neutral and coast most of the way there. They passed an overloaded, top-heavy firewood truck that most likely was coming from somewhere in Cufeo. The *campesinos* derisively referred to these old rattletraps as *cacharros* because oftentimes the

_.. bodies were literally held together with wire and bailing twine. Tomás shuddered to think what would happen if one ever lost its brakes on this hill.

When they arrived in Valdivia, he slung his pack over a shoulder and headed down Avenida Picarte towards the Plaza de la Republica, the city center. Many of the old buildings downtown had been destroyed or severely damaged by the earthquake, and some had been replaced by incongruous modern concrete structures. Turning left at the Plaza onto Perez Rosales, Tomás soon left the new structures behind. There was an abrupt transition to weathered wooden houses with corrugated metal roofs, which made Valdivia feel like a small town even though over eighty thousand people lived there. Ten minutes from the Plaza, Tomás arrived at the small house his Peace Corps buddy rented. Tomás knocked on the door. When no one answered, he pulled out a key and let himself into the small living room.

He dropped his pack onto the couch and pulled out a towel and some clean clothes. He made a beeline to the shower, passing through the kitchen and eating area. At the far end of the house, there was a bedroom to the left and a bathroom to the right. In the bathroom, he grabbed some kindling and firewood from a neatly stacked pile in the corner, and started a fire in the firebox underneath the water tank. The water took about ten minutes to heat up. He carefully adjusted the cold and hot before jumping in—he didn't want to scald himself like the first time he had taken a shower here. God, what a pleasure! He closed his eyes and luxuriated in all that hot water. How great it was to be alive. Noticing that the water going down the drain was black from the soot in his hair, he reached for the shampoo, eager to wash away the remains of last night's folly.

When he returned to the living room he found his friend sitting in the easy chair reading the paper.

"Hey Oso, how's it going?" Tomás asked, reaching out to shake his hand.

Oso put down the paper and Tomás saw his right hand was in a cast.

"Uh oh. What happened to you?"

Oso looked a little sheepish.

"Punched a horse."

"You're kidding. And just how did that happen?"

Oso was thirty-five years old, which was ancient for a volunteer, and had been in Chile for a year. He was about five ten and probably weighed at least two-forty. He had a gut, but he was solid—heavy shouldered and big boned. He had been a pulling guard for Jim Brown at Syracuse University and nobody messed with Oso. Because of his build, shaggy head, and lumbering gait, his co-volunteers had nicknamed him "Oso," which meant bear in Spanish. The nickname had stuck.

"You know that timber cruise the Chilean foresters and I have been working on in Chiloe?"

Tomás nodded as he sat down on the couch.

"It was really tough going and all of us were beat. We were at it for days, walking across those mountains and fighting the fucking *quila*. We needed a break, and one of the Chileans suggested we ride down from camp to get some bottles of *pisco* to make *pisco* sours."

Oso stood and backed up to a corner of a window, and rubbed his back against it. He even had the mannerisms of a bear.

"We had dinner in town, bought the *pisco* and limes and stuff, and headed back. On the way up we decided to get into the *pisco*. That stuff is about forty-five proof and I guess we got a little rowdy, and I may have spurred my horse too hard up the mountain. Anyway, when I got off him at camp, the little fucker turned around and muckled onto my stomach—so I drilled him between the eyes."

He looked at his hand.

"I may have busted it, but at least the horse went down to both knees. The Chileans couldn't believe it."

"Jesus, Oso. You're a piece of work. Can you do your mapping and tallies all right?"

"It's slow, but yeah. I've been doing projections and overlays here for two weeks. Where have you been, stranger?"

"Cufeo, doing the inspections. But I had to get out of there. Mind if I crash here for a few days, or do you have some hot romance going on that I'd screw up?"

"Feel free."

He sighed.

"I think ol' Oso just sort of scares the *Chilenas*. If I ever did score, it'd probably be because the girl wanted to marry me so she could get U.S. citizenship and a plane ticket to the land of luxury."

More volunteers married in Chile than in any other country, but Oso and Tomás agreed that it seemed that the lure of a life in the U.S. often outweighed 'true love.' Both of them were idealists, but they were pessimistic about ever finding real romance in Chile.

Oso said, "I think it's about time for me to go back to Nena's."

"Nena's? Again? Every time I come into town, you're ready to go there. Jesus, Oso, you're not a bear—just a horny old billygoat. Maybe we should change your nickname to *cabrón*."

"Watch it there, partner."

Tomás persisted.

"When was the last time you went to Nena's?"

"Two nights ago."

"Good God, Oso. How can you afford to keep going there? That's the most expensive whorehouse in town."

He extended his bad hand out and proudly turned the cast back and forth. There were several signatures on it.

"The girls signed it. They felt sorry for me and I got a freebie last time. Speaking of, are you buying dinner tonight?"

"Absolutely. How about a thick steak and fries? I've been thinking about a steak all day."

"Good choice. Here, read the paper. Let me take a shower first."

He tossed Tomás the Valdivia newspaper, *El Correo*, and shuffled out towards his room.

Oso and Tomás had an agreement that Tomás could sleep on the couch whenever he came to town. In return Tomás would buy Oso some dinners and beers. Tonight they decided on the Palace Cafe, which was the most upscale restaurant in Valdivia. Unlike the other restaurants, the Palace served a good, thick steak, just like in the States. The restaurant had modern plate-glass windows and a long, curved, contemporary-style counter. They sat down at a black Formica-topped table in front of one of the windows facing the plaza. It was a typical Monday night. The restaurant was not crowded and the waiter soon took their order.

Oso leaned back in his chair and looked at Tomás.

"How's it been going out in Cufeo? Are you messing around with one of the Martinez sisters yet?"

Tomás told him that he had moved out of the Martinez farm and into the storeroom of the schoolhouse. Oso couldn't believe it.

"Jesus, Tomás, that must be comfortable as hell! Why did you do that?"

"Because the Martinez farm is way off to one side of Cufeo, and I wanted to be closer to all the other socios. But the school's not so bad. And I take my meals nearby with a family...although that hasn't been much fun."

Oso laughed when he heard about the Señora bringing him *empanadas*, but was serious when Tomás told him about the desperately poor families he had been visiting lately. Tomás described the day at the *carrera* and how alien it had made him feel. He said nothing about last night.

"And so," Tomás concluded, "I felt I needed a break from the *campo*. You know, a little R&R."

Oso nodded. He understood completely. The steaks came, accompanied by generous portions of fries, and they dug in. They ate in silence. Tomás had not had a steak in a very long time and he devoured it. Oso took a swig of his beer.

"Tomás, what you need is to come with me to Nena's."

"No, what I need is to find a liberated university chick with long straight hair, who doesn't wear a bra, and believes in 'free love.'"

But Valdivia was a long way from Haight Ashbury, and his chances of finding some co-ed running around in sandals, beads, and tie-dye were slim. There were two small universities in Valdivia, but every co-ed he had seen so far was dressed to the hilt in stylish, expensive-looking clothes. It was mostly the wealthy who attended the universities.

Oso chuckled.

"Good luck, friend. I've met a few a few young ladies in town and taken one or two out to dinner. In fact I had dinner here with one last week. But I'll tell you what. Forget trying to get one to sneak off somewhere so you can get a little. It's like the old days—like out of a Victorian novel or something. Everything has to be so goddamn proper. If you find someone you like, then maybe the first thing you do is go for a walk around the park, but always with a little brother or sister or one of her friends as a chaperone. If you get beyond that and become *palolos*, then you might start holding hands and sneak in a kiss now and then. Then if you're ready to make the plunge and become *novios*, maybe you'll start getting some nooky. It's a long process, and I'm a little too old to play that game."

Oso sighed and put his napkin on the table.

"I'd rather just go to Nena's."

"Yeah, I can understand that. I don't think I could play that game either. Just a big waste of time. And anyway, the last thing I want is to get tied down. Like they say, 'I got places to go and things to do.'"

They finished their steaks and Tomás asked, "Do you want anything for dessert?"

Oso shook his head.

"Me neither."

Tomás called the waiter over for the check. It was good seeing Oso, and this evening—low key and relaxed—was just what he needed.

The next morning, after Oso lumbered off to the office, Tomás walked to the center of town for a leisurely breakfast. He had his two eggs over easy and two cups of brewed coffee. He bought a newspaper and also a *Condorito* comic book and sat down on a bench in the shady Plaza. The two publications were a good balance for working on his Spanish—the newspaper for vocabulary and grammar, and the comic book for slang and idioms.

At about 11:30, Tomás walked over to the Ministry of Agriculture, which occupied the third and fourth floors of a new concrete building next to a river. He climbed up to the third floor, where he was greeted by several office workers who were milling around, talking and joking. Without exception, the men all wore three-piece suits and polished shoes. A pretty secretary sat at a large desk in the middle of the room. On top of the desk was a metal stand holding an array of government rubber stamps and seals—the standard of Chilean bureaucracy. Tomás asked her if Sr. Ojeda was in. He was Tomás's boss, and direct link to the pine tree nurseries. Tomás liked to keep him up to date with the work being done in the *campo*.

The secretary smiled and said, "He's at the nursery today, but he should be in all day tomorrow. Do you want to leave him a message, Tomás?"

Even though Tomás hardly knew her, she used "tu"—the personal form of 'you'—when she spoke to him. Quite a change from the formality of the *campo*. He told her it was nothing urgent and he would stop by again tomorrow. He walked down the corridor to Oso's office, knocked, and stuck his head in. Oso was leaning over a very large desk covered with maps. He looked up.

"Hey Tomás. *Que pasa?*"

"Not much. Want to go grab some lunch?"

"Sure. Just give me a few minutes."

Tomás reached for a chair and pulled it up to the window. There was a great view of the river and the promenade below where there was a lively market six mornings a week. Farmers brought produce in from the country and fishermen brought their catch up the river from the Pacific Ocean, eighteen kilometers away. Tomás watched as some of the vendors closed up their stands. They were getting ready to go to lunch too.

Over the next two days Tomás took it easy. He checked in with Señor Ojeda, ate meals and drank beers with Oso, and even took in a shoot-'em-up Mexican western which was nearly impossible to understand. In the theater, all the aisle seats were taken. Because of the earthquake, everybody wanted aisle seats so they could get out fast if they had to.

Oso left to do field work again in the mountains. He half-jokingly warned Tomás that if he found that free-spirit co-ed and brought her back to his place, he had better wash the sheets before he left town. Tomás told him not to punch any more horses.

After two more days Tomás decided he was ready to return to Cufeo. On his last night he went to dinner at the La Bomba Bar & Restaurant which was just down from the plaza on the corner of Arauco and Caupolican. La Bomba was the opposite of the Palace Cafe. The two-story building formed a blunted V as it extended down both sides of the block. Other than the rat's nest of electric and phone wires that marred the head-on view, it was a handsome structure. The tall Victorian windows and the intricate cornice work were painted a rusty red which looked good against the cream colored walls. It was a testament to the building's construction that it had survived the earthquake intact.

Tomás entered and followed a skinny carpet down a long hallway towards a sign that said *Comedor* with an arrow pointing to the right. Two rooms actually made up the dining area, but only one was in use tonight. The room was half full and when an elderly couple looked up as he passed their table, Tomás said, "*Buen Provecho.*" They lit up immediately and smiled and thanked him. It never failed, he thought. Wishing diners "Bon Appetit" always got a smile and a thank you—probably doubly so in his case because they never expected that a *gringo* would be savvy enough to do it.

Although the walls had been papered over and were wrinkly and stained here and there, there was no denying the beauty and quality of the woodwork throughout the dining room. The windows looking out on Arauco were tall and formal, and looked elegant with their thick burgundy curtains. There was a broad molding where the walls met the ceiling, and the wainscoting was hand-planed and finely crafted. The round, heavy wooden tables and chairs had not been stained. Quite a change from the 'mod look' of the Palace. The clientele was different too. Here the patrons were middle aged and older, and conservatively dressed. La Bomba had the feeling of an old club. The waiter came over and Tomás ordered a *cazuela de vacuno,* a soup with everything but the kitchen sink thrown in. In the middle was a sizeable hunk of beef, barely hanging on to the bone. A good *cazuela de vacuno* plus a piece or two of fresh bread and a glass of red wine could tide him over for a full day.

After dinner, Tomás walked towards the front of the building and turned into the bar area near the front door. There were two rooms here also. The actual bar was in the nose of the building, and the windows looked out on both Arauco and Caupolican. There was a vacant table near the bar, and Tomás sat down and ordered a beer. He saw an abandoned *Correo* on another table and went over and brought it back. Around him, men were playing *cacho,* a popular dice game similar to poker. He spent a relaxing half hour watching them and reading the paper. But it was getting late.

As he was reaching for his wallet, he heard, "Don Tomás. How are you?"

Tomás turned and was surprised to see the *gerente* Manuel smiling at him. He was impeccably dressed in suit and tie, and Tomás couldn't help wondering what in the world he was doing in La Bomba.

As if reading Tomás's mind, the *gerente* said, "I come here every now and then when I am in town, for a cup of wine and to read the paper."

He looked down at the *Correo* on the table.

"It seems you do too. I also have friends who come here and we like to discuss politics."

He looked around the room.

"But it seems none have come in tonight. Can I invite you to a cup of wine... or," noticing his beer glass, "another Pilsner?"

"No thank you. But please sit down. I was only relaxing and watching these men play *cacho*.

Manuel sat and clapped his hands for the waiter.

"*Una copa* of Santa Rita white, please, and also whatever beer," he said, holding up Tomás's glass, "my friend here was drinking."

Manuel waved away Tomás's protest.

"Have you ever played *cacho*, Don Tomás?"

"No. Never."

Manuel went over to the barman and asked for one of the leather cups with dice.

When he returned he said, "Let's play a few games. I'll teach you."

Tomás got the hang of it after the first game and they were half-way through the second when a player near them let out a whoop. He stood up and did a little jig around his table.

Manuel smiling, explained, "He just scored a *grande de mano*. That is when someone rolls five of a kind on the first roll of one of his turns. Anybody who does that automatically wins the game. I think he was very happy because it was near the end of the game and he had been losing badly."

After their second game, Manuel ordered another round of drinks.

Tomás asked, "Don Manuel, when I turn off of the main road above the school in La Paloma to go down to your land, there is a little cross on the side of the road. Why is that there?"

Manuel shook his head sadly.

"Aah, now that is a very sad story. About thirty years ago my father brought a young orphan girl from Valdivia out to our house, where my brother lives now. When she was old enough she took care of our sheep, going out in the morning and staying with them all day until the evening when she would bring them in again. There was no school in La Paloma back then. One evening she and the sheep did not return and we went out looking for them. We found the sheep just before dark. But we did not find the girl."

The waiter came and put their drinks down. Manuel took a big swig of wine and smacked his lips in pleasure before he continued.

"We looked for her for three days with no luck. Finally, about two weeks later, our dog was chewing on something in front of the house and it turned out to be a small human leg. It had to be the little girl's and, although we did not think our dog killed her, we watched him closely to see if he would return to where he had found the leg. He never did, so we brought in a professional mountain lion hunter who eventually found her remains down in a *quebrada*. He was absolutely sure that the little girl was killed by a lion—not by our dog. We buried what was left of her by the side of the road where you saw that cross. We thought that was a good spot because she always enjoyed sitting there and watching people ride by."

Tomás couldn't help yawning after Manuel finished his story.

He noticed and said, "Come on, Don Tomás; finish your beer and let me show you where I live before you return to your friend's house. It is not far from here."

They left to the sound of the dice and leather cups hitting the table and walked down Arauco, away from the Plaza. After several blocks they entered a working class neighborhood. Manuel pointed out his house, one of many in a long, solid façade of identical two-story dwellings.

"These houses all look alike and it is good my number is 111. That makes it easy to remember if I have a bit too much wine," he joked, smiling.

They stopped in front of his door.

Tomás was about to thank him for the beers and say goodnight when Manuel said, "It is still not so late. How about one last drink at a place I know only a couple blocks away?"

Tomás didn't have to catch the early bus the next day, and he had gotten a second wind from walking in the fresh air. It also made sense to establish a good rapport with the *gerente*..

"Okay... *Como no?*"

Manuel slapped him on the back.

"Let's go then."

They started walking down the street. After a couple of minutes Manuel turned to Tomás.

"This bar is also a *casa de putas*. I hope that will not offend you."

"No, Don Manuel. Not at all."

Tomás was surprised when the whorehouse turned out to be located only a few blocks away from the Peace Corps office. He had probably walked by it a half dozen times. It was an ugly yellow and green two-story wooden building, with a naked light over the beat up front door. Not much was going on inside. A silent jukebox was in a rear corner near a small bar that was painted red. Two unattractive women in skirts too tight for their middle-aged bodies were standing at the bar, and they watched them walk into the room. There were two men talking and drinking red wine at one of the tables to their right. They looked up briefly, and then continued their conversation. Another man slept with his head on the top of a table in a corner. Tomás couldn't believe that Manuel was wearing a suit and tie here—the place was a dump. It looked like it hadn't been cleaned in months, and the small, unforgiving fluorescent lights revealed every speck of dirt. The naked lime green walls were filthy, and the low ceiling was gray from all the grime. The center of the room was clear of tables and chairs, and Tomás guessed that was where people danced because all the varnish was worn off of the floor. A constant buzz came from one of the fluorescent lights. Tomás thought he'd have to bring Oso here sometime—he wouldn't believe this place.

As they sat down at a wobbly table, Manuel told Tomás that *campesinos* from Cufeo came here sometimes if they wanted a late night drink. Tomás wondered if this was the bar Claudio had been talking about where Manuel was seen drinking and talking politics into the wee hours the night before the cooperative meeting.

A door between the jukebox and the bar opened and a surprisingly pretty young girl entered the room, tucking in her blouse. When she saw Tomás and Manuel, she hurried over to see what they wanted to drink. She barely glanced at Manuel, but gave Tomás a big smile. Tomás smiled back, and his estimation of the joint suddenly jumped a couple of notches. Manuel blatantly looked her over from head to toe.

"Señorita, I think you must be new here. Please bring us a bottle of Santa Rita white. With three glasses if you would like to share it with us. We must all get acquainted."

"Of course, Señor. *Con mucho gusto.*" She went off to the bar.

Manuel leaned toward Tomás.

"Listen, Don Tomás. She is pretty, no? And I think maybe she likes you a little."

Tomás watched her return. She was indeed pretty and had a nice body. She was wearing a tight skirt like the other women, but looked good in it. The skirt was also shorter and showed off a fine pair of legs. Tomás wondered what her story was. 'What's a nice girl like you doing in a place like this?'

When she sat down he said, "My name is Tomás and this is Don Manuel. What is your name?"

"Irene."

She pulled her chair up close to Tomás.

"Where are you from, Tomás?"

He told her he was from the States and was working with Don Manuel and other farmers in a reforestation program out in Cufeo. The three clinked glasses and took a drink.

"Have you worked here long, Irene?" Tomás asked.

She had very pretty dark eyes and long dark hair. Her lips were full and reminded Tomás of Sophia Loren. It was hard for him not to stare at those lips.

"No. I have been here for two weeks. But it is only temporary. I will be leaving soon to work in another place the Señora owns in Osorno. And believe me, it is a much nicer place than this," she said, disdainfully looking around the room.

"Is the Señora one of the women at the bar?"

"Oh no, Tomás. She is not one of them," she said haughtily. "She is in Osorno now. She spends more time there than here. But she will return tomorrow."

She drained her glass and turned to Manuel.

"May I have another *copa*, Señor?"

"Of course, dear. Here," he said filling her glass to the brim, "And do not be shy. Drink up. *Salud*," and the three of them clinked glasses again.

They finished the bottle of wine and Manuel ordered another. Irene went off happily to get it. Three quarters of the way through the second bottle, Irene began to giggle, and Manuel's eyes were glazed, and he was slurring his words. Tomás suspected that he had been drinking a good bit even before they had met at La Bomba. And Tomás was feeling pretty good himself.

Irene hit him up for jukebox money. She chose some slow Latin tune and when she came back to the table, she reached down and pulled him to his feet. Tomás was not much of a dancer, but he wasn't sure if what they were doing qualified as dancing. It was more like two glued bodies shuffling to slow music.

After a couple songs they draped their arms around each other and began to nuzzle. When they finally sat back down, Tomás noticed that Manuel had gotten another bottle of wine and drunk a third of it. He filled Irene's glass and his own. She reached for hers with her left hand because her right was caressing Tomás's thigh. Manuel excused himself and struggled to his feet. He held on to his chair as he took aim for the door at the rear of the room, and then staggered off. Tomás looked questioningly at Irene.

"The bathroom is back there," she said.

They went back to drinking and fondling each other. When Manuel returned he hung onto his chair again and did not sit down.

"Don Tomás," he said rather formally and trying to stand erect. "I think I have had enough to drink tonight and I might possibly be a little bit *curado*. I think it is time for me to go home. But first," he said reaching clumsily for his half filled glass, "one for the stirrup."

He drained it without spilling too much, and with an unsteady hand very carefully set the glass back on the table. Still holding on to the chair with one hand, he swooped his hat off with the other and bowed to Irene, who laughed.

"Good night, Miss Irene. And goodnight to you, Don Tomás."

With that he put his hat on and turned and staggered to the door, carefully shutting it behind him. It dawned on Tomás that he had just been left with a fairly significant bar tab.

Although it was hard for him to concentrate while her hand caressed his thigh, Irene and Tomás talked until they finished the bottle of wine. He started to ask her how much he owed when she interrupted him.

"Tomás, would you like to stay here with me tonight?" Her hand moved up his thigh to his crotch.

"What do you think?"

She gave him a little squeeze.

Smiling, she said, "I think you would like that."

"Irene," he said sincerely, "believe me, you have no idea. But I did not know that I would be coming here and I did not bring a lot of money. I probably do not have much more than enough to pay for the wine."

"Oh, but Tomás, do not worry about that. I will not charge you to stay with me."

"But what about the Señora? Won't you get into trouble?"

"She thinks that I am still with the *bandera* and does not expect me to be with anyone. But it is over now and I can be with you."

"What do you mean you are 'with the flag?'"

"Oh," she said without the slightest tinge of embarrassment, "that is how we women say it is our monthly time. But you must leave in the morning before the Señora returns."

Tomás nodded and Irene gave him another little squeeze. The other men had left long ago and the two women had disappeared through the rear door and had not returned. He paid Irene for the wine, and she put the money in a small box that she locked in a drawer behind the bar.

"We will go to my room as soon as I finish cleaning up."

She locked and bolted the front door. A few minutes later, as she bent over to wipe one of the tables, Tomás came up from behind and put his hands on her shapely rear end. It felt like she wasn't wearing panties. She straightened up and leaned back into him with a sigh. He put his arms around her waist and kissed her neck.

"Tomás! Wait. Let me finish."

She broke away and went to wipe off the other tables and straighten the chairs. When she was finally finished, she took him by the hand and led him out of the room. In the hallway, they were greeted by the stench of urine. The bathroom was obviously somewhere nearby. They went up a narrow steep flight of stairs, and Tomás suddenly wondered if he could make it through the rest of the night without peeing. He decided he couldn't.

When they reached the landing, he asked, "Irene, is there a bathroom up here? I have to make *pichi*."

"Me too; but the toilets are below and they are not very nice. You can do it here."

Tomás looked around. All the doors were closed in the hallway and he did not understand.

"Where?" he asked.

"Right here," and she lifted her skirt and squatted.

Almost immediately a torrent of urine splattered on the landing and ran down the stairs. Good God! He could not believe it. He had taken part in some pretty wild and debauched fraternity parties, but he had never seen a co-ed do anything this crude. Not even close. Irene looked up at him expectantly from her squatting position. Well, 'when in Rome' he thought as he unbuttoned his levis. He tried to pee, but it took a while. Irene stood up and waited. Finally he let go with a stream, aiming it down the stairs. His father was an avid duck hunter, and he had once explained to Tomás that the longer the barrel, the farther the shot went. Talk about a perfect example! He could not believe how far his stream went. He thought even Irene was impressed as she watched it splatter on the far wall beyond the downstairs landing. She giggled.

"*Por Dios*, Tomás! That is very good. If the toilet were there, you could use it without going downstairs."

He peed for what seemed like forever. When he was finally done, Irene giggled again as he tried to stuff his hard-on back into his pants.

"Oh, do no not bother with that, Tomás. Come on!"

And she took his hand and led him down the hall. At least she's leading me by my hand, he thought. They entered the last room on the right and Irene turned on the light. There was a double bed with a picture of Christ above it, a bureau and mirror, and a straight back chair. A single window looked out onto the dark street and Irene pulled the curtain across it. She kicked off her shoes, took off her blouse and bra, stepped out of her skirt, and jumped naked into bed.

"Brrr! Tomás, hurry!"

Tomás stumbled over a pant leg in his haste, but was soon in bed beside her. The sheets were cold and damp, like the sheets in the Martinez home. But with a warm and very soft body to cuddle up to, they warmed up in a hurry. Irene was totally uninhibited, and they wrestled and groped and tried things he had never imagined. They made love twice before Tomás, satiated and exhausted, finally conked out.

It seemed like he had just fallen asleep when Irene was gently shaking him.

"Tomás, wake up. Wake up. Remember you have to leave before the Señora comes, and it is already late."

He looked at her blearily and nodded. He was extremely thirsty.

"What time is it, Irene?"

"Almost ten o'clock. The Señora usually gets back around eleven. Hurry and get dressed."

It did not take him long. Irene put on a bathrobe and slippers, and led him down the stairs to a rear door. He hoped he looked better than he felt. Too much wine. But, other than his hangover, he felt happy and grateful to Irene. At the door he turned to her.

"Thank you Irene. You have been very kind to me. I hope to see you again sometime."

"It was fun, Tomás. If you want to see me again— and I hope you do—do not come here," she said as she looked around at the dirty walls with disdain again. "I will soon be in Osorno at a much better place. You must come find me there. It is called 'El Paraiso.'"

"I would like that," he said and he kissed her lightly on those full lips before leaving the building.

Tomás returned to Oso's and took a hot shower, split a pile of shower-wood, and neatly stacked it in the bathroom. He loaded up his pack and thought he would grab a bite to eat on the way to the bus station. He was a different person from the one who had come into town just under a week ago. Shouldering his pack and ready to try again, he opened the door and said to himself, "Ready or not Cufeo, here I come."

CHAPTER EIGHT

Lote Once (Lot Eleven)

It was a late sunny afternoon and Tomás was sitting on the edge of the schoolhouse deck thinking that summer was passing quickly. He wondered what he would do once school started. He wanted to remain in Caman—but where would he stay? If the Gomez family offered full room and board, he'd have to refuse. He just didn't think he could ever be comfortable there with the Señora.

The sun felt good on his face, and he was beginning to get sleepy when a movement caught his eye. He saw Juan limping up the road with a soccer ball under his arm. Like Jaime, Juan lived closest to the field and was the guardian of the team's equipment and jerseys. Juan waved and veered towards him. Other than his soccer shoes, Juan wore the standard Cufeo work outfit of patched pants, tattered white shirt with the sleeves rolled up, and a brimmed black hat. He was always wearing that hat, even when he was in the goal.

As Juan approached the deck, he held his arms up to the sky and said, "How about this day, eh? It is perfect for *futbol.*"

Juan was always upbeat and was described by his neighbors as *chistoso* because he joked a lot.

"Do you want to kick the ball around with us this afternoon?" he asked Tomás as he sat down on the edge of the deck. He kept his bad leg out straight.

"Yes, of course—*con mucho gusto.*"

Two riders popped into view high up on the La Paloma road. Tomás and Juan watched them until Juan recognized them as teammates. He turned to Tomás.

"You did not ride to any of the farms today?"

"No. I am letting Lobo rest before I go to Lote Once. Don Ramon says that it will be a very long trip."

They watched the riders again.

"He also says that I should buy another horse because I am wearing Lobo out with all my trips to the farms and tournaments."

Lote Once was the most remote and highest area of Cufeo. The *campesinos* often called it Antarctica because it was not unusual for it to snow there. For the farmers to transport their firewood and charcoal down to the highway and to bring supplies back up was an extreme hardship.

Juan took his hat off and carefully laid it on the deck. He ran his fingers through his thick black hair.

"Why have you not come over and looked at my work yet?"

"Because you live so close."

Tomás did not say that Juan was known as a very hard worker and that if anyone were on schedule with the clearing and fencing, it would be him.

"I thought I should go to the more distant farms first because of the good weather. But, if you like, I can come over tomorrow while my horse rests."

Players were arriving at the field, so they stood up. Juan dusted off the back of his trousers and put his hat back on.

"Tomorrow would be perfect. How about mid-day? Then you can eat lunch at my house afterwards."

Tomás accepted and Juan threw the ball out to some players in the middle of the field. "Good," Juan said. "Now let's go kick the ball."

Late the next morning Tomás walked the half mile to the Montoya farm. It was a beautiful sunny day and very warm—easily the warmest day of the summer. The house was set back from the road, and the gate out front had five stout horizontal bars. Rather than pull the bars back, he decided to climb over. Just as he was lifting his leg over the top bar, a dog that could have been Tobi's twin rushed up barking. He had forgotten his stick so he didn't dare get off the gate. Perched like a treed coon, he waited for Juan to come call the dog off. Instead, Maria Elena came around the porch corner, wiping her hands on her apron. Damn, he thought.

"Go on Muchacho," she said. "Go on and lay down."

The dog trotted nonchalantly back to the corner of the house where it lay down and started to lick itself.

"*Buenos dias*, Don Tomás. I see you have met Muchacho."

"Oh, the little dog. Yes, we have met," he said matter-of-factly as if he had only waited on top of the gate because he was being polite, rather than because he was scared of the dog. He climbed down off the gate.

"It is about time you paid us a visit, with you living so close. But come. I will show you where to find Juan. He told me to send you to the new clearing he is working on down the hill. I would take you there myself, but I am preparing lunch."

Her hair was in that thick, long braid again, and he realized that he had never seen her when it wasn't. Even though the day was so warm, Maria Elena wore a heavy long skirt under her apron. As they walked side by side, he could not help but notice how gracefully she moved. They passed a garden that had several rows of high bushy plants that were covered with thick pods. He wondered what they were.

"This is a very well kept garden, Señorita Maria Elena. What are those plants over there? I have never seen them before."

"Oh, those are *habas* and they are ready to pick. Would you like to try some at lunch?"

"Sure, if it's not too much trouble."

They continued walking.

He said, "The *empanadas* you made at the *carrera* were delicious—very juicy."

She smiled. God, he thought, she really did have a killer smile.

"Thank you. Were they as good as the ones Sergio's Señora brought you?"

"Er—better. That is, yours were much better," he stammered.

Her eyes danced and she seemed to be enjoying the moment. Did she think he was messing around with the Señora? Who else knew about those *empanadas?*

"It must be nice, Don Tomás, to have *empanadas* delivered right to your doorstep."

He didn't know what to say. They arrived at a little wooden gate set in a rusty barbed wire fence. On the other side, a narrow footpath was worn into the pasture. It headed straight downhill. Maria Elena's playful look was gone.

"Here we are. Just follow that path and it will lead you to Juan. Lunch will be ready whenever you two decide to come back up to the house."

He opened the gate.

"Thank you, Señorita Maria Elena."

She looked at him for a moment.

"You do not have to say Señorita every time you say my name. Please just call me Maria Elena."

"But you call me 'Don' Tomás."

"Yes, that is true. But it is different. It is proper to call you so. I know you want to be polite, but it is all right to address me by only my first name."

"Okay—Maria Elena."

She gave him a bright smile before turning towards the house. He went through the gate and down the hill.

He soon found Juan with sleeves rolled up, hacking away at some thick underbrush with an axe. When Juan saw him, he stopped and put the axe down, head first, with the long handle leaning against his waist. He took off the black brimmed hat and, pulling a handkerchief from a rear pocket, wiped his brow.

"Don Tomás, good morning. My sister told you how to find me. That is good. By God, it is hot today! But that is no surprise if you saw the sunset after *futbol* yesterday."

He carefully folded the handkerchief and put it back in his pocket.

"It was like *'una vaca pelada.'* That always means hot the next day. But," he added, "when it is like a 'skinned cow' in the morning, then that means rain."

Tomás smiled.

"We have an expression like that too. It is a rhyme that says the sailors will be happy with the weather the next day if there is such a red sun in the evening. But if they have the same sun in the morning, then they must be careful."

"I imagine the things of nature are the same everywhere. It is important to pay attention to her, eh?"

He limped over to a broad stump, leaned his axe against it, and sat down.

"This would be a good day to sit in the shade of the porch and drink *chicha dulce* and tell stories."

After a few moments he sighed and pushed himself back up from the stump.

"But if we did that, then nothing would get done. So come and look at my work."

They walked around the clearing. There were tall, orderly piles of *quila* and brush everywhere.

"With this weather, everything will dry out fast and I will be able to burn soon. But to be safe, I will burn on a cool cloudy day when there is no wind—or better still, when there is a light rain. After burning, I will continue last year's fence until it encloses this area too. Then I will be ready to plant the new trees. The work is hard, but not so hard as last year."

Tomás followed him down the hill. The terrain became very steep as they approached a new barbed wire fence. Last year's plantation was on the other side. Tomás could not imagine cutting the brush and dragging it into piles to burn on such a steep slope—or fencing it either. He said so.

"Yes," Juan answered. "It was difficult and I worked hard. But," he smiled, "being *cojo* with one leg shorter than the other makes it easier for me to work on such a slope."

Tomás wasn't sure if he was serious or joking.

"Don Juan, with two good legs or with one leg shorter than the other, it would still be very difficult to work here."

Tomás pointed to the plantation.

"And your *pino*. They look so healthy. Very few have died and the rows are perfect."

He wondered how Juan had kept the rows so straight and the pine so perfectly spaced. Juan obviously took a lot of pride in his work.

"Yes, and they are growing fast. Look at how much they have grown already."

Juan squatted down and, reaching through the fence, bent the little branches of a young pine between his thumb and forefinger. He looked up at Tomás.

"The light green is this year's growth. I think my little trees are very happy here."

He stood up and put his hands on the small of his back, stretching while they looked down a row.

"I have not removed the brown ones yet because they are so easy to see that I will not miss a single one when I re-plant in the winter."

They walked around for awhile longer and Tomás admired the hazy view of Volcán Osorno. He had read it was the second most perfect volcano after Fuji. He asked Juan if it ever lost all of its snow.

"No, although everyday it looks a little different. Sometimes you can see it and it looks very big and close. And other times you cannot see it at all. But even when it hides, it is always my companion while I work. But come, it is time to eat. Let us see what Maria Elena has prepared for us."

When they entered the house, the first thing Tomás noticed was the potted flowers and plants everywhere—on shelves, tables, the floor, and even on the stairs. They looked healthy and happy, and certainly brightened up the large room that was a combination of kitchen, dining room, and living space. Maria Elena was sitting in a comfortable-looking cushioned armchair, in front of a window that had a good view of the volcano. She had been reading but put the book down on a side table when they came in.

Juan hung his hat on a peg next to the door and said, "As you can see, Don Tomás, my sister would rather read than prepare our meal like she should be doing."

But he was smiling and Tomás saw that the dining table in the middle of the room had been set. There was a vase of freshly cut flowers in the center. Something was bubbling in a large pot on the stove that smelled delicious. Bowls and plates had been put out on a counter next to the stove.

Maria Elena stood up.

"My brother always tries to be funny and sometimes he is and sometimes he is not. When he is not, like now, I forgive him because he works so hard."

In a corner there was a small cast iron parlor stove with a potted red flower on it. It was the first non-kitchen stove that Tomás had seen in Cufeo. Juan noticed him looking at it.

"We sit for many hours by that stove in the winter. It is a good place to repair saddles and clothes, and shell the beans, and separate the seed potatoes, and do the many other things that there is no time to do during good weather. And," he continued proudly, "my sister reads to me when I am doing these little things. In the summer my room is there," he said pointing to a door to one side, "and Maria Elena is able to have both rooms upstairs. Besides her bedroom, there is a sewing room where there are, if you can believe it, even more of these flowers. In the wintertime I move up to the sewing room for the heat that comes up from the stoves. But now, on a day like today, even the kitchen stove makes too much heat."

It was indeed warm in the house even though all the windows were open. There were no screens. Other than houseflies, no bugs ever seemed to enter; Tomás had yet to see a mosquito.

Juan asked, "Sister, have you made any *limonada?*"

"Yes Juan. But wash up first."

As Tomás waited for his turn at the sink, he wondered why these two lived alone. Where was their family?

Juan must be at least in his mid twenties and Maria Elena something near that. Why weren't they married? They were certainly old enough. But he didn't ask. Sooner or later he'd find out. Behind the sink, a window looked out to the gate, and Tomás saw that the sink drained directly below the window. Some ducks came waddling over and were soon grubbing around in the soapy water.

When he and Juan were seated at the table, Maria Elena brought over glasses of lemonade and steaming bowls of soup. In the center of each bowl was a large chunk of chicken. Juan took a big swig of lemonade as Maria Elena joined them at the table. The soup was very spicy and, like most of the food in the *campo*, it was heavy on the cilantro. Tomás complimented Maria Elena on her cooking and her flowers.

"There are so many different flowers, Maria Elena. Do you have a favorite?"

"Yes, but it is not here in the house—it grows wild. It is the *copihue* which has the shape of a bell, about this big," she said holding her thumb and forefinger several inches apart. "It has a beautiful red color and will begin to bloom very soon. It will stay in bloom into May. You will see it everywhere up in the *quila* and trees because it is a vine."

Maria Elena put her spoon down and wiped her perfect mouth with a cloth napkin.

"There is a pure white *copihue* too—but here in Cufeo we have only the red. In the forest it can climb ten meters up into the trees. Juan told me you will soon be going to Lote Once."

"Yes, tomorrow."

"It is too bad you do not make the trip in a couple of weeks. Then you would see a lot of *copihue* in bloom there. Juan and I go to Lote Once at the end of every summer to pick some for the house and have a picnic.

We would go more often if I could pull Juan away from his *futbol.*"

Juan rolled his eyes while stuffing his mouth with a piece of bread.

"We pick the flowers and sometimes the fruit, which we call *pepino.* You can also make a tea from the roots, but that kills the plant. It is too beautiful to kill. The Mapuche Indians have a story about how the *copihue* came into the world. Would you like to hear it?"

"Yes, very much."

Maria Elena took a sip of lemonade.

"Many, many years ago, the land was inhabited by two Indian tribes: the Mapuche and the Pehuenches. There was a beautiful Mapuche princess called Hues and a handsome Pehuenche prince called Copih, and they were very much in love. But because the two tribes were bitter enemies they could tell no one of their love. They had to meet secretly. They were found out by their fathers, who were very angry. And when they learned that the pair planned to meet on the shores of a lake, they set off to bring them back. Copiniel, the Pehuence chief, and Nahuel, the Mapuche chief, found the lovers arm in arm on the edge of the lake. Nahuel was so angry that he threw his spear at the prince, striking him in the heart. He fell into the lake, dead. Copiniel then threw his spear at the Mapuche princess. The spear struck her in the heart as well and she too fell into the lake. They both disappeared. Both tribes mourned for a long time, and after a year they came to pay their respects at the lake. They arrived late in the day and spent the night there. When they awoke the next morning they saw a very strange sight. Two crossed spears rose up from the middle of the lake, with bell-shaped flowers wrapped around them. The flowers were red like the blood and white like the snow. Seeing this miracle, the two tribes declared an everlasting peace and decided to call the flowers *copihues* for the union of Copih and Hues."

"That is a very nice story, Maria Elena. It is a little like Romeo and Juliet," Tomás said, and then immediately regretted it. Why would he ever mention Romeo and Juliet here in the *campo*?

To his surprise Maria Elena answered, "Yes—but very little. It is similar because the two lovers both died and they were also from families that were enemies. But Romeo and Juliet killed themselves and, unlike the Indians, the families never made peace."

Juan smiled proudly.

"Have I not told you, Don Tomás? She reads all the time. But Maria Elena, look at these bowls. We are still hungry."

Maria Elena stood up and cleared the table. Tomás watched her as she put three pieces of meat in a frying pan while dumping a huge pile of fava beans into a pot of boiling water. They looked like lima beans. Maria Elena showed Tomás a couple of the long thick pods. They were fuzzy on the inside. When the meat and beans were ready, she loaded their plates and brought them over. It was the first time Tomás had been served meat in both courses. Juan dug into his pile of beans.

"Ahh. *Que rico*," he said chewing contentedly. "These are our very first *habas* of the season, Don Tomás."

Tomás watched Juan pick up each bean like a piece of candy and bite off a corner. He squeezed it between thumb and index finger and popped an inner bean into his mouth. He discarded the outside shell onto a plate in the middle of the table.

Maria Elena said, "Some like to eat the bean with its skin, but Juan and I prefer to eat only the bean inside."

She popped one into her mouth and added the rejected skin to Juan's pile on the plate. As he watched them eat the beans, he noticed they both had perfect teeth. People here either had very good teeth or very bad. And bad teeth were never repaired—they were pulled.

He tried a bean and indeed it was tender. The plate in the center of the table soon was piled high with the discarded shells. The ducks and chickens were in store for a treat. Juan finished his *habas* and wiped his hands on the cloth napkin. He looked over at Tomás.

"Your Spanish has improved very much."

"I study every night." And he told them about his ever-growing vocabulary list and the grammar book. "But it is being up here in Cufeo where I have no choice but speak Spanish that really helps me."

Juan looked at his sister and then back to Tomás with a mirthful expression on his face.

He asked, "Do you remember your first meeting with the Cooperative when you spoke to us?"

"Yes, of course."

Finally, Tomás thought—finally he was going to get some accolades for his little pep talk that he had worked so hard on during those first weeks after arriving at the Martinez home.

"I was very nervous, but I think it went okay," he said, fishing for compliments.

"I have to tell you," Juan said, "that after that meeting I talked to many of the *socios* when they passed by here on their way to and from town. Most of them had no idea what you were talking about."

"No! You are joking, right? You are being funny, eh Don Juan?"

But Juan looked serious. Tomás turned to Maria Elena who had her napkin diplomatically in front of

her mouth; her eyes were dancing again. He looked
back at Juan.

"This is not really true?"

"Yes, it is the truth."

Tomás pictured all the men in their dark hats and
mantas nodding so seriously at him as if they were hanging on to his every word. But the whole time they were
just sitting in their little chairs wondering what in the
world he was talking about. He felt the fool. No wonder Emilio never mentioned how he had done. The
whole thing was so absurd he had to shake his head and
laugh. Juan and Maria Elena joined in. Juan told him
that one Sunday a couple of weeks after the meeting,
some of the *socios* had come over to visit. While they
sat on the porch drinking *chicha*, they discussed his little 'speech' and tried to guess what he had been trying
to say. Soon they started making up things and each
tried to outdo the other with something more bizarre.
Juan had Maria Elena and Tomás in stitches when he
described how old Don Pedro had imitated him. The
old goat, Tomás thought. He had nodded more than
anyone in the schoolhouse and had looked like he was
agreeing with everything Tomás had said. But Don
Pedro and Juan, as well as the others, meant no disre-
spect, and he could see the humor of the situation.

Tomás gave Juan a little bow and said, "I am only
happy that I could provide you and the others with so
much entertainment."

Maria Elena got up wiping her eyes with the edge of
her apron and began to clear the dishes.

"For dessert I have some *sopaipilla*. It is delicious
with a little honey on it. I will also wrap some into a little bundle for you to take on your trip tomorrow, Don
Tomás."

Tomás gestured toward the pile of fava shells and
his empty plate.

"Please, only one small piece for me. I am already *bien satisfecho.*"

She carried the plates into the kitchen area and returned with the fried bread and a jar of honey, which she placed in the center of the table. As she sat down, she passed him the honey.

"Have you seen all the trees in the hills that have the beautiful white flowers now, Don Tomás?" she asked.

He nodded.

"Those are the *ulmo* trees, and the bees make their best honey, like this honey, from those flowers."

He reached for one of the golden brown pieces and put honey on it. It was delicious and impossible to eat just one. He reached for another and asked why it had a little hole in the middle.

"Oh, that is where I pinch the dough so each piece can breathe. If I do not do that, it will swell up like a little soccer ball when it is cooked."

After four pieces he finally stopped eating and pushed his chair back from the table, as if that might keep his stomach from bursting. He looked at Juan.

"I do not know how you will return to work. On such a warm day and with so much excellent food in my stomach, I think I will soon be very sleepy."

Juan winked at him and Tomás wondered if a wink were universal.

"The only difficult part in returning to work, Don Tomás, is walking the first three meters. I have to pass by that very comfortable chair by the stove before I can get to the door. That will take a lot of effort. And I just may have to stop and rest a little before I am able to continue outside."

"*Este maldito caballo!* Don Tomás run to the left. Quick! Don't let him get by."

Lasso in hand, Tomás ran as fast as he could towards a corner of the Rodriguez pasture where they finally had Lobo surrounded. Ramon approached from Lobo's right and Ramon's nephews, Javier and Alex, were between them. The boys and Tomás had tried unsuccessfully to catch the damn animal for over an hour before they gave up and walked back up to the house to ask Ramon for help. If they had Ramon's brother's horse, it would have been easy. But Pablo was off tending to some livestock business, so they had to go after Lobo on foot.

They carefully walked up with lassos ready. Ramon was just about in range and started to slowly swing his rope above his head. If he got his throw off, it would be all over—he never missed. Lobo watched them, eyes wide and ready to bolt. Suddenly he made a break for it and ran right past Tomás, not eight feet away. Tomás desperately flung his lasso, but the rope hit his flank. Lobo's tail was stretched out straight as he galloped off. Ramon ran up too late and had no chance to throw.

"*Mierda*, Don Tomás," he said trying to catch his breath. "This horse of yours. Aii, he is wild! But who can blame him? He is ridden more than any other horse in Cufeo and is worked too hard. You have to get another horse. And maybe, if you split the riding between them, Lobo might not be so *lobo*."

With a sigh he looked over to Javier and Alex.

"Come on boys, let us try again."

By the time they had Lobo saddled, it was late morning which was not a good time to be starting out for Lote Once. But Tomás felt he could not postpone the trip since he had already sent word to the farmers that he was coming. Ramon untied Lobo and handed him the reins.

"You will have to stay with one of the *socios*, Don Tomás. It will be too late for you to return today."

He didn't say anything. There was no way he was going to impose on a family for dinner, lodging, and breakfast while kicking some kids out of their bed in the process. He had another idea. After putting some grain in a saddlebag, he mounted and, thanking Ramon and the kids for all their help, rode over to the school.

He had decided he would camp out somewhere along the trail after visiting the farms. That would be easy enough. The sky was clear and the weather plenty warm. He would sleep under the open sky like a real cowboy and count the stars. It would be his little adventure. He lashed his sleeping bag to the rear of the saddle and filled his saddlebags with everything he would need. Finally, he put on spurs, *manta*, and hat, and set off.

He rode all afternoon. He passed the La Paloma schoolhouse and the little cross near the trail that led to Manuel's farm. After that, it was new territory. Occasionally he passed a farm and he would wave and shout a greeting if he saw someone. But mostly he and Lobo plodded past vast expanses of pale green pasture dotted with dark stumps. There was no litter along the road—no broken bottles, no plastic bags, no paper, no tin cans. Almost nothing was thrown away. If a bottle were non-deposit, then it became a container for something like cooking oil or vinegar or maybe a candle holder. Nescafe cans were transformed into kerosene lamps. String bags rather than plastic bags were used to carry supplies because they were strong and could be thrown over a shoulder and repaired and used for years. Newspaper was saved for starting fires of course, but it was also used to wrap up food like Maria Elena's *sopaipilla,* or cut up into little squares and stuck on a nail in an outhouse. String and twine were always saved. The other day he watched Ramon shape a new hammer handle out of a piece of hard, reddish colored *luma* wood. When Ramon was almost done he reached for a piece of glass that looked like the broken corner of a window pane. Using it as a scraper, he peeled off the tiniest shavings until the handle was as smooth as marble. About the only thing Tomás ever saw discarded by the roadside were old worn-out shoes that couldn't be repaired. He found them even along the most isolated trails. They were the Cufeo equivalent of blown-out retreads.

He hoped like hell that the *socios* would be at home and not off at town getting supplies or out visiting somewhere. Several days ago he had given notes to a farmer returning home by oxcart. Although the farmer would not be going all the way to Lote Once, he assured Tomás that he would pass the notes on. People took the responsibility of delivering letters and messages very seriously. Oftentimes receiving a timely note could save hours of unnecessary travel. Or a note might be an urgent plea for help. Everyone helped out, because they never knew when they might be the ones in need. The schools played a large role. A note could be given to the teacher who in turn would pass it on to a child. And the children were important not only in making the delivery, but because they could read and write—sometimes the parents could not. It might take days for a note to arrive at its destination. But it always did. It was like an informal pony express.

He was very high up in the hills now, and there were fewer views of the surrounding countryside. Tall trees lined the road, though every now and then a hillside would drop away and he could see for miles. There was checkered farmland way off to the east. He could see the pencil lines of the Pan American highway and a few other secondary roads. It was a clear day and the volcanoes were glorious. For the first time he could see the Andes—tall, thick, and shimmering on the horizon. As Lobo and he pressed on, the hardwoods closed in and the road narrowed into a double rutted trail. They passed two small clearings hacked out of the forest. Each had a shack built out of rough slabs in the middle. He waved at the people who came out to see who was passing by, and he began to get a clear picture of what Cufeo had been like when it had been homesteaded.

He stopped occasionally to pick leaves from the different trees. He was trying to identify and learn all the Chilean trees, but it was difficult because there were so many—*radal, avellano, tineo, trevo, olivillo, lumo, lingue, roble, ulmo, rauli.* They were all jumbled in his mind. Some were well over a hundred feet tall, with large spreading crowns and diameters six feet through. It was hard to imagine cutting them down and into logs without modern equipment. But with only axes, wedges, crosscut saws, and oxen, the *campesinos* somehow managed. At his Peace Corps training in the Seattle area, professors from the University of Washington had taken the volunteers on field trips to the surrounding humid forests of magnificent Douglas Fir and Western Hemlock. But he had never seen anything as spectacular as these hardwoods. This was indeed virgin forest.

There were four *socios* in Lote Once. With all of this virgin forest, he found it hard to believe that they needed to plant trees, until he saw the serious erosion on the slopes that they had cleared for pastures and crops. He realized right away that they wanted to plant pine to stabilize those areas. The farms were like the poorest ones he had visited before—shacks with dirt floors and ragged children running around.

But he was conditioned now so it didn't bother him as much.

It was the same at each farm. He was barked at by dogs, then greeted by the *socio* and introduced to his *señora*, while the kids stared at him like he was from the moon. The *socio* would walk the property with Tomás and show him the work he was doing. He was served *onces* at the second farm. It was cool at this elevation and the doors and windows were closed. It was dim and so smoky that Tomás's eyes watered while he drank *mate* and ate bread with *ulmo* honey. He had dinner at the fourth farm. Although it was still light, the hour was late when the meal was finished, so he was invited to spend the night. He politely declined, surprising the *socio* and his wife. They said he should not leave at this late hour. But he did anyway. As he rode off, they stood in front of their home and looked concerned.

The sun was well below the tall trees and he began to look for a place to spend the night. He remembered passing a little clearing between the first and second farm, where someone had been cutting firewood. He thought that might be a good spot. He spurred Lobo on and they arrived just before dark. He wanted to get a fire going while he could still see. He quickly took the saddle off Lobo, gave him some grain, and attached a *manea* to his front hooves. The hobble was made out of thick leather, but if it got wet, the leather could stretch enough so that the buttons might pull out of their loops. As a precaution, he put a rope on the horse and tied the other end around a stump. There was no way he wanted to walk back to Caman.

He spread out his *manta* and unrolled his sleeping bag on top of it. He would use the saddle for a pillow—just like in the cowboy movies. He gathered chips of firewood for kindling and tried to light a fire. But everything was too damp and just smoldered and went out. The sun must only hit this area for a couple hours a day. He soon used up all the newspaper and gave up. He pulled a big flashlight from the saddle-bags. It was very dark now, and downright chilly. He didn't think there was a moon, but it was hard to tell because the clearing was so small and the trees so tall. He had no choice but to turn in. So much for sitting around the campfire like a trail hand. But he was tired from all the riding and at least he would get an early start tomorrow. He climbed into his bag and fell asleep almost immediately.

He had no idea what time it was when Lobo began snorting and hopping around. He was wide awake in a heartbeat, listening hard. He thought he heard some-thing. A couple of seconds later, he heard something for sure. It sounded like careful footsteps somewhere in the clearing behind him. The hair rose up on his arms. Very slowly he unzipped his sleeping bag and reached out for the flashlight by the saddle. He heard another step—no mistaking it now—and it was much closer. He wished he had a pistol, or a machete, or something to defend himself. When his bag was totally unzipped, he peeled out of it, stood up, and turned on the flashlight all in one move. There was nothing where he pointed the light; but as he started to sweep it around, a man lunged at him out of the darkness, swinging a thick stick at Tomás's head. Tomás threw his arms up in self-defense and the club hit the flashlight, knocking it out of his hand and into the corner of his eye. Stars exploded in his head, but he had the pres-ence of mind to backpedal as he covered his head with his arms. He was struck again, this time on his right forearm and it went numb to the shoulder. He kept backpedaling. He could hear Lobo thrashing around behind him. He tripped over something and fell back-wards onto the ground. As he tried to scuttle away his head was unprotected, and he expected the 'coup de grace' from his attacker. But the attacker tripped too, and fell down hard. As he fell, the end of the thick stick grazed Tomás's head, and Tomás grabbed it with both hands and viciously yanked it away. The man rose to his knees, but Tomás was already on his. He could just see the outline of the man's head and took aim. He swung hard and hit him square. The man grunted and launched himself at Tomás—but not before Tomás had swung again and connected. The man screamed. Tomás cocked the stick for another strike as a fistful of dirt and wood chips struck him full bore in his eyes. He swung anyway and hit the man somewhere. He quickly wiped at the debris in his eyes. When he could see again, the man was just about up and Tomás hit him on a leg. The man grunted and turned, and started to run away. Tomás got up to go after him, but didn't go more than a few feet before he tripped hard again and fell flat on his face. What the fuck did he keep tripping over? He crawled over to the flashlight and turned it in the direction the man had run. There he was, just at the edge of the woods. The man turned towards him, and Tomás saw that the man was wearing dark pants and jacket and had long dark hair. He may have had a mustache but Tomás wasn't sure. There was blood all around his mouth and he had a hand covering his nose. He disappeared into the trees. Tomás was not about to follow him.

He looked over to Lobo, who was shaking. He walked over to calm the animal—and to calm himself. It was a good thing he had taken the precaution of the lasso around the stump because the *manea* had pulled out. Lobo was straining against the rope and it was taut, about a foot off the ground near where Tomás had been sleeping. So that's what he had tripped over, and his assailant too. That rope may have saved his life.

Why hadn't he listened to Ramon and stayed with someone? He shone the flashlight nervously around. His head throbbed. He gently felt the corner of his eye. It was already swollen and he knew he would have a shiner. There was a little blood where the stick had grazed his head. His right arm hurt like the dickens, but he could move it and nothing was broken. He wondered if the guy would come back. He didn't think so. He had done some real damage. But he might have a buddy or two. He put on his boots, and, clutching the stick, he stood guard for the rest of the night, dozing occasionally with his head against Lobo. He figured Lobo would give him an early warning if the man returned.

At first light he saddled Lobo, who was as eager to leave the clearing as he was. Lobo was even perky as they went down that endless hill. He laid the stick across the front of the saddle and ate some cheese with the last of Maria Elena's *sopaipilla*. The trees he had thought so beautiful on the way up now seemed like perfect places for an ambush. He wondered if he could identify his attacker. He didn't think so. But there must be something. He pictured the man just before he left the clearing, when he had turned with a hand covering his nose. Tomás turned like the man did and struck the same pose. The man had covered his nose with his left hand—and it was Tomás's right arm and right eye that were hit. He'd bet anything the man was left handed. He shivered. He had been very lucky. He could have been killed. Thank God for that rope. If he wanted to survive for another year and a half here, he had to start making better decisions. Camping out in Lote Once had not been a brilliant move.

Hours later he approached the La Paloma schoolhouse, a relief because it meant he was close to home. He threw the stick off to the side of the road. As he came down the last hill to Caman he could see the schoolhouse, and Ramon and Maria Elena in front of the Rodriguez gate. Maria Elena was on horseback. They watched him approach. When he stopped and said good morning, their mouths dropped open.

"*Por Dios*, Don Tomás, what happened?" Ramon asked.

Ramon quickly opened the gate and came around to Tomás, who slowly and awkwardly dismounted. His right arm was no help so he couldn't hang on to the saddle. Instead, he sort of slid down on his stomach. Maria Elena jumped off her horse and came up to him. She gently turned his head towards her and looked closely at his eye. Then she noticed the dried blood on his hair. She carefully removed his hat and examined his wound. Don Ramon repeated his question.

"What in the world happened, Don Tomás?"

"A man attacked me last night—after dark—and whoever it was hit me with a stick."

"What were you doing riding in the dark? You couldn't have been that late getting up there," Ramon asked as he took his turn at examining him.

"I wasn't riding. I was camping in a clearing off to the side of the road. I didn't want to take anyone's bed so I..."

Maria Elena glanced quickly at the sleeping bag lashed behind the saddle, and then lashed into Tomás.

"You what!? Camped out by the road? Don Tomás, what on earth were you..." She stopped in mid sentence and turned to Ramon. "*Tio*, did you not explain the dangers in Lote Once to Don Tomás?"

"I thought he was going to..."

Maria Elena didn't let him finish. Her eyes were flashing.

"I guess you did not tell him about how things can be up there, *Tio!*" Turning back to Tomás, she said,

"There are some very bad types up in those hills and it is a very dangerous place to be out alone in the night. There are also many mountain lions in that area of Cufeo."

Ramon asked, "Did you get a good look at him? Would you recognize him?"

Tomás shook his head.

"Then if it was up in Lote Once and you cannot identify him, the *carabineros* will never go up there and..."

Maria Elena interrupted Ramon again, "What were you thinking? Camping out? Even a child has more sense than that!"

It was the first time anyone had spoken so directly to Tomás since he had been in the *campo*. Ramon tried to calm her.

"Now Maria Elena," he began, but she wouldn't listen.

"I know these words are strong, *Tio*. But it is the truth."

She looked at Tomás again and not so gently replaced his hat.

"You're lucky your wounds are light and that you weren't killed."

She mounted her horse and looked about to turn away when he said, "Maria Elena, I ate your *sopaipilla* this morning. It was delicious. Thank you."

That took her by surprise and for a second she didn't say anything, while Ramon chuckled. Tomás thought that there was maybe a whisper of a smile tugging at her angry lips.

But she only said, "You were very lucky to be alive to eat it!"

With that, she abruptly turned her horse and spurred it into a brisk walk up the road.

"Don Ramon, she is very angry."

Ramon watched her ride up the hill.

"Yes she is. My niece can be very spirited. But she has reason. I should have told you more about Lote Once. There is much you do not know about life here. You should be more cautious."

He turned and looked at him.

"Come, let's get those wounds of yours washed and you can tell me more of what happened."

He shut the gate and they walked up towards the house.

After a few steps, Ramon said, "For the last several weeks Pablo and I have been wondering what you will do once school begins."

Tomás shrugged his shoulders.

"As you know, Pablo and his family will be returning to Valdivia so Javier and Alex can go to school there. After that they will only come up here on weekends and I will be taking care of the farm alone again. And, because the house will be almost empty, we wondered if you might want to live here?"

The offer took him totally by surprise. But what a great surprise. It was perfect. Absolutely perfect! He quickly accepted.

"Don Ramon, that would be very good. But only if you are sure that this is what you want and that I will not disrupt your life. Or that of Don Pablo and his family."

"On the contrary. It would be good for both of us. I would have company and so would you. I can teach you many things. And if you live here, then I would have someone to watch the house sometimes and I could visit friends. When Pablo and the family are gone, I am like a prisoner."

"Then agreed, Don Ramon."

They shook hands.

"Good. Now let's get this saddle off of Lobo and let him rest, and get you cleaned up. And I want to talk seriously with you about buying another horse. Pablo and I have some ideas."

As they approached the outbuildings, Tomás flexed his arm. It was stiff and hurt at the slightest movement. But at least he could move it. His vision was blocked a little in the upper corner of his right eye, and he thought he must have a pretty good shiner. He looked at Lobo and saw that his ears were perked up. Lobo was looking forward to his grain and being set free. He wondered if the animal remembered anything from last night.

CHAPTER NINE

Salton (Grasshopper)

At the end of summer Tomás moved into the room attached to the front of the Rodriguez farmhouse. It was small, maybe six feet by twelve, and was the most private room in their home. The only furniture was a little writing desk and a straight-back chair, perfect for studying at night. From the desk he could look out of the single window to the large vegetable garden and the road and school beyond. The window looked like it had been repaired recently and had all its panes. It had probably been fixed for him. At one end of the room was a door to the outside and the outhouse was only thirty feet away—a good thing for someone still adjusting to an unfamiliar diet. At the other end was his bed—several sheep pelts on the floor with his sleeping bag on top. There was just enough space left in the room for his trunk, whenever it arrived. An interior door with glass panes covered by a linen curtain led into a large dining room which connected to the kitchen. Like the Martinez house in Los

Guindos, the kitchen was where all the action took place and the dining room was used only on formal occasions. Last night had been such an occasion. The family had celebrated his arrival with an *asado.*

An *asado* was a traditional Chilean cookout where a lamb was roasted on a spit. In the *campo,* preparations went on all day, beginning with the selection of the lamb to be slaughtered. Ramon said that because the *asado* was in his honor, Tomás should rope the lamb. Ramon handed him his lasso. Over the summer he had practiced on fence posts, but he had a long way to go with moving targets. To his mortification, the whole family came out to watch. Pablo and his wife Miriam stood smiling by the corral fence. Pablo was a few years younger than Ramon, and taller and less stocky. No one would ever guess they were brothers. Miriam was short and solid, maybe five feet two with her shoes on. She was a bundle of energy and laughed easily and often. But there was no mistaking the substance to her. Like Emilio's Señora in Los Guindos, she was the one who kept the family ship on an even keel.

Ramon pointed out the lamb while Javier and Alex climbed the fence next to their parents, and perched on top for a birdseye view. As he slowly entered the corral, he hefted the lasso. Unlike his green nylon rope, Ramon's lasso was made out of one solid and tightly twisted piece of leather. It was heavier than the nylon and would throw much more true, especially if there was any wind. Ramon had taught him to make the big loop that would go around the animal's neck and then several smaller coils for the estimated distance of the toss. The loop and the coils he held in his right, throwing-hand, and the rest of the rope was in his left. Slowly swinging the rope above his head, he waited for a clear shot as the sheep jostled each other and ran around. He saw his chance and threw. He did not lead the lamb enough and missed completely. Everyone laughed and yelled out words of encouragement. The sheep now were totally upset which would make his second toss all the more difficult. He wondered how many throws it would take, or if Ramon or Pablo might have to step in and bail him out. But he was successful on his second throw—sort of. The lasso somehow snagged a rear hoof. He hung on while the lamb hopped awkwardly about, straining against the rope and bleating loudly. He hoped the lamb would not twist his leg off as it tried to get away.

Ramon entered the corral laughing and asked, "Don Tomás, is this a special way they lasso the sheep in your country?"

"Yes. By roping a foot, then the body is not damaged and it makes for a more perfect piece of meat."

The family thought that was pretty funny. The boys jumped down from the fence and helped to tug and push the struggling animal over to one of the little outbuildings where a horizontal pole extended from the eaves. Ramon and Pablo hoisted the lamb up to hang upside down from the pole. Tomás could not help swallowing a little. He was not a blood and guts kind of guy and this would be the first time he witnessed a slaughter.

Pablo tied on a full length white apron and pulled out a long thin-bladed knife, which he honed for a moment or two. Miriam approached carrying a shiny metal basin, and when she stood ready at his side, Pablo slit the lamb's throat. The lamb made a harsh gurgling sound as its blood splattered into the basin, and Tomás couldn't help noticing that the deep red color of the blood matched Miriam's painted fingernails. When the bleeding stopped, Miriam mixed some garlic, cilantro, salt, and a little lemon into the basin and let it sit for about five minutes. After the blood coagulated, she

cut it up into little squares as if it were a dish of brownies. This concoction, called *niache,* was the traditional
first dish of the *asado.* Miriam offered him a piece.

He was not adventurous when it came to eating food
like this, and having seen where it came from had not
helped his appetite any. He asked her to cut the piece
in half and took that. It did not taste bad, but it was still
warm and it made him gag. He looked over to Ramon
and Pablo. They had begun to gut and skin the lamb.
His nostrils inadvertently tightened as he smelled the
lamb's innards. He tried to tell himself this was only
reality. Where did he think all those neatly packaged
legs of lamb in the supermarket came from? Come on,
Tomás, get a grip.

When Ramon and Pablo were done, he took a picture of them with his instamatic camera. They stood
on either side of the now headless, gutted, and skinned
carcass. The taller Pablo was unshaved with long dark
sideburns and a derby-like hat. His long apron was
spattered with blood and guts, and his black rubber
boots had little pieces of meat and fat stuck to them.
Ramon was wearing a beret and a short leather work
apron. He smiled at the camera and playfully put his
right hand on top of the head of the lamb. He held the
knife in his left hand, and the fleece—bloody side up
so it would dry and could be scraped later—was draped
over a fence behind him.

Earlier in the morning Ramon had split some firewood and started a fire next to a low stump, away from
the house. He periodically fed the fire until there was
a large pile of coals. Pablo took half the carcass and
hung it in the root cellar to cool. He would butcher it
later and sell or barter the meat to neighbors. He and
Ramon then skewered the other half with a long hardwood pike and carried it over to the fire. They placed
one end of the pole on the low stump and balanced

the other on a pitchfork stuck straight into the ground, resting the pole where the rounded metal tines met the wooden handle. With two feet of pole extending beyond the pitchfork as a handle to turn the lamb, it became a giant rotisserie.

Ramon sat down on an old wooden crate within reach of the pole, and the boys sprawled on the ground nearby. Every now and then, as Ramon turned the lamb, Alex and Javier basted the meat with a sauce that Miriam had prepared in a large green bottle. Little holes had been punched into the twist-on bottle cap, which enabled them to sprinkle it over the meat. Tomás dragged over another crate and sat with Ramon. Watching the lamb slowly cook and gazing out beyond to the volcanoes, he thought of backyard cookouts in suburbia U.S.A., with fancy grills, long stainless spatulas, and thick leather cooking gloves. All that seemed so unnecessary—he couldn't imagine that it got any better than this.

The meal was a feast. The lamb was succulent and everything else was garden fresh. There were new potatoes with home-churned butter and parsley on top. There was the last of the *habas* and a salad of lettuce, tomatoes, sweet green peppers, and onion. They dipped pieces of bread into a big bowl of Ramon's *pebre* sauce which was heavy on the cilantro and hot peppers. Miriam had prepared some green hot peppers. Pablo told Tomás to dip the end of one in salt and take a bite. He tried one and found it was a great accent to the meat. After awhile his lips burned from the peppers. When Ramon saw him fanning his lips he told him to wipe salt on them. It stopped the burning immediately. For dessert there were fresh blackberries with whipped cream. There was not much conversation during the meal because everyone was stuffing themselves. After the meal when he tried to carry the dishes out to the kitchen, he was told to stay put. Pablo said it was a man's world and anything to do with dishes was women's work. Miriam didn't say anything, but it was only a matter of seconds before she had Javier and Alex clearing the table.

Pablo was sitting at the head of the table. After finishing his berries and cream, he pushed his chair back and turned to him.

"Don Tomás, I have waited until now to tell you some good news. I believe that I have found the right horse for you."

Everyone looked up with interest.

"He is young but already strong and well formed. He is owned by Don Pedro and when I told him the horse was for you, he offered to sell him for a very good price."

Pablo knew animals so if he said he had found a good horse, then there was no doubt. A good part of the family's income was from firewood and charcoal, but it was the money from his shrewd buying and selling of livestock that enabled them to live in Valdivia.

"He is very tall and should be able to carry you for many hours each day without tiring. And he will only get stronger as he gets older. And if you have such a horse, Don Tomás, then you must have some *huaso* clothes. You should be properly dressed on such a fine animal."

Miriam looked heavenward and said, "You and your *huaso* clothes, Pablo. We could very much use the money you spend on all your fancy hats and jackets."

She turned to Tomás.

"My husband has a trunk full and he fusses like an old lady when he chooses what he will wear."

Pablo responded angrily.

"It is very important to be dressed properly, woman! You know that. For my club meetings, the parades, for the *media luna,* and especially for my business. I cannot show up at the *fundos* to buy animals dressed like a *campesino* woodcutter!"

Pablo glared at her as she took plates out to the kitchen. An awkward silence fell around the table.

Tomás had seen Pablo dressed as a *huaso* —Chilean cowboy—several times. He was a long-time member of the Huaso Club of Valdivia, and rode in parades and attended rodeos. He wore a large flat-brimmed hat and a brightly colored little *manta* called a *chamanto.* The *chamanto* covered a snug, fancy jacket, and tooled leather leggings—*pierneras*—protected his pants. His large jingling spurs were always highly polished.

Miriam came back into the dining room and sat down. Pablo looked hard at her, but she ignored him. Tomás cleared his throat.

"So, Don Pablo, do you know how much Don Pedro wants for this fine horse?"

Pablo tore his eyes away from Miriam.

"Five hundred '*lucas*' and believe me that is an excellent price."

The official exchange rate was nine *escudos,* or '*lucas*,' to the dollar.

"And he is in no hurry for the money. Don Pedro wants to continue training the horse for a few more weeks."

Pablo looked over at Miriam.

"Is there no tea in this house, woman?"

Miriam gave him a look before she got up and went back into the kitchen. Satisfied, Pablo turned back to Tomás.

"The important thing is you will have your new horse in plenty of time before winter. You will need a strong horse then. Your Lobo is worn out and it will be much harder on him when the roads are slippery. And besides," Pablo said trying to look sternly at his sons, "now that you will have another horse, these two will not have the excuse of helping you catch Lobo, and they can spend more time on the weekends helping with the firewood."

Alex groaned. He was ten and very much the dreamer and thinker of the family. He would find any way he could to get out of physical work. Javier, twelve, was just the opposite—he was a worker and much more serious. Yet, as different as they were, they were very close. Tomás smiled at them.

"Are you two ready to go back to school?"

Javier said, "No! I want to stay here and help *Tio* Ramon."

Pablo beamed with pride as he looked at his son. Javier could already ride like a man and he worked hard at cutting and splitting firewood. Occasionally he helped his father drive livestock.

Miriam answered, "We know that, Javier. But it is very important for you to go to school in Valdivia. Years from now you will understand that it was the right thing to do."

Javier frowned.

The dog started barking outside and soon there was a knock on the kitchen door. Javier got up and went to see who it was. They could hear him talking to someone, and after a few minutes he returned with a folded piece of paper which he handed to Tomás.

"It is from the Martinez family in Los Guindos," he said.

"Who brought the note, Javier?" Miriam asked.

"Flor Gomez."

"Well, I hope you invited her in to sit down with us."

"Yes Mama, but she said she must go home. She has come from the bus and has supplies that need to be taken care of. She said that the Señora Martinez was on the bus and the Señora gave her this note for Don Tomás."

Tomás unfolded the note and was surprised by the excellent penmanship.

Dear Don Tomás,
I hope this letter finds you in very good health. As you know, the tournament here is next Saturday and Jaime wants you to also know that the team will be getting together Friday afternoon to finish building the ramada and to practice. We wonder if you could come over Friday and eat dinner and stay for the night in your old bed. Saturday morning you could rest and then play in the tournament. It is not necessary to let us know first. Please only come if you can. The whole family (especially Lilia) is looking forward to it.
With much tenderness,
Isabel Baeza Martinez.

Tomás read the note to the family and then turned to Ramon.

"Looks like you will be eating dinner alone on Friday and Saturday. I will not get back until after dark. I will bring you some *empanadas*."

Pablo, Miriam, and the boys would be leaving for Valdivia in the morning. Miriam asked if Tomás liked *empanadas*.

"Who doesn't?" he answered, and he could see the wheels turning in her head.

Pablo stood up from the table.

"That is good, Don Tomás. When we have you all dressed up on your big new horse, you can ride up to the *ramadas* and eat *empanadas* and drink wine out of a steer's horn. We will make a real *huaso* out of you."

Tomás arrived at the Martinez home early on Friday afternoon, and was greeted with a big hug from the Señora and polite handshakes from Rosa and Ana. Lilia was all smiles, but stood shyly back. Tobi greeted him like a long lost friend. He petted the dog for a few minutes before setting Lobo free to graze. Emilio was out fencing, and Jaime was over at the soccer field with the team, building the *ramada*. He headed over to the field to help.

That evening at dinner they caught up with the news from both sides of the highway. He was complimented several times on how well he was speaking, and he responded by saying he owed it all to his young teacher here. Lilia sat next to him, and they made plans to look for *chupones* in the morning. She told him she knew some secret places that the other kids in the *campo* had not yet discovered. He promised not to tell anyone where they were.

The next morning they picked *chupones* and *mora*, laughing often as they filled their straw baskets. He couldn't help noticing that Lilia was growing up and filling out. It wouldn't be long before she became an eligible young lady of the *campo*, just like her older sisters. But for now, Lilia was still a young girl who ate one blackberry for every five she picked. He tasted a *chupone*, which had a faintly sweet flavor, but he much preferred the blackberries. He wondered if the corners of his mouth looked like Lilia's.

After they returned to the house, Lilia proudly presented the two baskets to the Señora, who said, "That is very good, Lilia. But, I am surprised there are so many."

The Señora looked at him.

"And I see Lilia was not alone in eating the *mora*, eh Don Tomás? I think maybe the two of you should go outside and wash your faces."

After they took turns at the wash station, Lilia went to help the Señora render the *chupones* and *mora* into marmalade and jam. Tomás found Emilio clearing brush and they chatted amiably for awhile. Now that

Tomás had moved in with the Rodriguez family, Emilio said he would have Jaime bring his trunk up in the next couple of weeks. Tomás returned to the house to find Jorge and Jaime sitting under the eucalyptus tree. They stood up when he arrived and the three of them headed over to the soccer field. A few minutes later Lilia ran by, trying to catch up with Ana and Rosa. As Jaime and Tomás talked, Jorge paid no attention. He was too intent on watching Lilia in her skimpy polka dot dress.

The soccer tournament could not have gone better. Los Guindos won and the team was awarded a fat lamb in front of the cheering home crowd. There would be a celebratory team *asadao* sometime before winter, but for now the lamb would join the Martinez flock. Tomás ate his fill of *empanadas* and the Señora, who was working in the *ramada*, carefully wrapped up a half dozen for Ramon, along with a jar of blackberry jam for the Rodriguez household. After saying goodbye to the Martinez family, he rode home with Juan and teased him much of the way because it was Caman they had beaten in the finals.

As late summer turned into fall, life went smoothly. Most of the *campesinos* would be ready for their pine deliveries in the winter. Ramon turned out to be an excellent cook and baker. Most mornings he and Tomás ate fresh bread with honey or preserves and drank *mate* from personal cups. For lunch Ramon prepared a tasty soup, and occasionally a plate of potatoes with a small bowl of his *pebre* sauce on the side. For dinner they would have the rest of the morning bread and noontime soup. During dinner they listened to the radio. Ramon had a favorite *novela* that he religiously tuned into every evening. The program was about the misbehaving members of a high society family in Santiago. Adultery was common, household servants were seduced, and it was as racy as any soap opera in the States.

One night Tomás asked Ramon how many brothers and sisters he had.

"There were originally five of us. There is Pablo, of course, who is the youngest. Then there is Ricardo. He is the one that lives near Casa Blanca. He is married and he and his Señora have four children. Then there is me, and then there is my older sister, Angela, who lives in Santiago and, like me, is not married. My oldest sister, Maria, was the mother of Juan and Maria Elena. But she died with her husband in the big earthquake eight years ago. Do you know about the earthquake, Don Tomás?"

Tomás nodded and asked, "Was she killed in Valdivia?"

"No, but close. Maria, her husband, and Juan were returning on the late bus. I was at their house with Maria Elena. You have seen the big lake by the highway a little way before Valdivia. That was about where the bus was, on the level stretch before the hills, when the road suddenly split open. The bus struck the deep trench head on and flipped and rolled over. The driver, Maria and her husband, and seven others died, and many others were injured. Juan's leg was crushed and that is why he is a cripple. He had three operations, but his leg never grew back right—it was just too badly shattered. You should have seen him play *futbol* before he was hurt. No one could get the ball from him. People came out from Valdivia and wanted him to play for their clubs.

"After the accident, Juan spent a lot of time in the hospital and Maria Elena was by his bed almost always. She read to him for many hours a day and I think that is when she learned to love books so much."

Ramon stood up and made a cup of tea.

"How old is Maria Elena?" Tomás asked.

"Twenty."

"I would think she would be married by now."

"Yes. One would think so."

Ramon sat down with his tea and stirred sugar into it.

"Many young men, even some from Valdivia, have tried to win her—but they never succeeded. I think she cannot leave her brother."

He took a sip of tea and reached for the sugar again.

"Juan could not do much for over a year after he left the hospital. Maria Elena did everything and, although we all helped her when we could, she never asked for help. She can cut firewood, kill and prepare the animals, and even lasso the animals. I think that if she played *futbol*, she would be good at that too."

Ramon took another quick sip. Satisfied he brought the cup closer to his edge of the table and leaned back in his chair.

"The earthquake was on the twenty-second of May, and every year on that day we go to pay our respects to Maria and her husband. As you can imagine, the cemetery is always full of visitors that day. Maybe when I go this time you could watch the house for me, eh Don Tomás?"

"Of course."

Ramon finished mopping up his soup with a piece of bread and looked at his watch.

"Time for my *novela*," he said and walked over to the corner where his radio sat on a little shelf all by itself.

Ramon would not charge him for room and board, so instead they worked out a system where Tomás would buy their supplies. It made his staying there ridiculously cheap, and he told Ramon that. But Ramon would have it no other way. Each time Tomás went to Valdivia, they made a list of the things they needed. Staples like vegetable oil, flour, salt, sugar, Nescafe, *yerba* for their *mate*, bouillon cubes, yeast, and of course, batteries for the radio. One night Ramon had sworn at the radio when it started to fade in the middle of his soap opera.

"This damn radio is a 'battery eater,'" he exclaimed as he stood up and stomped over to the cookstove.

He opened the oven door and pulled out four used batteries, quickly placing them in the radio during a commercial. He put the weaker batteries in the oven. "There. This will give them more life."

Pablo came up to the farm one day carrying a few *huaso* items in a string bag. Tomás didn't think that unusual, but during *onces* Pablo surprised him by saying they were a gift.

"Now," Pablo said, "you will look like you are supposed to when you ride your new horse."

He handed Tomás an old pair of nickel spurs, which he told him to shine. The spurs were surprisingly heavy and had intricate geometric patterns etched into them. Although tarnished, they were beautiful. Then Pablo gave him a brightly striped *chamanto* which looked to be in perfect shape. It too was heavier than it looked and, as Tomás fingered the material, he guessed that it was made out of a heavy nylon. Finally, Pablo handed him a pair of beat-up *pierneras*. One needed a new buckle in the back, but they were very cool, and made Tomás think of motorcycle days when they would have come in handy during foul weather. Besides a buckle for the *pierneras*, the spurs needed new leather straps. Pablo told him where there was an excellent leather worker in Valdivia who could do the work.

"And just down the street from him there is a store that sells clothes for the *huasos*—hats, *mantas de Castilla*, riding boots—everything. You need a good wide brimmed hat and real riding boots that will not slip in the stirrup. And you should buy a *manta de Castilla* for the winter weather."

Two days later Tomás left for Valdivia with the spurs, *pierneras*, and his shopping list. Money was not an issue. His salary of seventy-five dollars a month was automatically deposited in *escudos* in his bank account and, although seventy-five dollars did not sound like much, his life in Cufeo was so cheap that he was rolling in dough.

Valdivia was a welcome change. He had not been in town for quite some time and it was great to catch up with Oso for a few days. He bought a *huaso* hat and a pair of short black leather riding boots. He also bought a *manta de Castilla* which was so large and heavy that it would be a pain to carry back up to Caman. He would have to lash it to the top of his pack.

He also picked up the money for his new horse from the Peace Corps office, and bought everything on Ramon's list, plus a few things not on the list, like a package of razor blades for Ramon. Whenever Ramon shaved, he would take the flat little blade out of his razor and painstakingly attempt to hone it on a smooth stone. Judging from the results, it didn't do much good, and it must have hurt like hell. Ramon would hack and scrape, and his face would end up looking like a war zone. But Ramon never asked for razor blades because he thought them a personal, not a household, item.

When Tomás finished buying for the farm, he went shopping for the Martinez family. He wanted to buy them presents for delivering his trunk, which would come any day now. He went to an *artesania* shop that sold crafts and souvenirs from around the province. They had an illustrated children's book about a little boy and girl who lived in the *campo*, and he bought that for Lilia. He also bought a porcelain salt and pepper shaker set of black and white oxen—the same colors as the Martinez's oxen—that were hitched to a cart that held napkins. He thought the Señora would like to put that out in the front room on the big table. For Rosa and Ana, he found two brightly colored kerchiefs. He went to a *confiteria* where imported and specialty foods were sold, and he got two large bags of pop-corn kernels—one for Ramon and him, and one for the Martinez family. He particularly liked the Spanish name for popcorn—*palomitas*—which translated as 'lit-tle pigeons.' And he couldn't resist getting a bag of hard candy for Lilia, to go along with the book.

Tomás returned to the Rodriguez farm sweating heavily from lugging all the merchandise up from the highway. He was just in time because Jaime showed up the following afternoon with his trunk. Ramon helped Tomás bundle up the presents so nothing would break, along with an explanation of each item and who it was for. Tomás also wrote careful instructions on how to cook the popcorn. He handed the package to Jaime and thanked him again for bringing up the trunk. They said good bye with an *abrazo,* and Jaime led the oxen out through the gate and down towards the highway.

Three days later Tomás received a note from the Señora Martinez.

Dear Don Tomás,
A million thanks for all your presents. Each was perfect and very thoughtful and I especially loved my pair of oxen. I have put them on the big table out front. You should not have gone to all the trouble and spent so much money on us. But we still want to thank you very much. I also have to tell you about our adventure with the palomitas. Lilia wanted to be in charge of cooking them and so she followed your instruc-

tions; but not exactly. First, she put too many of the yellow kernels in the pot. Then when she heard them begin to make noise she was very curious and took off the lid to look. Two or three hopped out of the pan onto the floor and she ran after them to pick them up. Unfortunately she took the lid with her and it was then that all the little kernels decided to hatch. It was like a machine gun, and little pigeons began flying around the kitchen. We all started to laugh as Lilia ran around trying to pick them up—it really was very funny. But Lilia still had the lid and Rosa had to run over and take it from her and cover the pot or they all would have escaped. Rosa shook it like you said so very few of the palomitas were burned. Also I think it was a good thing that Rosa and Ana had swept and washed the floor earlier in the morning!

Anyway, I wanted to thank you and let you know about our little adventure. Lilia also wants me to especially thank you for the pretty book.

With much tenderness,
Isabel Baeza Rodriguez

Tomás read the Señora's letter to Don Ramon and they laughed as they pictured Lilia frantically running around. Tomás had cooked some popcorn the night he returned from Valdivia. It was the first time Ramon had eaten popcorn too.

Pablo came up from Valdivia. When he learned that Tomás had the money for the new horse, he said he would go to Don Pedro's straight off. He was gone for most of the day, which was not surprising because business in the *campo* always included socializing. It was almost impossible to travel in Cufeo without passing the farm of a friend or relative, where one was always invited in to share some food and catch up on gossip. The day passed slowly for Tomás. He was excited and impatient to see his new mount. He studied for awhile and helped Ramon with some chores, splitting stove wood and fetching water from the spring—anything to make the time go by. Finally in the late afternoon he saw a rider leading a horse down the Casa Blanca road. He walked out to the gate to wait.

He knew little about horses but there was no denying that his new horse was big—taller even than Pablo's. He was gray and handsome, and young too. Pablo watched as Tomás patted the horse's neck and carefully walked around his backside.

"That's right, Don Tomás," he said. "Until you know a horse, you should be cautious. But Don Pedro himself has worked with this horse for some time now and he is very *manso*. Come, let us take him to the pasture so he can make friends with your Lobo. And let us hope that Lobo does not teach him any bad tricks, eh? Tomorrow we will saddle him and you can see how he is to ride."

At Pablo's insistence the next morning, Tomás put on all his new *huaso* clothes. He didn't have fancy *huaso* style pants, but the *pierneras* covered most of his jeans. Pablo loaned him a wide, double-buckle *huaso* belt, and gave him an old brown *huaso* jacket with white trim. Tomás slipped the bright *chamanto* over the tight jacket and put on his brown *manta*, folding it back onto his shoulders. Finally, he donned the new hat that he had bought in Valdivia. Pablo tilted the hat to a rakish angle and then stepped back. With hands on hips, he inspected Tomás. He smiled.

"*Perfecto.*"

Ramon had gone out to get the new horse and had saddled him.

As he led the horse up, he reported, "He is not like your Lobo. I walked right up to him and put the rope around his neck. He is very tame."

Ramon looked Tomás over from head to toe and whistled.

"Very Good! You have the look of a real *huaso*. And now I think it is time for the *huaso* to mount his new horse."

The horse was so tall that Tomás had trouble getting his foot up in the stirrup—he had to lift his foot with his hand.

"I think this will take a little time to get used to," he said after he heaved himself up into the saddle. "He is very tall and the ground is very far away."

The brothers laughed. Pablo said, "Aii, he is such a pretty horse. You should ride over to the Montoyas. Juan and Maria Elena will be impressed."

"I think maybe it's better if I go up the road towards La Paloma and see how he does with the hills there and..."

"Oh no, Don Tomás," Ramon joined in. "You will not wear all these fine clothes often—only on special occasions. And this is a special occasion. It is your first ride. Someone should see you like this—a *huaso* on his beautiful horse."

They persisted until he finally agreed. He set off, but with reservations. He did not want to impress anyone. God knows that he had tried doing enough of that in the past and it rarely worked out. And he was not a *huaso,* and it felt ridiculous to be dressed up as one. Plus he was way over-dressed for the warm day, and beginning to sweat.

He arrived at the Montoya gate and turned the horse sideways so he could slide the bars back out of the way. After all, he thought, no self-respecting *huaso* would dismount to remove them. Besides, the dog would probably come out and he did not want to be treed again—especially dressed up in these duds. The top bar slid back just fine. But as he bent over farther to slide the next one, all hell broke loose. Suddenly something let go and he was headed for the ground. His left foot flew out of the stirrup and he inadvertently jammed his spur into the horse. The horse reared up on his hind legs and launched himself over the gate. Tomás tumbled to the ground, luckily managing a shoulder roll instead of landing on his head. He ended up in a pile and could not see a thing because his *manta* had flipped over his back, covering his head. He flailed around, catching his breath. When he finally lifted the *manta* and peered out, there was Maria Elena, eyes wide in disbelief, standing on the porch staring at him.

"Are you all right, Don Tomás? I saw you fall from the window."

Muchacho the dog came running around the corner of the house and went berserk. Maria Elena yelled at the dog to be quiet.

The dog stopped barking and she asked again, "Are you all right?"

"Yes, I think so."

He slowly got up and tested his legs.

Maria Elena was beginning to smile and discreetly covered her mouth when Tomás said, "I do not think anything is broken."

He picked up his hat and started to dust himself off. It was hard to do with any dignity.

It was his obvious mortification that set her off. All of a sudden she started to laugh. She tried covering her mouth with both hands but it didn't work. She burst into hysterics and collapsed onto the porch deck, laughing hard and holding her sides.

"I am sorry, Don Tomás," she barely managed to say, "but I cannot help it. You came over the gate like a big brown ball and rolled up here to the porch. You were very graceful," she added, and started laughing again.

"I think maybe all I am good for is to entertain you people here."

"No, no! Do not think that. These things can happen."

She wiped her eyes with the edge of her apron.

"But what did happen?" she asked.

They looked over to the horse who stood calmly nearby. The saddle was upside down, hanging below its stomach.

"I thought maybe the cinch broke," Tomás answered as he walked up to the horse. "But I guess not. It's still attached."

Maria Elena helped him pivot the saddle back into position and they tightened the cinch. She stroked the horse.

"He is very beautiful. Did you just get him?"

"Yes."

Tomás took off his *manta* and tied it behind the saddle. Maria Elena admired his *chamanto* and then noticed the leggings and shined spurs. He explained that he was all dressed up because of her uncles who had insisted that he come here on his first ride.

"That sounds like my uncles, and I thought this *chamanto* looked familiar. If I am not mistaken, it used to be Pablo's."

She looked back at his horse.

"But you know what I think happened? I think that when the saddle was put on, your horse stuck out his belly. Some horses do that. After a few minutes their stomach goes back to normal which makes the cinch loose. With a horse like this, you have to wait a little after you saddle him and then re-tighten the cinch before you mount. Then it will stay."

"Don Ramon saddled him. I will have to tell him what happened. It seems there is not a day here when I do not learn something." He started to mount, saying, "I will return now and…"

"No, no, Don Tomás. You must stay for lunch and show Juan that you are now a real *huaso.*"

She began laughing again.

"And I cannot wait to tell him about your grand entrance over our gate."

"I think that is not really necessary, Maria Elena. I think that maybe ..." but he stopped when he saw her expression.

She put her hands on her hips.

"I heard how you teased Juan all the way home from Los Guindos about who won the tournament. Fair is fair, and I think it is fair for him to hear about this. And he has to see you dressed up. And your pretty horse too. Come on. Let's take care of your horse and go find Juan."

As they led the horse towards a shady spot, Maria Elena started laughing again. Tomás sighed because he knew that news of this would spread all around Cufeo.

When he returned to the farm after lunch, Ramon and Pablo came out to meet him.

"Well, how did it go? Were they impressed?" Ramon asked.

"Oh they were impressed all right," and he told them all about what had happened.

Ramon started guffawing and, just like Maria Elena, he had to sit down because he was laughing so hard. Pablo stared at Tomás in disbelief. Tomás was sure Pablo could not believe that he had made such a fool of himself. Pablo just shook his head. Ramon, with tears in his eyes, asked him to tell the story again. When he came to the part where his horse sprang up from a standstill and leapt over the gate, he searched for the right analogy. He thought of one, but did not know the word in Spanish. He went inside to get his dictionary. When he returned, he sat down next to Ramon while he looked up the word 'grasshopper.'

"Don Ramon, he jumped over that gate like a big *salton*."

The corners of Ramon's eyes crinkled as he smiled at Tomás.

"Don Tomás, I think you have just found a name for your new horse."

CHAPTER TEN

La Entrega (The Delivery)

"Hey Oso. How about some lunch?" Tomás asked as he stuck his head into Oso's office.

Oso looked up from the pile of papers on his desk and sighed. He took the cheap and well-chewed plastic pen out of his mouth, tossed it onto the desk, and rubbed his eyes.

"La Bomba?"

"*Logico.* Best *empanadas* in town."

Tomás had come in on the early bus and had spent the morning with Sr. Ojeda coordinating his first pine tree delivery. Everything was all set. He was to meet the driver with a jeep and trailer in front of the Ministry building early next Wednesday and they would pick up the seedlings at the nursery. From there it was just a matter of dropping them off at different locations for the *campesinos.* With luck they would be done by midday. Tomorrow he would return to Cufeo and spread the word that the delivery was on.

Oso pulled his dark rain parka off the back of the chair and threw it over a burly shoulder. They left his office and went down the stairway to the street, with Oso's shoes clicking sharply on the smooth, mirror-finish concrete stairs. If he weren't so big, he could almost have passed for one of the government bureaucrats. He was wearing black leather shoes instead of his usual muddy hiking boots. His dark pants were pressed and his white shirt was crisp and clean. Quite a change from the khaki pants and shirt, and the stained cruising vest with all the pockets.

"You're looking a little spiffy these days old man," Tomás said.

"Yeah, well, with all this damn rain I'm stuck here at the office and I figured I might as well dress the part. But not for much longer, my friend, because once I get caught up with the paperwork and finish the projections from the last cruise, I'm outta here for two weeks 'vacay.' You can slog around in the rain and mud delivering your little trees, but for me, Machu Picchu here I come. I can't wait!"

A light drizzle was falling and Oso put on his parka. In a few minutes they passed the central plaza and walked down Arauco to the restaurant. Across the street from La Bomba there was a small group of people waiting at a corner bus stop. The rain had picked up and most of them had their heads covered with umbrellas, newspapers, or anything else they had. One woman, though, stood unprotected. Tomás would recognize that long, thick braid anywhere. He had not seen her for a couple of weeks.

"Oso," he said. "I'll be right in. Grab a table would you? I see somebody I know from Cufeo."

Oso nodded and entered the building.

Tomás crossed the street and approached Maria Elena. She was dressed in a long, dark skirt and dark jacket. She held two string bags at her side, filled with items wrapped in heavy paper. She was looking the other way.

"*Buenos dias*, Maria Elena."

She turned around quickly and returned his smile; a small burst of sunshine on a dismal day.

"Don Tomás! What a surprise. I do not see you in the *campo* where we are neighbors, but in Valdivia we meet. What are you doing here?"

He told her about arranging the pine delivery and asked if she would like to join them for lunch.

"And you should get out of this rain—you are not even wearing a hat."

The water was starting to drip off her forehead and stream down her face as an old blue and white bus noisily approached. Maria Elena said Miriam was expecting her.

"I am sorry, but I really should...."

She paused when she saw his obvious disappointment. The bus pulled up to the curb and the line of people began shuffling towards the open door. She looked at the bus and then back at him again.

"But maybe I do have time for a cup of tea."

"Come on, then," he said as he reached for one of the string bags. With their heads bent against the rain, they hurried across the street. Maria Elena jumped lightly up to the sidewalk. Once inside the restaurant, they stomped their feet in the entryway and took off their wet coats. She was wearing a light green cabled sweater and a smooth woolen skirt. He thought she looked terrific. As they walked down the narrow hallway to the *comedor*, he worked up the courage to ask her if she would address him as Tomás while they were in town.

They stopped in front of the dining room doorway and she smiled sweetly.

"Yes, if you like."

They found Oso at a table near the parlor stove. The stove's heat took the dampness out of the air and the room was a comfortable temperature. If Tomás ever had any doubts about how attractive Maria Elena was, they were immediately dispelled when Oso looked up from his menu. His mouth dropped open ludicrously and Tomás almost burst out laughing. As he introduced her, Oso stood up and pulled out her chair.

Once she sat down and had the bags safely under the table, she said, "Thank you. Oso? That is your name?"

"Yes. It is a nickname that my so-called 'friends,'" he said, glancing at Tomás with a raised eyebrow, "have given me. My real name is Bruce which is 'Bruno' in Spanish. But everyone seems to want to call me Oso."

Maria Elena reached for a napkin and began to pat her face.

"Which of the three names would you like me to call you?"

"Oh, it really makes no difference, I guess."

"Then Oso it is. I have never known an *oso* before."

They all chuckled. A waiter came over and asked them if they were ready to order.

"Would you change your mind, Maria Elena, and eat lunch with us?" Tomás asked. "Or at least have a shortbread or cake or something with your tea?"

"No thank you, Tomás. Please, only a cup of tea. That really would be fine."

"What about you Oso?" he asked.

Reluctantly shifting his gaze from Maria Elena to the waiter, Oso ordered a cup of coffee and told the waiter he would have lunch a little later. Tomás also ordered coffee while Maria Elena asked Oso about his work. He said he was cruising timber on a large tract of government land on the island of Chiloe.

"And what is 'cruising timber?'" Maria Elena asked as she put her elbows on the table and leaned forward, resting her chin on her folded hands.

"That is a term foresters use when they take an inventory of trees. We lay out sample plots—or areas—on a systematic basis where we record the species, quantity, girth, and height of the trees. We also take increment borings where we drill into some of the trees with a tool that removes a core of wood, so that we can look at the annual rings. There is a ring for every year the trees grow and the separation between the rings tells us how fast or slowly they are growing. We bring all the data back to the office and then plot out the stands of trees on large maps, and compare them to aerial photos that show the timber types. This is how we determine approximate volumes and values and try to form an intelligent management plan."

Oso's Spanish was excellent and he knew his stuff. Maria Elena was intrigued.

She asked, "Are there any *alerce* there?"

Alerce was the Chilean counterpart to the sequoia in northern California. It could have a diameter of up to four meters across and could be thousands of years old. Oso said that there were a few stands in the more remote areas.

The waiter brought their tea and coffee, serving Maria Elena first. Tomás noticed that she put no sugar in her tea. In the *campo* she always stirred in a little honey.

She said, "I think the *alerce* is one of our national treasures. There are still some way up in the hills of Cufeo, but only where it is too difficult for the woodcutters to haul them out. They are so old and beautiful, and I hope that one day there will be laws to protect them. The forest can disappear so quickly. My brother and I are only two generations away from when there was only virgin forest in Cufeo."

Oso nodded.

"That is why forest management on a sustainable yield is so important. It is such a waste of your resource to just cut it all down. And that is what is happening with your *alerce*—or Patagonian cypress, which it is also called."

Oso turned to Tomás.

"The wood looks a lot like our redwood lumber and is used for just about everything, especially construction. Those decorative shingles that cover a lot of the old churches around here are all made out of *alerce*. That's because they're so rot resistant and last forever. But like Maria Elena says, the trees are hard to pull out of the woods. Oftentimes the loggers will girdle them first with an axe so they will die standing. That way they dry out and lose much of their weight making them easier to transport to the mill. A single log can be more than a legal truckload."

He turned back to Maria Elena.

"I cannot say what will happen to your *alerce* forests where I work, Maria Elena. All I can do is provide your government with useful information and hope for the best. But speaking of national treasures, Tomás, you did not tell me that there was such beauty in Cufeo."

Maria Elena and Tomás looked at each other and simultaneously rolled their eyes and laughed.

Maria Elena said, "Oso, I think you are a lady's man, no? But, you must come out to see the real beauty of Cufeo sometime. Maybe not now when the weather is so bad, but next summer. How long will you be here in Chile?"

"Oh, at least until this time next year. My two year commitment will be up then. But regardless, I will not leave before my work is finished."

"Then you must come out next summer and we can ride around Cufeo on horseback. I will show you some of the forests up high, and there are beautiful views everywhere. You will see why I love it so much. You can also see the new *pino* plantations and you might even see Tomás play *futbol* in a tournament. He is very good, you know."

Tomás looked at her, surprised.

"Yes, Tomás. Both Juan and I think you play well—for a *gringo* that is. But," she said after taking a last sip of tea and putting her cup down, "I do have to go. Miriam and *Tío* Pablo will worry if I do not get there soon. Oso, such a pleasure to meet you," she said extending her hand as she stood up.

"Likewise Maria Elena. I will look forward to our ride next summer, although I certainly hope to have the pleasure of seeing you before then."

He held her jacket out for her to put on.

"Thank you, Oso. You are indeed a gentleman," she said, and curtsied.

"I'll walk you out to your bus stop, Maria Elena."

"No, no Tomás. There is no need for both of us to get wet. When do you return to Cufeo?"

"Tomorrow morning on the early bus. I want to contact everyone about the delivery."

"I will be on the early bus too. Maybe we will be able to sit together. Or at least we can walk up the hill with Juan. I have bought a lot of merchandise and he will be bringing the oxcart down."

"I will look forward to it. Please give my regards to Don Pablo and the Señora Miriam."

After she left, Oso glared at Tomás.

"Tomás, it seems you have been holding out on me."

"Not bad looking, eh?"

"I guess! And well spoken. A nice girl."

They had their usual for lunch. He ate some baked *empanadas* and a salad, and Oso had his *bistec a la pobre*—beefsteak with a fried egg on top—with a huge pile of fries on the side. He told Oso how Maria Elena's parents had died in the earthquake and how she had taken care of her older brother. Oso listened quietly.

"That must have been tough," he said. "But at least she had her uncles and family nearby."

Tomás also told him about how her brother was laid up for such a long time and how she had to do everything, from cooking and cleaning to slaughtering and butchering to chopping firewood.

"Ramon says she does it all well. She is one amazing young lady. And pretty to boot."

Oso had a faraway, dreamy look in his eyes.

"But if you are getting any romantic ideas, old buddy, forget it. You would just be wasting your time. Ramon believes that she will never marry because she won't leave her brother."

"Now that is a pity," Oso said. "Do you remember when I told you I would never consider getting involved with a Chilena because she was probably just looking for a passport to the U.SA.? Well, maybe that might not be so bad, considering."

"Oso, you're unbelievable. You talk tough, but when you meet a smart, good-looking girl, you puddle. You are nothing more than a big teddy bear. But I believe she would never leave Cufeo, let alone Chile."

Tomás caught the waiter's eye and held up his left hand and mimed writing on it. The waiter nodded and went to get the bill.

"We'd better get a move on. You've got your maps, and I have to buy supplies for Cufeo. Lunch is on me."

That night he packed as many supplies as would fit into his pack. Some of the things that could get wet—like bottled and canned goods—he put into two string tote bags. The next morning it was still dark when he got up to take a quick shower—or as quick a shower as he could considering he had to start a fire to heat the water. After his shower, he tiptoed back to the front room and stuffed his sleeping bag into its sack and lashed it to the bottom of his pack frame. He put a waterproof cover over the whole pack and put it on, shrugging his shoulders up high while he tightened the waist strap. The pack was very heavy, and doing this took a lot of the weight off his shoulders. Carefully leaning so that he didn't tip over, he picked up the tote bags and took one last look around. He opened the door and locked it quietly behind him. The wet streets were empty and glistened in the streetlight. He would be extra early for the bus, but he wanted to save a seat for Maria Elena.

He arrived at the station at quarter to six. The bus would not be leaving for another forty-five minutes. However, there was already plenty of activity. The driver's young assistant was climbing the metal rungs on the side of the bus, hauling up bulky sacks and throwing them on top. Four passengers stood patiently waiting for the bus door to open. They had small bags and bundles at their feet. The ticket office was not open yet, but that made no difference for the local *campo* buses because fares were always collected in transit.

He handed up his backpack to the assistant saying, "There are a few delicate things inside."

The boy smiled good-naturedly and set it down carefully on the roof.

"What is your name?" Tomás asked him.

"Juanito."

"Thank you, Juanito. I am Tomás. Thank you for being so careful with my pack."

He walked over and took his place in the little queue and kept an eye out for Maria Elena. It was just after six o'clock when the driver squeezed past them and opened the door of the bus. Tomás took an aisle seat and selfishly tried to reserve the window seat by putting

his string bags on it. A few minutes later he saw an old
beat up Toyota pickup arrive, with Pablo sitting in back
on a mound of supplies. Maria Elena got out of the
passenger door while Pablo handed some *escudos* to the
driver. Then all three began to hustle things over to
the bus. Tomás didn't know whether to run out to help
and lose the seats or stay put. He lowered the window.
After Maria Elena dropped off a load by the ladder and
was returning for another, he yelled out to her.

"Maria Elena, come in and take this seat. I will help
Don Pablo with the rest of the things."

She looked up at the window. She had beads of
sweat on her forehead.

"Are you sure?"

Tomás waved at Pablo, who had noticed him in the
window. Pablo waved back as he hurried back to the
truck.

"Yes. Come in and take this seat. Hurry now so I
can help Don Pablo."

"Okay, but first let me go get some of the smaller
things."

She ran off to the truck and quickly returned with
her arms full, and came aboard. He stood up to let her
in to the seat.

As he started to leave, she said, "Thank you, Don
Tomás."

He flinched inwardly at hearing the "Don" again.
But she was right—being on this bus was like being
back in the *campo*.

"*Con mucho gusto*, Maria Elena," he said formally.
"Please watch my things."

He hurried out to help Pablo.

The bus was packed and the ride was slow because
of the many stops. He realized it had been pure fantasy
to think he could sit with Maria Elena. This was the
crowded *campo* rush hour and men were expected to

give up their seats for the *señoras* and the elderly. Pablo
and he stood scrunched together in the rear of the bus.
The windows were closed and the air was thick with the
smell of cilantro. Even at this early hour, it was on everyone's breath. Occasionally he could see Maria Elena
chatting merrily with the old lady sitting next to her.
But mostly he was trying not to lose his balance on the
curves, and not bump into fellow passengers or step
on someone's toes. They finally arrived at the crest of
their hill, and Pablo and Tomás slowly made their way
to the front. By the time they stepped down from the
bus, Maria Elena and Juan were grabbing large sacks
from Juanito. Pablo and Tomás pitched in and everything was soon on the ground. They thanked the boy
before he nimbly jumped back onto the bus, which had
already started moving.

When the oxcart was loaded, there was quite a
pile. But the big black and white oxen didn't seem
to mind—they peacefully stood there with the *garrocha*
leaning up against the yoke. Tomás started to shoulder his pack but Juan, as Tomás expected, would have
none of it.

"Don Tomás, give me your pack. One more sack
will not bother these animals." He took it from him
and as he carried it, he said, "What? Are you crazy,
man? This must weigh at least twenty kilos!"

"Yes, it is heavy. But it is a very good pack and if you
adjust it properly, it is not so bad. Here, let me show
you."

Tomás took the pack from him and held it out so
Juan could put his arms through the padded shoulder
straps. When he had it on, Tomás told him to hike his
shoulders and tighten the waist belt.

When he lowered his shoulders, Tomás asked,
"Now, how is that?"

Juan limped around a bit testing the pack. His leg seemed to be bothering him more than usual.

"That makes a very big difference. Much better, Don Tomás."

He limped around a little more.

"Yes, it is a very big difference—but still, I would not want to carry this all the way up to Caman."

He bent forward experimentally and with the pack so high above his shoulders, it caused him to suddenly lurch forward. He caught his balance quickly.

"But, by God, it is certain that I would not like to pick *habas* wearing this."

As Tomás helped him take the pack off, Juan asked if his pack were always this heavy. Tomás said he had bought more supplies than usual because he knew Juan was coming down with the oxcart and would offer to bring his pack up for him. Juan laughed.

"Don Tomás, you are learning the ways of the *campo*. That was *muy vivo*."

Juan picked up the *garrocha* and told the oxen to pay attention and began to lead them up the hill. Maria Elena, Pablo, and Tomás amicably followed. When they approached the steep area, Tomás picked up his pace and caught up with Juan, who was breathing hard. This part of the road was hell for him with that bum leg. Tomás told him that the trees would be coming sometime next Wednesday.

"That is good. I will come down early Thursday. The weather is perfect to plant," he said, putting his head back and squinting up at the misty light rain that had started to fall.

"My boss in the Ministry of Agriculture told me that the trees will come in burlap bags with five hundred in each. I will separate the bags into piles for each *socio*. You will have eight bags."

Seedlings planted two meters apart in rows also two meters apart meant that there were twenty-five hundred trees per hectare. Juan would be getting four thousand trees in each of five deliveries and would plant a total of eight hectares. The staggered deliveries were necessary so that the *campesinos* would be planting fresh seedlings. If they received all of their trees in one delivery, the roots would dry out before they were planted and many would not survive.

They labored up the God-awful section. The oxen slipped and struggled. Juan also struggled, and Tomás saw him grimace several times. When they finally made it up to the level stretch, Juan stopped to give the oxen—and himself—a rest. The oxen's huge chests were heaving and they were blowing so hard that they sounded like shrill whistles.

"It looks like your leg is bothering you more than usual."

"Yes. It is this weather. It always hurts me more during the rainy months. And," looking disgustedly back down the hill, "this *maldita* section of the road is always the worst. It costs me and my animals every time we go up or down it this time of year."

Tomás and Juan arrived at the Montoya farm. Maria Elena, who had gone on ahead with Pablo, was nowhere to be seen. She had pulled out the bars of the gate and left it open. As Juan and Tomás stopped in front of the gate, thick smoke started coming out of the kitchen stovepipe, and Tomás knew that she had just lit the cookstove. He pulled his pack from the oxcart.

"Thank you, Don Juan," he said as he strapped it on.

"*De nada.* I will see you later when I bring Pablo's things over to the farm. And maybe Ramon will prepare some *mate* for us."

Tomás told him he wouldn't be at the farm because, for the next two days, he would be riding non-stop to tell people about the delivery.

"Then *vaya con Dios*," he said and led the oxen through the gate.

Sometimes, especially during lousy weather, Tomás really had to force himself to get out of his down sleeping bag. This was one of those times. The nylon felt like silk against his skin and his cocoon was toasty warm. The morning, however, was raw. A dismal gray light filtered through Oso's faded curtains, and he could hear a steady rain on the tin roof. What a perfect day to stay in the sack, and what a terrible day for the delivery. But come on now, time to get up. He didn't move. He made a deal with himself that he would count to a hundred and then get up. Around eighty he nodded off to sleep again—only to jerk wide awake moments later and look at the clock. Jesus, that's all you need Tomás—to sleep through your meeting with the chauffeur. He sighed and crawled out of his warm bag and started to dress.

He arrived at the Ministry's front steps at about quarter after seven. He was fifteen minutes early so he took shelter under the portico. The front doors were locked since the office workday did not officially begin until nine. He shook the water from his poncho, which was the same color green as his lace-up rubber boots. He wished he owned some rain pants, but he didn't— his well-worn jeans were all he had. He also wished he had a cup of hot coffee as he sat down on the broad granite step in front of the door and watched the rain fall. At seven forty-five he began to get a little restless, but by eight fifteen he was downright nervous. Last night, over a beer, Oso had warned him not to count on the delivery being, as Tomás had referred to it, "a piece of cake." Oso knew very well how the Ministry functioned and he emphasized that if something could possibly go wrong, it would.

Eventually the janitor appeared on the other side of the glass door and let him in. The heat in the building felt wonderful. Tomás wondered if the janitor doubled as a watchman and stayed all night. But where the hell was the driver? Tomás had no idea, nor did he have a clue as to how he could track him down. He went up the stairs to the main office and sat down at a desk. He'd have to wait for someone to show up and help him out.

The first person to arrive was a low-level bureaucrat who fortunately knew a lot about how everything worked. He told Tomás that the chauffeur was most likely at the Ministry's garage on the other side of town. He explained that all the Ministry's vehicles were parked there at night and the chauffeur would have to go there first. Tomás accompanied him to the radio room and he called the garage. Sure enough the driver was there. He was waiting for the trailer frame to be welded because it had been overloaded yesterday and had cracked. The mechanics had just retrieved it from where it had been left south of town, and they said it should take about a half-hour to fix. As soon as it was ready the driver, named Lorenzo, would come over to pick Tomás up. Tomás thanked the young man for making the call and returned to the main office to wait. He could hear Oso's "I told you so" already.

Lorenzo arrived over an hour and a half later. He was fair-skinned, portly, and maybe six feet tall. His sparse hair was gray and his mustache was closely trimmed. Tomás thought he was probably of German descent, which wasn't unusual for southern Chile. Industrious German families had settled here in the mid 19th century. They owned large successful farms, built factories, and influenced much of the local architecture. Several stores and restaurants in Valdivia, as well as a high percentage of the mills and small factories out on the edge of town, were German-Chilean owned.

Lorenzo was dressed impeccably in a three-piece suit and his shoes were shined. Tomás thought that this was odd dress for a jeep driver who was about to go all over hell on muddy roads.

"Where have you been?" he asked. "The mechanics said the jeep would only take a half hour to repair."

"Oh, I stopped to have a cup of coffee and read the paper. It is early yet," the driver said flippantly and, as if Tomás were dismissed, he turned to talk with some of the other office workers who were standing around bullshitting.

Tomás said, "Ahh, excuse me Lorenzo…"

The driver turned back and looked at him.

"Are we all set to go to the nursery?"

The driver exhaled loudly and said, "Yes, I suppose so."

"Well, let's go then. We are late and we'll have to hurry if we are going to get the trees delivered today."

"It is never good to hurry, Gringo. We can always finish tomorrow if we have to."

Tomás didn't like the man's attitude and he started to heat up.

"My name, Lorenzo, is Tomás. And we cannot finish tomorrow because Sr. Ojeda has the trailer scheduled for his own use tomorrow. Let's go—now!"

"Okay, okay. Don't get excited."

The driver picked his hat up off a desk and slowly poked and prodded it into just the right shape. It was one of those sporty alpine types—green felt with a feather attached to the side. Tomás thought he was purposefully moving very slowly. Maybe Lorenzo thought that if he took his time he would not lose face in front of his co-workers. Or maybe he was just trying to annoy Tomás. If he was trying to annoy Tomás, he was doing a good job.

They went outside to the jeep and trailer. It was a small yellow hard-top Hotchkiss jeep with the letters S.A.G. painted in blue on the door. Tomás noticed the angry new weld on the trailer frame as he walked around to the passenger side. Lorenzo got in and after he slowly arranged himself, they drove southeast towards the nursery outside Osorno, passing the hills of Cufeo on the way. Thankfully, all was ready when they arrived at the nursery. Tomás helped the workers throw the burlap bags of Monterey pine onto the trailer. To counter-balance the heavy trailer, they loaded the back of the jeep with as many bags as they could squeeze in. Lorenzo never got out to help, and when Tomás opened the rear door to toss the bags in, cigarette smoke poured out. When they had arrived, the driver had made it quite clear that he did not do manual labor, and he remained in the jeep reading the *Correo*. No wonder he could dress the way he did, Tomás thought. The nursery workers ignored Lorenzo. Tomás guessed that they were used to his behavior. When they were done loading, Tomás shook hands all around and they were off again.

As they approached the Pan American Highway, he said, "Lorenzo, the first drop-off spot is…"

"The first spot is lunch. I am hungry and there is a good restaurant in Osorno we can go to."

When they reached the highway, he turned right towards Osorno instead of left towards Cufeo.

"But Lorenzo, we have to start the deliveries. It is late. Maybe we can get some sandwiches and sodas. We do not have time to go to a restaurant."

"Look, Gringo. Just so you understand. If I do not eat lunch at home, I eat lunch in a restaurant. I do NOT eat sandwiches."

"But there is still time now to make the deliveries.
If we go have lunch somewhere, then there won't be.
The *campesinos* think the trees will be delivered today
and they will be coming down tomorrow. For them to
come down from way up in the hills in such weather is
very difficult. And for them to make the trip for nothing would be terrible."

"That is their problem, not mine. They are used to
it. They will just have to come down again if the trees
are not there."

"But I gave them my word. If we do not deliver
them today, then I will have to go back to Cufeo and try
to stop them somehow. That will mean riding everywhere. You know there is no phone or radio up there
and..."

Lorenzo interrupted.

"Did you not understand what I said, Gringo? They
are used to it and for you to try to contact them is stupid. They are just *campesinos*. But if you feel you must,
then that is your problem."

They stopped and went into a restaurant on the outskirts of Osorno. Tomás was so angry he could barely
finish his bowl of soup. He flashed back to Peace Corps
training and remembered what one of the returned
volunteers had told him.

"At times you may be accused by people who don't
want us there of taking jobs away from the Chileans.
Technically this might be true. But most of the time,
the educated Chileans would not choose to do what you
will be doing. Many feel it is beneath them to deal with
the *campesinos,* and consequently there is a tremendous
lack of communication between the government workers and the *campesinos*. The *campesinos* expect to be
treated badly in the offices and they are. And it simply
becomes a Pavlovian sort of thing—if you repeatedly
get mistreated somewhere, then eventually you won't

return. So the *campesinos* don't go to the government
offices and have as little to do with the government
bureaucrats as possible. And most of the bureaucrats
couldn't care less about them. A big part of your job
will be to provide that missing link between the *campesinos* and the Ministry of Agriculture. Without that link,
very little reforestation will be done by the *campesinos.*"

After Lorenzo finished his three course meal, they
got back on the road. The first stop was La Clavela.
Lorenzo, of course, was no help. The only time he got
out of the jeep was to relieve himself of some of the
vino blanco he had drunk at lunch. Tomás noticed he
used part of his newspaper to clean the sticky red clay
off his shoes before he clambered back into the jeep.

Tomás unloaded and stacked the pine as quickly as
possible into different piles. He timed himself and,
as they sped off again, he asked Lorenzo what was the
latest they could return to Valdivia. Lorenzo said the
jeep had to be in the Ministry's fenced-in area before
five o'clock when the gates were locked. Looking at his
delivery list, he did some quick calculations. Clearly
there was no way they would finish today. Okay. What
was the best thing to do? The majority of the trees were
designated for the Caman road. That was the drop-
off for Caman, Lote Once, most of La Paloma, and for
some that lived on the eastern side of Casa Blanca. It
definitely made sense to make sure those trees were
delivered. He told Lorenzo to go to the Caman road
next. They would skip Piedra Azul, and he would take
a bus out tomorrow to spread the word that the trees
had not been delivered there.

It began to rain hard, and he was soaked and chilled
to the bone by the time he finished unloading the trees
on the Caman road. He climbed back into the jeep hoping to warm up, but Lorenzo got stuck when he went to
turn around. He jackknifed the trailer and then pro-

ceeded to spin the tires so much that the jeep was buried almost to the axle. They had to disconnect the trailer and jack up the jeep. Tomás threw stones and some pieces of wood and anything else he could find underneath all the tires. It worked and they got out. They re-hooked the trailer from a different angle and started back down the road. He was glad that Lorenzo was as wet as he was now, but he soon tired of Lorenzo's non-stop swearing and bad mouthing of the *campesinos*—like it was their fault he got his fancy shoes muddy.

They reached the highway again and he began to give directions for the Los Guindos drop-off. Lorenzo interrupted him and said he had had it for the day— that they would return to Valdivia NOW.

Tomás exploded.

"God damn it, that's it!" he yelled.

Lorenzo jumped in his seat. Tomás quickly reached over and turned the motor off and yanked the keys out of the ignition.

"Now you listen to me, Lorenzo. You have to be the laziest Goddamn son-of-a-whore I have ever met. You act like you are the most important thing on God's earth whereas you are a driver—nothing more. Just a fucking driver! No, I take that back. You are also a *huevon*. We have the time to drop off some more trees. Los Guindos is very close and has the best road and turn-around area of all the drop-off places and maybe you, EVEN YOU, might not get us stuck. If you do not want to do that, then you can take your fat ass out of this jeep and you can wait here for the next goddamn bus which," Tomás looked at his watch, "should be here in about forty-five minutes. But the Los Guindos trees, at least, will get delivered today."

He had thrown out some pretty serious insults— *huevon* was a big-balled moron—and he did not know what Lorenzo was going to do about it. But he didn't care. He did not give a fuck how big Lorenzo was or what trouble he might get into. If Lorenzo wanted to mix it up, he was ready to go.

He reached for the door lever and said, "So what is it? Los Guindos or the bus?"

My way or the highway. What's it going to be you fat fuck? To his amazement, Lorenzo immediately changed his tune.

"Easy, easy, Gringo…er, Tomás…"

He became very conciliatory.

"There is no reason to get excited now. We can make that last delivery—there is no problem. Just take it easy. We are not that far from Valdivia and you are right, there should be time for a delivery if it is easy to get to. Only give me the keys and tell me where to go."

I'll tell you where to go, you puke! Tomás took a deep breath.

"I think, Lorenzo, maybe we understand each other a little better now. These deliveries, I know, mean nothing to you. But I want you to know that they mean a lot to me. In fact, right now they are about the most important thing in my life." He paused to get a better hold of himself and after a few seconds said, "Please, take a left and after a very short distance you will see a gravel road going off to the right. Take that and go up there for another kilometer or so to the turn around."

Tomás handed him the keys and Lorenzo started the jeep. Maybe, he thought, a new pecking order had just been established—like when he hit Tobi with the stick. And maybe that's how things worked around here. You had to stand up and be counted, and once you did, things went a little more smoothly. As they drove up the Los Guindos road, he started to shake—his hands, his whole body. It was the adrenaline. There was no way Lorenzo could not have noticed. He looked at his watch, trying to hold it steady, and knew that indeed this would be the last drop-off of the day. That meant that most of the trees for the Casa Blanca area would not be delivered either.

They arrived at the drop-off spot and, unbelievably, Lorenzo helped him unload the pine. It went quickly.

Lorenzo tried to save face by saying, "Oh well, I am already wet and muddy."

On the way back to Valdivia he considered having Lorenzo drop him off at the entrance to Casa Blanca, so he could walk up and tell the *socios* there. But it would be dark soon. He also needed to talk to Sr. Ojeda the next morning before he took the jeep. And the remaining trees had to be unloaded so the trailer would be free for him. Plus he was wet and tired. He stayed in the jeep and they returned to Valdivia.

First thing the next day, Tomás arranged with Sr. Ojeda to have the jeep for the following Monday morning to finish the delivery. With the constant rain, the seedlings would be fine in the burlap sacks for a few days and Tomás didn't think it was necessary to heel them into the ground. He told Sr. Ojeda all about the delivery and he expressed a very candid opinion of Lorenzo. Sr. Ojeda promised to speak to Lorenzo, but as Tomás stood to leave the office, Sr. Ojeda said that it also sounded like he and Lorenzo had a lot of bad luck.

As he shouldered his pack, Tomás said, "Bad luck or not, if I had been alone, I could have easily completed the delivery. But I do not have time to worry about that now. I have to catch a bus so I can walk up into the hills to tell the farmers that there is no reason to come down with their oxcarts until next Tuesday. I only hope I make it in time. I also hope," he said looking hard at Sr. Ojeda, "that I do not have to go through this every week this winter."

He took the bus to Piedra Azul and learned that fortunately no one had come down for their trees due to the lousy weather. He walked up and contacted several of the *socios,* and they in turn rode further up to tell other *socios.* From Piedra Azul he took a footpath which would bring him up the backside of Central Caman and to the Rodriguez farm. There he would saddle Lobo or Salton and continue on to Casa Blanca. He slogged up the trail in the rain. Only nine and a half more deliveries. He couldn't wait.

CHAPTER ELEVEN

El Camino (The Road)

Tomás was returning from Lote Once on the path
that zigzagged alongside the main road. This was the
worst part of the trip, and it was safer to ride on the
path because the road was so heavily eroded and rutted.
And now, with all the rain, he could hear a stream rushing down it. He was counting on Salton to bring them
home because he couldn't see a thing.

Taking short cautious steps, Salton felt his way with
his front hooves, locking his rear ones as he skidded
down the slippery, narrow trail. Tomás gave the horse
full rein and hung tightly onto the front of the saddle,
trying to become one with his body. He thought of Juan
down by the highway, leaning over as he tried Tomás's
pack on. Juan had lurched forward from the unaccus-
tomed weight above his shoulders. Tomás didn't want
to cause Salton any such problems—the horse didn't
need any shifting bulk on top of his back.

He had hoped to have been further along and to have avoided going down this section in the dark. But the days were short and he had taken too much time walking the new pine plantations. At least, he hoped; he would not have to make the trip up again for another couple of weeks. He had made this one because he had to know if the farmers were ready for more trees. Delivery number five would be in two days. The deliveries had been going okay—certainly better than the first—with only a few minor glitches. Lorenzo managed to get stuck a couple of times, but nowhere near as badly as on the first delivery. They had also reached an unspoken agreement. If they got off to an early start, then there was plenty of time for a leisurely lunch. If not, then lunch was *empanadas* or something basic and quick. Lorenzo did not bitch, and although he never helped at the nursery—he had his image to maintain after all—he did help unload the trees at the drop-offs. He brought a rain jacket and a plastic cover that fit snugly over his fancy green felt hat, and he even had a pair of galoshes the likes of which Tomás hadn't seen since the nineteen fifties. Lorenzo would slip them on over his shoes and buckle up. Usually by the time he had his rain gear on, Tomás would have half the trees unloaded. But Lorenzo did try to help, and Tomás appreciated the effort. Their next delivery would mark the halfway point. After that the deliveries would become smaller and smaller as the farmers began to fulfill their commitments.

Winter was a rude change from the warmth and bright blues and greens of summer. It rained constantly. It was gray. Nothing dried out. The crudely tanned sheep pelts that served as his mattress began to sweat and smell. His clothes were cold and damp when he put them on in the morning. He could see his breath as he dressed. The house never warmed up completely, and he and Ramon huddled in the kitchen around the cookstove and brazier. Strong drafts that came through the walls and windows made the candlelight flicker. Even the flame inside the glass chimney of the kerosene lamp was unsteady, and his eyes soon tired when he tried to study. But the weather was a common denominator—it gave everyone something to complain about. It was a season to suffer through, and the animals didn't like it any more than they did. Sometimes when he went out in the driving rain to help Ramon bring in the sheep, he would pass Salton and Lobo huddled under a clump of *quila,* with their rear ends pointing windward. They looked comatose. He wondered if they thought about anything—like sunny days and long green grass. Oddly, colds or the flu were not commonplace at this time of year. Maybe it was because everyone was so isolated. But when misfortune struck, it struck hard.

One afternoon, he and Ramon were drinking *mate* after a late lunch. It had been raining steadily for forty-eight hours and had only just let up. There was a knock on the door. Ramon got up and opened it. A young boy of about twelve or so stood there, drenched. Ramon ushered him inside. Before the boy could say anything, Ramon had him take off his wet hat and *manta* and sidle up to the kitchen stove. Tomás brought a stool over so the boy could sit down as Ramon slid the kettle over the firebox. Once the boy had a cup of hot tea in his hands, Ramon asked the purpose of his visit.

The boy was the grandson of a widow who lived a mile up the road. Last night the old *trabajador* who had worked for the widow for years had a stroke in the little shed where he slept. He could not move and they could do little for him. The widow had her grandson walk down to the highway very early in the morning—which must have been during some of the heaviest rain—and wait until a trucker came to pick up firewood. The truckers usually made at least one morning trip regardless of the weather. When one arrived, the boy explained the situation and the trucker agreed to return in the afternoon and take the old man to the hospital. The boy was here to ask for Ramon's help to hitch up their oxcart and to load the man onto it.

Ramon said of course he would help and they would leave as soon the boy finished his tea. Tomás asked if he should come. Ramon hesitated, then nodded. When all three were bundled up, they set off and walked up to the widow's house. Tomás helped Ramon bring in the oxen and watched him hitch them up to the cart. He made it look so easy—there was not a wasted move. They folded up a *manta de Castilla* and placed it on the bed of the cart as a mattress. Then they went to the worker's shed.

Opening the rickety door, it took a second or two for Tomás's eyes to adjust to the dim light. Over in a corner was a bed of straw. On top was an old man covered by a *manta*. His complexion was gray and only his eyes moved. He watched them come over and bend down to pick him up. He looked from one of them to the other, but when he saw Tomás, his eyes froze. He did not take his eyes off Tomás as they carried him over to the cart. They covered him with every other *manta* the widow owned and put a sheet of plastic on top, tucking the edges underneath. They tried to make him as comfortable as possible, although Tomás didn't know if that made any difference because it looked like the man couldn't feel a thing. He only stared. And he looked awful. Tomás and Ramon walked down with the boy as far as Ramon's gate, and said goodbye and good luck. The boy thanked them. They watched the boy slowly lead the oxen down the road. It started to rain again. The next day they learned that the old man did not make it to the hospital. He died in the cab of the truck.

The road leveled off, which meant Tomás was not far from home. When Salton made a sharp left and stopped suddenly, he knew they had arrived. He brought Salton up sideways to the gate and felt for the single heavy wire loop that secured it. Heading up towards the house, he could just see a faint light coming from the kitchen window. The sheep were to his left. They were spending the winter nights in the large fenced-in garden so that the soil would be well fertilized come spring. They spooked when he rode by, and he thought they must still be on edge from the mountain lion's raid two nights ago. Ramon had found a partially eaten ewe close to the house, not ten feet from the door leading into Tomás's room. The large cats were emboldened by the horrible weather which made it difficult to hear, smell, or see anything—plus the dog, which was supposed to be guarding the sheep, was usually under the house on the worst nights. It made Tomás think twice about going to the outhouse in the middle of the night.

The rain was beginning to let up. Although it had been only misty for most of the day in Lote Once—like being in a cloud forest— it had been raining hard for the last couple of hours. Amazingly his thick *manta de Castilla* had kept him dry except for some dampness on the top of each shoulder. He had stopped in front of the shed and started to dismount when Ramon came out, carrying a lantern. He was wearing a tattered rain jacket and a wide-brimmed hat, and he was shaking his head.

"Aii! Don Tomás, you must be ill-used from such a long ride."

Tomás got off the horse and almost fell as his knees buckled. They were cold, stiff, and sore. But it was the weight of the *manta de Castilla* that made him stumble. It must have weighed at least an extra twenty-five pounds. The *manta* did not shed any of the rain—it absorbed and held it like a sponge. Ramon's arm shot out and caught hold of the *manta* before he fell.

"Don Tomás, go into the house and get out of your wet clothes. I will take care of Salton."

"Thank you, but my clothes are dry—except for my *manta*. It must weigh ten or fifteen kilos. Unbelievable."

Ramon hung the lantern on a large nail near the shed door and reached for the reins.

"At least go into the shed to take the *manta* off. There is a cord in there that you can drape it over, and tomorrow morning we can beat it with a stick; otherwise it will not dry out for the rest of the winter."

He led Salton over to a post where he hitched him and started to loosen the cinch. Tomás did as he was told and walked stiff-legged to the shed. He could just see the cord and he hung up the *manta*. He unbuckled his *pierneras* and hung them next to the *manta*. Ramon ducked inside carrying the saddle and the burlap-bag saddle blanket. They wiped down Salton with some dry burlap bags and rewarded him for the wet day's work with an extra-generous dollop of grain.

"Don Tomás, if your clothes really are dry, then go to the *fogon*. Here, take the lantern. I have built up a good fire for you to warm yourself and I have potatoes cooking in the coals. I also have made some *salsa* which I will go and get."

Ramon turned and went out in the dark towards the house. What a prince he was, Tomás thought.

A *fogon* was a simple outbuilding where the *campesinos* kept a fire going all winter, where they could warm themselves on the cold rainy nights before bed. The Rodriguez *fogon* was thirty feet or so behind the house. It had a dirt floor and vertical siding that was more-or-less weather tight. A square hole was cut in the metal roof, and the tin was peeled back to allow the smoke to escape. But because an angled flap of roofing was still attached on the north side, it formed a shield against the strong, wind-driven rain, so very little fell into the fire. Sometimes it would get smoky inside, but the warmth was well worth it.

Tomás entered the *fogon* and set the lantern down on one of the four hewn logs that served as benches around the fire. He held his hands out to the fire. Once they were warm, he started to rub some life back into his stiff knees. Finally he turned his backside to the fire. God it felt good. Life's little pleasures. After a long moment he surfaced from his trance enough to notice that Ramon had raked some coals between two bricks that were off to the side. Straddling the bricks was a steaming kettle of water, and on top of one of the benches were cups of *mate* and a sugar bowl with a little spoon sticking out of it.

Ramon came in carrying the bowl of *pebre* sauce, which he set down next to the *mates*. Seeing the sauce, Tomás's stomach started to growl and suddenly he was starved. Ramon took off his hat and jacket, gave them a shake, and hung them up on large rusty nails. He hung the lantern from the ceiling, grabbed a round-nosed shovel, and started digging through the coals. He soon uncovered the potatoes which he plopped down next to the *mate* cups. In a few minutes a half dozen were sitting there.

"Better wait a few minutes," he said sitting down on a log. "They are still too hot."

Tomás had to swallow the saliva that had formed in the back of his throat. When his backside was toasted, he sat down. Ramon poured steaming water into their *mate* cups. He handed Tomás his and they sipped *mate* while staring into the fire. Finally Tomás couldn't wait any longer and reached for one of the potatoes. He dusted off the ashes and ladled some of Ramon's sauce on it. He took a bite.

"A million thanks," he mumbled, mouth half-full. "I didn't realize how hungry I was. These potatoes are the best things I have ever put in my mouth."

"Hunger is always the best sauce, Don Tomás. *Buen provecho.*"

Ramon reached for a potato, and they sat in companionable silence, eating potatoes and sipping *mate*. For the umpteenth time Tomás thought about how simple life was in the *campo* and how much he enjoyed these simple pleasures. It had started to rain hard again, and the noise on the tin roof only heightened his feeling of well being.

The golden light from the roaring fire danced merrily on the rough plank walls. This was where the family did any of a number of winter chores—mending saddles, small carpentry projects, or anything else that might make a mess in the house. Miriam toasted ground wheat for *chicha con harina* in a large rectangular pan suspended over the fire. During rainy weekends, the boys patiently cracked marble-sized *avellano* nuts with a hammer, exposing the inner white seeds which they roasted in the same pan.

The temperature was dropping and Tomás leaned towards the fire. He closed his eyes and basked in the heat. He soon became sleepy. It was here that the long winter nights were wiled away with homespun tales. Ramon was usually the story teller, and Pablo always sat next to Miriam, who knitted by the firelight. You could almost set a watch by when Pablo would dip and nod and eventually fall asleep with his head on Miriam's shoulder. Last time they were all together, Ramon told a story about two boys named Andre and Juan. They were Alex and Javier's age, of course, and had run away from home because their father made them work too hard. On the trail, they had all sorts of adventures and they soon learned to live off the land. Ramon spoke in his gentle, clear voice.

"Late one afternoon they came to a beautiful little clearing in the woods. There was a stream nearby and it was a perfect place to camp. They made beds with leaves from the forest and with the long grass from the clearing. They spread their *mantas* on top of them. The weather was nice and they were in a very good mood. Andre went around gathering mushrooms and berries for dinner while Juan collected fallen branches and pieces of wood for a fire. They took the pointed sticks they used for carrying their little bundles of clothes and went to the stream where they speared a fat trout. At the muddy edge of the stream, they noticed the footprints of many dogs that had stopped there for a drink of water. The boys thought this strange because the nearest farm was far away. And the tracks were also very big. But they didn't think too much about it, and went merrily back to the clearing to start a fire and cook dinner.

"They ate their dinner and then sat around the campfire, feeling very proud of themselves. They did not have to work anymore and there was no one telling them what to do. The sun went down and it cooled off. Juan got up and threw more wood on the fire. It was very dark outside of their circle of light. Suddenly they heard a long howl off in the distance. The boys knew that it was the howl of a wolf, and they looked at each other with their eyes wide. A few minutes later there was another—closer this time. Soon there was howling everywhere.

"'Those tracks by the stream,' Juan whispered. '*Por la chupailla*. They were from wolves.' The wolves got closer and closer. Their howling made the hair on the boys' arms stand on end and they suddenly wished they were at home—or that their father were here because he would know what to do. But they were all alone and all they had for protection were the two pointed sticks and the pocketknife they used to clean the fish. But the boys were clever too. They knew the wolves did not like fire, so they threw more wood on." Ramon stood up and threw a piece of firewood on to the fire. Sparks flew up and out of the hole in the roof while Javier and Alex waited impatiently for him to continue. He sat back down.

"The cries of the wolves became more and more excited. Soon they were just outside the edge of light thrown off by the fire. The boys could not see them but they could hear low growls as the wolves circled them in the darkness. They could even smell the wolves now. They smelled of dried blood and rotten meat. They smelled horrible. The boys kept throwing wood on the fire; but they were running out of it. If they could just hold the wolves off until daylight, they would be okay. But the night was passing slowly and there was no way the firewood would last. They knew it was just a matter of time before the wolves came at them. Finally they were down to their last piece of wood. They stood as close to the fire as they could and held their pointed sticks out in front of them." Ramon leaned over to reach for another piece of firewood, turning his back to the boys. "Andre, the younger boy, reached for the last piece just like this and he was about to throw it on the fire when..." Ramon suddenly dropped the piece of firewood and whirled on the boys with a contorted face. With teeth bared, he let out a tremendous growl. The boys jumped a foot and Pablo woke up. Miriam smiled, but didn't look up from her knitting. And Tomás thought of Tobi attacking him while he was brushing his teeth.

"Don Tomás, wake up!"

He jerked awake. Ramon was laughing.

"You were like the cat—ready to fall in the fire."

Tomás sat up away from the fire and, bleary-eyed, said, "I guess I am pretty tired."

Ramon pulled a handkerchief from his pocket and used it to lift the kettle up off the bricks. He re-freshened his *mate* and gestured to Tomás. He declined. The flames of the fire had mostly died down and the rain had stopped. The only noise was an occasional crackling from the fire. Ramon put his handkerchief away and took a long sip of *mate*.

"Go get some sleep, Don Tomás; otherwise you'll never make the early bus tomorrow. I will stay here for a bit and put the fire to bed."

Tomás nodded sleepily and said goodnight. Ramon began shoveling a thick coat of ashes over the fire. Tomorrow afternoon, Ramon would rake away the ashes, exposing the embers to the air again, and the fire would be blazing away in no time. Tomás stepped outside, but immediately returned with an excited smile.

"Don Ramon! It is snowing hard with very big flakes."

"I wondered. I thought it unusual that the rain stopped so suddenly."

The morning dawned bright and clear and very cold. Tomás had that same excited feeling he always had with the first snowfall at home in New England. When he walked down to catch the bus he marveled at this new look of winter. The all-white volcanoes stood out clearly against the deep blue sky, while a three-inch white carpet covered the pasture and capped the dark stumps and wooden fences. The snow sparkled in the bright sunlight and it was hard to believe that this was the month of August. Looking way down into the valley, he could see where the snow stopped and checkered fields began. He wished he had his camera, even though a single picture couldn't possibly take it all in.

He and Lorenzo made the pine tree delivery and thankfully the snow did not add to their usual problems at the drop-offs. Much of it was gone by the time they were finished, and two days later the *campo* was just soggy and muddy again. It had warmed up and the gray sky threatened more rain. He arrived at the farm with his pack full of supplies, and as he stomped and wiped his boots on the little porch, Ramon opened the door.

"Don Tomás, I am glad you are back. Here, let me help you."

Tomás was soaked with sweat from the climb. He entered the house and Ramon lifted the pack from his shoulders. He eased the tightness in his shoulders by stretching up and touching the low ceiling.

Ramon asked, "Have you heard about Juan?"

He lowered his arms slowly.

"No. What?"

"He went down yesterday morning to get the trees you delivered. On the way back he slipped while leading his oxen up the steep section and injured his bad leg. The snow had not melted there yet and the road was more treacherous than usual. He should have waited, but he was too excited to begin the last of his planting. We are not sure whether he re-broke his leg or if he only seriously sprained it. But after he fell he could not put any weight on it at all and he was in terrible pain. He tried to crawl back to the cart and get out of the snow but it hurt too much. So he just lay there in front of the oxen hoping someone would pass by and help him. But because of the snow no one came. Finally, Maria Elena became worried and walked down looking for him. By this time he was soaked and she found him half frozen. She was not strong enough to lift him without hurting him, so she wrapped him with her *manta* and ran all the way back. Luckily Pablo was here for the day, and we rode down and loaded him onto the cart and brought him up. We went slowly and were as careful as possible, but the trip up was very painful for him. Maria Elena went to Casa Blanca to get Don Pedro's Señora."

Don Pedro's wife was the best healer in Cufeo and was always consulted in times of crisis.

"She is with Juan. Now that you are here, I will go and see how he is. I do not know when I will return. There is soup that can be heated up on the stove if you become hungry and you know where the bread is."

After Ramon left, he began unloading the supplies. Ramon returned at dark, saying that the Señora thought the leg was not broken; but the knee had swollen up like a balloon. She believed that Juan had at least sprained it and possibly torn something because the area had so quickly turned black and blue. The Señora would return in a few days after the swelling had gone down to examine him again and see if she thought he should go to the hospital in Valdivia. The only good thing about the whole situation, Ramon said, was that Juan already had a pair of crutches in the house.

The next night as he and Ramon sat at the kitchen table eating soup, they talked about Juan's situation. Juan was frustrated that he couldn't finish the planting and it was almost impossible to find good *trabajadores* because they were already planting for the other farmers.

Ramon said, "I have sent word to Pablo and Miriam to see if Javier and Alex can come up to help this weekend. I am sure they will. And Maria Elena, of course, is determined to start planting with help or without it. But I am told it is best to have at least two people— to work in pairs. How many trees did you deliver for Juan?"

"Four thousand."

"And how many trees can two people plant in a day?"

He thought about that for a second or two.

"I have been told that on a good site two men can easily plant five hundred in a day. Juan's site is fairly level and he has done an excellent job clearing. But with the boys it would probably be something less than that."

"Aii! Then they need more help than Javier and Alex. That is a lot of days for the little trees to sit outside and not be planted. And someone has to see to Juan, although I would not want that job. He will be very difficult and it will be hard to keep him in the house. He will be hobbling around on his *muletas* in no time and I know he will want to supervise. He wants his little trees planted straight as an arrow and it will be difficult for him to let someone else do the work. Oh, he will be miserable to be around. Poor Maria Elena."

Suddenly something smelled awful. Ramon jumped up and yanked the tablecloth back.

"*Aii! Mierda!* You damn, miserable cat. You dirty animal. Go! Out! Outside! Get out of here!"

Ramon ran over to open the door and grabbed a *huasca* from the wall. He slammed it all around the cat as it slid frantically across the floor trying to make a beeline for the door. Tomás noticed that even though Ramon could have easily struck the panicked animal with the whip, he didn't. He never did, he just hit all around it on the floor.

Ramon had his favorite animals on the farm and they were his everyday companions during the long spells that he was alone. One of these companions was a big gray cat he named Molestoso which meant 'someone who bothers you all the time.' Ramon talked tough to it, but Tomás knew that he loved the cat.

During the winter, Ramon would shovel coals out of the kitchen stove into a brazier that he put under the kitchen table while they were eating. The cheap plastic tablecloth hung down below the table top and kept the heat under the table, warming their feet, legs, and knees. No matter how drafty or cold the house was, the brazier would keep them warm while they ate and listened to the radio.

Ramon always felt a little sorry for the cat during the wintertime, so when Pablo and Miriam were not around he would let it inside during dinnertime to warm up. Before bed he would put it out again to catch the mice and rats that raided the grain shed. When Ramon opened the kitchen door, Molestoso would stride purposefully in and jump straight away onto one of the stools that had been shoved under the table. Purring immediately in the warmth, he would curl up and fall asleep. Then, as the coals died down, the cat—still sound asleep—would lean closer and closer to the ebbing warmth until finally part of him was in the coals. The cat's fur would singe, which stunk to high heaven. This had happened several times, and the cat's coat was checkered with burned splotches. Tomás had no doubt it would happen again many times before winter's end.

Ramon left the door open to air out the kitchen, and after hanging the little whip back on the wall, returned to his stool.

"Don Ramon, I would like to help with the planting. With the two boys and Maria Elena, we could make two teams of two—at least over the weekend while the boys are here. I could also help most of next week."

"Yes. Yes. That would be good. The four of you would work well together, although you had better team Alex up with Maria Elena. I do not know why, but she is the only one who can keep him working. But you do not have another delivery next week?"

"Not until next Thursday."

"That's good then. But the boys will have to go back Sunday afternoon. Maybe I can get Flor to come over and watch the house next week. Then you and I could plant early in the week with Maria Elena. If we could just find a worker for only a day or two, between us all we might finish the planting by mid week, providing it does not rain too hard. Don Tomás," he suddenly sounded formal, "on behalf of Juan and Maria Elena, thank you for your offer and I am sure they will accept. It is good of you and a good plan. And tomorrow morning, I will go discuss it with them and also go over and ask Flor. But now," he said looking at his watch, "it is time for my *novela*."

Late Friday afternoon Javier, Alex, and Tomás walked over to the Montoya farm for *onces* and a planting lesson from Juan. Maria Elena served them tea and some fresh bread with home churned butter, honey, store-bought cheese, and *mortadela,* which was a sausage meat spread. She also fried an egg for each of them. It was quite an *onces,* and Tomás was sure it was to show how much they appreciated their offer of help.

Juan was seated by the little heating stove with his leg elevated and a pile of planting tools by his chair. He had moved back to his summer room rather than trying to negotiate the stairs.

"Don Tomás, how many trees have you planted?" Juan asked.

The boys and Tomás were seated at the dining table.

"None—not even one," he answered honestly.

"Not even one!"

Tomás shrugged and Juan rolled his eyes.

"Well then, that makes it obvious. Maria Elena should be in charge."

"Of course she should. Not a problem."

Tomás looked over to her standing by the kitchen range.

"Just tell us what to do, Maria Elena."

The two boys were not paying attention because they were too busy stuffing their mouths with pieces of bread that they had slathered with honey. Miriam would never have allowed them to put so much honey on their bread.

Juan began the planting lesson.

"The first thing you will do is set the lines for the trees with these range poles here."

He motioned to the straight poles, about two and one half meters long, that were sharpened on one end.

"Don Tomás, you will measure a couple of meters off of one end of my fence and stick a pole in the ground there. Then one of the others should do the same at the far end."

The boys were paying attention now.

"Maria Elena will then take this *piola* here," Juan explained as he indicated the large rolls of heavy twine, "and tie it to the first pole. Then stretch it taut and tie it to the second pole. It has to be tied high enough to be above any stumps that might be in the way."

"Juan," Maria Elena interjected, "I do not think it necessary to describe every little thing. We can..."

Juan held up a hand to silence her.

"Please sister, let me go over this. I want everyone to understand and I want it done right."

She sighed and Juan continued.

"Then you only have to measure along the *piola* and plant a tree every two meters. Now, you should work in teams of two. Maria Elena and Don Tomás should

make the holes with these two *barretas,* and Javier and
Alex will place the little trees in the holes. Give each
one a little shake first so the roots are straight. And
then, with your feet," he said looking directly at the
boys, "CAREFULLY stamp the holes closed around the
little trees. Simple enough, eh?"

The three of them nodded. Tomás looked at the
barretas. They were crude, skinny shovels made out of
old truck springs that had short steel tubes for handles.
They looked like the letter 'T.'

"Now, the *barreta* is exactly one meter long so all
you have to do is lay it down on the ground twice to
measure two meters and then dig your hole there. Any
questions? Don Tomás?"

He shook his head. Juan turned to the boys.

"And you two *cabritos?* This is very important. Are
you ready to work hard for your Aunt and Uncle?"

They nodded seriously. '*Cabrito*' meant little goat,
but was used affectionately in the *campo* when referring
to children—like 'kids' in the States.

"Then," he said, adjusting his leg into a more comfortable position and leaning back in his chair with a
sigh, "Maria Elena, would you please refill my *mate* for
me?"

Early the next morning, two very sleepy boys and
Tomás walked over in heavy fog to the Montoya gate.
They could barely see Maria Elena standing on the
porch. She divvied up the planting tools by her side
and asked Tomás to carry one sack of trees. As they
slowly walked across the pasture, everything looked
eerie and mysterious. No one said anything. They
were still too sleepy and they had a long day ahead of
them. At least it was not raining.

They started out slowly, but soon each team developed a system and got into a rhythm. They planted
all day. It was hard work. Juan had been smart to tell

the kids to be the planters. Being so small and lithe, they scurried around like busy little squirrels burying nuts, and were a tremendous help. By dark, they had planted a sack and a half, which Tomás thought was pretty good for three out of four neophytes. He heeled the remaining trees into the ground, and they wearily headed back to the Montoya house. Maria Elena thanked them at the porch before they continued on home. After dinner they went out to the *fogon*, but there were no requests for stories and the boys did not last long before they peeled off to bed. Bidding Ramon good night, Tomás followed shortly after.

They woke to light rain the next morning and the day passed slowly. It was no fun. It rained lightly the whole day and they were all soaked. When the boys had to leave early to catch the afternoon bus, Maria Elena put down her *barreta* and said, "Don Tomás, the weather is terrible and you are soaked. Why don't you call it a day too, eh?"

Maria Elena looked as tired as he felt. He told her he was no wetter than she was and he knew she would keep working until dark. He said he'd stay. She smiled appreciatively.

"Then I will be back as soon as I walk these," she looked gratefully at her nephews, "two very hardworking young men to the gate."

The boys looked tired but proud, and they puffed up a little. Tomás thumped them on their backs, shook hands with them as if they were adults, and wished them a safe trip to Valdivia. Maria Elena walked them to the gate. He planted trees until her return.

"Do you want to dig or plant?" she asked.

"Dig."

"Agreed." She picked up one of the cloth pouches full of seedlings and tied it around her waist.

They set to work.

Many trees later, Maria Elena asked, "Tomás, do you miss your home?"

He looked down at her as she patted a seedling. Her eyes were so beautiful—almond shaped and so dark. Were they really dark brown or black? It took him a second or two before he realized she had omitted the *Don.*

"No, not at all."

She looked shocked.

"You don't?"

"No. My family is not close like yours. Everyone is scattered around the country and our roots are not so deep. I only saw my grandparents maybe once a year at Christmas and I can't remember the last time we got together with aunts and uncles and cousins. My parents also sent me away to school when I was about Javier's age."

He dug another little hole and Maria Elena put in a seedling.

"A few years after that, I began to spend much of my time during summer vacations traveling. My parents encouraged this and I honestly think they preferred telling their friends about my travels than having me at home."

He measured out another two meters. Out of the corner of his eye he could see Maria Elena frowning.

"I think that is sad, Tomás. Is your family rich? Is that how you can go away and travel and not help at home?"

"No, I would not say we are rich. Half rich maybe—in money, that is. My family certainly has more money and automobiles, televisions, a boat, and other things that no one has here in the *campo.* But there are things we don't have—certain values. Things you can't buy—like close family."

She bent over, seedling in hand. She shook it gently before placing it in the hole. She looked up at him.

"What will you do after the Peace Corps?"

"Travel. I can't wait to see other parts of South America. And after that I would love to buy—have dreamed of buying—a motorcycle in Panama, and then ride up through Central America back to the States."

Maria Elena nodded and went back to work. She did not ask any more questions and Tomás suddenly felt a distance between them. They continued to work side by side—lost in their thoughts. After awhile Tomás asked, "Maria Elena, what about you? Don't you ever want to marry and have a family?"

She planted two more trees without answering and Tomás wondered if he had been too personal.

Finally she sighed and said, "Yes, I do. But I do not know if I ever will."

He stopped digging.

"Why?"

She arched her back. Tomás imagined it was plenty sore and stiff considering the effort of the past two days. She looked him in the eye.

"I do not know if I can ever leave Juan. I do not think he will marry and I also know he does not want me to leave—or at least never live very far away. I think he would welcome a brother-in-law in the house and enjoy having more help with the work on the farm. But I do not think that would be healthy for me or the man I marry. So, I just do not think things will ever work out—considering the situation. But yes, I would like to have my own family. What woman would not? But," she added with a bitter sweet smile, "soon I will not have to worry about such things. I will be too old for someone to ask me."

"Maria Elena, are you serious? You are very beautiful and the years will never pose a problem for you. A man would be lucky to have you as his *señora*—no matter how old you are."

Tomás surprised both of them with that. They looked at each other and Tomás felt something electric pass between them. Finally he broke the silence and the moment.

"Besides, you are strong and capable. What man would not want you to do all his work for him, eh?"

She laughed and they began planting again.

It was just before dark when they took care of the loose seedlings, picked up the tools, and returned to the house. Maria Elena invited him in for a light supper. Juan ate in his chair while Maria Elena and Tomás sat at the table. They reassured Juan that things were going well. They told him how many trees had been planted and that the rows were perfect. Juan was understandably depressed and there was none of his usual jokes and banter. Tomás knew he was terribly frustrated because he couldn't help. But at least he was beginning to hobble around on his crutches, which would take some of the pressure off of Maria Elena. Halfway through dinner Tomás realized how exhausted he was. He declined *mate* after the meal and said he would return the next morning with Ramon. Juan and Maria Elena thanked him several times for his help over the last two days. In unison they bid him goodnight.

It was partly sunny the next morning when he and Ramon arrived at the Montoya farm. Guillermo, the tall bearded soccer player who had carried buckets of water with Tomás at the fire, was leaning on the gate, talking to Maria Elena and Juan. Guillermo would help with the planting. He was a free lance *trabajador* who worked for several farmers, but was planting for Don Pedro this winter. When Don Pedro's Señora had returned home after tending to Juan's knee, she told her husband about the injury. Don Pedro offered

Guillermo's services for two or three days. Maria Elena and Juan had quickly accepted.

The four of them left Juan sulking on his crutches and walked out to the plantation. Guillermo and Tomás each carried a bag of trees. Guillermo would work with Tomás while Maria Elena would team up with her uncle.

As Tomás laid his bag on the ground and opened it, Maria Elena said matter-of-factly to Ramon, "*Tio,* I should do the planting. Men are not so gentle when they stick their little trees into the holes."

The men stopped their preparations and looked at each other in shocked surprise while Maria Elena bent over and began to fill her pouch with seedlings. Ramon's mouth had dropped open, and Guillermo slowly shook his head and smiled.

When Maria Elena straightened up and faced them, Guillermo, merriment in his eyes, said, "This is true, Maria Elena? None of my girlfriends have ever complained about that to me. But I will make sure I am more careful next time I go to Valdivia."

"Valdivia? What are you talking about?" Maria Elena asked in puzzlement, and then she noticed the Cheshire cat smiles.

You could see the exact moment when she realized what she had said and how the men had interpreted it. All she could manage was a little "Oh," and she suddenly looked very embarrassed. Tomás wouldn't have thought it possible for such a dark-complexioned person to blush like that—but she did. She went beet red. The men could not help laughing. Poor Maria Elena. She was mortified. After a moment or two, Tomás took pity and tried to give her a little space. He tied on one of the pouches and, after quickly filling it with seedlings, turned to Guillermo.

"Come on Don Guillermo. Let us begin planting our row over there."

He started to walk away.

"All right, Don Tomás. But," Guillermo couldn't help adding, "I want you to be gentle when you stick your little tree in the hole."

Guillermo burst out laughing again and Ramon joined in. Maria Elena looked down and started fiddling with the trees in her pouch.

Maria Elena did not say more than a word or two to them for the rest of the day. If her eyes happened to meet Tomás's, she would blush and look away. But everyone worked hard and they planted over two bags of trees. If the weather continued to cooperate, they estimated it would take another day and a half to finish. Guillermo would lodge with Juan and Maria Elena, and as a sign of the respect that he commanded, he would sleep inside their house. Ramon and Tomás refused to stay for dinner, saying that they had to get back for chores and so that Flor could go home.

The next day the sun actually came out again—two days in a row!—and Maria Elena seemed to have recovered sufficiently to talk to them without blushing and looking away. The weather put a spring in everyone's step as they cheerfully walked out to plant. Guillermo and Tomás quickly got into their rhythm and hardly spoke as they planted tree after tree. It was a good time to think. For some time now, Tomás had wondered what particular project he could initiate that would benefit the community. He wanted to continue with the reforestation, of course, but he also wanted to start something on his own. When he came up with the answer, he realized the seed had been in the back of his mind for months—maybe ever since that first ride up to La Paloma for the cooperative meeting. But it had germinated with Juan's accident. He had thought long and hard about it and had decided to broach the subject with his co-workers when they stopped for lunch.

When they put down the tools and tree pouches, Maria Elena spread a *manta* on the ground. She shared this with her uncle while Guillermo and Tomás sat on nearby stumps. It had turned into a gorgeous day, and they ate silently, basking in the sunshine.

After a few minutes, Tomás put his bread and cheese down.

"If I were to ask the three of you what single thing, above all else, makes life difficult here—and if you could change it—what would it be?"

They looked at each other before they began listing all the hardships. No electricity. A terrible road. No telephone or radio communication. No hospital or doctors. No running water or indoor plumbing. They almost gleefully went on and on. Tomás continued eating and did not say a word. After they finished listing everything, they debated between mouthfuls which was most important. It went round and round until finally the consensus was *el camino*. To have a good road meant that trucks could take their products directly from their farms to the market and bring supplies back up into the hills. A vehicle could bring a doctor up or take a sick person down. The old *trabajador* might not have died, they said, if he could have gotten to town earlier. A good road could mean the first step towards electricity which could provide light, water pumps, indoor plumbing, some power tools, and a phone line where you could call out during an emergency. And, as in the case of Juan, a good road would be safer and cause less wear and tear on both people and animals. Yes, hands down, they said, the road.

"That is what I think too."

They looked at him, wondering why he had brought the subject up.

"This winter I have been talking with different government agencies about assistance programs available to rural communities. I learned that one of these agencies has a cost-share program that includes road construction and repair—as long as that road leads up to a settled community. I think Cufeo would qualify."

Guillermo immediately said, "With INDAP. I have heard they have such a program."

Why was this guy only a *trabajador*, Tomás wondered for about the twentieth time in the last two days.

Guillermo pulled up his left foot and, while inspecting the torn sole of his work boot, continued.

"But, Don Tomás, it will not do us any good. There is no money here. We could never come up with our share."

Maria Elena disagreed.

"But, Don Guillermo, what if we organized events—fundraisers?"

"Maria Elena, we would have to raise thousands and thousands of *escudos*," Guillermo countered.

"But we do not know what it would cost," Tomás interjected.

Maria Elena added, "I think you would be surprised at what fundraisers can do. When the women sell *empanadas* and wine at the *carreras* and the *futbol* tournaments, a lot of money comes in. And you know better than I do how much money is bet on the horse races. If we could get people to somehow contribute all that towards a new road..."

Ramon was quiet. Playing the devil's advocate, Tomás joined in.

"And what if larger than usual events were organized? Let's say an effort was made to attract people from Paillaco, Valdivia, and Reumen. Maybe even Osorno."

"That is right," Maria Elena said. "We could...."

"I think," Ramon said interrupting her, "it is as Don Tomás said. We do not have any idea what it would cost. Maybe we should get some sort of idea first before we get too excited. Only then can we determine if there is any chance at all."

"Then you think it is worth a try?" Tomás asked. "Do you think I should try to find out more about it when I go to Valdivia for my next delivery?"

They nodded as one.

The pretty INDAP secretary came back and said that Sr. Mueller would be right out and that he could wait in one of the chairs over by the large office window. He hadn't been sitting for much more than a second or two before a tall blond young man approached from the hallway. He stopped in front of Tomás and introduced himself, telling Tomás to call him Kurt.

Kurt led him into his office which was spacious and comfortable. There were several beautiful framed black and white photos of the lakes and volcanoes of the province hanging on the walls. The window behind his desk looked down on the main plaza, where people were taking advantage of the nice day. Some were strolling arm-in-arm while others were seated on benches, watching children play or feeding the pigeons. Kurt surprised him when he switched to perfect English.

"My secretary told me you are with the Peace Corps. Where are you from in the States?"

"Just outside of Boston."

Tomás asked where he had learned English.

"I have a degree from R.P.I. in New York State. I studied engineering there for four years. And how about you? What do you do here? I hope you do not work for the CIA."

University students and political leftists accused the Peace Corps of being infiltrated with spies from the CIA.

"Not likely, Kurt." Tomás told him all about the Cooperative and the reforestation loan.

Leaning back and folding his hands on his chest Kurt asked, "And what do you think of Chile?"

Tomás gestured towards his photos.

"It is so beautiful, and the people so *simpatico*. But I have to admit that I am still getting used to the way things are done here. Everything seems to take longer than in the States."

Kurt laughed.

"Now isn't that the truth. All the *tramite* is frustrating—even for me, a *Chileno*. I mean, look at these rubber stamps here," he nodded towards the little metal stand on the desk. Tomás counted eight. "Each document I process has to be stamped just right. If only one is stamped wrong it can screw up the whole works and it may be days or weeks before the document is returned and I have to start the whole process over again. It can cause totally unnecessary delays. And that, of course, is just the first little step in any project I do. But why have you come to see me, Tomás?"

Tomás described the road and explained the hardships. Kurt leaned forward.

"From what you say, there is no doubt that Cufeo qualifies for the program, and yes, the biggest problem would be for them to raise their share of the cost."

He swiveled his chair and looked out the window for a minute before he turned back to Tomás.

"An application will have to be submitted with," he patted the top of the rubber stamp stand, "all the particulars. But this is something you cannot apply for. This has to be done by the community. A committee representing the community needs to be formed and it should come here to formally apply. Do you think that poses any problems?"

Tomás said he didn't think so but it would take a little time.

"When you have a committee, get back to me and we will set up a meeting and take it from there. I think we can help. At least I hope so."

He held out his hand.

"A pleasure, Tomás."

Over the course of the next several weeks, Tomás rode around Cufeo and helped organize meetings at the schools to discuss the road and the INDAP program. The rains were beginning to ease so there were good turn-outs. He explained the necessity for a Road Committee, and it was decided that the Committee should have a member from each of the three main areas serviced by the road to Caman. It was no surprise that old Don Pedro from Casa Blanca was selected. Likewise it was no surprise that the consummate politician and talker, the *gerente* Manuel from La Paloma, was also chosen. However, what did surprise him was that in this man's world, Maria Elena was chosen to represent Central Caman. That was the Road Committee—the three of them. He set up a meeting with Kurt, and the Road Committee and he went to Valdivia to apply for the cost share. Kurt met them out front in the waiting room.

They entered his office where he held out a chair for Maria Elena. As Kurt began to explain how every-thing worked, Tomás tuned out for a while. He figured it was the Committee's job to get all the details straight and sign on the dotted line. When he tuned back in he noticed how well Kurt interacted with everyone. He smiled a lot and was polite and exceedingly helpful. Maria Elena returned each of his smiles with one of her own. She was quite charming. Tomás had never seen her interact like this before. During his first meeting with Kurt, Tomás had not thought about how a woman might react to him. He realized now how attractive Kurt was—tall, well built and well spoken, friendly, and handsome, with a natural confidence and presence. He was what girls in the States would call a hunk. He was also probably very well off. Tomás began to watch Maria Elena's interaction with him more closely.

As much at ease as Maria Elena seemed, Don Pedro was the opposite. He was clearly uncomfortable, squirming in his chair and twisting and fidgeting with the hat in his hands. His freshly shaved, weathered face had been nicked in several places, and he had missed a spot that bristled with a few short white whiskers.

Manuel, though, was in his element. He was nattily dressed and did most of the talking, using flowery language to describe the community's struggles, will to persevere, and other claptrap. Kurt was polite to Manuel, but he certainly paid more attention to Maria Elena.

Finally, the forms were signed and carefully stamped, and put in a little outgoing basket to be processed. Kurt explained that the next step would be for all of them to get together again in a few weeks here at the office. By then the weather should have significantly improved and he would take them in his jeep to look at the road and do a cost estimate. Then they could figure out if they had a snowball's chance in hell of coming up with the cost-share. Everyone stood and shook hands. Taking Maria Elena's hand in both of his, Kurt inclined his body in a little bow, and said it had been a pleasure to meet her. Tomás noticed that there was no ring on his left hand. Turning to the rest of them, Kurt said that he would do anything he could to facilitate the project.

Outside in the plaza, they headed towards a nearby café for coffee and a discussion of the meeting. They were all very up-beat.

Manuel was excited and even old Don Pedro said, "That went very well. I am so surprised. I cannot remember ever having such a meeting in a government office and I think Sr. Kurt really does want to help us. I also think," he said turning to Maria Elena and winking, "that it was a good idea to have you on the Committee, Maria Elena. He seemed to pay a lot of attention to you."

So it was obvious then, Tomás thought. Kurt was interested in her.

Maria Elena blushed and said, "Oh, I do not know about that, Don Pedro. But I agree. I do think he wants to help. And he is very *simpatico*."

They entered the little café. Tomás had to agree that the meeting had gone well. Maybe exceptionally well. As for the attention Kurt showered on Maria Elena—he did not like that at all.

CHAPTER TWELVE

La Idea de Don Pedro (Don Pedro's idea)

"Aii," Don Pedro exclaimed as he took his hat off and rubbed the top of his head.

Don Pedro, Manuel, and Tomás were bouncing around in the rear of the Landrover, while Maria Elena sat in the front. Kurt was driving. He had insisted that he could make it around the worst section of the Caman road and now he was giving it a shot.

"An oxcart might be slower," Don Pedro muttered, as he carefully put his hat back on, "but it has a lot more headroom."

Kurt continued dodging stumps. The Landrover bumped and lurched over rocks, exposed roots, and half rotted logs. Manuel had been uncharacteristically quiet during the ride out from Valdivia, and now had a slight sheen of sweat across his pale brow. He did not look good. When Tomás had met him this morning, his face was puffy and creased, and he smelled of stale alcohol. In the confines of the Landrover, the odor was more noticeable, and Tomás wondered if he was going to puke.

Kurt and Tomás had just finished walking up and down the bad section of the road, twice. Tomás had helped take some measurements and Kurt had taken a few shots with his transit, so he could calculate the amounts of fill that would be needed to soften the slope. He had studied the lay of the land and expertly pointed out where and what sized culverts would be needed to divert runoff. When Kurt learned that the road up above was not nearly as rough, he decided to try the detour, and they now lurched one final time as they turned back on to the road. Kurt set his odometer and they continued slowly up to Central Caman. This would be as far as the road would be improved— that is, if the community could come up with the cost share.

A week later, Kurt's estimate for the road came in at a staggering one hundred and eighty thousand *escudos*—twenty thousand dollars. The community would have to come up with half that. Kurt said he would lock in the estimate for a year, but if the community took any longer to raise the cash, they would have to reapply and the estimate would have to be adjusted, to keep up with Chile's double-digit inflation.

The nay-sayers, like Guillermo, shook their heads and said it was an impossible amount. But after the initial shock, the Road Committee went to work—especially Maria Elena. She traveled all over the *campo*, planning fund raisers, organizing the women, meeting with the captains of the *futbol* teams, and getting the concession stand for every event—including the Los Guindos tournament across the highway where there would be no roadwork. She even enlisted the children at the schools to pick the bright green *romerillo* ferns that could be sold for a few pennies to merchants in Valdivia. The ferns were exported to Europe for Christmas decorations and floral arrangements.

Through Pablo's connections with the Huaso Club of Valdivia, Maria Elena received permission to run a concession stand at the rodeo during the Semana Valdiviana, and she recruited Miriam to help. Maria Elena worked so tirelessly on the road project that Tomás wondered if it was because the road had hurt her brother so badly, and now she wanted to make sure that that would never happen again.

At about a third of the way through the soccer season, Tomás met with the Road Committee at Don Pedro's farm to discuss the idea of a grand finale fundraiser. They were sitting around a large table in the kitchen, drinking tea and discussing possibilities. They all agreed that it should be held in the fall, after the soccer tournaments were over, and it seemed appropriate to hold it in Central Caman where the new road would end. Manuel and Maria Elena said they should have an afternoon *carrera* followed by an evening fiesta with music and dancing. They envisioned whole lambs grilled over outdoor spits and barbecued meat sold throughout the day and night. Several *ramadas* would be built and the deck of the school used as a stage for the musicians. Tables and benches would be set in the soccer field for eating. Manuel said he had spoken with the owner of the still undefeated 'big gray' from Casa Blanca, and with a man in Paillaco who also owned a horse that had never been beaten. They agreed to race. The owner of the 'big gray' went further and said that if his horse won, he would donate half of his winnings to the road fund.

Don Pedro was silent until Maria Elena and Manuel finished. He agreed that their plan was a good one, but he insisted something else was needed to make the fundraiser a truly grand and memorable and—especially—money-making event.

"The horserace will certainly bring the men in from Cufeo, Valdivia, and Paillaco, if we get the word out. And I cannot think of two better horses for the race. But I also think we need something more; something to draw in a larger, mixed crowd. I have an idea that might just do the trick."

They looked at him expectantly.

"I have given it a lot of thought and I believe we should have not one, but two races; one in the late morning and another in the afternoon—a double feature like they have sometimes at the movie theater in Valdivia."

Don Pedro paused and leaned back, scratching what looked like a two-or-three-day-old stubble while he let the idea sink in. Maria Elena and Manuel slowly nodded as they thought about it. Don Pedro leaned forward again.

"It also has to have something that will draw people who do not usually attend *carreras*. We want to make this a grand fiesta, so we need more than just the older men who come to bet on the horses and drink wine. And we certainly do not want a lot of drunken men at the fiesta later in the day. If we can get the younger men and older boys to come early, then the young women and girls will come too. And the mothers will want to keep an eye on their daughters, so they will come. With the women and younger people here, I think the men will behave themselves, and in this way we can truly have a very large and successful event. And," he added, "the earlier everyone comes, the more money they will spend."

Don Pedro looked at them closely.

"But the big question is, who races in the first event?"

Maria Elena and Manuel looked at each other and back to Don Pedro. They didn't offer any suggestions. A sly grin slowly spread across Don Pedro's face.

He said, "You, Don Manuel, are a well known leader in the community and the *gerente* of the Cooperative. You have lived here all your life and you know everybody and, of course, you are on the Road Committee."

Manuel was wondering where Don Pedro was going with this.

"Yes, that is true."

Now that the weather had improved, Manuel was spending more time in the *campo* than in the bars of Valdivia, and he looked the better for it. Don Pedro leaned towards him.

"And I remember that when you were younger you also raced in many *carreras*. Is that not true also?"

Manuel started to look a little wary.

"It is true I raced when I was younger. But with all due respect, Don Pedro, that was a long time ago. I haven't..."

"Wait, Don Manuel. Please let me finish. And the horse you ride now—he is the same one you used to race?"

"Yes, but..."

"And he is still a young enough horse, is he not?"

"He is fifteen and not so young now. But yes, he could still race. But..."

Don Pedro held up both hands for silence and turned to Maria Elena.

"Maria Elena, if we wanted to attract the young men of Cufeo—other than with pretty girls like yourself," Maria Elena looked heavenward, "what is an interest they almost all share?"

Before she could answer, Tomás blurted out, "*Futbol.*"

Don Pedro turned quickly to him, "Exactly, Don Tomás. *Futbol.* So, what about a *futbol* player that everyone knows but wouldn't expect as one of the riders in the first race?"

They chewed on that for a little bit and decided it was a good idea. But who?

Maria Elena said, "I do not know any *futbol* player who has raced in a *carrera,* or any who might even be interested. And," noting Don Pedro's continued sly smile, "if you are thinking of Juan, forget it, Don Pedro. He certainly cannot do it with his bad leg."

Juan had recently gone from crutches to using a cane. His knee was coming along slowly, but Maria Elena was still doing most of the chores—which made the time she spent working on the road project that much more of a sacrifice. Tomás was playing for Caman this summer, and they all missed having Juan in the goal. They only hoped that he'd be able to play at some point.

"No, no. Not your brother. Think about it, Maria Elena. Who plays *futbol* in all the tournaments and is always noticed? And who, at the same time, is very much interested in the road project?"

Tomás thought of all the players that stood out. Miguel from Los Guindos? But he had no interest in the road on this side of the highway. Guillermo? He was a very good player and with his size he always stood out. And he was interested in the road. But he didn't even own a horse. He could certainly ride. But with that big frame of his? Maybe...

Maria Elena looked questioningly at Don Pedro. Suddenly she smiled and he quickly matched her smile with his own.

"Of course, Don Pedro. Perfect."

She looked at Manuel. And then at Tomás. And then back to Don Pedro.

"Perfect. That would draw a lot of people. Yes. Perfect."

Maria Elena and Don Pedro continued to smile while Manuel and Tomás looked dumbly at one another. Manuel, Tomás knew, did not have a clue. He only went to *futbol* tournaments to drink wine in the *ramadas*.

Clapping her hands excitedly, Maria Elena said, "Don Manuel and Don Tomás! You two will be in the first race."

"So tell me more about this fiesta and your horse race," Oso said as he and Tomás walked up the Caman road.

It was the perfect weekend for Oso's visit. Tomás and Maria Elena had everything planned. Maria Elena would give Oso a tour of Cufeo, with him tagging along. The next day, the three of them would ride over to the soccer tournament in Los Guindos. Oso would watch him play while Maria Elena worked in the concession stand. He also wanted to introduce Oso to the Martinez family and show him their farm. The weather was going to be beautiful, clear and cool, for the next few days.

"The race will probably be a joke. But at least it should draw a lot of people who wouldn't come otherwise, and that's the point. Everyone loves it when the *gringo* makes a fool of himself. It will give them something to talk and laugh about for weeks."

Manuel had balked at Don Pedro's idea in the beginning. But when he realized that there was no chance he could lose and that he would be on center stage for a very large crowd, he let them talk him into it. Tomás accepted because he knew it would attract more people, which meant more money for a very good cause. But he had plenty of reservations—not the least of which was the recurring vision of Manuel, galloping way ahead of him, turning around in his saddle and motioning for him to hurry up. Manuel is smirking and the crowd along the track is roaring with laughter.

"I will race in the morning and then there will be a real *carrera* in the afternoon. After that there will be a dance in the evening, complete with musicians. There will be an *asado* all day and, of course, there will be plenty of *chicha* and *vino*. The money we raise from the food and drink—and possibly from some private contributions—could be significant. It should be quite an event, certainly the biggest thing to ever happen around here."

Oso was perspiring freely. He was hatless, and carried a change of clothes plus his sleeping bag in a blue nylon sack that he had thrown over his shoulder. After hearing so many of Tomás's stories about the *campo* dogs, he had armed himself with a stick. He looked over at Tomás.

"There is no way I am going to miss that race. But do me a favor and don't fall off. I don't want to have to carry the pieces back down this hill. How much farther is the farm, anyway?"

He was breathing heavily, and stopped to pull a bandanna from his back pocket and wipe his brow. Tomás thought of his penchant for French fries.

"Not far. About a half mile. That's Maria Elena's house over there," Tomás said pointing to the right. "And that's the infamous gate I told you about."

Oso chuckled.

"I have done some pretty embarrassing things before, but I don't know if anything could top that. If it had been me, I think I might have just stayed hidden under that *manta* rather than show my face. Or maybe I would have pretended to have been really hurt, so Maria Elena could have nursed me back to health."

"In your dreams, big guy. Only a veterinarian could nurse you back to health."

Oso looked at him in mock disgust. They rounded the corner and the farm was just ahead. Oso kicked a little stone off to the side of the road and then looked back to Tomás again.

"But you know what? I am thinking I may just put the word out and see how many volunteers I can talk into coming to your *carrera*. That would be an easy sell. I can see the billing now. GRINGO VOLUNTEER VERSUS SEASONED CAMPESINO—THE RACE EVERYONE IS TALKING ABOUT. TO BE HELD HIGH UP IN THE FOOTHILLS OF THE ANDES, OVERLOOKING THE BEAUTIFUL VOLCANOES OF SOUTHERN CHILE. And with the *asado*, the *vino*, and all the farmers' daughters, I'll bet I could get ten—maybe twenty—volunteers to come."

"Wait a minute, Oso. It's going to be bad enough without..." Tomás stopped and thought about it. "Actually, you know, that's not such a bad idea."

The volunteers would spend a lot of money and he'd bet that Ramon would let them camp out in the pasture. If people knew a bunch of *gringos*—and maybe some *gringas*—were coming, it would be an added attraction. He could visualize the whole scene: the crowd, the roasting lambs, the *ramadas,* the colored tents in the pasture, and, unfortunately, the race.

"But Jesus, Oso, I hope I don't make too much of a fool of myself in that damn race. And, like you say, I hope I don't get hurt either."

He unhooked the gate and they walked past the empty corral towards the house. The sky was azure blue and the sheep were grazing peacefully out in the pasture. Lobo and Salton were slowly walking along the fence line in the distance. It was a beautiful *campo* morning. As they approached the kitchen steps, Oso saw Molestoso, completely checkered now with brown singe marks, sunning himself on the porch.

"Good grief! What happened to that cat? Is that mange?" Oso asked, carefully stepping around him. "God, it looks awful!"

Tomás laughed as he held the door open for Oso and explained about the *brasero* under the kitchen table.

Late the next morning he was on Lobo, Oso was on Salton, and Maria Elena rode between them on her chestnut mare. She spurred her horse ahead and turned onto a narrow path that led up to a plateau with a truly beautiful view of the surrounding countryside. He had stopped here a couple times before, on his trips to Lote Once.

Maria Elena reined in her horse and said, "This is a good spot to let the horses rest a spell. And it is so pretty here."

They dismounted and admired the view. Oso snapped a couple of pictures, and got his bearings by locating the different roads off in the distance. Maria Elena patted her horse's neck.

Tomás said, "You know, I would really like to see one of the mountain lions around here. Not too close of course, but close enough to see it well. I'd also like to see a condor. With all the time I spend on horseback riding these hills, I have never seen one."

The Andean Condor was huge, with a wingspan of ten or eleven feet. In comparison, the wingspan of a bald eagle might top out at six and a half to seven. Maria Elena told Tomás that condors lived only in the higher mountains. She had never seen one, but had read that they had ugly bald heads and they could soar forever.

"Oso," she asked, "have you ever seen them while cruising your timber?"

"No. They don't usually visit forested areas. They like to nest above the tree line in caves or on remote ledges. I have seen a few way up in the Andes when I crossed over to Argentina on vacation. But that is the only time."

After the horses had rested, they headed back down to the main road.

Oso said, "I used to feel a little sorry for you, Tomás, all alone out here in the *campo*. But living and working here sure beats sitting in an office in Valdivia."

"I don't think you would say that if you were here during the winter. Believe me, you don't know how many times I thought about that nice hot shower of yours back in Valdivia. But still, I do love it here."

Maria Elena laughed.

"Yes, a hot shower now and then would be very nice."

Tomás thought of the occasional sponge baths he took out in the *fogon*. He wondered where Maria Elena bathed. A lovely picture began to form in his mind.

"But are you serious, Tomás," she asked, "when you say you love it here?"

"Does that surprise you? I love almost everything about Cufeo, though I realize that I have it a lot easier than you and the others."

He spurred Lobo lightly. Lobo had that sleepy look in his eyes and had begun to fall behind.

"I get a salary deposited in the bank each month without any of the back-breaking work the men do here. Have you noticed how fit every man you see is, Oso—no matter how old? That is because they work so damn hard—day in and day out—chopping wood, throwing cordwood around, cutting brush, walking up and down these hills. It is a tough life, but at least it keeps you in shape."

The road became much steeper, and he and Oso followed Maria Elena single file. After a slow half-mile climb they were able to ride three abreast again. He thought about today's long ride and wondered how Salton was doing with Oso on his back. Then he thought about Oso slugging his horse in Chiloe. He told the story to Maria Elena and she laughed hard. She batted her eyes at Oso and said he must be very strong. Oso blushed.

The countryside changed from overgrazed pasture with terrific views to thick hardwood forest. Oso looked around with great interest. It was obvious he was enjoying this ride immensely. They rode for some time in silence. The only sound was from the plodding and occasional stumbling of their horses.

Finally Maria Elena said, "See that tall dead tree with the long seam running down its length? It is close to where we turn off the main trail."

Tomás knew that they were only on the outskirts of Lote Once. The *socios* he had visited lived quite a ways farther up. Maria Elena slowed her horse so she could look at both of them.

"Remember. Very few people know about this spot and I want it to stay that way."

They nodded and followed as she urged her mare forward. It was a narrow and little-used downhill trail with lots of switchbacks. They had to push branches of *quila* out of their way, until it leveled out. Then they entered a magical grotto, filled with ferns and some absolutely tremendous trees.

In English, Oso exclaimed, "Holy Shit. These are *alerce*, Tomás. Holy shit! Look at them."

They stopped in a wide clearing around the base of one of the behemoths. Maria Elena was smiling proudly. Tomás looked at the tree. The base had to be at least ten feet through. He looked up and it went on forever. Down low there were no branches, but farther up the stem tapered, and there were thick branches that were covered with so much moss and lichens that they looked like the hairy legs of a tarantula. It was so silent that it was almost eerie, like an ancient and sacred place. The forest floor was peppered with miniature ferns. He had never seen such tiny ferns. Oso was spellbound, and Maria Elena did not say a word. Finally, Oso got off his horse, handed Tomás the reins, and began to walk silently around the tree. He was smiling when he reappeared on the other side, running his hand along the trunk.

"What a beauty," he said to no one in particular.

They tied up the horses to some *quila* on the edge of the open space.

"I have never counted them, Oso, but I think there have to be at least fifty of these trees here. Aren't they beautiful?"

There was no need to answer.

"Come. There is a little path that connects the trees."

After a short walk through the *quila* they came to another *alerce*. It was even bigger than the first. Tomás touched the thick, reddish-gray, flaky bark. It had a spongy feel to it. The tree must have been close to two hundred feet tall and had those same hairy, tarantula branches. They walked to two more before Maria Elena spoke.

"So what do you think?"

"Spectacular," Oso said, pulling his small camera from a pocket. "I have to take a picture. You two step up to the tree so I can get some perspective."

He stepped back as far as he could and looked through the viewfinder.

"*Mierda*, it is too damn dark to take a picture."

"Never mind, Oso. You will be able to take plenty of beautiful pictures in a few minutes," Maria Elena said.

They returned to the horses, and Maria Elena took their lunches out of her saddlebags, which she handed to Tomás. She then walked over to a sizeable branch and dragged it off to the side, revealing a faint path. They followed her through a thick tangle of *quila* and came to another open area around an *alerce*. They continued on around it to where the path entered the *quila* again. Eventually the *quila* gave way to hardwood forest and the path started to go downhill. Soon they were going down some switchbacks. It was very damp and they carefully stepped over slippery roots. There were big trees and tangles of undergrowth everywhere, and Oso told him that this was a typical temperate rain forest. They crossed a wide stream, jumping from stone to stone, and hearing a waterfall somewhere below. Finally they saw brightness through the trees. Maria Elena smiled cryptically.

"We're almost there."

When they reached the forest's edge, Maria Elena stepped aside, motioning for them to continue forward. He and Oso stepped out onto a broad shelf. The first thing they saw was the jagged, knife-point-shaped volcano Puntiagudo, with its snow-covered tip sparkling in the bright sunlight. It looked big and so close. Off to the left was the waterfall that they had been hearing. Its broad white ribbon plunged a hundred and fifty feet, past emerald-green ferns and moss, down to a clear pool surrounded by huge flat rocks. It looked like a great place for a swim.

Immediately below them was a clearing of at least two hectares which had been created by hardwood trees that had fallen down eroded slopes. Or maybe they had fallen during the earthquake, Tomás thought. They were layered at different angles, but the whole jumble was smoothed out by a thick green carpet of vines everywhere on the fallen trees.

Maria Elena asked, "Have you ever seen anything so beautiful?"

They shook their heads.

"And, believe it or not, it is even more beautiful at the very end of the summer and into the fall. Remember, Tomás, when I told you I came to Lote Once for picnics with Juan, and that we would pick *copihue* for the house?"

She turned and pointed down to the clearing.

"All those vines on the fallen trees are *copihue*. When they are in bloom it is like a bright red sea."

He looked out and tried to imagine. It must be absolutely spectacular. Maria Elena sat down on the edge of the shelf and let her feet dangle over the side. They joined her. Other than the click of Oso's camera, they were silent for some time.

Finally she sighed and said, "This place is so beautiful. It is so perfect. It is like heaven on earth."

He agreed. If a person believed in heaven, then something like this would do just fine for eternity.

Oso said, "And it certainly is a fine place for a picnic. So, come on already, Tomás. Open up those packages of food. I'm starved."

CHAPTER THIRTEEN

El Robo del Lobo (The Theft of Lobo)

The Casa Blanca *ramada* was lit by two kerosene lanterns hanging from corner posts. Claudio, Don Pedro's son, had taken over bar duties after the tournament while the women, including Maria Elena, bundled up the cooking gear and went home. At Manuel's urging, Tomás remained to help him talk up the road-benefit fiesta. But the small crowd at the *ramada* was buzzing instead with the news from Los Guindos.

The Los Guindos team had been uncharacteristically eliminated in their first game. The reason was obvious. Jaime and Jorge had been no-shows, and Los Guindos had lost badly. As the team prepared to leave, Miguel walked up to Tomás, holding a folded piece of paper.

"Don Tomás, here is a note for you from the Señora Isabel."

He took it, asking, "Where were Jaime and Jorge? You really missed them today."

"There was a fight and they are both hurt bad. Jorge is in the hospital in Valdivia."

"A fight? *Por Dios.* When? And who did they fight?"

"The two of them—they fought each other. It was very bad. They almost killed each other."

He couldn't believe it. At least he couldn't believe Jaime had gotten into a fight. He was so mild mannered—a live and let live kind of a guy.

"What in the world did they fight about?"

"I don't know. I have seen Jaime, but he will not talk about it. He looks awful. And the Señora Isabel and Don Emilio say nothing."

Miguel's teammates rode up.

"I must go now. I will tell the Señora I delivered her note."

Miguel mounted up behind a teammate and left. He watched them ride off before he unfolded the piece of paper.

Dear Don Tomás,
Please come over and see us as soon as you can. It is very important.
Isabel Baeza Martinez

Everyone had noticed the absence of Jaime and Jorge, and it didn't take long for news of the fight to circulate. Eventually, as the night wore on, talk centered on the grand fiesta. Manuel brought up the race between the 'big gray' and the horse from Paillaco several times. The conversation inevitably shifted to the race between Manuel and Tomás. Manuel basked in the attention and playfully poked fun at Tomás by asking how much of a lead he thought he should spot him. Some chuckled with Manuel, but some did not. Tomás played along good-naturedly, but as it grew late and more wine was drunk, he was ready to leave.

Manuel looked over at him from where he was leaning on the rough wooden bar.

"Don Tomás, I am a little short of money. Invite me for one last *copa*."

Tomás hesitated and then said, "Okay. But not just for you—a round for everyone. And a toast first."

He dug into his pocket for some bills while Claudio refilled all the glasses from a wicker-covered demijohn of red wine. He cleared his throat.

"As you all know, the money spent here tonight will benefit the road project. So you can tell your *señoras* that you have been drinking for a very good reason."

The men laughed. Everyone was in a good mood.

"The road project has united this community and it is good to see everyone working so hard towards a common goal." Tomás raised his cup. "So I say to you, here's one for the road."

The men lifted their cups and said in unison, *"Sí, Don Tomás. Uno para el camino!"*

A few minutes later Manuel had finished his *copa* and wandered off into the dark to relieve himself. Claudio approached Tomás and quietly asked him which horse he was going to ride in the race.

"I think Salton. Salton is Don Ramon's choice."

Guillermo, who, Tomás had learned, was nicknamed 'El Barbudo' because of his beard, was standing next to him at the bar. They were teammates now. Guillermo put his cup down on the counter. "You must try to get off to a good start, Don Tomás. The horse of Don Manuel has always been very quick off the line; if Don Manuel gets ahead enough in the beginning, he will cut in front of you. He is a clever rider and that is his style. If he gets too far in front he will make you eat dirt, and it will be very difficult to get around him."

Claudio spoke again.

"Don Guillermo is right. And I think Don Ramon is too. Salton should be your horse. Lobo is too small and he does not have enough strength. And you must practice. Salton is young and must be shown what to do. If you are lucky, he will be like his father—strong and fast. There is a big difference though, between speed and quickness. Salton's father is not quick off the line, but he is strong enough to make up for it. I do not know if your horse has that same kind of strength. And the track at Caman is not long, and I think that is not good for your horse. But talk to Don Ramon. He can give you good council. Did you know that he used to race? And that he raced several times against Don Manuel years ago?"

That surprised him. He would have to ask Ramon about that. Claudio quickly changed the subject when Manuel came into the light, tugging on his fly.

Claudio asked, "Don Manuel, how about one last *trago* on me?"

Manuel nodded his thanks and held out his glass with a smile. When Claudio tried to fill Tomás's cup, he shook his head and covered it with his hand. This was a new development, he thought. Maybe some people were actually taking this race seriously. And maybe Manuel was not so popular after all. And maybe there were people who would like to see him win.

He waited for Manuel to finish his wine. Manuel had to pass through Caman on his way home so they would ride back together. They walked over to the horses. Because it had been overcast in the morning, he had brought his big black manta and left it draped over his saddle. Manuel mounted his horse. Tomás looked for Lobo. He knew that he had hitched him next to Manuel's horse, but Lobo wasn't there. He thought somebody must have moved him. He looked in all directions.

"Don Manuel, I don't know where my horse is. I tied him up here, near yours, but he is gone. He must have gotten loose. Maybe he followed Maria Elena and Don Juan back to Caman..."

"Or maybe he is just grazing on the other side of the schoolhouse. I will have a look."

Manuel turned his horse and loped off into the darkness. After a few minutes he rode up to the *ramada* and spoke with the men there. Tomás walked back up and everyone looked concerned.

Manuel said, "No one has seen your Lobo. We think he has been stolen." Removing his left foot from the stirrup and extending an arm, he said, "Mount up behind me. We will go look for him."

He put his foot in the stirrup and, tugging on to Manuel's arm, hoisted himself up. Everyone wished him luck. Manuel suddenly spurred his horse and they were off at a gallop. He frantically clutched Manuel's waist. He had never ridden double before, and it was fortunate that it was flat when they started out because it was easy to get into the horse's rhythm. Uphill was easy too. But galloping downhill was something else entirely. The horse jostled and pitched, and the darkness didn't help his equilibrium any. Manuel's broad back and the edge of the saddle prevented him from falling forward, but he had to hold on tightly to Manuel's waist to keep from skittering off of one side or the other. Falling off was a definite possibility. They galloped for what seemed like an eternity. As dark as it was, it seemed insane to ride so fast. Occasionally he saw the dim kerosene light of a house close to the road, and dogs would come out and bark. But after a while he became totally disoriented, and had no idea where they were. He just held on.

Finally, Manuel reined in his horse. It was breathing heavily. He knew that they had stopped in front of a farm because dogs began to bark. But he couldn't see the farmhouse. He had no idea how Manuel had known there was a farm here. Manuel loudly announced their presence. A door not thirty feet away opened and a man holding a small lantern appeared on the threshold.

"Good evening, Don Carlos," Manuel said. "Please excuse the inconvenience of such a late appearance at your door but it is Manuel Vargas and Don Tomás. Don Tomás's horse has been stolen from the tournament in Casa Blanca. Have you seen it or any strange movement around?"

He recognized Carlos Zambrano so at least he knew where they were now. Carlos was not a *socio*, but was interested in planting trees next winter. He had talked with him several times.

"Aii, *mierda*! Your horse has been stolen, Don Tomás?" he asked as he walked up. "What kind of people do we have around here now? It must be one of the *trabajadores*. But, Don Manuel, I have not seen anything unusual although many passed by on their way to and from the school today. And I did not see either of your horses, Don Tomás. Which one was stolen?"

"It was Lobo, Don Carlos. The small brown one."

Manuel said, "Don Carlos, would it be all right to dismount for a few minutes to rest and stretch? We have ridden very hard—and it gives one such a thirst."

"Of course. Forgive me. Here, come up to the porch."

Manuel tied his horse to a fence and Carlos led the way over to a little bench.

"Please rest and I will bring you some wine for your thirst."

Manuel took off his hat and gave it a shake against his thigh. His voice took on a weary tone.

"Don Carlos, thank you very much and, again, please forgive our bothering you at this late hour. But Don Tomás's horse. This is such a bad thing."

Manuel looked down to the ground, totally mortified and sad now. Tomás suddenly realized that besides being a charlatan, Manuel was quite an actor.

"Yes, clearly, yes. This is very bad. *Por Dios.* But, please excuse me and I will bring you some wine."

Carlos set the lantern down on a little table and disappeared into the darkness. When he returned he handed Tomás and Manuel each a large glass of red wine, and waited politely for them to drink it. Tomás drank out of politeness but refused a refill. Manuel, however, did not, and had another glass while he continued to lament the theft. After Carlos had yawned once or twice, Tomás suggested to Manuel that it was late and they should go. They thanked Carlos, who promised to keep a close eye out. Tomás mounted up behind Manuel and they were off at a gallop again. After a ways, Manuel slowed down to trot. Tomás tried to steady his voice and speak loudly enough so that Manuel could hear him over the clip clop.

"Where are we going now, Don Manuel?"

Manuel turned half way around in his saddle and said, "If someone stole your horse, there are only three roads he could have taken. We have been on one now, and we will go to the other two. I know a family on each road where we can ask about your horse. Make sure you hold on tight."

They began to gallop again. He did not fall and they went to the two houses on the other roads. The scenario at each was the same: Manuel begged their forgiveness for the late hour, explained that Don Tomás's horse had been stolen, asked if there was any strange activity, and requested that since they had been riding hard, could they possibly have something for their thirst. Tomás's stomach was already in rebellion from all of the bouncing around behind Manuel, so he refused any more wine. Manuel, though, put away a large glass of wine at each house. Tomás didn't know how he did it, after drinking all day at the tournament.

By the time they left the third house, Manuel was very drunk and they no longer galloped. Tomás had no idea what time it was, but it had to be very late—or early—as the sky was beginning to change from black to gray. Finally they headed down the Casa Blanca hill and, after passing the schoolhouse, arrived at the Rodriguez gate. It was a huge relief to slip down off of Manuel's horse. He bid Manuel good night and thanked him for all of his efforts. Manuel dismissed the thanks with a grandiose wave of his hand that caused him to lose his balance and almost fall to the ground. He caught himself at the last moment. The horse must have been accustomed to such behavior because it did not shy. Instead it took advantage of the moment to bend down and eat some grass. It must be starved, Tomás thought. Manuel pulled its head up and mumbled something before he turned towards the road to La Paloma. He was weaving in the saddle as he slowly rode away. Tomás watched him until he disappeared over the hill. Somehow Manuel stayed upright. It was as if his bottom was glued to the saddle.

When he started up the little porch stairs, the front door opened and Ramon hurried out. He looked upset.

"Don Tomás, where have you been? I have been worried about you." Looking all around and then back to him again, he asked, "And Lobo? Where is your horse?"

Suddenly Tomás was exhausted. It must have shown because Ramon ushered him inside without another word and sat him down at the kitchen table. He told

Ramon the whole story. Ramon didn't say anything, although he occasionally shook his head from side to side. His face was flushed and he looked angry.

Ramon said, "This is bad. Of all the horses to steal, it would be yours. Listen to me. Our community will not stand for this. We must find your horse and saddle and *manta*. And as for Manuel," he said omitting the 'Don,' "let me guess the three farms you went to last night."

He held up his left hand and raised three fingers. He pointed emphatically at each finger.

"Don Carlos Zambrano, Don Ivan Coronado, and Don Alberto Baeza."

Tomás looked at him in surprise.

"But how did you know?"

"Because, Don Tomás, those are the only three places in Casa Blanca that sell wine as a little side business. Manuel knew what he was about and it was not about finding your Lobo. Come on. Let's saddle Salton. I want to go track your horse."

They went out into the dawn and brought Salton in from the pasture. Ramon put Pablo's saddle and bridle on him. Ramon mounted and Tomás walked alongside as far as the gate. They heard *trele* sounding the alarm from high up the Casa Blanca road, and looked up to see a little brown horse slowly coming down.

Ramon said without hesitation, "That is Lobo."

"How can you tell? He is so far away."

Ramon kept his eyes on the horse.

"It is Lobo, all right. I can tell from the way he walks. And," he turned to Tomás with a thin smile, "considering what has happened, what are the odds that there would be another riderless horse at this time of day, heading straight toward us?"

It was Lobo, and Salton's nostrils flared when he caught his scent. He whinnied to his pasture mate, and in response Lobo began to trot. He had come home on his own but the saddle, bridle, and *manta de Castilla* were gone. Tomás put his belt around Lobo's neck and led him over to the shed to grain him, while Ramon decided to head to Casa Blanca to see what he could find out. He watched as Ramon slowly crested the Casa Blanca hill, and then made a beeline to his sleeping bag.

Ramon was gone all day and Tomás slept for most of it. When Ramon returned in the early evening, it was quite a role reversal. Tomás went out to meet him and help him with the saddle. Tomás had reheated yesterday's soup and he served Ramon, who was starved. He ate half a bowl of soup before looking up to tell Tomás what he had discovered.

"I think I have found the culprit," he said as he broke off a piece of the two-day-old bread and dipped it into his soup. "I rode up to the school and asked the neighbors if they had seen any strangers or anything suspicious. I told them about your horse and saddle. I went from house to house until I came to the Widow Carlota's farm, not far from my brother Ricardo's place…"

Ramon took another spoonful of soup and looked up to see if Tomás knew where that was. He knew it well because the widow had a big cherry tree whose branches extended over the road. Every summer she tried but failed to prevent the soccer players on horseback from picking it clean.

"She told me that a *trabajador* from the farm next to my brother's had come by late in the morning yesterday and bought two glasses of *chicha con harina* for breakfast. He said that he was on his way to watch the soccer tournament. There was nothing unusual about that. But, because of so much *movimiento* on the road with people going to and from the tournament, the Widow

Carlota went out at dusk to make sure everything was secure. When she was returning to her front door, a rider passed by. She could not swear to it because he had his head turned away from her, but she thinks it was the same *trabajador*. And she wondered why he was on horseback since he had been on foot before. Also, he was wearing a *manta de Castilla* that he had not had in the morning."

Ramon got up and took their bowls and placed them in the sink.

"Don Ramon, do not worry about those. I will clean up the kitchen. What else did you find out?"

Ramon puttered around a bit, stoking the stove and pulling the kettle of water over the firebox. Tomás thought he was proud of his detective work and was enjoying the moment. He was building up the suspense just like he did when he told his stories out in the *fogon*. He reached for his *mate* cup and filled it with *yerba*.

"I found out from the widow where he lives and it is right off the trail that leads to Ricardo's. I headed that way and paid close attention to the tracks. As you know, that trail is not so heavily traveled, not like the roads around here or near the school in Casa Blanca. As I got close to the worker's shack I saw the tracks of a shod horse that I thought might be Lobo's. I did not want to alarm the worker, so I made sure there was no one around to see me get off of Salton to take a closer look. And," Ramon looked at him triumphantly, "they were Lobo's tracks."

Tomás thought that this was something out of a TV western. And it was for damn sure that Ramon knew Lobo's tracks. He had shod Lobo last fall and had had quite a time doing it. Lobo had tried to kick Ramon several times until Ramon finally put a twitch on him to calm him down. He had taken a loop of Tomás's nylon rope and put it around Lobo's muzzle and upper lip. Inserting a short stick as a handle, he twisted the loop tighter and tighter around Lobo's upper lip until it looked like it was going to pop. He had Tomás hold it while he turned to Lobo and said, "There. That will get your attention and let me work without all your fussing." Fitting and shaping Lobo's shoes had required quite a bit of hammering on the anvil. Ramon had said that one hoof in particular had an odd shape.

"Then what did you do?"

"I rode past the worker's shack towards Ricardo's, trying my best to look like I was just passing by on my way to pay a brotherly visit. There was no one around that I could see, but after I passed the shed, I did not see Lobo's tracks again. I am sure that this is the man who robbed you."

"Now what do we do?"

Ramon brought his *mate* over to the table and reached for the steaming kettle.

"I discussed it with Ricardo. He and his family are going to keep a close eye on any movement over there. He knows the man and where he is chopping firewood for the Perez family. Ricardo will have his sons wander in that area from time to time as if they are looking for some of their animals. It should not arouse suspicion."

True enough. Animals were always getting out of pens or pastures and had to be brought back. Even though the Montoya's sow had a large triangle of one inch diameter sticks fastened around its neck to prevent it from passing through a fence, it was always getting out somehow and wandering the countryside. With Juan still hurt, Tomás had helped Maria Elena search for the sow several times.

"As it is," Ramon continued, "some animals have disappeared near Ricardo's since last winter, about the same time that this man started working in the area.

Ricardo suspects him. But right now we do not want to alert him in any way. We will wait and see what he does."

"Does this happen often, Don Ramon—I mean—stealing horses?"

"No. They are too easy to trace and there is not such a good market for horsemeat. But as for the other animals—yes, it can happen at any time. That is why we have to maintain *mucho ojo* here, and why I am not able to leave the farm for any length of time."

Ramon re-freshened his *mate*.

"About three years ago almost everyone in this area of Cufeo had animals stolen. It did not matter what kind—oxen, cows, pigs, or sheep. We often found the trails of the animals and they always led to the highway, but then, with the pavement, we could follow them no further. And, besides, we thought that somehow the animals must have been picked up and taken away. But we watched and watched and never saw a truck parked anywhere. And it would be impossible for a trucker to pass by exactly when the thief was coming down out of the hills with an animal. We took turns and watched for weeks and we never saw anyone, but our animals kept disappearing."

Tomás stood and walked over to the sink. He poured what was left of the hot water into the basin and added some soap. He ladled some cold water from the bucket on the floor and began to wash their bowls.

"So you never caught them?"

"They were caught but it was only by chance. It was actually a *futbol* player from Valdivia who solved the mystery. His team had been put out early in a tournament in Piedra Azul and, rather than return to Valdivia with his team in the back of a firewood truck, he stayed to drink wine and watch the rest of the tournament. By the time he left, there were no more buses to Valdivia.

But he walked down to the highway anyway. He had to get back to Valdivia somehow because he had been told by his boss that he would be fired if he was ever late again for work. He was supposed to be there early in the morning, so he tried to hitchhike. But, as you know, there is very little traffic—especially late on a Sunday afternoon. And no one who can afford a car wants to stop and pick up a man in the middle of nowhere. So he began walking. He walked for quite a ways until he came to that section on the highway, a little east from where we catch the bus, where it is so steep that the bus never stops. Right there is a tremendous culvert under the road for the runoff from the hills. The culvert is so big that you could ride through it on a horse if you wanted. When the *futbol* player approached the culvert, he smelled something rotten. He thought that probably some animal had been hit and had died on the side of the road. But then the smell got much stronger, so he decided to see what it was."

Tomás had finished washing and drying the dishes and was about to hang up the towel when a movement outside caught his attention. It was Molestoso stalking something in the barnyard. He hung the towel on its nail next to the window and returned to his stool at the table. Ramon waited for him to get settled.

"He climbed down and saw that the ground near the culvert had been rutted and dug up by some animal. Something that looked like entrails had been pulled out of the earth and partially eaten. He looked around and saw a lot of freshly packed earth, and he guessed that more than one thing had been buried there. When he went into the culvert, he was amazed to find a whole butcher's shop set up, with a large wooden table, meat saws, cleavers, and knives."

Ramon leaned back and put his hands behind his head.

"I will not bore you with the rest of the details, but the *futbol* player finally made it to Valdivia and alerted the *carabineros*. He did not get fired and became something of a hero. The *carabineros* put some men out in the hills to observe the area around the culvert, and eventually they caught the perpetrators."

Tomás thought Ramon had probably learned the word perpetrators from his nightly radio programs.

"Including the rustlers, the butchers, and the trucker," Ramon went on, "it was a ring of six thieves. When the meat was butchered and ready to sell, someone would lay a branch a certain way on the side of the highway. A truck would pass through late at night, and when the driver saw the branch he would stop and pick up the meat and hides."

Later that evening they listened to Ramon's *novela,* and afterwards, when it was time to turn in, Tomás remembered the Señora's note. With the theft and Ramon's detective work, he had forgotten completely about it.

As Ramon headed for the stairs, he asked, "Would it be all right to borrow Don Pablo's saddle and bridle tomorrow? The Señora Martinez sent word asking me to come over."

"Of course."

Ramon started climbing the stairs, but stopped halfway and looked over.

"I heard about Jaime and Jorge. Do you know what that was all about?"

Tomás held his hands out to his sides, palms up.

"I have no idea."

Ramon continued up the stairs and Tomás wondered where he had heard. It was amazing how fast news traveled in the *campo*, especially when it was bad.

He left as early as he could the next day and arrived at the Martinez's house by mid morning. Tobi barked as he pulled up to the corral. He looked over and saw Jaime sitting alone at the table under the eucalyptus tree. Jaime looked at him, but didn't say a word. His left eye was swollen shut and he had his head cocked a little sideways so he could peer out of his other eye, which wasn't much better. Some hair had been shaved off of his head so that an ugly cut could be stitched. Raw abrasions with salve smeared over them covered the left side of his disfigured face, and his upper lip was split open. His left arm was in a sling and the other rested on the table. The knuckles of both hands were a bloody pulp. And Jorge was in the hospital, Tomás thought. What the hell did he look like?

The Señora hustled down the steps and came up to him.

"Thank you for coming, Don Tomás. Here, let me take Lobo for you."

She took care of the horse while he continued to stare at Jaime.

Finally he said, "I have seen you look better, Don Jaime."

Jaime tried to smile but it looked like his face hurt too much to pull it off. The Señora came up and abruptly took Tomás's arm.

"Come, Don Tomás. Let's go for a walk. There are some things I must tell you."

They headed out towards the gate and walked in silence for a couple of minutes before the Señora stopped and faced him.

"Something very bad has happened. But before I tell you, you must swear to me that you will not tell a soul."

He looked her straight in the eye.

"I swear."

She looked at him for a long moment before she nodded and took a deep breath.

"Jorge violated Lilia."

That hit him hard. Different emotions passed through Tomás in onrushing waves. He was furious—he felt sick—he felt weak—he was furious. He felt the Señora's hands cover his and he looked down. He didn't realize he had balled them into fists. He didn't know what to say. He felt so sad and sick to his stomach.

But then a wave of anger passed through him again and in a low voice he did not recognize he spit out, "That son-of-a-bitch!"

The Señora held on to his hands, a little harder now, and her eyes filled with tears. He thought that this wonderful, rock-solid pillar of a woman must be shattered inside. And Lilia? Oh God.

"How is she?" he whispered. "Was she badly hurt?"

The Señora briefly wiped at her eyes and took his arm, and they began to walk again.

"There was blood and some tearing. That is healing, but her spirit is not. She will not get out of bed. It has been almost a week now. She does not say anything. She will barely eat. She only stares. I don't know what to do. I sent you the note because I thought if you came to see her maybe it would help…"

They reached the gate and they both put their forearms on top and looked out.

After a short while the Señora said, "And there is also the chance of a baby…"

She turned to him.

"Lilia became a woman not long ago."

He looked down the road while he processed everything. They were silent. The sky was bright blue and there was a warm breeze. How could something so terrible happen here, surrounded by such calm beauty? He lightly blew out through pursed lips and looked at the Señora.

"That certainly explains what happened to Jaime. How did he find out?"

They turned around and headed back to the house.

"Lilia had gone out to bring in the sheep. There was a bad spot in our fence where the sheep had been getting out lately, and crossing over to our neighbor's land. The sheep wandered near where Jorge was cutting firewood. Lilia was gone for such a long time that I sent Jaime to look for her. He found her sitting in our stream, crying. She would not say anything to him. She would not look at him either. Jaime told her to get up and come back to the house, but she wouldn't move. So he went into the stream and picked her up. She struggled and cried the whole way back to the house.

"It didn't take long to figure out what had happened. When Jaime put her down, one of his arms had blood all over it, and her little dress had blood on it too, down below. I immediately suspected the problem and pushed him out of the kitchen so I could examine her. There was no doubt. It was obvious she had been raped. I told Jaime that Lilia had been raped and to go and get Emilio right away."

The Señora smiled sadly to herself.

"I think it is the first time that Jaime has not done what I have asked. He didn't go get Emilio. He knew that it was Jorge who raped Lilia, and he went to find him."

They arrived back at the house. Jaime was still sitting under the eucalyptus tree. The Señora and Tomás went inside, and climbed the stairs to the bedrooms. He had never been upstairs before. It was dim, and the roof angle made for a low ceiling towards the eaves. There was a single bed to their left. Straight ahead was a cord hanging from the ceiling that stretched from one gable end, where there was a small window, to a walled-off bedroom at the other. A curtain, tied to the cord, was pulled back, revealing two double beds. Lilia was in the double bed nearest the window, where pale shafts of morning light just reached her. One of her eyes was swollen and black and blue. Rosa and Ana were sitting on chairs next to her. They got up and sadly faced them.

The Señora said, "Don Tomás has come to visit you, Lilia."

Lilia did not move and she did not look his way. She only stared at the ceiling. Rosa and Ana squeezed by them and headed to the stairs. Both lightly touched Tomás's forearm when they passed, as if to thank him for coming. The Señora moved to the foot of the bed while he sat next to Lilia and thought hard about what to say. He tried a light approach.

"Lilia, what are you doing in bed this time of day? It is so beautiful outside. The *mora* are fat and black and I thought if I came over you would want to pick some with me. This is no day for you to be lazy and stay in bed."

She turned slowly towards him. There was no emotion, no connection. She looked through and past him. It broke his heart. He looked up at the Señora and her eyes were full again and she had a hand covering her mouth. He looked back to Lilia.

"I am so sorry about what has happened Lilia. But you must be strong and get better and…"

He moved his hand and laid it gently on her thin forearm. When he touched her, her eyes panicked and she flinched and jerked her arm away. She moved away from him and began to shake. He was shocked.

"I am sorry, Lilia," he said as softly as he could. "I did not mean to frighten you. I will not touch you again, I promise."

He turned helplessly back to the Señora.

"Now you see, Don Tomás. She is the same with all of us. I do not know what to do. I do not know if she even knows who we are."

They turned back to Lilia and silently watched her.

After a time, the Señora sighed and said, "But come, Don Tomás. Come downstairs and let me make you something to eat."

"Thank you, but if it is all right, I would like to stay with Lilia."

She nodded and went downstairs. Tomás didn't say a word as he watched Lilia stare at the ceiling.

After a while he said, "Lilia, I want you to know that I love you very much and I would never do anything to harm you. You are the little sister I never had and it hurts me to see you like this."

Lilia turned towards him again. He wasn't sure if she even understood him.

"Everyone here loves you very much and we all want you to get better. But you have to try. I know it will be hard, but try to forget what has happened and think only of the love your family and I have for you. You are far away from us. Please come back."

He wanted so much to stroke her head and brush her hair back away from her face, but he didn't dare.

Finally he stood up.

"Lilia, I will go now. But I will return soon. Maybe then you can pick *mora* with me."

He smiled down at her but there was still no response. He turned and headed down the stairs. The Señora met him at the landing. Rosa and Ana were behind her. He shook his head. They walked slowly towards the kitchen, but he stopped by the front door.

The Señora asked, "Won't you have lunch with us, Don Tomás? Emilio should be returning soon."

He did not think he could sit through a meal surrounded by such sadness. And he could imagine how Emilio was taking all this.

"No thank you, Señora. But I do want to go out and talk with your son."

"Yes. That would be good. Thank you for coming."

They hugged goodbye. He stepped out into the bright sunlight and headed over to Jaime. He sat down at the little table and looked at him. Jaime made another attempt to smile and then turned his head towards the pasture. Tomás wondered if he could see any of it. They sat there in silence.

Eventually Jaime turned towards him and said, "I almost killed him, Don Tomás. It was very close. If Papa had not arrived, Jorge would be dead."

He turned towards the pasture again.

"When Mama said Lilia had been raped, I knew it was Jorge. It had to be. I knew how he has looked at my sisters, and I have kept my eye on him. But Lilia? I never even thought that possible. She is so young…"

Tomás remembered Jorge closely watching Lilia in her little polka dot dress as she passed them on her way to the tournament.

"I ran to where he was working. He was stacking firewood and had his back to me. When he heard me, he turned and saw me running towards him, and he did not seem surprised. He looked from me to where he had left his axe and he started for it. But I leaped on him and I started to choke him. I wanted to kill him, Don Tomás.

"We fell over the cordwood pile and I landed on top of him. I grabbed a piece of firewood and struck him as hard as I could on the head. But he is such an animal! It was like he didn't feel it, and he is so strong. He got the firewood away from me and wrestled me until he was on top, and then he hit me, again and again. They were like hammer blows and I weakened fast. He had a knee on each of my arms. Then he began to laugh. He laughed at me!"

The fury came into Jaime's face as he relived the moment.

"He laughed and spit in my face. He said, 'How delicious, your little sister—so tight and oh so sweet. I already want her again. But maybe when I am done with you I will go up and fuck Rosa and Ana instead.'"

Jaime exhaled and somehow a couple of tears found their way out of his swollen eyes.

"I went crazy. Somehow I wiggled and bucked and found a strength I did not know I had. I freed an arm and felt around for something to strike him with. I found a thin, jagged chip of firewood, and as he bent close to try to hold me down again, I stabbed him in the eye. He screamed and released me and covered his eye with his hands. I scrambled free and grabbed a big piece of firewood. As he began to get up, I struck him on the side of his head. But he didn't go down. He bellowed like a bull and charged me. But I had the madness now and I struck him and struck him, staying on his blind side. There was blood pouring from everywhere on his face. He pulled a piece of wood from the pile and swung and hit me on my shoulder."

Jaime glanced to his arm in the sling.

"I felt it crack, but that just made me madder and I hit him again and again until he went down. Then I jumped on him. I wanted to strike him with my fists. I wanted to feel my hurting him. I hit him until he didn't move. Finally I stood up and caught my breath. And then, God forgive me, I went over and got his axe. I was going to split him in half..."

Jaime looked at Tomás with a grim smile.

"But that is when Papa arrived and stopped me."

Tomás did not know what to say. Jaime turned toward the pasture again.

"I am so scared, Don Tomás," he said softly. "There is a good chance that Jorge will die and I am scared that the *carabineros* will throw me in prison. I am scared that I will be taken away from my family and will not be able to help Papa on the farm. And I am so scared for Lilia. You have seen her now. She is broken and I do not know if she can be fixed."

Tomás shook his head.

"I can't believe the *carabineros* would arrest you. Not for something like this. Jorge raped a twelve-year-old girl. I don't think there is a judge or a jury in my country that would ever send a man—especially the girl's brother—to jail for what you did. And here in Chile? *Por Dios, hombre,* children here are sacred. What Jorge has done is the worst of crimes."

"I hope you are right, Don Tomás."

Tomás was not religious, but he said, "I will pray for you. For you and for Lilia."

They sat in silence for a few minutes before he told Jaime to heal quickly and that he should be going. He said that he would be back soon to see how he and Lilia were doing. Jaime thanked him for coming and Tomás left him under the eucalyptus tree. He mounted Lobo and slowly headed down towards the highway, his head full of the violence and injustice of the world.

CHAPTER FOURTEEN

La Fiesta (The Festival)

Three days after his trip to see Lilia, Tomás was hacking at some firewood near the *fogon* when he heard the dog bark. He went around the house to take a look and Ramon came out the front door. An overweight boy was coming up to the house with oxen and cart. In the middle of the cart was his saddle.

"Gordo," Ramon said, smiling as he came down the steps, "I see you have solved the mystery."

Tomás joined Ramon at the foot of the porch stairs. The boy stopped the oxen a few feet away and leaned the *garrocha* against the yoke. When he smiled, his plump round cheeks compressed his eyes into slits. Nicknames like *gordo* and *flaco*—skinny—often replaced first names and were used with no slur.

Ramon shook the boy's hand and introduced him.

"Gordo is my nephew, Don Tomás—my brother Ricardo's second son.

He turned to his nephew.

"Gordo, go sit on the bench in the shade while I fetch some *chicha dulce* from the cellar. You must tell us what has happened."

Ramon returned with a wine bottle full of *chicha* and three glasses. He filled Gordo's glass first, and the boy took a long drink before beginning his story.

"My brother and I kept a close eye on the *trabajador* like we said we would, *Tio*, and yesterday we saw him walk down towards the highway carrying a small bundle wrapped in brown paper. Miguel and I went to tell Papa and he said we should search the worker's shack. So we rushed over and at first we didn't find anything. But the dirt under his cot looked new so we dug into it."

Gordo took another drink and looked at Tomás.

"We found your saddle and bridle, all wrapped up in burlap bags, buried there. When we told Papa, he said we had to get word to the *carabineros* before the thief disappeared in Valdivia. He sent Miguel to the Casa Blanca school to notify the teacher there, who has a little pick-up truck. Papa thought he could drive in and notify the authorities. But on his way down to the school, my brother learned that the man had hitched a ride on a firewood truck and was already headed to town. There was no time to lose, so Miguel ran the rest of the way to Casa Blanca and told the *Profesor*. He closed the school right away and left for Valdivia. He passed the old firewood truck on the way, and alerted the *carabineros* on the outskirts of town. When the *carabineros* nabbed the man they opened up the bundle he was carrying, and found your *manta*, Don Tomás. When they asked him about the saddle, he said that if a saddle had been discovered in his shack, he had no idea how it had gotten there. He said that the *manta* was his and he had bundled it up to make it easier to carry. The *carabineros* want you to come in and identify the *manta* right away, Don Tomás."

Tomás was amazed at the efforts made on his behalf.
And grateful.

"I will go in first thing tomorrow, Gordo. Thank
you. You and your brother were very clever. Please
thank both your brother and father for me."

Gordo smiled proudly and his eyes were slits again.

Tomás took the early bus to Valdivia the next morning, marveling at how well the *campo* network worked.
At the same time, he wondered what would happen to
the thief. He was not here to put poor people behind
bars, and the *trabajador* was dirt poor. What chances
had he ever had? Yet there were other poor, hardworking people who had never resorted to stealing.
And what about the embarrassment of Ramon and
Ricardo for their community? He recalled Ramon's
angry words when he said "Our community will not
stand for this." There was a good chance too that
this man was responsible for several missing animals.
Tomás's thoughts shifted to Jaime and he wondered
if the *carabineros* had come for him. Maybe he was in
the same jail.

He walked to the jail from the bus station and
was ushered into a large, windowless room with a single desk and two long wooden benches. A sergeant
in a brown woolen uniform sat at the desk. His white
leather belt and holster were polished to such a lus-
ter that they looked more like plastic than leather. He
sent a corporal out through a rear door to get the suspect. When he returned with the man, the corporal
was holding a *manta de Castilla* under his arm.

The man was about Tomás's height, with long black
hair. At first he wouldn't look at Tomás, but when he
did, Tomás saw that he had a mustache and an angry-
looking scar across his nose. Tomás was reminded of
his attacker from Lote Once. The man was about the

right height and had the same hair and a mustache—plus his nose looked like it had been crushed.

The sergeant said, "This is the man who works at the Perez farm and a saddle was discovered under his bed. The school teacher from Casa Blanca told me that the saddle is yours. Is that true?"

"Yes. It was issued to me by the Peace Corps and was stolen along with my horse when I was at a *futbol* tournament. The horse came back by himself the next day, without the saddle. The saddle was returned to me yesterday and is at the farm of Don Pablo and Don Ramon Rodriguez. If you would like verification that it is mine, you can call the Peace Corps secretary, Sra. Elsa, or stop by to talk to her at the office on Calle Picarte."

"That will not be necessary, at least for now. We were also told that your *manta de Castilla* was stolen. This man says that this one is his. Can you somehow identify it as yours?"

Nodding toward the suspect, Tomás asked, "Can he? Is there some way he can positively identify it?"

The sergeant turned to the man.

"Well, can you?"

The man looked defiant.

He shook his head and said, "There is no way to identify it—it is just a *manta de Castilla* I have had for a year or so."

Tomás wondered what they did to punish thieves here. He turned from the suspect to the sergeant.

"If it is mine, it will have a little 'G' on the reverse side of the label below the collar."

The sergeant walked over to the corporal, who unfolded the manta.

The suspect blurted out, "That's right. I forgot about that." Turning to Tomás, he asked, "How did you know about that?"

The corporal found the label and turned it over to show the sergeant, who nodded.

The sergeant asked, "What does the 'G' stand for?"

"*Gringo.*"

The suspect said, "No it doesn't. It stands for *guapo.*"

The sergeant looked at him and laughed.

"Sure it does. And I suppose 'handsome' refers to you?"

But the thief persisted.

"It belongs to me, I tell you. It's his word against mine."

Tomás had to admit the guy had balls. He had an idea.

"Sergeant, why not get us each a piece of paper and we will make 'Gs' and you can compare them to the one on the *manta.*"

"I don't think that is necessary, Sr. Young."

"Please do it."

The sergeant nodded to the corporal who got pens and paper. Tomás wrote his capitals with a swirly backwards slant and knew that the other guy wouldn't come close. But that is not why he wanted the man to make his 'G.' Tomás watched as he awkwardly scratched out his letter. The man was left handed. Tomás would bet anything this was the man who had attacked him in Lote Once. The sergeant showed the man Tomás's 'G' and the one on the *manta.* The thief looked down at the floor.

The sergeant asked, "Do you want to press charges, Sr. Young?"

Tomás looked from the thief to the sergeant and back to the thief.

"Do I want to press charges? Yes sergeant, I certainly do."

The horse race with Manuel loomed on Tomás's horizon like an exam he was unprepared for. It was approaching way too quickly. He was busy with the road project and playing in *futbol* tournaments. Plus, he had initiated a new food-for-reforestation program where the farmers would receive Alliance for Progress food— flour, powdered milk, vegetable oil, and margarine—for their work. There would be many new farmers planting this winter, including Pablo and Ramon. Ramon would also receive an extra share for bringing up the food by oxcart and doling it out to the various farmers.

One day slipped into the next. He was visiting different farms almost every day, and before he knew it the fiesta and horserace were only three weeks away. He had visited the Martinez family a few times and, thank God, Lilia was not pregnant and Jaime did not go to jail. Indeed, after the *carabineros* saw Jaime's condition and tried to ask Lilia some questions, they wanted the family to press charges against Jorge. But they refused; they did not want the rape to be public news. They also knew that if Jorge went to prison, it would be his death warrant—there was no way he would survive once the prisoners learned of his crime. The Señora felt that Jorge had been punished enough; he had lost his eye, and his brain was damaged after so many blows to the head. And he would never be able to return to Cufeo because word, of course, did get out, and everyone knew what he had done. Even with an addled brain, Jorge knew enough to never set foot in Cufeo again.

Other than a few ugly scars, Jaime healed, but Lilia did not. Her wounds were too deep and there was very little progress. The last time Tomás visited, Lilia was gone.

The Señora explained, "We took her to live with Emilio's parents in Osorno because we thought there were too many things here that reminded her of what

happened. And there is a special doctor there who might
help. And maybe when she can go to school again..."
Her voice trailed off and she looked miserable. Lilia's
absence was huge. The light of her presence may have
dimmed after the rape, but there had always been hope.
Now that she was gone, there was no light at all.

Maria Elena opened up a savings account in
Valdivia for the road project and she made all of the
deposits. The bank balance was becoming respectable as, little by little, the proceeds from various activities added up.

Last weekend had been the La Paloma soccer
tournament, and Maria Elena was expecting Manuel
to bring her the proceeds. But Manuel didn't show
up, and Tomás began to get a bad feeling. Manuel
had been quite drunk at the tournament and had irri-
tated several *campesinos* by urging them to spend lots of
money for 'his' road project. He had strutted around
like a drunken, puffed-up banty rooster, and Tomás
had found the scene embarrassing.

Tomás decided to pay a visit to Manuel to find out
what was up. He saddled Lobo and headed out, but
before turning off the main road, he visited the Señora
who had run the concession stand. He wanted to know
for sure that Manuel had been given the tournament
money. He found the Señora in front of her house
with a sturdy homemade broom, sweeping the barnyard free of firewood chips, small branches, and pig
and chicken excrement. She was short and shapeless
in her thick dark sweater and broad skirt. Only a small
amount of swarthy leg was visible above her white socks,
and her thick leather work shoes did not have laces.
A man's wide-brimmed hat was tilted back away from
her forehead. Her high cheekbones and her smooth,
taut skin hinted at Mapuche heritage.

She stopped sweeping and smiled up at him. Tomás did not get off of his horse. They greeted each other and chatted about the weather and the local gossip for a little while. She walked over to the porch, laid the broom against a post, and picked up a pot full of potato peelings from a bench. She began to scatter the peelings for the chickens as they continued to talk. The chickens fought over the scraps. One had a particularly large piece and Tomás watched as two others chased it around and around the barnyard, trying to take it away. The conversation turned to the recent tournament and he asked how the concession stand had done.

She smiled proudly and said, "Very well. I do not know if everyone is drinking and eating more these days, or if they just want to help the road project, but we sold many *empanadas* and a lot of wine...."

She paused and her smile faded.

"Some though—especially Don Manuel—drank too much. That was not so good."

"Do you have any idea how much money you made?"

"Yes, to the *centavo*. Wait a moment and I will tell you exactly."

She carried the empty pot into the house and he heard her open and close a drawer.

She returned with paper in hand saying, "I walked down to give the money to Don Manuel early Sunday morning, but he was still asleep because he was so pickled the night before. So I gave the money to his Señora. Let me see. After all the expenses, we were left with eighteen hundred and thirty-three *escudos* and forty-five *centavos*."

"*Por Dios*, that is wonderful. That is the most for any tournament so far this summer. Maria Elena will be very happy, and it certainly will make the road account look better."

The Señora looked surprised and then asked suspiciously, "Maria Elena has not received the money yet?"

Oops, he thought. He backpedaled. He did not want to raise any flags—especially since he had no idea if there was cause for alarm.

"Oh, I am not sure. I have not seen her this week but I know she will be excited that the tournament brought in so much."

The Señora and Tomás exchanged a few more pleasantries before he took his leave. Riding away, he thought it interesting that she had kept such detailed records of the money. He wondered if it was because she did not trust Manuel. Tomás was beginning to see the man from others' eyes now and it seemed like a very good idea to know exactly what the tournament's proceeds had been.

He rode down the hill to Manuel's farm. He was relieved to see a horse saddled and tied up in front and smoke coming out of the chimney. As he approached, Manuel came out of the door, wearing spurs. He did not look good, and he certainly was not his garrulous self. He even looked a little nervous.

"Don Tomás, what can I do for you?"

Tomás did not receive the customary invitation to dismount but he did so anyway.

"Good morning, Don Manuel. I had hoped that I would find you home."

Still speaking abruptly, Manuel said, "You are lucky. I have just returned from some business I had in Valdivia."

"Aah," Tomás said. "That explains it then."

"Explains what? Here, let me take your horse."

As Manuel reached for the reins, Tomás could see that his hands were shaking. He took that as a bad sign.

"It explains why you have not brought the tournament money over to Maria Elena."

"Oh that....well, er...I plan on taking it over later this week."

He looked very nervous now. The door opened and the Señora came out and coldly nodded good day to Tomás. She did not invite him in; the atmosphere was icy indeed.

"Good morning, Señora," Tomás said politely, tipping his hat.

She nodded again but was quiet. Tomás turned back to Manuel.

"Don Manuel, it is Friday—it IS the end of the week."

Manuel looked a little startled. Possibly he did not realize what day it was—another bad sign.

"But don't worry. If you give the money to me now, I can take it to Maria Elena so that she can deposit it on Monday."

Tomás had never seen Manuel at a loss for words before.

He opened his mouth, then shut it, opened it again, hesitated, and finally said, looking utterly miserable, "I do not have all of it, Don Tomás."

Tomás thought he would find this out all along, but the reality still hit him hard. Now what was he supposed to do?

"What do you mean, Don Manuel?"

He became belligerent.

"What do you think I mean? I mean I do not have it all. I spent some of it in Valdivia."

Tomás just looked at Manuel. He could feel the eyes of the Señora boring into him.

After a few moments, Manuel continued.

"I...well...er...I spent some of it on some wine and things...."

God, Tomás hated this. What a situation. How was he supposed to deal with someone at least twenty years his senior who had ripped off his community? And he was a member of the Road Committee. If this got out, it would jeopardize the whole project. It was a huge betrayal of the community's trust and hard work. There was absolutely no justification.

"And how much is 'some of it?'" Tomás asked in an even tone.

"Maybe half."

He went over and sat on a bench, looking up at Tomás while resting his forearms on his knees. The Señora remained at the door, glaring at Tomás with bulging eyes. She looked like she was ready to explode.

"That is a lot of wine, Don Manuel."

Manuel looked at him, calculating for a second or two, and then his eyes took on a furtive look.

He waved his hand in a cavalier dismissal and, not looking Tomás in the eye, said, "Oh, it was not so much."

"Really, Don Manuel?"

Tomás knew what he was up to.

"Let me see. I am pretty good with numbers. Half of eighteen hundred and thirty three *escudos* and forty-five *centavos* would be approximately nine hundred and seventeen *escudos*. That, Don Manuel, is one hell of a lot of wine to drink in four days."

Manuel was no dummy. He knew now that Tomás had suspected something all along. He sighed and stared down towards the rough plank deck. His Señora, meanwhile, erupted and rushed at Tomás. She stopped as Tomás held his ground and looked at her coldly.

"Yes, Señora?"

"How dare you come here and confront my husband!"

He did not say anything.

"He is a hardworking man."

Maybe when Manuel was not drinking or talking, Tomás thought. But that was not fair. He knew Manuel was hardworking. It was just that he could not control his drinking, and it had seriously affected his judgment.

"How much real work have you ever done? Eh? Let me see your hands."

She reached for them and Tomás let her turn them over. She was surprised that there were some calluses. Thank God he helped Ramon split wood at the farm, he thought.

"Hmmph! I guess you have done a little work," she admitted grudgingly and abruptly let go of his hands.

He slowly lowered them.

"Señora, we are all born into different situations in life and some certainly do have it easier than others. I do not deny that. But there is one thing we can all have if we try hard enough. And that is honesty and honor."

He turned to Manuel.

"Don Manuel, I expect you to pay back all of that money and to deliver it to Maria Elena by next Wednesday. If you do that, then I promise that this will remain just between the three of us. I will tell no one."

Manuel, looking desperate and holding his hands out to the side, said, "But where am I supposed to get it? Tell me that."

"That, Don Manuel, is your problem, not mine. You have betrayed your community and your friends. If I were you, I would find the money somewhere—any-where—and make it right."

"And if I do not?"

Tomás looked him straight in the eye. He hoped Manuel believed him because he meant it from the tip of his toes to the top of his head.

"Then, Don Manuel, I will ride to every house in Cufeo—from Lote Once to Los Guindos—and I will tell everyone that our little *carrera* has been cancelled. And I will also explain why—that I will not race against a man who is a thief and who has betrayed the confidence and trust which his community has placed in him. You can say whatever you want to whomever you want to try to justify what you have done. You can also decide who you think the community will believe. But by next Wednesday, Don Manuel, or I will start riding early on Thursday morning."

Tomás glanced from him to the Señora, who was now looking slumped and resigned. Without saying goodbye, Tomás mounted his horse and left.

That night Tomás was quieter than usual. After dinner and his *novela,* Ramon turned off the radio and asked him if something was wrong. Tomás wanted to tell him about Manuel but he could not. Manuel's absconding with the funds, though, was not the only thing on his mind. During the long ride home, he had thought hard about the race and decided that he didn't want to just put in an appearance—he wanted to be competitive. Manuel had certainly provided him with plenty of motivation.

"No, Don Ramon, nothing is wrong, although I guess I do worry some about the race." He hesitated a second or two before he added, "Don Claudio told me that you used to race in the *carreras* when you were younger."

"Yes, that is true. I raced many times."

"He also told me that you raced against Don Manuel."

"That is also true," he said without inflection.

"Is there any way that Salton and I can beat him?"

He smiled softly and a little sadly, Tomás thought, before answering.

"Do you want the truth, Don Tomás?"

"Of course."

"No… not unless something very unusual happens… like his horse stumbles or maybe if there is a lot of rain and the track is pure mud. Then Salton's strength could be an equalizer. But in good conditions—and believe me I am sorry to say this—your chances are not good at all."

Tomás expected that answer, but he would not leave it at that.

"Don Ramon, even though my chances are not good, I want to try to win that race. Will you help me?"

To Tomás's surprise, Ramon leaned back on his stool and laughed loudly and heartily. Tomás was taken aback. He may not have a chance in the damn race but that didn't mean it was something to laugh at.

Ramon must have read his thoughts because he stopped laughing quickly and, after wiping his eyes, said, "Don Tomás, I am not laughing at you. It is that niece of mine," and he started chuckling again.

What did Maria Elena have to do with this?

"I owe her two liters of *chicha* now," he said, shaking his head. "Over a month ago she bet me some of her *ulmo* honey against the *chicha* that you would decide to get serious about this race and ask for my help. Because you never brought the subject up at all, I thought the bet was a good one. But, damn, I was wrong. It seems that she knows you pretty well. *Por Dios*, I am tired of losing bets to her. It seems that she always wins."

Ramon leaned forward and put his thick forearms on the table, suddenly serious.

"I would be happy to help you, Don Tomás. Nothing would make me happier than if you beat Don Manuel. But I want you to understand that even with much preparation—and time is getting short—your chances are not good at all. He is an excellent rider and even though he and his horse are not as young as they were, they both have a lot of experience. And Salton is very young and inexperienced—both of you are."

"I know all this, but I want to try."

Ramon looked at him for a few moments.

"That is what Maria Elena told me. She said that no matter what the odds were, it was in your nature to try to win. It would give me great pleasure to help you. But it is late and we should go to bed. Tomorrow when we drink our *mate* we will make a plan."

Ramon got up from his stool, lit a Nescafe-can kerosene light, grabbed the chamber pot, and headed up the steep stairs. Tomás took the table lamp and went out to his sheep pelts and sleeping bag.

The next morning was cool for summer, and Tomás did not want to leave his warm bag. When he finally did get up and stumbled into the kitchen, he found it toasty warm, and Ramon was sipping his *mate* at the table. Tomás shuffled over to the sink. He did not know why he felt so tired. He ladled cold water into the tin wash basin and splashed it on his face. When he joined Ramon at the table, Ramon was all business.

"I thought a lot about it in bed last night, and the first thing we have to do is get some oats for Salton. If you bring a sack from Valdivia, I will meet you at the bus with both horses and Salton can start his training by carrying his oats back up to the farm."

He pulled the kerchief out of his back pocket. Using it as a potholder to open the oven door, he kneeled down, peered in at his bread, and poked and turned it this way and that. With the blade of a large kitchen knife he tilted it up off the rack, and then shook his head when he saw the bottom.

"Aii, it is only cooking on the top again."

Using a special little shovel, he ladled coals from the firebox into the oven directly below the bread, and shut the oven door. Tomás waited for him to sit back down so he could prepare his *mate*—the kitchen was too narrow to get past him while he was checking his bread.

"We will start him on a kilo of oats a day and then increase it little by little as we exercise him. By the end of his training he should get two kilos in the morning and two at night. What farms do you have to visit in the next couple of weeks, Don Tomás?"

"I am pretty well caught up, but I do have to make at least two trips to Casa Blanca."

"Good. Then we will have plenty of time to work with Salton. I think the trips to Casa Blanca will be a good first step in his training."

"Why?" Tomás asked, while filling his *mate* cup with steaming water.

"There are level stretches of road and long easy hills over there. Here the hills are too steep. I will draw you a map to show you where you should alternately run and walk him. By galloping him up the long hills and then walking the level areas, it will build up his strength without tiring him too much. We will have Salton do at least a week of that before we even think of putting him on the track."

Ramon walked over to the far kitchen door and went outside. He split some wood and soon returned with an armful which he dumped into the empty box next to the stove. He opened the firebox door and after pushing the coals around, stoked the stove. The bread smelled wonderful. Drinking *mate* on an empty stomach was not the best thing to do because it was so high in caffeine. Tomás was getting a little wired and his armpits had started to sweat—'*mate*-pit,' he called it. Ramon checked his bread again; it was ready, so he pulled it out. He placed the round loaf on a small board and brought it over to the table. He let it cool for a few minutes while he ground up some hot peppers with a mortar and pestle, and prepared a bowl of his spicy-hot *pebre* sauce. After he sliced the bread, Tomás reached for a piece and dipped it into his sauce. He took a bite. And then had a sip of *mate*. Heaven. He wondered which he liked more—*mate* with oven-fresh bread dipped in Ramon's sauce, or with Maria Elena's hot *sopaipilla* and honey.

"After those sessions," Ramon said as he also dipped a thick slice and took a bite, "we will get you accustomed to riding on a *pellon*. It is good that the race will be here in Caman so we can go out onto the track and practice whenever we want. Once both you and Salton are accustomed to the *pellon*, then you and I will begin racing—with me on Lobo. But we must be sure to always do that when it starts to get dark."

"Why so late?"

"Because Salton has never raced and no one knows what to expect of him. You don't want to give anything away. Certainly the odds are not good, but with the bloodline of your horse, he might surprise us. So I think the plan should be to work Salton hard for the next two weeks. First we train him in Casa Blanca, then on the track with Lobo, and then we will begin to cut back to only light exercise. By then—with luck—both of you will be ready."

Over the next two and a half weeks, Tomás did exactly what Ramon prescribed. He brought up the grain, he exercised Salton on the Casa Blanca hills, and after a few rides he felt completely comfortable with only the sheep pelt for a saddle. There were no stirrups, so it was basically like riding bareback, which was fun at a full gallop. It was only when he tried to rein Salton in that he had a problem. It was tough to pull the reins without stirrups to brace himself with, and he ended up bouncing awkwardly against Salton's broad neck as they slowed down. But other than that, it all went fairly well except for the starts. They practiced that over and over again.

It was an interesting side note to the *carrera* that Salton's father—the 'big gray'—would be racing at the same track on the same day. Unfortunately, as Ramon and Tomás quickly learned, Salton, like his father, was slow coming off the line. They worked and worked on the starts but it didn't change. Ramon would gauge if they were 'nose to nose' when they passed the starting line. If they were, he would give a shout and they would race the full length of the track. Lobo always jumped to a full-length lead. Salton just couldn't get into a low enough gear. He always caught up with Lobo, but Tomás could never make him pass either. Tomás thought that maybe Salton was content to only go neck-and-neck with his pasture mate. On a couple of evenings they switched horses to see if Ramon could get anything more out of Salton, but he could not get Salton to pass the smaller horse either. When they finished their last practice before the race and were walking the horses back to the farm, Ramon shook his head sadly.

"Maybe with a *huasca* we could get him to run faster, although I never liked using one. A rider should be able to communicate with his animal without a whip. But what worries me most is that he does not seem to have the spirit of his father. Who knows? Maybe if he races another horse besides Lobo he might want to go faster. I know he can run much faster. I know it! But I cannot make him. I am sorry. I have failed you."

"Please do not say you are sorry, Don Ramon. I am so grateful for all the time you have spent helping me. If Salton doesn't want to run, then so be it. It has nothing to do with you."

They reached the gate. Ramon unhooked the latch and swung it open.

"And, believe me, no one will be surprised if Salton and I do not do well."

Ramon, however, kept shaking his head. Tomás was not so happy either, and God knew he was dreading the race. Manuel had delivered every last *centavo* to Maria Elena, which was great. But Tomás had seen him twice since then, once on the bus to town and once when they passed on the La Paloma road. Not only did Manuel not greet him, but he did not look at him either. Tomás knew that when they raced, Manuel would show no mercy, and would do his absolute best to make Tomás look bad in front of all of Cufeo.

Oso was the first Peace Corps volunteer to arrive, and he pitched his tent two days before the fiesta. He helped Tomás greet and settle the others as they showed up at the farm. Together they organized the volunteers into a cheerful workgroup to help with last minute preparations. Central Caman was buzzing with activity and Tomás was too busy to be nervous about the race. Oxcarts were bringing food, wine, and building materials. Two large *ramadas* were cleverly constructed using the soccer goals as part of the framing. There was also the *ramada* that had been built earlier in the summer for the soccer tournament. Holes were dug and outhouses were built over them. Barbecue pits were prepared, and wood was stacked alongside. Lanterns were hung over the school deck for the musicians, and tables, benches, and chairs were arranged around a large open area for dancing in front of the deck.

Seventeen volunteers had arrived from all over Chile, and Ramon's pasture was dotted with their brightly-colored nylon tents. The little tent city could be clearly seen from the road, and had become quite the attraction. Tomás had not seen most of the volunteers since his training, and it was fun to catch up. They were very much impressed by his job site, and one after another told him that he was living the Peace Corps experience they had always imagined but had come to believe did not really exist.

After cooking dinner on an assortment of high-tech campstoves, the volunteers bought liters of *chicha* from Ramon. Tomás showed them how to play *tejo*, a cross between horseshoes and quoits. Years ago, Pablo and Ramon had set up *tejo* pits beside their house, and Javier and Alex liked to play whenever they were around. The game was simple. Two boxes set on the ground, forty feet apart. Each box was about a meter square and was filled with clay soil. A string was stretched taut across the middle. The object was to toss discs made of lead from one box to the other, trying to get closest to the string. Water was sprinkled on the clay soil to soften it so the discs would stick where they landed.

Tomás stole off quietly just before dark to find Salton and exercise him lightly, one last time, at the track. He rode bareback instead of bothering with the *pellon*. As they went through their paces, Tomás thought that maybe he could not communicate with Salton as well as some riders might, but after all the time they had spent together lately, at least they were on the same page. He had gotten into the habit of talking to Salton, and he told him that tomorrow was the big day and he hoped that the horse was less nervous than he was. And that he would try to do his best. Salton's ears always pivoted around when Tomás talked to him, as if he were really listening. Tomás grained him, and set him free for the night. He watched him amble off to find Lobo. Thinking about the race, he stood there, bridle in hand, for a long time.

Tomás tossed and turned and took forever to fall asleep. He had just conked out when he was awakened by the sound of rain lightly tapping the wood shake roof. He opened his eyes and looked up at the dark ceiling, wondering if the rain would make a difference in the race. More importantly, he hoped the weather would clear for the fiesta. Everyone had worked so hard; they did not need foul weather to keep people at home. He fell back asleep but not for long. He was awakened again, this time by the feeble crow of Ramon's old rooster.

He got up thinking that, for once, he had risen before Ramon. But as he entered the kitchen, there he was, lighting the fire in the stove.

"Good morning, Don Tomás," he said with a smile. "All ready for the big day?"

"I hope so."

He walked to the sink and splashed cold water on his face. That was usually a jolt, but he was already so wound up that he hardly felt it. He took the tin drinking cup from the shelf, filled it, and headed outside to brush his teeth. The ground was wet but it was no longer raining. He walked around the corner of the house to where he could see the tents. Some of them sagged a little from getting wet and there was no activity yet. He turned to look at the volcanoes to the east. The view always changed with the weather. This morning was one of those beautiful, fanciful vistas where thick billowy fog had settled into the valleys between the steep, dark hills. The volcanoes Choschuenco and Puntiagudo loomed faintly on the horizon. Snow had fallen there, brushing them with white that was just a shade off from the pale sky. It gave the volcanoes a spectral air. Ramon had told him that on mornings like these, the fog would always burn off by midday and the sun would come out in full force. It was going to be a beautiful day for the fiesta.

He was not hungry but forced himself to eat with Ramon and the rest of the family who had come up for the big event. After breakfast he went outside and walked to the gate to see what was happening. He gazed over at the school where there was a bustle of activity. Women were busy lighting charcoal fires in the *ramadas,* and Maria Elena was heading towards one of the soccer-goal *ramadas,* carrying a large wicker basket that was covered with a white cloth. Several men stood around drinking *mate* and staring, mesmerized, at roaring fires in the barbecue pits. Every now and then one of them would reach for a piece of firewood and throw it on. Sparks would shoot fifteen feet up in the air. There was plenty of movement on the roads too. He could see people descending by horse and foot from Casa Blanca and La Paloma. A firewood truck full of people standing in the back, arrived from the highway.

Oso appeared from behind him and leaned up against the gate. Maria Elena saw them and waved. She brushed her hands off and wiped them on her apron. Saying something to a woman next to her, she took off her apron, laid it on the counter, and headed their way. She was intercepted by two men on horseback and stopped to talk to them.

Tomás turned to Oso.

"I want to thank you for helping to organize the volunteers into that work crew. It was a big help and I know everyone was appreciative."

Oso dismissed that with a wave of his hand.

"They are pretty impressed with the whole scene here. But I'll tell you what. Not one of them, including me, would like to be in your shoes today."

He stuck out his hand which Tomás took.

"Good luck, Tomás."

"Thanks, Oso."

Maria Elena broke away from the riders and approached the gate.

"You two gentlemen seem a little serious this morning." Holding her hands up to the sky, she beamed, "The sun is already trying to look down on us. It is going to be a beautiful day for the fiesta."

Maria Elena's hair looked recently braided. It was pulled tightly back from her face and her skin shone. Tomás thought she looked absolutely beautiful. Apparently Oso did too because he became tongue-tied when he asked her how the preparations were going. Maria Elena teased him and asked if maybe he had drunk too much hard *chicha* last night.

"And you, Tomás. I hope you are clear headed. Are you ready for your race?"

"I guess I am as ready as I'll ever be. But I hope you did not bet any *ulmo* honey on the outcome."

Maria Elena blushed.

"I have to admit, though, I wish Don Pedro had never come up with his idea."

Tomás saw Juan pull into the soccer field. His oxcart was laden with the carcasses of several lambs ready for the spits. He must have been up slaughtering at first light. Maria Elena saw him too.

"Oh! I'd better get my apron back on and help Juan. And the women."

But before she left, she moved closer to Tomás; her hands on the gate were inches from his and her face not more than a foot away. She smiled so softly into his eyes that he felt he would melt.

"Tomás, ride well and ride safe. I wish you luck."

He could not have looked away even if he had wanted to, lost as he was in her gaze. He barely managed to thank her.

She held his eyes for a few more moments before saying, "I must get to work."

"And I must grain Salton."

"And time for some breakfast," Oso said. "I'm as hungry as a bear."

The rest of the morning Tomás spent alone, except for when he went with Ramon to inspect the track. They walked the length of it and Ramon kicked at the surface in a couple places. It was definitely soft.

"It is really going to be important to try to get Salton off quickly. If you fall too far behind you will, believe me, be eating mud today. Are you nervous, Don Tomás?"

"Damn right I am."

"Are you scared?" he asked.

Tomás thought about that for a second or two.

"No...I don't think so. But I do have a serious case of the *mariposas*."

Ramon looked baffled. Tomás explained the expression of 'having butterflies.'

"Well, that is okay. But you do not want to be scared. Remember that a horse can feel what you are feeling and if you are scared, then he will be on edge and less confident. But if he feels your excitement and positive energy, then that is much better."

They returned to the farm. Tomás waved to a couple of volunteers who shouted good luck. Ramon said, "I have to give mash to the pigs and then I will put on my good clothes for the fiesta. In an hour or so you should get Salton and we will exercise him very lightly. We can go to the rear pasture where there is enough room. When it is time for the race, I will go over to the starting line with you."

Tomás felt a lump in his throat. Ramon had helped him so much for this race that Tomás wanted to do well as much as for him as for himself. He thanked Ramon again for all his help.

After they exercised Salton, they checked and adjusted the *pellon* one last time. Tomás tried to make light conversation with Ramon.

"Well, at least there will be no one betting on my race. No one is that crazy. They can save their money and spend it on food instead, which will be good for the road fund."

Ramon looked at him across Salton's back.

"But there are many bets on your race, Don Tomás, although I have to tell you no one is betting on you to win. They are betting on how many lengths you will lose by."

Tomás laughed.

"Well then, I would very much like everyone to lose their bets today."

Tomás reached for Salton's reins and led him towards the road. The three of them slowly walked up to the gate. Tomás was amazed at how many more people had arrived. When he had gone to the rear pasture, he had heard what sounded like a truck or two rumbling up the Caman road. Now he saw four old firewood trucks parked near the rear of the schoolhouse, alongside a Landrover and a few four-wheel-drive pickups. The road was passable in the dry season, but just barely. If a trucker risked it, he was usually related to the family where he was picking up the firewood. Today they were making the trip because they could charge their passengers.

As they crossed the road, another truck full of noisy partygoers slowly approached from below. The soccer field was full of people of all ages and the track was already lined with spectators. Although it did not help his nerves any, Tomás couldn't help being pleased by the size of the crowd—the fiesta would bring in a bundle today.

Salton had never experienced anything like this. His ears were perked up and his nostrils flared as he took in all of the smells of other horses, cooking meat, and the large crowd.

When they arrived at the starting area, Tomás grabbed hold of Salton's mane and vaulted up onto his back. Manuel was already there, taciturn and ready for business. He held a small leather riding whip in his left hand, and he wore stubby spurless spurs on his ankle-high black riding boots. Tomás did not have a whip and wore his everyday spurs which were about the size of a quarter. He leaned forward to rub Salton's head between his ears. As Tomás pulled up alongside, Manuel gave him a cold stare. Then the *griton* came up to them and explained the rules. The crowd was really buzzing now, although to Tomás they seemed somewhere off in the distance. He was getting into a zone.

He did, however, turn to Manuel and, extending his hand across the lashed poles that separated them, said, "Good luck, Don Manuel."

Manuel looked startled. He hesitated and then very reluctantly shook Tomás's hand. His handshake was like a dead fish, and he didn't say anything. The judge asked them if they were ready. With his heart in his throat, Tomás nodded yes. The judge turned and walked over to the starting line. People moved away from him as he bent over slightly and eyeballed the last post. Not looking at the riders, he lifted his hand and then let it drop. Manuel and Tomás took off, but there was no yell as they passed the judge. Even Tomás could see that Salton had been at least a head behind Manuel's horse when they left the starting area. The crowd around them had quieted for the start, but now buzzed noisily. A few laughed when Tomás, trying to reign in his horse, almost fell off. He finally got turned around and returned to the starting area where Manuel was already waiting.

As they prepared to start again, Tomás remembered what Ramon said about body communication. Salton was definitely feeling his vibes and knew that something was up. Somehow—maybe it was because of the crowd and that it was not Lobo at his side—Salton knew that this was serious. He felt different somehow; like he was steeled or coiled.

The judge dropped his arm again and they were off. This time he yelled. The crowd roared from somewhere far away. Salton came off the line more quickly than he ever had before, but it was not nearly quick enough. In what seemed like a split second, Manuel had jumped to a three-quarter-length lead and was pulling away. In the process, intentionally or not, he pulled to the left a little too early, and the rear flank of his horse bumped hard enough into Salton to make him miss a step. Some of the crowd yelled in disapproval, especially when they saw that it let him pull farther ahead.

Before Tomás knew it he was two lengths behind and, as Ramon predicted, he and Salton began to eat mud. The hooves of Manuel's horse were throwing up chunks of topsoil at point blank range. It was like being peppered full bore in the face with hard peas from a pea-shooter, except the peas were golf-ball-sized. It hurt like hell. And Salton did not like it any more than Tomás did. Salton pulled a little to his left and Tomás let him have full rein. Tomás could hardly see anyway as he squinted through his muddy slits of eyes. He just tried to be part of Salton's body, in total sync with him as he ran.

As they veered to the left, two things happened. The first was that he was nailed squarely in the eyes with what must have been a sizeable chunk of mud, and he could not see a thing. The second was that he felt a liquid change in the way Salton was running. It reminded Tomás of a motorcycle he used to have, that was a real dog until it reached about four thousand RPMs. At that point it would take off like a rocket, becoming very smooth, with no vibration at all. That was what it was like with Salton. Once he got up to speed, he took off in another gear. And he was so smooth! Even though he could not see a thing, Tomás knew that they were flying down the track, and that they must be gaining on Manuel. But it was all Salton—Tomás just crouched forward and low, and hoped to not disrupt his flow.

He paid no attention to the crowd—it must have been loud—but all he noticed was a distant dull roar. But he was in tune with the thundering of Manuel's horse, which got louder and louder until he knew that they were side by side. The sound of both horses was deafening. And then, suddenly, the race was over.

Salton kept running for a little ways. Tomás did not pull in much on his reins, but Manuel must have reined in his mount because Salton began to slow down too, and all of the smoothness was gone. He had no idea who had won, and there was so much mud in his eyes that he could barely see a thing. It hurt like the dickens when he tried to blink. He pulled in on the reins, and when Salton slowed to a walk, he gently patted his neck, cooing to him while the animal caught his breath. Salton was sweaty and Tomás could feel his chest heaving mightily. They turned around, and Tomás aimed towards the noise of the crowd, holding him to a walk. Salton was still very excited. Tomás kept patting him and telling him how well he had done, and promising that he was going to have a special picnic of oats this afternoon.

"Don Tomás!"

It was Ramon's voice, a little out of breath. He must have run up to them, Tomás thought.

"Don Tomás, what a race! You did so well. Oh Salton, my boy, what a champion you are. What a heart you have."

Ramon's voice sounded on the verge of tears. Tomás had never heard him so emotional.

"Don Ramon—then did we win?"

"You do not know? I was going to ask you. They are still discussing it at the finish line. Oh what a race!"

Tomás smiled with huge satisfaction. Then it had been close—very close—close enough that the officials were not sure. Whatever the outcome, he would be happy. Damn! We did all right. He patted Salton again.

"Don Ramon, I do not know who won. I cannot see a thing—some of the mud hit me in the eyes. But it was a good race, was it not? And it was all Salton. I just gave him full rein and he was magnificent. He has this other gear..."

Tomás looked towards where he thought Ramon was.

"It was amazing. It was like..."

Ramon interrupted him, concern heavy in his voice.

"Don Tomás, bend down here and let me look. You are covered in mud, but I did not realize. Bend down!"

Tomás did as he said and Ramon turned his head one way and then the other.

"Aii! It is not just your eyes. I am surprised you can even breathe—you have mud everywhere. Come on, let me lead you two home. Let's wash your face and get the mud out of your eyes."

As he led them away, Tomás could hear him pat Salton's sweaty neck.

"And you, Señor Salton. I am going to wash your face too and take you for a long walk. I do not want your magnificent legs to get stiff, although the way you looked, I think you could have run all the way up the hill to Casa Blanca."

Ramon patted him again.

"You deserve a pile of grain this afternoon, my boy."

"That is what I told him too. You were right, Don Ramon. You knew he could run faster. He has another gear or something. And it was so smooth. It felt like we were flying. And..."

But they were surrounded now by people offering congratulations. The outcome had still not been announced but that did not stop people from appreciating the race. Tomás heard Guillermo and Pablo, and then Juan and Oso and a few of the volunteers in the crowd. He nodded and smiled but did not say much. He left it up to Ramon to get them out of there and back home. His eyes felt terrible and he wanted to wash them out pronto.

Ramon brought them through the gate and to the rear of the house. Tomás dismounted and sat down on the long chopping log. Ramon went into the house and returned with everything Tomás needed to wash his face. While Tomás flushed his eyes with clean water over and over again, Ramon cleaned Salton and then took him for his long walk.

By the time Ramon returned, Tomás could see, but his eyes were definitely scratched. He could not stop blinking no matter how uncomfortable it was.

Ramon looked at his eyes and said, "If I did not know better, I would think you have been getting drunk for a month. Your eyes are all bloodshot, but I think you will live."

Suddenly he looked serious.

"I have just come from across the road. The judges have proclaimed Don Manuel—by the closest of margins—the winner of the race. I am sorry, Don Tomás."

The news did not bother Tomás. Above everything else he felt tremendous relief that it was over and, who knows, maybe it was for the better. It would have been a huge loss of face for Manuel if he had lost.

"Do not worry about me. I am very happy the way things went, except for maybe one thing."

"And what is that?"

"I am thirsty and hungry and we are wasting time. Let me change my clothes and let's go to the fiesta."

He dressed in record time and they rushed over to Maria Elena's *ramada* for some *empanadas* and sweet cider. The other race was scheduled to take place within the hour and they wanted to have their stomachs full by then. On the way Tomás was congratulated and thumped on the back several times—quite a difference from that first *carrera* when he made everyone around him uncomfortable. God, that seemed so very long ago, he thought. They arrived at one of the big *ramadas* that had been framed around a soccer goal. A small crowd was in front, two deep, and they had to wait their turn. He watched as Maria Elena expertly folded and shaped the *empanadas* and carefully dropped them into the hot oil. An empty green wine bottle that served as her rolling pin lay on its side on the counter next to a mound of *masa*. Don Pedro's Señora and two other women were serving the *chicha* and *empanadas*. When Tomás and Ramon stepped up to the counter, Maria Elena's face lit up.

"Don Tomás! That race has to be one of the best ever. It was very exciting."

He looked over towards the track where a crowd was already beginning to form again, and back to her.

"I wouldn't think you could see much from here."

Before she could answer, Don Pedro's Señora said, "Oh Don Tomás, did you think we could keep her working here during your race? Oh no. She would not help us then. She deserted us and left us with all the work."

The Señora smiled over at Maria Elena, who quickly turned her back to them and poked at some *empanadas* in the large pan. They sizzled and popped, and Tomás's mouth began to water.

The Señora continued, "But there was almost no one here anyway. Everyone was at the race. What a noise the crowd made. It must have been very exciting, Don Tomás."

"It certainly was, Señora. I only wish I could have seen more of it."

His eyes were watering and he wiped them with a handkerchief that Ramon had loaned to him.

"How are your eyes?" Maria Elena asked. "Ramon told us about the mud."

He must have come over to the *ramada* after he had found out the race results, Tomás thought.

"You came by here, Don Ramon, and you did not bring me back an *empanada?*"

Tomás raised an eyebrow, which was not easy.

"Well, now that I think of it, I did buy two, and I meant to bring one back for you, but it somehow disappeared on the trip over..."

At least he looked a little sheepish.

"Well, in that case," Tomás said good-naturedly, "I would like to order a half dozen now. Three for my excellent trainer here and three for me. And we want them nice and hot! And also two cups of your excellent *chicha* to toast my horse."

"*Si*, Don Tomás. *Con mucho gusto*," Maria Elena said, smiling and turning back to the sizzling pan.

Don Pedro's Señora filled two large glasses. Tomás pulled out his wallet and extracted a few bills, while Ramon took a sip of his *chicha* and rubbed his hands in anticipation.

As they ate, Maria Elena told Ramon that she was running out of baked *empanadas* and asked if she could use his oven. He said to go over whenever she wanted and bake away.

"Oh, but *Tio*, I do not see any smoke from your chimney. Is the stove going?" she asked innocently.

She knew very well that breakfast had been a long time ago and Ramon certainly would not be cooking a mid-day meal today. And she knew that Miriam would be working all day in the other large *ramada*. Of course the stove was out.

Ramon looked a little wary.

"The fire has been out for some time, Maria Elena," he said carefully.

"Well then, do you think you could start the fire and get the oven up to temperature for me? Please?"

She batted her beautiful eyes at him. Tomás thought if they had been batted at him like that, he'd have been over to the house in a flash—rubbing two sticks together if need be. But Ramon's reaction was different.

"Aii! Of all the *ramadas* to visit we pick yours. At any other place I would be left alone in peace."

Shaking his head and trying to look angry he took a bite of his last *empanada* and followed it with a slug of *chicha*.

When his mouth was clear again, he said, "After the race, Maria Elena. After the race I will get the oven to temperature and I will come by to tell you when it is ready. But there is a price. To do this I want a free *empanada*. No! Make that two *empanadas*—one for Don Tomás, too—in advance."

"Done, *Tio*," she said meekly and, turning away so he could not see her smile, she dropped two *empanadas* into the hot grease.

Juan, Ramon, and Tomás walked over to the finish line to watch the second race. Oso muscled his way in

through the crowd and joined them. Without saying
a word, he stuck out his hand and gave Tomás a solid
handshake and pat on the back before turning to face
the starting line. Oso always joked around with him
and was rarely serious. Tomás took his handshake and
his silence as the highest compliment.

The second race began and there was no false start.
The *griton* yelled and the crowd roared. Like last summer, the 'big gray' fell quickly behind and, also like
last summer, it did not take him long to make up the
difference. He won easily by at least two lengths. The
crowd broke up into noisy, gesticulating groups to pay
off their bets. Ramon went off to get the oven hot for
Maria Elena, and Juan left to do his chores. Oso and
Tomás walked through the crowded soccer field to one
of the barbecue pits where there were two choices—a
lamb dinner, with beans, potatoes, and bread cooked
in the coals, or a thick slab of lamb between two pieces
of fresh warm bread. A large tin of red *aji* paste was
on the table next to the eating utensils. Oso stood in
line to order a full meal for himself and a sandwich
for Tomás. After asking him to be sure to slather his
sandwich with pepper paste, Tomás went to get them
a couple of cups of wine. They would meet at a table
near the deck of the school.

They were joined by several volunteers, and Tomás
was congratulated many times. He had become something of a celebrity among his cohorts. Gradually all
the volunteers gathered at their table. As they chatted
about what they were doing all over Chile, they took
turns fetching liters of wine. The first volunteer that
Tomás had met at training was here, and he told Tomás
all about where he worked, which was three hundred
miles to the north. Richard was tall and thin, and from
the Bay Area where smoking pot bordered on religion.
He had given up pot when he joined the Peace Corps

but he missed it—nothing like a little toke to take the
edge off, he would say. Like Tomás, he worked for the
Ministry of Agriculture, although he was more involved
with forest fire protection than with planting trees.
He worked primarily with one cooperative that was
located about seven miles away from where he lived,
and, because the buses were never convenient, he used
a bicycle. During his bike rides, he watched the farmers till and plant their fields.

By mid summer the crop was tall and Richard
thought the plants resembled marijuana. About a
week or so later, as he pedaled by, he thought, damn,
that definitely looks like pot. He got off his bike and
took a closer look. And it WAS pot, acres and acres of
it. It turned out that the farmers were growing and
selling hemp to a factory where the tough fiber was
rendered into fabric for furniture. Richard thought
that this was a sign that he was supposed to smoke pot
again. So he did. He also believed it was his destiny
to provide for his friends, so he made midnight forays
to the fields. He picked the leaves from many different plants so that no one would notice. He filled garbage can size plastic bags and carried them back on his
bike. If any volunteer wanted pot, Richard was happy
to give it to him or her—by the garbage bag if desired.
And beware, all the volunteers said, if Richard brought
brownies to a Peace Corps party.

Tomás laughed at this story, but he also realized how
out of the loop he was. He had not heard of this or any
of a dozen other volunteer stories that had made the
rounds. When Richard asked him if he wanted some
pot, he shook his head. It was not worth the risk. And
when did he have time to smoke it, anyway?

The sun was sinking, and the musicians began to set
up on the schoolhouse deck. There were two guitars,
an accordion, a tambourine, and an instrument called

a *tormento,* which was little more than a slatted wooden box that the musician played like a bongo drum. The chairs and tables nearest the deck were quickly filling up. Tomás noticed there was a changing of the guard in the *ramadas.* The younger women were taking off their aprons and handing them to the older *señoras.* Now that everyone was congregating around the school, the magnitude of the crowd became evident. Tomás was very excited at the turnout and what it meant for the road fund.

The musicians started the evening with a *cueca,* the national folk dance of Chile. It was symbolic of the mating of a rooster with a hen. The dance began with the partners facing each other and clapping to the rhythm of the music. Both had white *pañuelos*—handkerchiefs—which the women held between the fingers of their left hand while the men laid theirs across a shoulder. As they danced, both whirled the handkerchiefs above their heads. The men scratched and stomped the ground around the women, feinting this way and that. The women twirled and danced around, lifting a corner of their skirts with their free hands. The men leered and the women smiled coquettishly. Often the men would cock an arm as if it were a wing and use it as a distraction as he approached his partner, imitating a pretty basic rooster move. They went round and round, sometimes becoming quite sensuous as the rooster got closer and closer to his flirtatious hen. It was fun to watch.

Tomás did not enjoy dancing so he did not venture out to the dance area. But that did not prevent him from having a good time watching the others. Juan was somehow making do with his gimpy leg as he scratched around Flor. Old Don Pedro danced often with his Señora. Whenever she was resting, he would patrol the edge of the dance area, beckoning with his *panuelo,* trying to entice young *señoritas* to come out and dance. A few brave volunteers were circling blushing *campo* girls, but no one turned more heads than Oso when he danced the *cueca* with Maria Elena. She smiled and swirled around gracefully while he lumbered and waved a paper napkin that he had pilfered from the cooking area. The band was enthusiastic and played one song after another. In between the *cueca*s and ballads, they cracked ribald *campo* jokes, full of idioms and off-color expressions that he had never heard before. The audience laughed heartily, but Tomás realized, that he still had a ways to go with his Spanish.

During the band's first break, he walked over to the nearest *ramada* where he forged through the crowd to buy a cup of wine. By the time he returned, the band had finished their break and started up another *cueca*. As he sat back down with the volunteers, he saw Maria Elena dancing with Kurt, and his stomach did a serious flip flop. Where the hell had Kurt come from? He was circling engagingly around her and she was one big smile. Try as he might, Tomás could not take his eyes off of them. One thing was obvious—both were having a very good time. And all of a sudden, he was not.

Through the course of the evening he drank too much wine. He tried to bolster up the courage to ask Maria Elena to dance, but she kept dancing with Kurt. And damn it, they looked like they were having such a good time. And what was worse, they looked good together; they were a very handsome couple indeed.

The music continued on into the night, and the lanterns shed a warm golden light onto the dancers. When the band played a slow dance, and Kurt and Maria Elena came out, he couldn't watch. He had to get out of there. He had to pee anyway. He stood and walked to the far end of the school. As he rounded the corner, Oso was suddenly at his side.

"Where are you headed, Tomás?"

"To take a piss," he said curtly.

Oso's eyes widened a little, surprised by Tomás's tone. But all he said was, "Lead the way, then. I am about ready to burst myself."

They relieved themselves behind a firewood truck. Tomás looked at the beat-up old heap and bet that none of its lights worked. Its passengers would probably be spending the night curled up in their *mantas* somewhere. There would be a lot of strangers hanging around Caman tonight, which probably explained why he hadn't seen Ramon for some time. He was at the farm keeping an eye on things.

As they zipped up, Oso asked, "Who's that guy with Maria Elena? I've seen him in Valdivia."

"Kurt. He is the engineer with INDAP who put together the cost share proposal for the road. He's got an engineering degree from the States and really knows his stuff. He speaks perfect English. And he's a nice guy."

"It seems Maria Elena thinks so."

Just what he wanted to hear.

"Yeah, it seems that way, doesn't it?"

They headed back towards the party. The music had stopped. There was some applause from the crowd on the other side of the school.

Oso said, "I did not see you dance with Maria Elena."

"No. I didn't."

"I think that was a mistake, Tomás," he said seriously as they walked around the corner of the school.

Tomás stopped.

"Just what do you mean by that, Oso?"

"What I mean is...."

Just then Richard came up with a big party smile and glazed eyes, holding an armful of empty green bottles.

"Hey Oso. Tomás. I just borrowed these bottles from Don Ramon and I'm going to get wine. Help me carry them over to the tents. The band is done and we are going to have a campfire and play the guitar."

"We'll talk later, Tomás," Oso said.

He turned to Richard and held out his hands.

"Here, give me some of those. Looks like we'll be up late tonight."

By the time Tomás returned to the table, the musicians were putting away their instruments. He did not see Maria Elena and Kurt anywhere, which didn't make him feel any better. He hoped that they had not gone off somewhere in the bushes.

Men had taken over the late night shift in the *ramadas*. The women and their families were beginning to leave, and soon only the serious revelers would be left. Drinking would continue into the wee hours of the morning, so there was still money to be made. But the more wine that was drunk, the greater the chance that a fight would break out—especially with a crowd this size, and with so many of them not from Cufeo. Tomás suddenly realized that he had not seen Manuel since the race. He wondered if he was still here. If so, chances were that he was drinking at one of the *ramadas*. As he looked around for him, he saw Maria Elena heading purposefully his way. She stopped at a formal distance in front of him.

"Don Tomás," she said evenly.

"Maria Elena."

They looked at each other for a few moments and neither said anything. She was not smiling. He wasn't either.

Finally she asked, "Why did you not ask me to dance tonight?"

"Because I am not a very good dancer... and anyway...." He hesitated and then just repeated himself, "I am not a very good dancer, Maria Elena."

"That does not matter. What did you start to say—
'and anyway'.... 'and anyway,' what?"

He realized now that she was angry. Well, so was he.

"And anyway, you seemed to be having a very good
time with Kurt. I did not think you wanted to be
interrupted."

Her eyes flashed.

"So when did you start doing my thinking for me,
Tomás? That is something for me to decide, not you."

"Are you going to tell me that you were not having
a good time with Kurt?"

She hesitated.

"No...I was having a good time, but..."

"So then you see why I did not bother you."

"Aii!"

She rolled her eyes heavenward.

"Tomás..."

She looked like she was physically trying to control
herself.

"Tomás," she repeated levelly, "Is this how you do
things? Is this how you ran your race today?"

"Oh, was I in a horse race tonight, Maria Elena?" he
countered.

"You were not," she snapped.

She was very angry now.

"I just know how you are when something matters to
you and," looking at him hard she said, "I guess some
things are just more important to you than others. Go
back to your table and drink wine with your friends.
That is where you seem most comfortable."

Without saying goodnight, she turned and left.

Watching her stride away, his anger burned out
quickly and was replaced by a sick feeling that ran
through his whole body. He suddenly felt like a fool—
an immature and jealous fool. Maria Elena went up to
Juan and butted into his conversation with Guillermo.

She quickly said something to her brother, and then went over to a nearby table and angrily grabbed her shawl. Throwing it around her shoulders she stormed off towards the road. Juan and Guillermo watched her leave. Juan shrugged his shoulders and shook hands with Guillermo before limping after her into the darkness.

Tomás sighed and sat down at the nearest table. He began to torture himself by thinking of all of the things he should have said to her. First off, he thought, I should have asked her to dance, like Oso said. I should never have…

He felt a hand on his shoulder and looked up. Kurt was smiling down at him.

"Hey Kurt," he said in English. "How's it going?" Composing himself, he stood up and shook hands, saying, "It's great of you to come out and support the fiesta."

"I wouldn't have missed it for anything. I heard all about the preparations from Maria Elena and so I had to come up."

When had she been talking to him? Damn it, Tomás, stop thinking like that! Kurt offered to buy him a glass of wine. He accepted.

After touching cups and taking a sip, Kurt said, "I saw your race today. You rode very well. And your horse did well too. Maybe one day he will challenge his father."

Now that would be something, he thought.

"Tomás, would you consider selling your horse to me?"

He didn't hesitate even a fraction of a second.

"Not in this lifetime."

"I thought not."

They drank their wine and began to talk about the road project. He told Kurt about all the fund-raisers and how the bank account was growing. Kurt said he really hoped they could come up with the money. He said how inspiring it was to see a community pull together and to work so hard towards its goal.

"Whether or not Cufeo gets the new road, Tomás, you should be congratulated on what you have done here."

Tomás downplayed his efforts saying, "Thank you Kurt, but I really have done very little. It really HAS been the community. But if there is one person who has put in a monumental effort, then it has been Maria Elena. You have no idea how hard she has worked for this."

"Yes. I can imagine. She is one very capable young woman. And beautiful too."

Oh you noticed, he thought sarcastically—then immediately felt chagrined by the thought. Jesus, who in their right mind did not find her beautiful? Kurt said something he missed.

"What's that Kurt? Sorry—I was spacing out."

"I said Maria Elena thinks the world of you, Tomás."

Tomás was all ears now.

"What do you mean? Why do you say that?"

"Because every time I am with her, she somehow brings the conversation around to you. About how much you have helped them, how good a person you are, how athletic, and so on. And now, if I see her again, she'll probably talk some more about your race today. No offense, Tomás, but I would be lying if I didn't say that I'd rather talk about other things when I am with her."

"I imagine you would, Kurt. But, frankly, I am surprised. And also very pleased to hear it —but still surprised."

From the depths of sheer jealousy to pure happiness in a split second: how were such things possible?

Was it healthy to go through such bursts of highs and lows?

His face must have revealed something of his emotional condition because Kurt said, "Well, aside from that race you ran, Tomás, I do believe I have made your day. But," as he drained the last of his wine, "it is time for me to go."

Tomás escorted him to his Landrover. They were silent until Kurt climbed in and started his vehicle.

They shook hands and Tomás said, "Drive safely, Kurt. It has been a long day with a lot of wine."

He nodded and put the Landrover into gear.

"And Kurt, thank you for telling me about Maria Elena. You certainly didn't have to."

Kurt understood that Tomás knew that he was very much interested in her, and that Tomás appreciated his honesty, considering the situation.

"Tomás, I wish you luck. She is a great girl and you might have a real opportunity there. Don't blow it."

With that he drove off, and Tomás watched his taillights bump down the road. He put his hands in his pockets and slowly walked towards the farm. Well, that certainly put a new spin on things. Kurt thought he had a "real opportunity" with Maria Elena. If he didn't blow it. God, like tonight. He felt like such a fool.

He came up to the gate and leaned against it. He looked across the road to the soccer field and lantern-lit *ramadas*. God knows he had always found her attractive. And he always enjoyed being with her, no matter what they were doing. But more than friends? Maybe Kurt was wrong. There had never been any sign. Well, maybe when they were alone planting the trees that one time. There might have been some spark then. Maybe it was true. Maybe there was a chance that Maria Elena was attracted to him. And why didn't he think that could be possible? Your lack of self esteem, Tomás?

But if it were true, where could it possibly lead anyway? She would never leave Cufeo and, at some point, he would be leaving. So what was the point? And Juan. What about him? That would certainly change things between them. And Ramon too. But, one thing was for damn sure, and there was no getting around it. There was absolutely no way he could have felt like he did tonight—watching her dance with Kurt—if he were not totally smitten.

CHAPTER FIFTEEN

El Viaje (The Trip)

Oso and Tomás were late. They hustled up the Montoya's porch steps and entered the house. It looked like they had stumbled on to a South American drug ring. Maria Elena, Don Pedro, Manuel, and Juan each had a pile of bills and coins in front of them, and there was a mountain of money in the center of the table. Don Pedro was bragging how well 'his' horse had done in the race.

"Aah, Don Tomás. Here is the young jockey now. I was just saying, who would have thought that you and Don Manuel would have had such a great race, eh? I should have sold that horse to you for a lot more money. And everyone I have talked to enjoyed your race more than the 'big gray's.' It was, if I may say so, a stroke of genius on my part."

Manuel was noticeably silent, and did not look up from his piles of bills and coins. Tomás had still not spoken with him since the race. He was sure that Manuel was not happy that it had been so close.

Don Pedro was clearly in good spirits.

"I see we not only have a jockey here today, but also a very light-footed dancer. Here, Sr. Oso, come sit next to me."

He made room for him at the table.

"I enjoyed watching you dance with Maria Elena. You must give me lessons sometime. I do not think I have ever seen the *cueca* danced quite like that before."

"Don Pedro, you are making fun of me," Oso said as he pulled up a chair and sat down.

Tomás sat between Juan and Manuel.

"I saw you dancing with your Señora," Oso continued, "and I think it is YOU who is light on his feet and it is YOU who should give ME the lessons."

Don Pedro sighed.

"Aah then, maybe you are right. But my Señora said I wore her out last night. What I need is a younger woman like Maria Elena to dance with, although from what I saw, I do not think she would have had the time. Except for maybe your dance, Sr. Oso, she seemed very occupied with Sr. Kurt."

Maria Elena blushed furiously and began to shuffle some bills. Tomás did not say a word. He pulled out a pencil and a small pad of paper and placed them on the table in front of him. Reaching out with both hands, he raked in a bundle of bills and coins—as if he had just won the pot in a poker game—and began to sort and count.

In about an hour's time they had finished adding it all up—twice to be sure. After serving some sweet cider and re-heated *empanadas*, Maria Elena subtracted all the expenses.

"After paying everything, we will have twenty-two thousand, five hundred and twenty *escudos*, and fifty-five *centavos*."

It was a huge amount—over twenty-five hundred dollars—and everyone cheered and applauded. Maria Elena smiled.

"This will take the bank teller a minute or two to count."

"And where does that put the account, Maria Elena?" Tomás asked.

It was the first time that they had looked directly at each other. Her smile vanished and she was all business. She opened her little passbook and did the arithmetic.

"With the fiesta money we will have forty-nine thousand, six hundred and forty six *escudos* and ninety *centavos.*"

Suddenly it was very quiet in the room. They all knew—Oso included—that ninety thousand *escudos* were needed for the road. It was early fall now and there were only a few more small events planned.

"It looks like we still have a long way to go," she said as she sat down heavily. "And I do not know how we will get the rest, with winter coming."

She looked very tired all of a sudden.

Juan said, "Don't worry, Maria Elena; we will think of something. The deadline is still more than half a year away and we have already raised over half what we need. So do not look so sad."

Everyone nodded in agreement, but they weren't fooling anyone. They knew that it would be tough to raise money during the winter months. Manuel got things moving again.

"Maria Elena, the first thing to do is to get that money safely into the bank. I think you should take it down to Valdivia tomorrow. If you want an escort, I would be happy to come down early and accompany you."

Tomás thought Manuel's concern for the safety of the money a bit hypocritical, considering, but his offer was a nice gesture. Maria Elena thanked him but declined, saying that it was too far out of his way. Oso said he would be returning on the early bus and offered to accompany her. He beamed when she accepted, mentioning that no one would dare to bother her with him at her side.

Dusting the crumbs off of the front of his shirt and jacket, Manuel said, "In that case, everything is settled. Thank you for the *empanadas,* Maria Elena. I must return now and take care of the animals before dark."

They all stood. When Tomás thanked Maria Elena, there was still no smile. Juan escorted them outside, and Oso and Tomás accompanied Manuel and Don Pedro as far as the Rodriguez's gate. They said their goodbyes and Don Pedro turned his horse up the Casa Blanca road. Manuel started towards La Paloma, but did not go far before he reined in his horse and turned around.

As Tomás was latching the gate, he said, "Don Tomás, may I have a word with you?"

"Of course, Don Manuel."

Uh-oh, he thought. He grimaced at Oso.

"I will see you up at the house."

When Oso was out of earshot, Manuel said, "Don Tomás, it is obvious that you have kept your word about the...er...problem I had with the tournament money, and I want to thank you for that. I also want to congratulate you on the race you ran. You say to everyone that it was only your horse that allowed you to do so well. But, I know—as well as Don Ramon or anyone else who has ever raced—what it is like to have that mud thrown into your face and your eyes. Considering that you have no experience, for you to not panic and give up has impressed me very much." He paused and then added, "I hope you still feel that you can shake my hand, because I would very much like to shake yours."

He leaned down from the saddle and extended his hand across the gate. Tomás took it eagerly, and felt their strained relationship ease immediately. A brief but good silence followed before Manuel turned his horse again and rode away.

Winter and the rains were quickly approaching. The bright blues and greens of summer and early fall were dulled now by sunless gray skies, and the world once again became sepia and earth-toned. Oso had finished his cruise and timber projections for the Ministry of Agriculture, as well as his two year commitment to the Peace Corps. He accepted a short-term job to help acclimate the next volunteers to arrive in Santiago, so he would soon be leaving Valdivia. Tomás would miss him tremendously.

Even though more farmers were planting trees this year, there would be fewer pine deliveries because the plantations were smaller. So Tomás could take some vacation time at the end of the winter. He planned to retrace Oso's steps through northern Chile, across to Bolivia, and up to Peru, with a visit to Cuzco and Machu Picchu as the grand finale.

Tonight, he and Oso were having a farewell dinner at the Palace. Tomás watched as Oso took a bite of rare steak and chewed contentedly, his eyes closed. Moments later he popped a fry into his mouth, followed by a swig of cold Escudo beer. When his plate was empty, Oso mopped it with a piece of bread. Finally, he wiped his mouth with the cloth napkin and leaned back in his chair. With hands folded across his ample stomach, he looked over to Tomás.

"When you come up to Santiago, I want to hear all about how you're doing with Maria Elena."

Tomás had told him about Kurt's assessment, and he was surprised when Oso quickly agreed. Oso thought that Tomás must be more than a little numb to not have picked up on Maria Elena's interest in him.

"We'll see what happens, Oso. But right now she is beside herself. She eats, sleeps, and drinks the road project, and worries that it will fail. Winter is practically here and the last of the fund-raisers have brought in maybe another fifteen hundred *escudos*. Like all of us, she has run out of ideas about how to raise more money. No one can afford to donate even part of their income from the firewood and charcoal. And how could you possibly entice anyone to travel to Cufeo for an event during the winter? Impossible. So we have to find something in the *campo* to bring in to Valdivia to sell. There are the sales of *copihue* and ferns to the flower shops, but that brings in pennies. I suppose *avellano* nuts could be gathered—if the pigs haven't eaten them all—and sold by the kilo. But it would be nuts to spend so much labor and time for so little money."

"So to speak."

"Yeah, right. But really, it's just crazy. So anyway, Maria Elena worries all the time."

Tomás got the waiter's attention and he came over.

"Another Escudo, please."

He looked at Oso who nodded.

"And another for my friend."

The waiter returned and filled their glasses halfway before putting the brown bottles down on the table. The two friends sat in comfortable silence, slowly drinking their beers and wondering what the future might bring. Tomás looked around the restaurant. Most of the customers were young, either university students or upper-middle-class professionals. The women were quite attractive, but he couldn't help thinking that not one held a candle to Maria Elena. Everyone was also better dressed than he and Oso, but that was no surprise either.

Oso interrupted his thoughts.

"I'll enjoy catching up with all of the volunteers from my program when they come through Santiago to take care of the stuff that they need to finish up before they leave. There are many that I haven't seen since our in-country training."

"How does that work anyway? What do you have to do before leaving?"

Oso pulled a toothpick out of a shirt pocket and started to work it.

"Oh, a bunch of stuff. You're responsible to get your trunk to the main office so that it can be shipped out. You have to give an assessment of your two years here. You also have your language proficiency tested by a Chilean instructor..."

"How do you think you'll do with your Spanish?"

"Maybe a four or a four-minus. I just wish my accent were better."

True enough. Oso spoke beautiful Spanish. He was basically fluent, grammatically good, and he had an immense vocabulary. They were graded on a system of one to five, with five being perfect. Tomás thought that maybe he spoke with less of a *gringo* twang than Oso, but he knew his grammar was not so hot because he had learned most of his Spanish from uneducated *campesinos*.

Oso told him that if any of the returning volunteers had some *escudos* left in their bank accounts, they could exchange them at the Banco del Estado for dollars at the official rate. The Peace Corps had an agreement with the government so that each volunteer could exchange up to a thousand dollars worth of *escudos* before leaving. Because of the roaring inflation which had been growing steadily since the earthquake, not just anyone could exchange *escudos* for dollars in the banks—there would be a run at the banks if they did. In the two years that Tomás had been in Chile, there had been a seventy percent surge for the dollar. Consequently there was a terrific black market for dollars, at double the official rate.

Toothpick lodged in the corner of his mouth, Oso continued.

"But I'll bet very few volunteers will take advantage of that. Unlike your situation Tomás, it is pretty hard to save money if you live in a town and have to pay for room and board, especially if you live in a city like Santiago, Concepcion, or Valparaiso. For the guys who don't have any money but want to travel around before going home, they can cash in up to half of their readjustment allowance in Santiago. But most will probably just fly straight back to the States."

Volunteers were given a readjustment allowance of fifteen hundred dollars after their two years, which was supposed to help tide them over until they figured out what they were going to do after their Peace Corps service. Tomás tried to estimate how many *escudos* he might be able to save before leaving Chile. He wanted to travel around South America, and cashing them in could help pay for the trip. He also wondered, if he remained in Chile, if he could get the total readjustment allowance here in dollars. If that were possible, then he could exchange it for double on the black market and have a good little nest egg. Now that would be a great scam, he thought. What an easy way to double his money. If only the Road Committee could somehow double their money that easily. He took another sip of beer....

"Holy Shit! That's it," he exclaimed loudly, making Oso and everyone sitting nearby jump.

"Oso," he said in a much lower, but very excited voice, "I just had a brainstorm. I know how we can raise the money for the road. It might not be exactly legal, but it would work. I would need you, though, to make it work."

"Jesus, Tomás. You about gave me a heart attack."

"Oso, listen! If you had a bunch of U.S. dollars and wanted to double your money, what would you do?"

"Easy. Exchange them with the merchants here on Calle Picarte. They're always pestering us for dollars."

"Right. And what if I were to get all of the *escudos* from the Road Committee up to you in Santiago and you talked some of the returning volunteers into exchanging them for dollars? I could bring those dollars back here, exchange them on Picarte, and *voila*, we'd double the Road Committee's money. They'd be in business."

Oso slapped his thigh.

"Brilliant, Tomás!"

He extended his hand and, like two grinning fools, they shook.

They spent the rest of the evening hashing out details for the plan. First and foremost, Tomás did not want to handle any of the money. So someone on the Committee would have to go to Santiago. Maria Elena was the logical choice. She had been in charge of all the money so far, and Don Pedro was old and probably would not want to make such a trip. And Manuel, in the big city with all of that money? He was just too much of a loose cannon.

Maria Elena could transfer the Road Committee's money to the main bank in Santiago and make withdrawals there, once Oso had everything lined up. Tomás would time his return from Peru so that he could escort Maria Elena back to Valdivia. There they would sell the dollars on the black market to the merchants. The *escudos* would go back to the Committee's account and they would have enough for their share of the road. However, since exchanging currencies on the black market was illegal, Oso decided that he would get the exiting volunteers to sign receipts for their 'donations,' in *escudos,* to the Road Committee. It would make no difference to the volunteers, since they'd be back in the States, and why would the Chilean government care anyway, since all of the money would be going towards improvement of its infrastructure? Oso would contact Tomás through the Peace Corps office as things developed in Santiago.

By the time they left the Palace, it was raining. They buttoned their jackets and pulled the collars up. Bracing themselves, they stepped out into a cold, wet Valdivia night.

It was still raining the next morning which made buying supplies and walking up the hill no fun. His pack was so heavy that by the time Tomás reached the Montoya's gate, he was lathered in sweat. He leaned the pack up against a gate post. Muchacho scooched out from under the porch and shook himself. Wagging his tail, the dog half-heartedly announced Tomás's arrival. As Tomás began to pet him, Maria Elena came around the corner of the porch and smiled politely.

"*Buenos dias,* Tomás. This is a surprise. Come on up out of the rain. It is bad weather to be out."

They bemoaned the weather for a few minutes until Tomás couldn't restrain himself any longer.

"Oso and I have a plan to raise the rest of the money that we need. I want to explain it to you and see what you think."

That brought out a big smile.

"Come into the house and sit by the stove. You can dry out and help me shuck *habas* while you tell me. This should be good. Whenever you two are together..."

She did not finish the sentence, and instead led the way into the house. Tomás sat in Juan's chair near the stove, and she handed him a basket of *habas*, an empty cardboard box, and a big bowl. They threw the beans into the bowl and the pods into the box for the chickens, while Tomás explained the plan. When he finished, what a smile was on her face. Her eyes positively shone.

She jumped up.

"It will work. It is so simple. Oh Tomás, thank you!"

She bent over and kissed him on the cheek and began to dance around the room, lightly clapping her hands. He did not say a word. The simple peck on the cheek took him by surprise—a very nice surprise indeed—and he felt about as high as he had right after the race. After a few moments she calmed down and returned, blushing, to her chair. She did not say anything and neither did he. Finally, she stood up and took the bowl of beans to the kitchen.

When she returned, she sat down and said, "So you will be leaving soon on your big trip. You must be very excited."

He nodded, although right now he wasn't so excited about the idea of not seeing Maria Elena for three weeks. Her deep brown eyes looked directly into his.

"I will miss you, Tomás. Maybe if you are not too busy you can write me a postcard. You could send it to Pablo's in Valdivia."

"I will. I promise." She would miss him, she said. Suddenly he felt like he was riding on a cloud. She turned to the window and saw Juan walking up towards the house. It was raining harder, and Juan was hanging on to his hat as he leaned into the rain.

"Here comes Juan for the midday meal. Would you like to stay and eat with us? You could tell him about the plan for the road."

"I would love to, Maria Elena. I have to admit that I am very hungry. I worked up quite an appetite walking up the... Aii!"

"What is it?"

"I just remembered," he said, abruptly standing up and walking quickly to the door. "I left my pack out at the gate. I'd better get it before it gets any wetter, or before Muchacho finds the food inside."

With his hand on the latch, he stopped.

"Maria Elena?"

"Yes, Tomás?"

"For some time now I have wanted to say this to you, but there was never the right moment."

She looked at him questioningly.

"I want you to know that I wish from the bottom of my heart that I had asked you to dance at the fiesta."

She smiled sweetly.

"I know that, Tomás. I have always known that. But thank you for those words. And thank you for your plan."

Tomás laid his *The South American Handbook* down on the little airplane-style tray table. He would be on this modern German-made *bus cama*—sleeper bus—for twenty-three hours before he arrived at the oasis town of Calama in northern Chile. That would be his first stopover on his way to Machu Picchu. He planned to take a tour of Chuquicamata, the largest open-pit copper mine in the world.

His vacation had begun three days earlier with a visit to Oso in Santiago. Tomás had explored the city during the day, and at night he and Oso had dined at cheap restaurants and had taken in some current American movies. Plus they had worked on their plan. Oso had spoken with several returning volunteers, and they were happy to help out. So, everything was all set, and Maria Elena would arrive in less than three weeks. Tomás had arranged his travel accordingly.

He reclined his seat and looked out the window at the passing countryside. He thought back to the scene at the Montoya house when Juan had returned for lunch. When Tomás had told him about the plan, Juan had become as excited as Maria Elena. Brother and sister immediately began to plan the trip to Santiago. Tomás had forgotten that Ramon's elder sister, Angela—Maria Elena's and Juan's aunt—lived in Santiago. They would contact her and were sure that she would offer lodging. Juan talked as if he would go too, but that was short-lived.

"But Juan, who will watch over the farm and take care of the animals? And who knows how long I may have to stay in Santiago getting the money exchanged."

"You cannot go alone Maria Elena. Who will watch over you?"

That set her off and she went into a full-blown tirade.

"Watch over me! Juan, I am twenty-one years old and I think I can watch over myself. Do you not know me? Do you not trust your own sister who has been on her own for most of these twenty-one years?"

She did not let him answer.

"If I want to go to Santiago alone, I will—with or without your blessing. Who do you think you are?"

Tomás shrunk in his seat and wished he were somewhere else. But it ended quickly.

Juan said softly, "Maria Elena, I am only your brother who loves you very much. And who worries about you traveling alone. I do trust you, sister. It is that I do not trust everyone else in this world."

She gave his hand a squeeze and held on to it. She said she would be fine and, besides, who would molest her with Oso at her side. Tomás thought, hey wait a minute. What about me? Although Juan still looked concerned, he put up no more protest and they resumed making their plans...

"Would you care for a *pisco* sour, Señor?"

Tomás looked up and the bus attendant was passing around a small tray of cocktails. These sleeper buses were like traveling first class in an airplane, with plenty of legroom, footrests, and seats that reclined all the way back. There were even blankets in the compartments above, and a couple of TV screens were mounted in convenient locations. They were much better than the Greyhounds and Trailways back home.

The bus attendant handed him the cocktail and continued up the aisle. *Pisco* meant 'little bird' in Quechua, the Indian dialect that originated with the Incas in Cuzco; but to most South Americans it meant a brandy which was first distilled in Peru in the 1600's when the king of Spain banned wine. Tomás took a sip. Drinking it straight, he knew, was harsh. But a *pisco* sour was something else. Made with sugar, egg whites, and lime juice; it was tart and sweet, and, like *mate*, had its own distinctive taste.

His vacation turned into a kaleidoscope of different sights and cultures. He took a bus from Calama to the mining town of Chuquicamata, a clean, modern city with a population of over twenty-eight thousand people. Half of the population was employed by the mine. He walked from the bus station to the mine's Public Relations office and joined the three-hour afternoon tour. It was brutally hot and he sweated continually. He learned that Chile was the largest copper producer in the world, and that Chuquicamata supplied about half of Chile's total output.

The operation was huge. The pit alone was almost four hundred meters deep. The immense deposits were discovered in 1911 and excavation began in 1916. And, like most Chilean copper, it was developed by U.S.-owned corporations, a real sore spot with the Chileans. It was only last year, in 1969, that, after twenty years of trying, the government of Chile was finally able to invest in the mines, buying about twenty-five percent from the Anaconda Corporation.

No one was allowed on the tour without long sleeves and pants. They were given hardhats and protective glasses, and were ushered into the giant smelter building. The heat from the overflowing crucibles made the desert air outside feel cool. While touring the huge open pit, Tomás picked up a couple of small green-colored rocks of low-grade ore. Back in the States he had several small items that he had collected on various travels. He would add these to his collection. He wondered if Maria Elena might like such a souvenir, so he bent down to grab a couple more.

From Chuquicamata, he continued on to the seaport of Arica, the northern-most town in Chile. It was known for its year-round beaches and lively casino. Chile had acquired Arica after the War of the Pacific in the 1870's and 80's, when, defeating both Peru and Bolivia, it had increased its territory by one third. In the process Bolivia had become landlocked, and now half of Bolivia's exports passed through the town.

The bus terminal was on the outskirts of town, and because he never liked the hassle of taxi barter, and also because he was on a serious budget, Tomás shouldered his pack and trudged through the dry heat to the center. He soon had a following of curious children in his wake. He was an oddity, and they stared at him with wide eyes. He could hear them whispering to each other in awe, "*Mochilero! Mochilero!*" A *mochila* was a backpack and a *mochilero* was a backpacker. The way they said it, though, made him feel like he was something out of a Spaghetti Western. He stared straight ahead as he walked, and he felt a little on the wild side.

After finding a cheap hotel, Tomás wandered around the streets and looked at the broad expanse of beaches. He visited the San Marcos Cathedral which was built by Eiffel, of Eiffel Tower fame. He read international newspapers at a fancy hotel bar. After dinner he went to the Casino and watched wealthy, large-gutted men and their bejeweled wives and girlfriends gamble. A couple of the women smiled at him when their husbands weren't looking, and he imagined a late-night liaison.

The next morning he had a sugary pastry and a Coke before boarding the train—not much sustenance for the eleven-hour ride to La Paz. His guidebook said he would have to switch trains at the border, and that there could be considerable delays while Bolivian officials searched for contraband. The train left Arica and after an hour or so it began to slowly climb into the Andes. About half way to the border, the train reached the plateau at over four thousand meters. Some of the surrounding peaks were totally covered with snow, while others were streaked like a Sarah Lee coffee cake. Flocks of alpaca and white-bibbed vicuña grazed on the tundra-like vegetation. Inside the train was freezing, so he pulled his sleeping bag around himself. He ate some food peddled by vendors who boarded the train at little stations in the middle of nowhere, and felt the better for it. Snuggled in his bag, he watched the scenery, dozing occasionally. Time passed slowly. His thoughts turned to Maria Elena.

What was he going to do about her? Did she really, as Oso put it, have the hots for him? Or was he jumping the gun here. Maybe Oso and Kurt were wrong. He knew she respected what he was trying to do in Cufeo, and maybe that was all there was to it. But Oso was pretty damn perceptive. And if he were right, then what about his plans to travel after the Peace Corps? What about Brazil, the Amazon, Columbia? What about buying a motorcycle in Panama and touring through Central America? This was the opportunity of a lifetime, and getting involved would squelch all that. It would have to be the real deal too. Anything less than a total commitment would be a violation; of her, of Juan, of Ramon, of the whole family. Was he ready for that? No. He was too young.

It was interesting, though, that as pretty as she was, he was never tongue-tied or clumsy around her—unlike Oso. They were comfortable with each other. It was a good fit. But what about having a family? Was that what he wanted? Did he want that responsibility? Because that was where it would end up—kids, settling down, and busting his butt in Cufeo forever. He could kiss everything else goodbye. Didn't he want to return to the States? No, not necessarily. He loved Cufeo. Sure it was hard, but it was real. But was he really part of it? Or did he just think he was? Face it, he was still on the outside looking in. And was he ready to settle permanently into a community? That meant involvement with the realities of everyday life. Traveling was a lot easier. Like now. The excitement of seeing new things with no attachments. Just take it all in and move on before you saw what went on behind closed doors—all the struggles and all the pain.

He got up to stretch and walked through the train. Although there was a little bit of steam heat, it was cold. Passengers had collars pulled up and hats pulled down tight. Many were wrapped in blankets, or wore heavy ponchos. Again he felt lucky to have his down bag. For hours and hours the scenery was bleak. Occasionally they passed a cluster of small buildings, but for the most part it was desolate—no trees, no green grass, only windy and cold.

Oso had told him about a Bolivian volunteer that he had met in La Paz. His project was to develop potable water and indoor plumbing for tiny rural schools in this area. The volunteer had said that his biggest problem was that there was almost no paper in these isolated communities, so the people were accustomed to using stones to wipe themselves. When the toilet paper he had provided ran out, they didn't replace it, and went back to using stones again. And they threw the stones down the toilets, continually clogging up the works.

It was beginning to get dark and he looked at his watch. The train was due to arrive in half an hour, but he could see no sign of La Paz on the horizon. He asked the conductor if they were running late; but no, he said, they were right on time. Tomás checked out cheap hotels in his guidebook for a few minutes before he looked out through the window again. Still no lights. La Paz was big—over four hundred thousand people. He should at least see a glow on the horizon. It was also the highest capital in the world at thirty-six hundred meters. Suddenly, the land on his side of the tracks fell away and he looked down into a huge bowl, filled with thousands of twinkling lights. Incredibly, the city lay below him. The lights went down forever, and the train very slowly began to head down towards them. It was a dramatic, circuitous route to the city's center.

He was tired from the long trip so he found a simple hotel, ate, and went right to bed. The next day he explored. He found the city captivating. The Indian women with their long thick black braids reminded him of Maria Elena. But they were mostly stout and they all wore dark felt bowler hats. The market stalls sold everything from fresh produce to black-magic talismans that brought good luck and warded off evil spirits.

La Paz was founded by the Spanish in 1548. The site was chosen for the protection it afforded from the cold winds of the plain above and because gold had been discovered in a nearby river. As he wandered about, he saw dozens of stalls and shops that sold gold jewelry. He thought about buying a pendant for Maria Elena when he visited a jewelry factory. But he did not buy her anything—he thought jewelry would be too personal. Instead, he bought a postcard with a picture of an Indian woman with a thick braid wearing a bowler hat. He wrote to Maria Elena, describing La Paz and the train ride over the Altiplano. He also told her he missed her and thought of her often. He sent it to Pablo's house in Valdivia, wondering how long it would take to get there.

After three days he left La Paz. He went to the tiny port of Guaqui and crossed over to Puno, Peru, via Lake Titicaca. The lake was actually two lakes. The boat passed by the Isle of Sol which, according to legend, was the site of Incan creation. It was a sunny day, and he wondered if the thin air explained why the calm water seemed such an extra-bright blue as it mirrored the sky. He saw some of the boats made out of *totora* reed which the Indians harvested on shore. The reed had other uses—thatching for roofs, fodder for animals, and food for the locals.

At Puno he boarded the train for Cuzco, four hundred kilometers to the north. The train slowly passed isolated, dusty churches and, though they were never below ten thousand feet, the windows were all open and the air was warm. At the frequent stops, vendors swarmed over the train to hawk their wares—orange soda and dark colas in little plastic bags with straws sticking out, roast lamb and stuffed peppers, and little ceramic figures.

He was worn out after the thirteen hour trip and hung out at Cuzco for a few days. There was a lot to see, which was good because he wanted to walk around and get all of the kinks out after so many long train and bus rides. But a few days were barely enough to take in the colonial churches and Incan stonework. He saw a twelve-sided stone, set in an Incan wall, that put the stone walls of New England to shame. Tomás tried to insert the blade of his pocketknife between each of the twelve joints. He could not—the joinery was that tight and precise.

He bought an intricate red Indian poncho for himself, two Indian Altiplano-style ear-flap hats for Javier and Alex, and two more for Juan and Ramon. He also bought a beautiful brown and white, impossibly soft alpaca sweater for Maria Elena. After carefully wrapping the gifts up in cardboard and plastic and lashing them to his pack, he set off by train for Machu Picchu.

Oso had visited the ruins the year before and had given him some good tips. He suggested that Tomás should spend at least a couple of days and bring food and water. He told him that backpackers could sleep in a stone hut at the edge of the ruins, that was watched over by two caretakers who were armed with machetes. The machetes were for the occasional poisonous adder which posed the only danger in the ruins. There was a luxury hotel nearby, but Tomás did not consider that an option. He left his pack in the stone hut and wandered blissfully around the Incan city. Because of its remote location, it was nearly intact. It had never been discovered by the Spanish and, consequently, was never destroyed. For centuries it had been overgrown by jungle, unknown until Hiram Bingham found the ruins in 1911. Subsequent archaeological expeditions from Yale did the excavation.

Oso had loaned him his Machu Picchu guidebook, and Tomás read about the layout of the different structures, courtyards, and temples. He also tagged along with a small tour group and listened to the guide. The ruins were interesting, but he could only walk around them for so long before everything began to look the same. But what made Machu Picchu truly spectacular was its location. It was set high on a mountain and surrounded by other mountains that jutted up from the lush Urubamba River Valley far below. In all directions, everything was steep and green.

That night he shared the hut with a handful of backpackers from different parts of the world. Two were volunteers working in Peru. All of them pooled their food, shared dinner, and smoked a little pot. He would never forget the rest of that night. Through dumb luck, the moon was full. He sat on the ground and leaned back against a large stone and looked out over the ruins. The moon was huge as it cleared the surrounding peaks and it bathed everything with sharp, silvery light. A few llama were grazing in front of him. They were let in at night to keep the grass closely cropped. Above him, to his right, loomed the dramatically steep Huayna Picchu with its rounded nose. He could hear the Urubamba River below. A little later, the soft music of a flute floated over the ruins. He turned and saw the tall, long-haired German backpacker, one of his dinner partners, sitting in front of the hut, playing. Tomás turned back to the moonlit vista and enjoyed the music. Machu Picchu was magical. Suddenly he wished that Maria Elena were by his side.

The next day he explored the surrounding area. He climbed into the caves of the Temple of the Moon, and hiked up Huayna Picchu which afforded an unbelievable view down to the ruins. He remained on top of the mountain for some time. He thought of Maria Elena and realized that there had not been a day of the entire trip when he had not thought of her. Every time he saw something interesting or spectacular, he wanted to share it with her. Did that mean he could not enjoy these things as much without her? No. Of course not. But was he sure? He stood up and started down the mountain. With his first step towards the ruins, he realized that he had passed the zenith of his trip and had begun the long trek back to Santiago. And to Maria Elena.

He hustled back, taking longer bus rides and fewer layovers. Although they had planned that Oso would meet Maria Elena at the bus station, it suddenly felt very important for him to do it. He wasn't sure if he had come to a decision about Maria Elena, but he knew that he was missing her tremendously and wanted to see her as soon as possible.

He surprised Oso with his early arrival, and Oso understood completely when he said he wanted to meet Maria Elena alone. He walked up Avenue Bernard O'Higgins to the bus station that served the south and, with about a thousand butterflies fluttering around in his belly, anticipated her arrival. He should not have been nervous. When the bus arrived and he saw her step down, he felt a warm rush and the butterflies evaporated in an instant. And when she saw him he knew Kurt and Oso were right— she lit up as if someone had turned on a switch.

"Tomás!" she exclaimed and rushed towards him with a huge smile. Her trademark thick long braid was swinging to and fro.

His face felt stretched he was smiling so hard as he quickly walked up to her. They stopped less than a foot apart and stood there grinning like fools. He told her how much he had missed her.

"Me too, Tomás. I missed you every day."

That lit him up and he wanted to take her in his arms; but he only said, "Come on. You must have a bag underneath the bus. We should get it before it disappears."

He took her arm and escorted her over to the cargo doors of the bus. The terminal was crowded, but they could have been the only two people on earth as far as he was concerned. He didn't notice any of the noise from the throngs of passengers or from the many diesel buses. Maria Elena looked terrific. He had wondered if this *campo* girl would fit into the urban scene, but he shouldn't have bothered. She was wearing a lightweight lavender cardigan sweater with the sleeves pulled up a little. Her pleated white blouse was open at the neck, revealing a simple gold chain and tear-shaped pendant against her dark skin. Under her arm she carried a bright red raincoat. Her black skirt was stylishly short and showed more of her legs and more of the true outline of her body than he had ever seen. Her shoes were low-heeled and practical, but smart. God, he thought, she was beautiful. Correction. Sexy and beautiful.

"Would you like a cup of tea or anything before we go to your Aunt's? I located her apartment before I went north on my trip; it is maybe a fifteen minute walk, or five minutes by taxi."

"Let's walk. My suitcase is not....Oh there it is, Tomás, the little brown leather one. Here is my baggage check."

They stopped for tea and talked about the news from Cufeo and their plans for the next couple of days. He told her that Oso had outdone himself and everything was all set. Oso estimated that it might take three or four business days to exchange all of the money. His large apartment, which he shared with two other volunteers, was near downtown, and it was also near a branch of the Banco del Estado and the Peace Corps office. It would serve as command headquarters.

Tomás was glad that Maria Elena's suitcase wasn't any heavier because the walk took a little longer than he thought. They arrived at her aunt's apartment, which was in a working class neighborhood, and they rang the doorbell. There was grillwork in front of the two windows that flanked the front door. Each had potted flowers sitting on the ledge.

The door was quickly opened by a lively little woman wearing a brightly-colored apron over ordinary clothes. When she saw Maria Elena she smiled broadly and gave her a big hug, and told her to spin around a couple of times so that she could get a good look at her.

She laughed and said, "My, Maria Elena, how you have grown into such a lovely woman. And who is this gentleman—your *novio*?"

Maria Elena turned pink and Tomás smiled at her discomfort. There was a strong family resemblance between Maria Elena's aunt and Juan—even her laugh was similar.

Maria Elena said, "Oh no, *Tia*. This is Tomás Young who is a very good friend and is helping us with the road project that I wrote to you about. And I know I mentioned Tomás in my letter."

He said hello and shook the Señora's hand.

"Aah. So you did, Maria Elena, so you did."

She stood there beaming at them for such a long time that he wondered if she were a little simple.

Finally, breaking the silence, he said, "Señora, where would you like your niece's bag?"

He looked past her and noticed that there were knick knacks everywhere in the room, on all the tables, cupboards, and shelves. She also had as many flowering plants as Maria Elena had in Cufeo; there had to be a dozen plants at least. He wondered if a penchant for flowers and gardening was genetic.

"Oh forgive me, Señor Young. Please, both of you come inside. I'm just so excited. I have not seen this… this woman… since she was a little girl."

"Please, Señora, call me Tomás."

"All right...Tomás. But follow me, please. You can put the suitcase down in Maria Elena's room and then we can all have *onces*."

He followed her as she bustled down a narrow hallway. He had eaten a tart with his tea and wasn't the least bit hungry. But when you were invited in Chile for *onces*, it was difficult to refuse. Maria Elena caught his eye. She knew exactly what had just passed through his mind—probably because she had had the same thought. There was no getting out of it for her either.

He met Maria Elena early the next morning at her aunt's where they breakfasted on tea and freshly-baked bread served with an array of jams and jellies. The Señora was bubbly and talkative. He noticed right away that Maria Elena was using the personal 'you' when addressing him, and he very happily followed suit. After breakfast they took a cab to Oso's apartment. Maria Elena gave Oso a big hug and a peck on the cheek. In return, he hugged her back, lifted her off the ground, and twirled her around as she feigned protest.

Tomás said, "Okay you two. How about we get down to business here? You keep this up and you're going to make me cry or something."

Oso, chuckling as he set Maria Elena down, quipped, "What's the matter, Tomás. Are you jealous?"

Tomás blushed and they laughed.

Oso turned serious.

"Well, here's the plan. For the next three days, beginning tomorrow, volunteers will meet us here at ten in the morning. Each one will exchange a different amount of *escudos* depending on how much of their own money they have to cash in. Maria Elena can walk over to the bank when she knows how much to withdraw, and return here with the *escudos*. The volunteers will take them to the bank, and come back here with the dollars. Simple enough, eh?"

"Yes," Maria Elena said. "Perfect. And that lets me meet the volunteers so I can thank them. Yes, it is a good plan, Oso."

She walked over to him, bent down, and kissed him gently on the cheek.

"A million thanks for what you have done. If not for you, I do not think we would ever have come up with the money in time. Tomás and I both know that it has taken a lot of effort and time."

"You are very welcome, Maria Elena. Believe me, it was my pleasure. And besides, it has been great catching up with all the volunteers. Some are friends that I have not seen for two years."

Tomás suddenly stood up.

"Oh, I almost forgot. I have something for you Maria Elena. Wait a moment and I will be right back."

He walked out of the large living room to the nearest bathroom. The apartment was well furnished and had very high ceilings. Much of the time, as he did now, Oso had this large and comfortable space to himself. One of his roommates was a forester who had the enviable job of laying out hiking trails in many of the beautiful national parks. He was away a lot, so Tomás was sleeping in his room. The other roommate was a fisheries expert who split his time between the government office here and studying shellfish at a fishery station near Viña del Mar—the French Riviera of Chile.

Tomás entered the bathroom where he took off the money belt he always wore under his pants when he was traveling. After transferring his depleted stash of dollars and travelers checks to the passport pouch under his shirt, he returned to the living room. He handed the money belt to Maria Elena and told her to wear it under her skirt.

"Very clever, this," Maria Elena said, examining it and zipping the zippers of the various compartments.

"Good thinking, Tomás," Oso said. "That probably is the safest way. I was wondering what she would do with all the cash. She obviously can't put the dollars into the bank and wire them south. Anyway," he said standing up, "I have to go to the Peace Corps Office today and get some things done. So you two are on your own. But how about dinner tonight? With Tomás buying of course."

Tomás frowned at the cheapskate.

"Oso, with your new job, you are being paid a lot more than a volunteer now. Dinner should be on you."

Maria Elena said, "Tomás, do not worry about paying for me. I have discussed the trip's expenses with Don Manuel and Don Pedro, and we all agreed the road fund should pay them. If everything works out like we hope, then we will actually have a little extra money to…"

Tomás interrupted her.

"No no, Maria Elena. It is not you that I worry about taking out to dinner. I would enjoy taking you out to dinner. It is this big oaf over here," he said jerking a thumb at Oso, "and his appetite that I worry about."

"And with good reason," he said, patting his stomach. "But how about we meet here at six this evening? Will that work for you two?"

Maria Elena raised her eyebrows when Tomás said no problem, they should be done with their sightseeing by then. This was news to her. Tomás knew she had never been to Santiago, and before heading north to Peru, he had wandered around the city, making plans for their time together here. He was going to be her own private tour guide.

"Well then," Oso said, "Let's go."

And they left the apartment.

Maria Elena and Tomás began their tour by walking to Cerro Santa Lucia, the seventy meter hill where Pedro de Valdivia founded Santiago in 1541. Back then it had been a tiny fortified settlement which barely survived repeated attacks by the Mapuche Indians. But Valdivia had managed to tough it out, and the conquest of Chile had begun. The hill was now a honeycomb of footpaths, steps, and fountains, crowned by the remains of the old fortress, set on bare rock at the top. They quickly walked up, passing many slower sightseers along the way. All of their walking in Cufeo had them in better shape than most.

They passed raven-haired young lovers snuggling and kissing on the many benches along the paths. Tomás tried not to look at them, and wondered if they made Maria Elena uncomfortable. If they did, she didn't show it. She seemed to not notice. The climb was well worth it; they had a great view of Santiago and a fairly clear view of the Andes, looming in the east. Tomás had read in old guidebooks that one of the beauties of Santiago was the clear view it afforded of the "surrounding and imposing Andes." Unfortunately, that had changed in recent years, as the smog from urban sprawl now made such sightings the exception rather than the rule. Aah, sweet progress, he thought.

They stood in the *torre mirador*—lookout tower— holding on to the iron railing which was already warm from the sun. The whole city lay before them. Tomás had a long list of sights and asked her to choose. She realistically narrowed down her selection so they wouldn't walk their legs off. She chose the Plaza de Armas with its massive Cathedral, the Plaza de la Constitucion with the Palacio de la Moneda— Chile's White House— and the Iglesia de San Francisco which was not only the oldest church in Santiago, but also the oldest building. They were all within walking distance.

So they headed back down the hill, passing the lovers again on their way.

Hours later they took a break and sat down in the busy Plaza de Armas. This was the historic center of Santiago, and all distances in Chile were measured from here. There was a large bronze statue of Pedro de Valdivia sitting on his horse. The horse was heavily muscled, and reminded Tomás of the muscle-bound black stallion that raced at Caman when he was living in the school. There were pigeons everywhere, and flower vendors and many other people on the benches. Everyone was very well dressed. There was a photographer with an old box camera on a tripod. He had a fuzzy fake horse with a little saddle for kids to sit on and have their pictures taken. A *huaso* hat lay balanced on the saddle. Maria Elena and Tomás sat in the plaza for a long time. Tomás noticed that the photographer didn't have a single customer.

The Mercado Central was only a few minutes' walk away, near the south bank of the Rio Mapocho. They entered through a large grillwork gate, and wound their way through a labyrinth of narrow aisles. First, they passed the *carnicerias* where meat saws were whining and the butchers, dressed all in white, cut and wrapped meat behind glass-cased counters. They soon came to the *pescaderia* which had every fish and certainly every clam and mussel imaginable. Tomás had never seen so many kinds of clams. They ranged from fingernail size up to six or seven inches across. Piles of spiny *erizos*—sea urchins—lay on the long wooden tables, next to fish, eel, octopus, and squid. Everything was accessible, and shoppers poked and prodded and asked vendors about their wares.

They continued through the narrow aisles, and wound around to a central eating area where there was a myriad of tiny restaurants behind glass windows.

The food couldn't be fresher, as it came from fish stalls just a few steps away. The competition for patrons was fierce. Waitresses or waiters stood near the doorways and tried to entice passing shoppers inside. Maria Elena and Tomás chose one specializing in seafood, and ate a cheap and excellent *cazuela de mariscos*, a seafood stew.

After lunch they headed over to the Feria Municipal La Vega which was across the river and a few blocks away from the Mercado Central. Maria Elena's aunt wanted to cook at least one big dinner for them before they returned to Valdivia. She had given them a shopping list because she knew that they would be near the markets, and she insisted that they go to the cheaper Feria Municipal for her things.

As interesting as it was to look at the architecture surrounding the Plazas and to read up on the history of Santiago, it was the markets that Tomás enjoyed the most. They were the throb and pulse of the community, where it was all happening, and where one could get a good feel for a place. And as much as he had enjoyed wandering around the Mercado Central, the much larger Feria Municipal La Vega was the place to go. The Feria was the wholesale market of Santiago, and it was huge. Trucks from all over Chile were there, unloading their produce or loading up their purchases. Inside there was an incredible selection of fruits and vegetables—mountains of grapes, plums and nectarines, apples, pears, and cherries. Pineapples and bunches of bananas hung from frames above the booths. Mangos, papaya, passion fruit, and many other tropical fruits he didn't recognize were perfectly stacked in tall, thick pyramids. There were onions, avocados, tomatoes and potatoes, beets, huge mounds of corn, hanging braids of garlic and red peppers, different colored wheels of cheese, vats of pickled peppers, and vats of green and black olives, all different kinds of nuts. Vendors competed side by side, their stalls immaculate, and the fruit shined and the vegetables looked washed and so very fresh.

The crowd bustled and hustled, and laborers carried large sacks over their shoulders. Many pedaled three-wheeled bicycles, with steel frames for carrying cargo mounted above the front wheels. It was busy, but as busy as it was, the vendors were friendly and smiled at them whether they bought something or not. It was interesting and fun. He loved walking around and shopping with Maria Elena, and watching her smile back as she interacted with the vendors. Time passed too quickly, and before they knew it they had to leave. They had to deliver the food before they met Oso for dinner, so they splurged for a cab to Maria Elena's aunt's apartment.

Oso had selected a restaurant from the many situated between the Plaza de Armas and Avenue Bernard O'Higgins. Because he would be paying tonight, Tomás was happy to see that the tables were set with little paper napkins. The prices would be reasonable. They ate roasted chicken and potatoes with fresh green beans, and a simple salad of tomatoes and shredded onion with vinaigrette dressing. Oso selected an excellent bottle of white wine for them to share. He said it was from a little winery located thirty minutes outside of Santiago.

After flan for dessert, they strolled arm-in-arm up to the Plaza de Armas. The weather was mild, so they sat down on little metal chairs set up in front of the round gazebo near the statue of Pedro de Valdivia. The Orchestra of Santiago was playing a program of loud Germanic oompah music. As they listened, Tomás stretched his tired legs out full length. Maria Elena, sitting in the middle, stretched hers too. They sat there for quite awhile, relaxing and digesting their meal while they listened to the music. It was a laid-back evening.

The bank maneuvers began the next morning. Everything went smoothly and each day, Maria Elena looked like she had put on a little more weight around her middle. After tucking the last dollar into the money belt on the morning of the fourth day, Maria Elena and Tomás bought tickets to Valdivia on the evening train. They were eager to change all of those dollars back into *escudos* and deposit them safely into the Road Committee's bank account. Oso would see them off at the station.

That afternoon while Oso was at work, they decided to kill time by taking in a matinee movie. "The Graduate" was still playing in a downtown theater. Tomás had already seen it with Oso at the beginning of his trip and thought Maria Elena would enjoy it. She did, and laughed often. After the movie, they went to a little café for Maria Elena's customary tea with honey. Tomás had a beer. He asked her what she thought about the movie.

"It was very funny Tomás. But I cannot believe the luxury of life in your country—new cars everywhere, swimming pools, the fancy houses. It seems like such an easy life. Can it really be like that?"

"Certainly not for everybody, but for many it is. It's pretty much how I lived at home."

She took a sip of her tea.

"You know, I guess I also found the movie sad. The boy was off all those years at the university without his family and when he returned his own mother and father did not know him. They did not know him or what he wanted. I realize that the boy was confused too, but his family did not even recognize his confusion."

She took another sip of tea.

"And where were the grandparents or the other sisters and brothers, or the neighbors to help out and do something besides drink their *cocteles*? It seems to me that those people had fancy houses and cars; yet they were missing many important things."

"Maria Elena, do you remember when you and I were alone planting your trees, after you walked Javier and Alex to your gate?"

"Yes?"

"And do you remember asking me if I missed my family and I said no?"

"Yes, Tomás, I do remember that."

"Well now you can see why. And I think I told you then that we have a lot of things that you do not have, but most of them are not so important."

She held his eyes for a moment and then sadly nodded. He changed the subject.

"Well, what about Katherine Ross—the girl in the movie. She was a—how would you say—knock-out."

"*Muy guapa*. She was *muy guapa*."

"Well then, I thought she was *muy guapa*. And her hair was beautiful, not as dark and long as yours, but very beautiful." He hesitated and then asked, "Why do you always have yours in a braid? Don't you ever just brush it out and let it hang free?"

"Of course. I brush it every night before bed. But I always braid it in the morning. Every morning."

"And why?" he persisted.

She looked a little embarrassed and began to fidget. She looked down at her teacup and ran her finger around and around the rim. Finally she looked up.

"Do you promise not to laugh, if I tell you?"

"You have my word."

"Well…and you promised, remember…"

She looked at him seriously and he nodded.

"When I was a little girl—about nine I think—my hair was already very long. For some reason, I told Juan that I was going to put it in a braid and not let anyone ever see it hanging free again until I married. My husband would be the first. He laughed at me and teased me, saying that was the stupidest thing he had ever heard and that I would never stick to it. You know how he can be. At any rate, I was stubborn..."

"Oh really. I never noticed."

She gave him a dirty look before she continued.

"And because he made so much fun of me, I persisted, until I had done it for so long that I may as well continue doing it until my wedding day. I did not know, however," she said with a bitter-sweet laugh, "how long that was going to be."

As he finished his beer he wondered if it was possibly in the cards for him to be the first to see her hair all brushed out. He put the glass down and said seriously, "I guess that is as good a reason as any."

He looked at his watch.

"We should get going to Oso's now. We don't want to miss that train."

He pulled out her chair for her.

"Thank you, Tomás," she said, looking at him before turning towards the door.

As he pushed the chair back in under the table, he didn't know if the "thank you" was for pulling out her chair, or for not laughing. As he turned to follow her, he thought again about her hair.

Oso, Maria Elena, and Tomás entered the station and made their way through a bustling crowd up to the train. They located the old Pullman sleeper, or Pullman Cama, as the Chileans called it. Tomás carried their luggage on board while Oso and Maria Elena remained on the platform. Tomás admired the rich mahogany paneling and ran a hand over the dark velvet seats. During dinner, the seats would be made up into bunks complete with thick black curtains for privacy. He put their gear into the luggage compartment, but not before taking the alpaca sweater out of his pack and placing it on the table between their seats. He had paid a lady in a downtown Santiago store to put it in a small box and wrap it in brightly-flowered paper. He asked a well-dressed gentleman across the aisle to please keep an eye on it. The man smiled and assured Tomás that he would.

Tomás returned to the platform and they began saying their goodbyes. Maria Elena's eyes were moist and tears began to run down her cheeks. She hugged and re-hugged Oso.

"Send me your address in the States when you have it. You have Pablo's address in Valdivia so you have no excuse to not write to me at least several times a year. You hear me, you old bear, you?"

Maria Elena was weeping freely now. She impatiently swiped at her eyes.

"Where are our seats, Tomás?"

He pointed through the window.

"Five rows in, on the other side."

She quickly hugged Oso again and stood on her tiptoes and kissed his cheek.

"Goodbye, Oso. You take care of yourself. And write!"

He nodded several times but did not say a word. Tomás could see that he did not trust himself to speak. Maria Elena reached out, and of all places, lightly patted him on his belly a few times. He smiled, his eyes filling. She turned and quickly climbed up into the train.

Oso and Tomás did not say anything. Both wished that the train would leave so that they could get this over with. Passengers went to and fro as the conductors and porters prepared for departure. Finally a conductor motioned for Tomás to get on the train.

Tomás turned to Oso and said, "Well old buddy, I guess this is really good bye. I will miss the hell out of you."

Simultaneously they held their arms out and gave each other an *abrazo* complete with back-thumping. They shook hands and then hugged and thumped each other all over again. When they stepped apart, both had tears running down their cheeks.

"Like Maria Elena told you," Tomás somehow managed to say, "write us from the States, okay?"

"You bet," he said with a teary smile. "Have a safe trip. And good luck with you know who."

"Thanks. I'll need it. And you, have a safe trip wherever you might go and a good life wherever you end up."

They shook hands one last time, and Tomás sadly watched him lumber off toward the platform gate. Oso gave a final wave as he left, and Tomás waved back. Then he climbed up into the train which began to slowly pull away from the platform. He didn't enter the coach for a few minutes. He wanted to compose himself first and he knew that Maria Elena would know exactly what he was doing.

When he finally took his seat across from her, she reached for one of his hands and gave it a squeeze of understanding. He almost lost it when she did that. They smiled sadly at one another and then looked out the window. The train slowly made its way out of the station and they began the long trek south.

Maria Elena pointed at the colorful package and asked, "Where did that come from? Is that yours, Tomás?"

He reached for it and handed it to her.

"No, it is yours. It is a little present I brought for you from Peru."

Her eyes widened in surprise.

"Go on, open it. That is, if you want to," he added.

"Of course I want to," and she quickly began to unwrap it, carefully folding and setting aside the flowered paper. "The paper is very pretty. I will save it to wrap things for Christmas."

She opened the box and her mouth dropped.

"Oh Tomás! It is beautiful," she said as she unfolded the pullover sweater. She held it away from her to get a good look at it, and then up to her to see if it fit. Then holding it against her cheek she said, "It is so soft. I have never felt such soft wool before—never."

"It is made out of alpaca," he said, smiling at her obvious pleasure.

"No wonder..."

She began to pet it.

"No wonder it is so soft." Looking up again, she said, "Thank you Tomás. It is very special. And it is special that you thought of me way up north in Peru."

"Maria Elena..."

"Yes?" she answered while looking down and closely examining the fine hairs of her sweater and looking at the label.

"Would you like to hear just how much I thought of you when I was up north?"

She looked up immediately, the tear streaks still evident on her cheeks.

"Yes, I would, Tomás. Very much."

She put the sweater carefully back into its box, and sat back against the velvet seat with her arms folded across her chest.

"So tell me. Tell me how much."

And he began to tell her all about his trip. He talked and talked, and occasionally she would ask a question. She was a rapt listener and as the country-side passed by, so did the time. They passed Rancagua and headed toward Talca as night began to fall. He told her of the special moments he wished he could have shared with her. With her eyes happy and glisten-ing, she said that he was sharing them with her right now. He told her about the dramatic descent down to La Paz and the Indian women there with the dark braids that reminded him of her. When he concluded with the description of that moonlit night at Machu Picchu, she reached over and held his hand.

"I wish I could have been there with you, Tomás. I really do."

She took her hand back, and he noticed that they were the only passengers in the car. The porters entered and began to change the velvet seats into bunk beds. Yikes, he thought, what time was it? He quickly looked at his watch.

"Aii," he exclaimed jumping up. "By God, Maria Elena, it's late! They'll stop serving dinner soon. We have to hurry and get to the dining car."

She stood up quickly.

"You go ahead and get us a table Tomás. I want to wash my face and hands. I must look a mess from say-ing goodbye to our Oso. I will only be a few minutes behind you."

He could tell that he just made it in time from the unhappy look on the waiter's face as he glanced from Tomás to his watch. The waiter obligingly seated him.

"There will be two of us, waiter. My dinner partner will be here in a few moments."

The waiter went off with a frown to get their menus. Soon, Maria Elena entered the car and spotted Tomás. She smiled and headed his way and, as he stood up, he wanted to whistle. She was wearing the alpaca sweater. It was just the right color for her and—my God!—how it heightened the softness and contour of her body. And he was not alone in his assessment. Every male under the age of seventy turned to admire her as she walked by. He held out her chair and she gave him her little regal nod of thanks as she sat down. The waiter came over with the menus. When he saw Maria Elena—being the Latin male that he was—he suddenly was all smiles and very solicitous.

The choices were chicken, fish, or meat. They both chose the steak, medium rare, and he ordered a bottle of Casillera del Diablo merlot. After the waiter departed, Tomás said that the sweater looked great on her.

"Yes, I think so too. And it fits perfectly."

She looked down to her chest and his eyes followed hers. He couldn't agree more.

"I also have gifts for the boys and Juan and Ramon."

He described the Altiplano Indian hats, and she said that Javier and Alex would love them. But she bet him that Juan and Ramon would never wear theirs. She stuck out her hand. He shook his head. He knew that she usually won her bets, and she certainly knew her brother and uncle better than he did.

"No bet," he said. "But we'll see."

They talked about everything—travel—movies—Oso—their families—life in Cufeo.

As the waiter was clearing the dinner plates, she asked Tomás, "What do your parents do?"

"My father sells *seguro*."

"What kind?"

"All kinds—automobile, health, homeowner's. You name it and he's probably got a policy for it." There was no insurance of any kind in Cufeo.

"This homeowner's insurance. What is that?"

"The company will pay to replace something stolen out of your home, or to rebuild it if something were to happen—like, say you parked an oxcart of *carbón* too close and it caught fire. But to have this *seguro*, it costs you money every month. And you might pay for it your whole life and never have a problem."

Maria Elena thought about that for awhile. It must have been such a foreign concept.

"And your mother? What does she do?"

"She cooks for my father and washes their clothes in a washing machine. She does dishes in a dishwasher and she drives to the *supermercado* to buy all their food. Other than that, she grows flowers. She is president of a garden club, so she spends a lot of time organizing competitions where women arrange their flowers and judges decide which are the best."

"Does she grow vegetables with her flowers?"

"No. Not even a radish."

Maria Elena shook her head in disbelief.

"What are their winters like?"

"Much colder than here. There is a lot of snow and ice, but my parents only use a very small amount of wood—in their fireplace. Most of their heat is from burning oil. All they have to do is turn a dial on the wall and the house will be as warm as they want."

Maria Elena was silent. He realized talking to her about the States made him uncomfortable. Life there was so different that it had nothing to do with them. Thankfully the waiter came with their dessert of apple pie.

Halfway through the pie, Maria Elena looked up.

"Tomás. Do you have a *palola* or a *novia* waiting for you back in your country?"

The question took him by surprise.

"No. No one."

She looked at him more closely.

"Truly?"

He smiled.

"Truly. I was too busy with my studies and sports during school to get seriously involved with anybody. And I traveled too much in the summers."

He looked straight into her eyes.

"And I guess I never met anyone really special—like you."

Their eyes locked.

After a few seconds she grinned and said, "That is good."

She picked up her glass and, still grinning, held it towards him.

"Could I have some more wine, Tomás?"

There were only a few diners left by the time they finished their dessert. He took care of the bill, leaving a handsome tip for the waiter who really had been very good. Maria Elena again tried to pay for her dinner, but he told her that taking the train had originally been his idea, and that part of the idea was to have a dinner like this —with him paying for it. She acquiesced and, as they started to get up, the waiter hurried over to pull out her chair. She thanked him, bestowing one of her trophy smiles. Tomás thought the waiter was going to melt.

Tomás watched her as they walked down the length of the dining car. She was wearing that short black skirt which was very likely the only stylish skirt that she owned. It certainly was the only skirt that she had brought to Santiago because she had worn it every day. Tomás could not help ogling her, and he looked up guiltily just in the nick of time when she suddenly turned.

"Tomás, I have a little confession to make and I want to ask you again not to laugh at me. Okay?"

"Okay."

"When I was little, Juan and I took a train ride in the summer, with my parents, to Puerto Montt. He and I raced around and ran from car to car. The train was old and slow and everything was very casual. The doors were always left open for ventilation in the summer and you could have jumped right off if you had wanted to. Juan and I were crossing between cars and this old train was very jerky. It suddenly lurched and I fell down on the metal floor, skinning my knee. And I almost rolled out the door. The track was rushing by and I was heading right for it. Juan grabbed my leg just in time, or I would have fallen off."

"You must have been terrified."

"I was. Terribly. I cried and cried, even when we returned to our seats with our parents. I used to have nightmares about it. And ever since then, as much as I love to travel on trains, I am still scared when I go from car to car. It was a good thing we were late for dinner because I made myself run and jump each time I crossed from one car to the next."

He laughed, picturing the sight.

"Tomás! You promised."

"No, no, Maria Elena. I am not laughing at your fear. That is not funny and it is very understandable. I am laughing at your jumping—I would have loved seeing you do that."

"Well, if you understand, then would you mind holding my hand when we cross the cars on our way back?"

With a swooping gentlemanly bow, he said, "Of course, Señorita; con mucho gusto," and he reached for her hand.

They crossed over to the next car but he did not let go of her hand. He held on to it the entire way, even though that had not been her request. She did not complain though, and judging from the warm smiles of their fellow passengers, they must have looked like the consummate young lovers. He also noticed a few envious looks from male passengers, and he could not help but feel proud. But it was indeed a serious business for Maria Elena to cross from one car to another. Each time she nervously gauged the distance and fiercely gripped Tomás's hand. They had just made their final crossing, and his free hand was on the door handle, when the train gave a big lurch. It threw them off balance, but he quickly caught himself by hanging on to the door. Still, it was enough to scare her. She let out a little scream and threw herself against his chest.

"Don't worry, I have got you," and he held on to her tightly for a few moments.

Her hands and forearms were flat against his chest and her eyes were squeezed tightly closed.

When she opened them and looked at him, he said softly, "And I am not going to let go of you—ever."

It was noisy, and the train continued to lurch. This was no place to get romantic. He opened the door to their car and let Maria Elena pass by before he closed the door and shut out most of the noise. She turned and stood facing him in the short passageway that led to their berths. He pulled her into his arms. He reached up, held her face, and gently kissed her. Then he looked into her eyes.

"Maria Elena, I love you so very much, and I have for such a long time."

She softly stroked his cheek.

"I know, Tomás, I know."

They kissed again and looked at each other so intently that he felt a surge of emotion take over his entire being. The floodgate was finally open, and his love poured out to her. He could feel hers in return. It felt like he was part of her, and she part of him. It was strange and intense. He wondered if she felt it too. He kissed her as deeply as he could. They surfaced and she swayed a little, and he did not think it was due to the motion of the train. They fiercely embraced, and their hard-pressed bodies could not possibly have been closer. He tried to breathe in all of her; her skin and hair smelled so good and he could just detect the scent of the wine she had had with dinner. He could feel her soft breath on his neck as he passed his hands slowly over and down the length of that long thick braid that he had wanted to touch forever. He put a hand on the small of her back. He never wanted to let go of her. He could have stayed like that forever.

After awhile her breathing became very soft and regular and he wondered if she had fallen asleep. But moments later she said, "Tomás…"

"Hmm?"

"Do you want the upper or lower?"

He pulled away from her, brushing a stray lock of hair from her face.

"What?"

"Do you want the upper or the lower berth?"

"Oh. Right. I don't care. Which do you want?"

He snuggled up again.

She did not hesitate.

"The lower".

"Okay," he murmured. "That is fine with me. We'll take the lower then."

She pushed away from him and with her arms straight, hands on his chest exclaimed, "Tomás!"

"Just joking, Maria Elena. Just joking, *mi querida.*"
He sighed.

"The upper will be fine," he said meekly, and she allowed him to pull her back in close.

They stood there cheek to cheek for awhile longer before she said, "Come on, Tomás. We have to get some sleep. We will be in Valdivia before you know it."

And he let her lead him away to their berths.

CHAPTER SIXTEEN

La Cuchillada (The Stabbing)

"Life is good, eh Salton?"

Tomás leaned forward and patted the big gray neck. It was a beautiful late October day—sunny but cool—and his favorite panorama of distant volcanoes backed by deep blue sky lay before him. He was returning from Lote Once where he had explained the food-for-reforestation program to a couple of farmers. They decided to participate and he had walked their land to determine the best areas to reforest.

A lot had happened since he and Maria Elena had returned from Santiago. And other than Juan, all of it was good. There had been no glitches in Valdivia. They had decided to leave their luggage at Pablo's house and exchange the money right away. Miriam was home alone and insisted on making them breakfast. The boys were at school, and Pablo was buying animals in Paillaco. Sitting at the little table in the kitchen, it did not take long before Miriam knew that something was up between them. They tried to temper their looks at each other, and their touches were limited to the inadvertent. But they were so charged that when they did touch—like when he passed her the honey for her tea—he was surprised when there were no sparks. By the time they were ready to leave, Miriam smiled knowingly and her eyes danced with merriment. He figured that all of Cufeo would know within the week.

Everything went smoothly with the money exchange and they deposited almost ninety-six thousand *escudos* into the Road Committee's account. They had done it. Maria Elena said she had to pinch herself—she could not believe it. She was ecstatic. They returned to the *campo* early that afternoon, taking turns carrying her little suitcase up the hill. The walk up to Caman had never gone so quickly. It seemed like they had just stepped off the bus when they arrived at her gate. He reluctantly left her there, and felt a void as he continued on to the farm. They had been together pretty much round the clock for the last six days.

Even though they kept their relationship as private as possible, it did not take long for rumors and gossip to abound. Everywhere he went, Tomás received smiles and winks and pats on the back. When he visited a farmer, he was always asked how Maria Elena was. They had become an item in the eyes of Cufeo, and their relationship was accepted by everyone—except for Juan. The new relationship rocked him. Maria Elena had told him immediately, and he made his feelings clear on Tomás's first visit. When he entered the house, Juan stood up from his chair and said coolly, "Don Tomás." There was no smile or pat on the back. There was not even the customary handshake. When Maria Elena took his hand and led him over to the table, Juan stormed out of the house without a word. Her smile vanished.

"I knew he would be like this," she said.

They could hear the blows of the axe as Juan began to split wood. He split piece after piece. Maria Elena's expression hardened.

"But it's not fair. I have taken care of him forever; cooked all his meals, washed his clothes, nursed him during his injuries. And now that I have finally found someone to love and I am happy, he gets mad. He is so selfish!"

Tomás brought his chair up close and covered her hands with one of his.

"He is scared of losing you, *querida*. And who can blame him? I don't know if I would act the same if I were in his shoes, but I certainly know I wouldn't be happy about it. This is something we all have to get used to."

She tried to smile, but it was a poor attempt. Juan continued to methodically split wood.

Tomás stood up.

"I will see you tomorrow. Right now I want to try to talk to him."

She walked him to the door. He held both her hands and lightly kissed her.

"Wish me luck."

He sat down on the edge of the porch and watched Juan split wood. He was very good at it. In one whack he split the smaller pieces cleanly in half. As he worked the bigger pieces, he always struck in the same place. When Tomás split wood at the farm, his axe rarely struck the same place twice.

Juan had worked up a good sweat, and when he reached for his handkerchief to wipe his brow, Tomás said, "You are angry with me."

Juan glared at him as he put his handkerchief away. "Yes; that is the truth."

He started to turn back to his work, but Tomás walked up close, giving him no room to swing his axe.

"Why? What is wrong?"

Juan leaned the axe up against the woodpile.

"What do you think, Don Tomás? Eh? I trust my sister to go to Santiago because you and Oso were to watch over her—so nothing would happen to her. Well, you watched over her alright. Very closely it seems. Just what happened on that train? Eh?"

He was getting worked up and Tomás was glad the axe was leaning against the woodpile.

"Listen to me! Oso and I DID watch over her in Santiago and she was never in any danger. And NOTHING happened on that train. I would never do anything to compromise Maria Elena's honor."

Juan continued to glare. When he reached for his axe, Tomás did not move an inch. They looked at each other. Finally Juan walked towards the tool shed.

"Don Juan, wait a minute."

He stopped.

"I just want you to know one thing, and that is that I love your sister. This will not change. Not now. Not ever. Better get used to it."

Juan didn't say anything. Tomás turned and walked away.

Ramon was not at all surprised by the turn of events. He had suspected that this would happen ever since Maria Elena had gotten so angry when Tomás returned, injured, from Lote Once. He gave Tomás a little lecture about respecting his niece, and how important the honor of a woman was in Chile. Tomás told him not to worry—Maria Elena's honor was sacred to him. One thing Ramon certainly did not mind was the frequent arrival of Maria Elena bearing warm *empanadas* and *sopaipilla*. And he could not help but notice their charged aura. He smiled often as he watched them interact.

Tomás decided to extend with the Peace Corps. The process was just a formality. He knew that there would be no problem with the Ministry of Agriculture because of the number of *campesinos* in the reforestation project. And his track record with the Peace Corps was good because of the success of both the road project and the food-for-reforestation program. After he received the formal approval in Valdivia, he made a beeline back to the *campo* and to the Montoyas. He entered their compound and bent down to pet Muchacho, who knew him so well now that he did not offer so much as a "woof." Maria Elena saw him from the kitchen window and was soon outside.

"You look like a Cheshire cat, Tomás. Why are you grinning so much?"

"Oh no reason, I guess—other than I hope you can put up with me for another year."

"Oh Tomás," she exclaimed and jumped into his waiting arms. "Your extension has been approved."

He nodded and hugged her hard. He doubted that Juan would be as happy with the news. Muchacho was pushing his head hard into his leg, upset that his ear rub had been so abruptly interrupted. Tomás freed a hand to tend to him and kept the other locked around Maria Elena's narrow waist. For anyone passing by, it was a very domestic-looking scene.

"Come, Tomás," she said after a few moments. "Come with me to the garden and see how I want to lay it out."

He took her hand and they strolled towards the garden with Muchacho, tail wagging, following close behind.

Tomás set up the meeting with Kurt to pay the community's share of the road costs. Kurt said it would be good PR for his agency to be seen working successfully, hand-in-hand, with a needy rural community, so they should expect a reporter from *El Correo* to be at the meeting. Tomás decided to not attend because he didn't want to draw attention to the Peace Corps's role. Manuel lobbied to be the one to present the check, and nobody disagreed.

Minutes before the scheduled meeting, the Road Committee stood on the steps of the INDAP building. Don Pedro wore a dark suit and his best white shirt with the top button buttoned. He kept running a finger between his weathered neck and his collar. He looked nervous and uncomfortable. His wide brimmed hat was in his hand and he was uncharacteristically silent. At least, Tomás thought, he had done a pretty good job of shaving. Usually he had little pieces of tissue stuck to various shaving mishaps. But today he was smooth-faced with no evident wounds.

Manuel carried a little brown briefcase with the bank check tucked safely inside. He was nattily dressed in a well-pressed suit, a starched white shirt, and a narrow dark tie. His shoes had a mirror shine, and he wore a narrow-brimmed flannel hat. He could easily have passed for one of the government bureaucrats entering the building. Like Don Pedro, he seemed nervous. He could not stand still, and was continually brushing off one arm or the other or adjusting his necktie.

Maria Elena, on the other hand, appeared calm. Tomás knew that she was excited that all of their hard work had finally come to fruition. He also knew that she would be happy when this was over. She was dressed in a medium-length wool skirt, a white blouse, and her Alpaca sweater.

He squeezed her hand.

"I'll be waiting in the café. Good luck." He held the door open and they filed in.

They were gone for over an hour. Tomás passed the time at the café drinking coffee and trying to translate the slang of a new *Condorito* comic book. He put asterisks by the captions he didn't understand so that he could ask Maria Elena later. When they finally joined him in the café for a celebratory coffee and tea, they were excited.

"Well, how did it go?" he asked as he held out a chair for Maria Elena.

"Thank you, Tomás. It went very well. Kurt was great. He made everyone feel at ease—or at least almost everyone," she said, smiling at Don Pedro. "When Don Manuel handed Kurt the check, he told us that the road construction would begin within two weeks. Three at the most."

Tomás was skeptical. Government agencies, all of them, were known to drag their feet forever before actually starting a project. The waitress came over and took orders. Coffee for the two men and tea for Maria Elena. Tomás asked for a glass of water.

Don Pedro, who seemed relaxed and his usual self, leaned back in his chair and said, "Don Tomás, you would have been proud of Don Manuel. Although he was so nervous his hands were shaking, he did not drop the check when he handed it to Sr. Kurt in front of the photographer."

Maria Elena added, "They took several pictures of Don Manuel handing the check to Kurt. Don Pedro and I were standing behind them, but I do not think you will see us because Don Manuel fluffed up like a big turkey for the camera."

"The article and picture will be in tomorrow's *Correo*," Manuel said excitedly. "I know because I asked the reporter."

"And I bet you will be at the doors of the *Correo* at five tomorrow morning with a wheelbarrow, fighting with the newsboys to get enough copies to fill it," Tomás said.

The waitress came over and handed out their drinks. Tomás held up his glass of water.

"But seriously; congratulations to all of us. Here's to the Road Committee for all of their hard work and for a job well done."

They clinked cups and glass, and all happily took a sip.

The Road Committee returned to Cufeo while Tomás stayed for, of all things, a Halloween party that was being given at the Chilean-North American Institute. His district rep had pressured him and two other volunteers from the area to attend. There were few North Americans in this part of the world, so he wanted the three of them to at least make an appearance.

Tomás felt ridiculous in his costume as they rode towards the party on a city bus. Every head was turned their way, and he felt that they deserved every stare and giggle. Thankfully they soon reached their destination, and the catcalls and whistles faded as the bus pulled away. The volunteers at his side had only recently arrived in Chile. On his left was Mike whose Spanish was about like his had been when he'd first arrived. Mike was working out of a SAG office in Los Lagos, about sixty kilometers to the west. On his right was Jack who had a masters degree in forestry and was teaching at the University Austral in Valdivia. Because his family was Basque and spoke Spanish at home in Colorado, Jack was fluent. He had taken over Oso's house, and Mike and Tomás would crash there tonight.

Their costumes were not very creative. Although they both had short hair, Jack and Mike had decided to go as hippies. They wore sandals, ragged blue jeans, t-shirts, lightweight ponchos, and lots of beads. Most of the catcalls were directed at Jack because his jeans were cut-offs, a definite no-no in Chile. Men did NOT wear shorts unless they were playing soccer or at the beach. Tomás was dressed as a Peruvian Indian. His cheap sandals had tire tread for soles, and he wore the bright red poncho that he had bought in Cuzco. He rolled his pants up to his calves, and he had borrowed Ramon's Peruvian ear-flap hat. He also wore a long strand of colorful round beads, made from seeds, that he had bought from a train vendor in Peru.

The Institute was lodged in a fine old Victorian house. It had several gables and ornate trim around the large windows and along the edge of the steep roof. It could use a fresh coat of paint, but it was still much nicer than the other buildings in the neighborhood. The Institute hosted cross-cultural activities and offered English courses for Chileans, and Spanish courses for foreigners. It celebrated both U.S. and Chilean holidays, which explained the costume party tonight.

They passed through the tall front doors and entered a high-ceilinged foyer. They were greeted by a good-looking witch dressed in black, and wearing a pointed hat. She was seated at a massive wooden desk, and gave them a bright smile that showed that two teeth had been blacked out. They introduced themselves and exchanged pleasantries while she printed out nametags. They could hear faint music from another room. It sounded like the Beatles. The kindly witch directed them toward the music, and they passed through another set of tall doors.

They entered a large, festively decorated room. Orange and black bunting draped from the walls to a central chandelier, and fake spiders dangled from their webs in the corners. Here and there, black cardboard cats raised their backs. At the far wall, tables covered with orange tablecloths and colored gourds were pushed together into a long banquet table. On each end was a large punch bowl, and plates of sandwiches and other snacks were scattered among the gourds.

Most of the young women were standing around a punch bowl at one end of the table, while the men were standing around the other one. Everyone had taken their costumes seriously. There were a few witches, some ghosts and goblins, but more than anything else, there were masked cowboys and cowgirls. The three volunteers guessed that if there was any alcohol to be had, it would be in the punch bowl where the men stood. They headed straight to it and were not disappointed. They filled cups and chatted about the Peace Corps and other volunteers they knew in common.

Over the course of the evening, inhibitions were softened by the alcohol, and some of the Chilean men began to ask about life in the States. Was the free love movement for real? Did they know anyone who had gone to Woodstock? Did every teenager have their own car? Did they really put a man on the moon? Oddly, Tomás thought, no questions about Vietnam. Most of the Chileans were young professionals, along with a few university students. The students, none of whom were studying forestry, were surprised to learn that Jack was a professor.

Tomás enjoyed listening to the American music while Jack and Mike danced. Jack was big, with a linebacker's build, and he towered over the Chilean girls. Mike had a winning, disarming smile. With his stumbling, shy Spanish, the girls flocked around him. When Tomás learned that Oso had trained them in Santiago, he told the story about Oso punching his horse. He also told them stories about Cufeo which had them wide-eyed. Tomás felt very much the seasoned volunteer.

Only half-melted chunks of ice remained in the punch bowl when the party began to break up. It was almost midnight and the three of them had a pretty good glow on. They wolfed down a couple more sandwiches and headed to the door to thank their hosts who were politely waiting for the last stragglers to leave. The buses had stopped running, so they walked towards the center of town along Avenida Errazuriz. The street passed the whorehouse that Manuel had taken Tomás to, almost two years ago.

As they approached it, they could hear lively Latin music, quite a change from the music at the party. Tomás told Jack and Mike about the place. Since they weren't ready to call it a night, they decided to go in—obviously not thinking too clearly because they were still dressed in their costumes. The walls were still filthy, and all of the tables were taken. It was a mixed clientele—city laborers, *campesinos*, and at one table were four greasy looking youths. There was only one whore who was not seated at a table. She was very drunk and was holding on to the jukebox. When she saw them enter, her worn face broke into a smile, and she staggered over. She thought they would be good for a drink or two.

Tomás had no idea what Jack and Mike thought of this dive because he didn't have time to ask. The old whore tripped as she came over and reached out for him to keep from falling. She missed, but succeeded in grabbing his strings of beads which broke, and the colored seeds cascaded to the floor. Tomás barely caught her elbow which saved her from going down hard; but she did go down. He helped her up, and looked at the beads scattered all over the room. If they weren't already the center of attention with their costumes, they certainly were now.

"*Por Dios!* Are you okay?" Tomás asked.

She dumbly looked around the floor before answering.

"Yes, I am fine. But your beads. I am so sorry."

Some of the *campesinos* and laborers were chuckling.

One yelled out, "Now you have done it, Maria old girl."

As she turned to see who had spoken, she took a step backwards and crunched several of the beads. She immediately looked at Tomás with such a comically guilty expression that he burst out laughing.

"It's okay, Maria. All those beads cost me no more than *una luca*."

She smiled with relief and looked down at the beads. After a moment, with hands on hips and slightly swaying, she turned back to Tomás.

"Well, there certainly are a lot of them."

She sighed and got down on all fours and started to pick them up, one by one. Tomás kneeled down to help and before long both of them were giggling at the absurdity of the situation. Tomás forgot about Jack and Mike who were standing in the middle of the dance floor. Conversation in the bar resumed. Soon Tomás heard a few insulting whistles and comments from the hoodlums' table, and he looked up. They were making fun of Jack's exposed legs. One of them loudly asked why a *mariposa* would come into a bar for real men. *Mariposa* meant butterfly, but, in this case, it was slang for queer and was a serious insult. The conversations stopped at the other tables, and Mike and Jack began to look very uncomfortable.

The smart thing would have been to leave immediately. But instead, Tomás became angry and made the unpleasant situation even worse.

He said to the wise-ass, "You must not have too many brains if you insult someone who could kick your butt from here to Osorno."

Not a very bright move, and it didn't take long to turn into one of those—"Oh, is that right?" "Yeah!

That's right!"—situations. Jack was challenged to a fight out in the streets. With a little shoving they headed to the door. Outside, the tallest squared off in front of Jack. Jack calmly took off his poncho and handed it to Mike. When the Chilean saw Jack's linebacker build bulging with muscles, he quickly changed his mind and backed off. But Tomás laughed at him, so the thug came right at him instead. No punches were thrown as they grabbed and wrestled each other. Tomás was a little quicker and managed to get a foot and leg behind the Chilean and pushed him. He fell awkwardly and hard to the ground. When he got back up, he reached into his pocket and pulled out a knife.

Suddenly everything was in slow motion for Tomás. In a fraction of a second, he decided that the Chilean had pulled a knife because he was scared. He decided not to back down. He reached into his pocket and pulled out the knife he always carried. He smoothly flicked open the blade and, just like in the movies, he got into a crouch and moved from side to side. He had never been in a situation like this before and he certainly had never pulled a knife on anyone. He was totally bluffing. They eyed each other. Tomás was focused intently and everything seemed extra sharp. He saw fear in the Chilean's eyes, and hoped his showed nothing. They circled each other, but did nothing. Finally Tomás straightened up.

Very calmly he said, "It is not worth it. One of us will go to the hospital and the other to jail. It is not worth it," he repeated.

He folded up his knife and put it back in his pocket. Relief surfaced in the Chilean's eyes, and he nodded and did the same. No one had lost face and it was over. His gamble had paid off. But, just at that instant, someone blindsided him. He got walloped on the side of his face and was knocked down to one knee. As he stood back up, there was some shoving and shouting in the dim light, and then suddenly the Chileans were gone. They just disappeared into the dark.

Jack asked, "Are you alright?"

Rubbing his jaw, Tomás said, "Yeah, I'm okay. Someone sucker-punched me."

"Yeah, I know. I saw him do it. When I went to grab him, I think another one of those creeps stuck me in the butt," he said, straining to look behind him.

He loosened his pants and stuck a hand under his belt and felt his rear end. When he withdrew his hand, there was blood all over it."

"Jesus," Tomás said.

He couldn't believe it. Suddenly it hit him. This had been no game. Those punks had meant business.

"Jesus Christ, Jack! Mike, are you alright?"

"I'm OK. They didn't do anything to me."

He turned back to Jack.

"Well the good news is the hospital is close by. Come on, let's get you checked out."

As they began walking, Jack said, "Wouldn't you know it. Of all the places to get stabbed! I am supposed to take my class up to the university's forestry camp in the coastal range on Monday. By horseback."

Mike and Tomás broke into laughter. Picturing Jack with his sore butt on horseback, riding slowly up a mountain, struck them as hysterically funny. Even Jack chuckled at the irony of the situation. They continued walking to the hospital. Tomás soon found himself taking unusually deep breaths. He thought maybe it had something to do with coming down off of the adrenaline rush, but when his back started hurting too, he stopped.

"Hey guys, wait a minute. I feel a little weird."

He reached around and felt under his shirt. It was wet and slimy. When he brought his hand out it was covered with blood.

"Shit! I've been stabbed too. In the back. Fuck me! Let's get a move on to the hospital."

He couldn't believe it. He had never felt it. And he realized that it had been very professionally done. It was like a pickpocket who bumps hard into his target and, at the exact same moment, lifts his wallet—the victim feels the bump rather than the hand in his pocket. Tomás must have been hit with one hand and stabbed with the other.

Jack received a few stitches and a penicillin shot in the butt. The doctor told him he could go home, but Tomás had to stay. An x-ray revealed that the knife had just punctured his lung and it had deflated a small amount. The doctor believed he would be all right and the lung should re-inflate on its own. If it didn't, then they would have to insert a tube and suck the air out of the chest cavity. Tomás was to stay at the hospital so they could monitor him. They sewed up his back, gave him some shots, and took him to a private room. He gingerly climbed into bed and fell asleep. Some time later, when it was still dark, he woke up in agony. He threw up several times and his back felt like it had been seared. Just rewards for having been so damn stupid, he thought.

The doctor was right. By having him breathe pure oxygen and doing some different inhalation exercises, his lung quickly filled to normal capacity. The doctor said he was very lucky; it could have been much worse. On the third day in the hospital he was still feeling a steady throb from the wound, and he hoped it wasn't becoming infected. There was a knock on the door and Ramon poked his head in. Tomás tried to look beyond him into the hall.

Ramon smiled.

"Don't worry. She is talking with the doctor. I must tell you, though, that she learned some of the details of the...er...incident. She is not happy. Better said, she is very angry with you."

Tomás wondered who had told her about it. In a small voice, he said, "The whole thing was stupid and it could have easily been avoided."

Ramon set his hat down on the end of the bed and brought a chair over. He looked like he had not shaved for a couple days.

"Before I forget," he said, "Juan wanted me to tell you to get better quick."

That perked him up. Maybe Juan was coming around a little.

"Tell him that's much appreciated. And tell him that at least he won't have to worry about me molesting his sister for awhile."

"How long is awhile?"

"The doctor wants me here for another day or two to take some more x-rays. Then I will have to take it easy for a few more days at least. And absolutely no horseback riding for a couple of weeks."

"Then you must stay with Pablo and Miriam in town."

Tomás shook his head. He didn't want to put them out. He said he could stay in Oso's old place, but Ramon wouldn't hear of it.

"And probably sleep on the floor; or at best, on a couch. And who will cook for you? And believe me, Miriam will not allow this. She will be very angry with you if you do not stay with them and...."

Ramon stopped in mid sentence as Maria Elena strode purposefully into the room. From the look on her face, Tomás knew immediately that he was in trouble. Ramon picked up his hat; he didn't want any part of it.

"Then it is settled. I will go now and talk to Pablo and Miriam, and I am sure they will come by later. I will come back this afternoon, Don Tomás, before I take the bus back."

Tomás tore his eyes from Maria Elena and said, "All right. And thank you for coming all the way in to see me. I am sorry I have interrupted your chores. Who is watching the farm?"

"Flor," he said as he walked to the door. "I will see you later this afternoon and," turning to Maria Elena, "I will see you on the bus, if not at Pablo's, eh?"

"Yes, *Tio*, at one or the other," she said without looking at him.

Ramon raised his eyebrows at Tomás before leaving the room. He shut the door silently behind him.

Maria Elena and Tomás looked at each other for a long while before she spoke.

"The doctor said you were very lucky. Another inch or two and it could have been life threatening."

She started to pace back and forth at the foot of the bed.

"I heard from Don Manuel where it happened and some of how it happened."

Manuel. Of course, Tomás thought. He would know of the goings-on at that place.

"Are you listening, Tomás?"

"Yes, Maria Elena."

Steam was almost coming out her ears.

"What were you thinking? That is about the dumbest thing I have ever heard. Going THERE, dressed as an Indian no less. How could you do something so... so stupid!"

He shrugged his shoulders.

"I was not going to stay there overnight or anything. I only wanted to show my friends the place and I was not thinking straight. I agree it was stupid. I should never..."

She interrupted.

"Now that is an understatement—not thinking straight."

"Maria Elena, I know that it was a dumb decision. Okay? And believe me, I am paying for it."

But there was no sympathy. She was relentless.

"You could have been killed, Tomás. Did you ever think of that? And what for? What a waste that would have been. What if…"

He interrupted her, "But I am very much alive, Maria Elena."

His back was killing him, and he felt that he had received enough abuse from her for one day.

"Lay off, okay?"

That was the wrong thing to say. She exploded.

"Lay off, you say? You do not think you deserve to hear this? After what you did? Here I thought I finally have found a man who is different from the others. One I could love and respect. How can I respect you after what you did? Eh? Tell me that."

"I am sorry, Maria Elena. That is all I can say. I AM SORRY. I AM SORRY I am not perfect like you. And I AM SORRY you cannot respect me. And that about says it all, doesn't it? If you can no longer respect me, then we have nothing. Nothing at all."

He was suddenly rip-shit and couldn't stop.

"You see that door over there," he said pointing. "Why don't you use it and leave me alone. I do not need any more of this."

She stopped pacing and they glared at each other. She nodded slowly.

"I see I was wrong about you."

She walked over and opened the door and gave him one last scathing look.

"*Adios*, Tomás."

Three days later he moved into Pablo's and Miriam's house. It was a small and plain two-story affair with a few small paned windows and gray weathered siding. Downstairs was much like the farm, with a large formal room that was never used, a narrow hallway with stairs, and a kitchen and pantry area where everyone hung out around the wood-burning stove. The biggest difference was the indoor plumbing—they had running water in the kitchen and a single bathroom on the first floor. Upstairs were three tiny bedrooms—one for Miriam and Pablo, and one for each of the boys. He was given Javier's room.

He was still pretty much bedridden, and the downstairs bathroom created the indignity of having someone else take care of his chamber pot. Miriam climbed up and down the creaking stairs to bring him his meals, and hovered over him like a mother hen. He hated to be such a bother. As he became more mobile, he tried to think of things he could do to help out. He made his bed and tried to split wood for the kitchen stove. But after one whack, he knew that it was a bad idea. Miriam wouldn't let him do the dishes, so he decided to explore the neighborhood. Pablo rented a few hectares behind the house which he had fenced in for the livestock that he bought and sold. A pair of matched young oxen were peacefully grazing there, and next to the house was a small fenced-in garden.

His body was healing, but he wished he could say the same for his spirits. "*Adios*" she had said so coldly. That was not a 'Bye, see you later.' It was more like 'So long pal! It was fun while it lasted.' It was a good-bye with finality. And there was no doubt that she had meant it. He had not measured up to her expectations. He had blown it. He was miserable.

But could it be over just like that, he wondered. Was that all there was to it? Could something he felt so deeply be gone so quickly? He couldn't believe it. But this was all new territory for him, so he didn't know. He did not sleep well. He tried to shake it off, thinking, well hell, that certainly simplified things. No strings and restraints now. He would see the road completed and after this year's planting, head on out. It was going to be a drag, though, working for another year with her nearby. But maybe he could somehow cut his extension short. That was it—button up his work and get the hell outta Dodge. Travel A.S.A.P.. Make way Brazil and Amazon basin, here I come! But he wasn't fooling himself and he felt lousy. He had no appetite. His stomach was a knot. He ached. Everyone in the house knew what was going on. Conversations were muted. No one mentioned Maria Elena. There was not the customary banter. Even Javier and Alex were quiet.

Five more days passed before he went to the hospital to get the stitches pulled and for a final x-ray. The doctor cleared him to return to the *campo*. He said that Tomás had healed fine, but to still take it easy. And absolutely no horseback riding for at least another week. Tomás told the family the good news and that he planned to take the bus out to Cufeo the following day. Pablo said he would go with him to carry his pack. Tomás didn't argue. The last thing he wanted was to try to carry his pack up that long hill.

Midmorning the next day he was packing when he heard the stairs creak and there was a knock on his door.

"*Adelante,*" he said and looked up.

Maria Elena entered. He froze, looking at her with a pair of underpants in his hand. She gently shut the door.

"Hi," she said softly.

She looked terrible. Her hair was well-combed and her braid was thick and tight. Her simple skirt and sweater were neat and clean. But her eyes and her face; it looked like she had not slept for a week.

"You look awful."

She smiled faintly.

"I know. I have not slept so well lately."

"Me too."

"Tomás, I am so sorry. And I can...I do," she blurted out, "respect you. I should not..."

He threw the underwear down and rushed to her. He put a finger on her lips to silence her.

"No, No. I am the one who is sorry, *querida.* I was so dumb and irresponsible. I have no excuse. But I promise you, I swear to you, I will never, ever do anything like that again."

He pulled her to him and held her close. God, she was so precious!

"Tomás...it is...that I do not know what I would have done if you had been killed. I just cannot imagine my life without you now."

She was crying softly. He could feel the tears on his neck. They held each other until he took her shoulders and gently pushed her from him. He looked at her.

"I am so thankful you came. I couldn't think straight and I felt so terrible. I thought you never wanted to speak to me again. But," he said nodding towards his pack, "you could have saved yourself a trip. I am going back to Cufeo today on the midday bus."

She brushed away the tears that remained on her cheeks.

"I know. Pablo sent word yesterday. That is why I am here....to walk up with you."

There was no longer a knot in his stomach. He was suddenly happy again. Everything was all right. Thank God.

"Then I hope you will be patient with me. It may take a little longer than usual. I am not walking so fast these days."

She reached up and fastened a shirt button that he
had missed.

"I do not care about that, Tomás."

She looked at him.

"Time does not matter when I am with you."

He thought back to when they had returned from
Santiago and walked up the hill together. He had been
so amazed at how quickly they had arrived at her gate.
She was right. Time was irrelevant when they were
together.

"I feel the same way, Maria Elena; exactly the same
way."

He cheerfully followed the doctor's orders. He
stayed off of Lobo and Salton for ten days which gave
him plenty of time to spend with Maria Elena. He
weeded and mulched her garden and helped with little
chores. He repaired this and that, and was surprised to
find that he was really pretty good with his hands. He
took many long walks with her. As the days passed, he
got stronger, and was able to help Ramon split wood
and with the food distributions. And Kurt was good to
his word. Shortly after Tomás returned from Valdivia,
Kurt began shooting grades and flagging the new road.
A large bulldozer and front-end loader were trailered
in and two dump trucks started hauling material.

The roadwork became quite an attraction. People
stopped on their way to and from the bus to watch.
Some came down out of the hills only for that reason.
The *campesinos* with oxcarts showed their respect and
gratitude by detouring the work area without being
told, going way around so that they would not be in the
way. Once the steep section of road was completed,
the work progressed quickly up the hill. Maria Elena
and other women began to show up where the road
crew was working, bearing *empanadas,* homemade

cheese, and fresh bread. Sometimes, if the crew was working in front of a farm, a señora would bring out hot soup. The road crew was doing a super job, and Tomás believed that the good will of the community had a lot to do with it. Kurt lunched several times at the Montoya farm and also at Ramon's. He and Kurt had become good friends.

As the work approached the school, the *Profesor* sometimes took his students down to watch the trucks, bulldozer, and loader. Oxcarts with firewood and charcoal descended from Casa Blanca, La Paloma, and Lote Once, and orderly piles began to sprout up near the school in anticipation of the firewood trucks coming up the new road. It was all very exciting. By the middle of the summer a large grader was trucked in and began to put on the final touches. The Road Committee decided to celebrate the new road with a ribbon-cutting ceremony and an *asado* at the school. They discussed it with Kurt and he was all for it. With some of the money remaining in the Committee's account, Maria Elena and Manuel bought supplies in town. Don Pedro located the lambs to roast—all of which were donated. Women from all around Cufeo contributed food, and there would be sweet *chicha* and wine. It would not be as big as the fundraising *fiesta*, but there would be a lot to eat and drink. And it would be free.

The weather was good and there was a big turnout. A long ribbon had been tied to stakes on either side of the road just before the junction to Casa Blanca and La Paloma. When the roadwork had been finished, the grader had been parked behind the school, but for the celebration it was moved to the middle of the soccer field and was decorated with brightly-colored bunting and streamers. It attracted all of the young boys like flies to sugar. Putting the grader on display had been Maria Elena's idea.

A V.I.P. area had been set up on the school deck, with tables and chairs for Kurt, the road crew and their families, and the Road Committee. A reporter and photographer were coming and Manuel, impeccably dressed again, had of course lobbied to cut the ribbon. A small caravan of INDAP vehicles and a few firewood trucks had arrived and stopped in front of the ribbon. Tomás was happy to see that it looked like the whole road crew had come. Kurt said a few words and Manuel waxed eloquent for too long, causing members of the crowd to good-naturedly tell him to get on with it.

They cut the ribbon with a pair of sheep shears. Afterwards, the crowd separated into small groups and headed off to get something to eat. Some of the children, including Javier and Alex, helped to serve food to those sitting on the school deck. Tomás wandered around the crowd, happy and proud for his role in the project. Everywhere he went he was greeted and brought into the conversation. Because of soccer, reforestation, and the road, he knew almost everyone and he considered many to be friends. For the first time in his life, he felt like he was part of a community. His relationship with Maria Elena was probably the biggest reason for this. It had allowed him to turn the corner. He was no longer on the outside looking in.

One clear evening, Maria Elena and Tomás took a walk to a favorite spot behind her house where the land sloped downhill and there was a great view of the distant hills and volcanoes. They sat close together on the short-cropped grass, leaning against a huge half-stump. It had a natural curve that comfortably fit their backs and they liked to come here to sit and talk. It was very peaceful.

They did not talk much tonight but they were totally comfortable in their silence. It was amazing, though, how often their thoughts were in sync. One of them would start to say something and the other would exclaim, I was just thinking that. How did you do that? And they would laugh. This evening, though, Tomás thought he would take her by surprise.

"Maria Elena…"

"Yes Tomás?"

She looked so beautiful with the evening's golden light on her face. She had been inspecting her braid which she always draped over her front when they were leaning against the stump.

"If I ask you a hypothetical question, would you give me a hypothetical answer?"

"Sure, why not? Ask me."

"After the Peace Corps, if I could figure out a way to make a decent living here that would somehow enable me to live in Cufeo… and enable me to buy some land…as near as possible to Juan…If I were able to do that…..and this is hypothetical remember…then could you……would you…..Maria Elena, would you marry me then?"

She tried to look serious, like she was thinking really hard, but the corners of her mouth were twitching. He was pretty sure that she was playing with him. But, then again, he wasn't absolutely sure. Whatever she was doing, she certainly took her sweet time to answer him.

Finally, she said, "Now this is only hypothetical, right Tomás?"

"Right," he said nervously.

"Well, if it is only hypothetical, then yes, Tomás, hypothetically, I would marry you."

Her eyes were dancing.

He looked out to the volcanoes for a second. Taking a deep breath he turned back to her.

"And, Maria Elena…"

"Yes, Tomás?"

"Maria Elena, what if my question were not hypothetical?"

"Then my answer would not be hypothetical either. And my answer would be the same. Of course I will marry you, you idiot! Why has it taken you so long to ask?"

With that she launched herself onto his lap, and they grabbed each other and started rolling around in the grass like two wrestlers. He was so happy he could die. He knew she was too because when he finally kissed her, their teeth clunked because they were smiling and laughing so much. They started rolling around again until he was a little out of breath. Maria Elena noticed and called it quits. They returned to the stump and cuddled like the two young lovers they were. No, he thought. Make that the two young *novios* they were!

As they talked, he felt it necessary to repeat that he would figure out some way to make a living for them after the Peace Corps. He already had some ideas. Maria Elena shook her head. She was not worried about that in the least. At dusk they decided to go up to the house. Maria Elena was excited and wanted to tell Juan right away. They stood and brushed the grass and dirt off of each other and headed up, hand in hand.

Muchacho met them near the garden and followed as far as the porch. Dogs, even Muchacho, were never allowed inside. They found Juan sitting in his chair, mending a soccer shoe by kerosene light. Tomás guessed that they had a look about them because Juan immediately put the shoe down and was silent. Juan probably knew what was coming, but his face was a mask. Maria Elena and Tomás had agreed that Tomás should tell him.

Tomás cleared his throat while Maria Elena walked over and sat at the dining table.

"Don Juan, Maria Elena and I have become engaged. We want to marry and we would like your blessing."

Juan tried to put on a good face, but was having a tough time. He was about to say something, but Tomás continued.

"And I want you to know that we are going to live here in Cufeo—with you for awhile if that is okay—until we can find our own property, which we both hope will be nearby. And I will never take your sister away to the States. You have my word on that."

Juan's grin was immediate and huge. For someone with a bad leg, he sure got out of that chair fast to shake Tomás's hand and give his sister a big hug and kiss on the cheek.

He limped quickly back to Tomás and said, "This is wonderful news. I am not surprised that you have decided to marry, but I am so happy that you will stay here in Cufeo. I have been so worried that you would take her away. But this is perfect and I am very happy for you, Don Tomás...and for my sister...and for me also."

"Don Juan...?"

"Yes, Don Tomás."

"If I am going to be your brother-in-law, do you think I could call you Juan and you could call me Tomás now?"

"Yes Tomás, my brother. We can do that."

They gave each other a full-blown *abrazo* with Juan exuberantly thumping his back. Tomás grimaced a little more from reflex than pain, and was glad he had healed properly. When they shook hands at the end of the *abrazo* and turned as one to Maria Elena, she was beaming at them and obviously could not be happier—even though tears were streaming down her face.

CHAPTER SEVENTEEN

El Casamiento (The Wedding)

The end of the summer had been hot and dry, enabling trucks to venture high up above Caman into the more remote areas for hardwood sawlogs. Oxen pulled the logs to clearings where they were loaded by hand from rough ramps built into side slopes. Often the trucks would travel in tandem, in case there were any problems. Two heavily loaded trucks now descended in low gear, and Maria Elena's and Tomás's horses shied from the staccato backfiring.

The wedding date had been set and was only a few weeks away. They were on their way to the *copihue* clearing for a picnic and were fine-tuning their wedding plans along the way. They would be married at the clearing in a small private ceremony. They would say their vows in a *ramada* that Tomás would build on the broad shelf that looked out to the waterfall and Puntiagudo. Oso would be their best man. He was working now for the Peace Corps in Paraguay as an Assistant Director. He had written back and said he was honored and wouldn't miss it for the world. Tomás planned to buy the finest *huaso* hats he could find for all the men in the wedding party. They had asked a priest from Paillaco to marry them. The priest was on a soccer team and had played in several tournaments in Cufeo. He said he would be delighted to ride up into the hills to perform the ceremony.

It was warm, but as they slowly rode down the narrow trail and entered the *alerce* grotto, the temperature dropped noticeably. Here it was cool and pleasant. They hobbled their horses and put little piles of oats on the ground in front of them. Carrying food and *mantas*, they walked to the clearing. When they stepped out onto the ledge from the forest's edge, Tomás was once again struck by the incredible beauty; but this time the *copihue* was in full bloom and it was just like Maria Elena had said—a sea of red. It reminded him of the field of poppies where Dorothy and her companions fell asleep in Oz. He spread their *mantas* under the shade of the hardwood trees. While Maria Elena organized the food, he lay down and put his arms behind his head. He admired the view. The sound of the waterfall was constant and soothing.

Maria Elena lay down beside him and he put an arm out for her to rest her head. They did not say anything as they breathed in the beauty around them. It was perfect. As if by signal, they turned to each other. He tried to communicate what he felt for her—his deep, deep love—with a tender kiss. He felt her melt into him and he kissed her again—with more passion this time. Their hands soon roamed over each other's body. They were so eager and hungry for each other. They touched and caressed until he forced himself to pull away.

"We had better stop, Maria Elena," he managed to say, a little breathlessly. "If we keep this up, I do not know if I could stop again."

She put a finger up to his lips.

"Tomás, it is okay."

He looked at her in disbelief. Was she saying it was all right to continue? To make love?

"But Maria Elena...your honor..."

She moved closer.

"It is all right, *mi amor*. I know you want to do what is right for both me and my family. But the wedding will be soon now. It is okay. And my family expects it too. I am sure they think we have already made love. And they know that you would not compromise me."

She sat up and began to unbutton his shirt. When it was unbuttoned he shifted his body so that she could take it off. They looked at each other. He pulled her head to him and kissed her again, very softly. His eyes went from her face to her shirt. His fingers felt clumsy as he began to unbutton it.

If, in their haste and passion, they were a little out of sync, he attributed it to being the first time. But still, he felt complete—fulfilled and happy. And they had their whole lives to fine-tune their lovemaking. He briefly wondered if they had made a baby as he fell asleep in her arms. He didn't know how long he slept, but he awoke with a smile. He could hear Maria Elena humming happily somewhere nearby. When he opened his eyes, the sight of her took his breath away. She was standing naked with her back to him. As she looked towards Puntiagudo, she was brushing out her hair which came down and covered most of her perfect rear end.

"Maria Elena!" he exclaimed.

She turned smiling at him. My God, he thought. She was his Venus. His lovely dark-haired Venus.

"Your hair," he stammered.

"Did I not tell you I was stubborn?" she asked, still smiling and walking towards him with the brush in her hand.

Her breasts were swaying gently and his eyes were all over her gorgeous body.

"Did I not tell you that the first man to see my hair would be my husband? Well, *mi amor*," she said as she dropped the brush onto a corner of the manta, "you are my husband—we are married now."

She straddled him and, folding her knees so they would take most of her weight, she sat down on his stomach. Smiling seductively, she tipped her head forward and the world was dimmed as her hair cascaded over and around him. Their faces were smiling mirror images. They were in their own private cocoon. He reached out and gently traced her skin with his fingertips from the sides of her waist down the curve of her hips and back up again. Her breasts were just grazing his chest. She leaned forward a little more and lightly kissed him. Her lips lingered briefly on his before she pulled away. She kissed him again, a little longer this time.

"Tomás?"

"Yes," he managed to whisper.

He was very aroused.

"Do you know what *conyugal* means?"

Her voice had a tone he had never heard before. It sounded husky.

"Yes. It is spelled almost the same in English."

She straightened up and with a flip of her head settled her long dark hair behind her, cloaking his erection. His hands went from her hips to her breasts, gently hefting them. He cocked his thumbs and lightly toyed with her dark nipples. They turned hard in an instant.

"Because we are married now," she said softly, "do you not think that a husband should perform his conjugal duties?"

He smiled up at her.

"*Si*, Señora. I most certainly do."

Without taking her eyes off his, she leaned forward and reached for him behind her...

After their love-making, while Maria Elena sliced the bread and cheese, he thought happily that practice does indeed make perfect. It occurred to him that Maria Elena had never brought her brush on one of their outings. In fact, he had never even seen the brush before. He could come to only one conclusion. She had known all along that they would be making love today. She had planned it. He put his hands behind his head and smiled up into the shaded green canopy.

The wedding was quickly approaching and they were still tending to details. Their blood tests were done, and they had taken care of everything that both of their governments required. He received a brief letter from his parents saying that they had not been given enough notice, and had already put money down on a cruise through the Greek islands for that very week. They were sorry to miss his wedding, they added, and sent a generous check as a wedding present. Guilt money, he thought, but just as well. As much as Maria Elena wanted to meet them, he knew that it would have been awkward—especially given the way that his father felt about the marriage. Maria Elena was not surprised, and she had only smiled—sadly, he thought—when he told her about the money.

They decided to have the reception two days after the wedding. That would give Ramon, Juan, and Pablo more time to prepare. They would do all the slaughtering and butchering of several lambs and even a steer.

The reception would be very large. Much of Cufeo had been invited, plus friends—including Kurt—from Valdivia and Paillaco. Besides Oso, the Peace Corps would be represented by the regional rep and his wife, and a half dozen volunteers. Even Maria Elena's spinster aunt from Santiago would be coming.

Maria Elena and he would not be allowed to do anything the day of the reception, but during these last few days they were extremely busy. He was building *ramadas* and outhouses, and sprucing up the pasture behind the house where it would take place. His pet project was laying out perfect *tejo* pits. He thought it would be the natural place for the men to hang out, so he located the pits in front of one of the *ramadas*. He made the boxes rugged and the distance between them could not have been off by more than a millimeter. He raked and manicured the area around them. Maria Elena teased him, saying that she hoped he would not spend his wedding night playing *tejo*.

For her part, Maria Elena organized all the food and recruited several women to help with the cooking. She procured eating utensils and cookware, and took care of the decorations and flowers. She also set up lodging for those who needed it. She went over her lists continually, paying attention to the smallest detail. By evening she was exhausted, and several times she fell asleep with her head on his shoulder as they sat at their stump. Tonight was one of those nights; he hated to disturb her.

"Maria Elena," he whispered, "you should get something to eat and go to bed. Tomorrow will be a long day for both of us."

With her eyes still closed, she nodded sleepily. Tomorrow she would go to Valdivia on a firewood truck, and would meet Miriam at a church to pick up folding chairs. He would leave early on Salton, with Lobo in tow. He was going up to the *copihue* clearing to build their wedding *ramada* and to bring back several burlap bags of *copihue* for the reception. He helped her to her feet and with an arm around each other's waist, they slowly walked up to the house. He kissed her goodnight at the door.

Shortly after sunrise he approached the Montoya farm. Maria Elena was already waiting for him with a pile of burlap bags draped over the gate.

"Good morning, *mi* Señora," he said as he got off of Salton and tied both horses up to the gate.

"Good morning, *mi* Esposo."

He reached out over the gate and pulled her by the shoulders close enough and so that he could kiss her. She reached through the bars to hold his waist.

After they kissed, he said, "I am tired of sleeping alone. I want to see your long beautiful hair again."

She sighed.

"And I want to loosen it for you. Soon, though, *mi querido*; soon you will see my hair every night."

"I cannot wait. And I am tired," he said looking down and trying to be funny, "of this gate they have built to keep us apart."

"You could climb over, you know, and kiss me properly."

"Thank you, Señora, but I will never leave if I do that. When is Hernán coming?" he asked as he freed himself from her arms and took the pile of burlap bags over to Lobo.

Hernán was the owner of the firewood truck that would take Maria Elena in to town. He and his helpers were picking up some wood from behind the school.

"Soon. But we will probably not leave until mid morning."

It took a long time to load those trucks. The truckers tried to get on as much as possible, so their loads were always tightly and efficiently stacked. And since the *carabineros* never weighed the trucks, they were always overloaded.

"Well, do not flirt too much with him on the way to Valdivia. Remember you are a married woman."

"But I have to at least be friendly if I am going to get all these rides."

Maria Elena hardly ever took the bus anymore. She was always finagling rides from the truckers.

"Well, *mi querida, vaya con Dios.* I should be back before dinner," he said as he mounted.

He started to ride away when she said, "Tomás, aren't you forgetting something?"

He reined in Salton and looked back at her. She pulled out a couple of the bars and crossed over to him. He dismounted.

"*Claro que si,*" he said, and took her in his arms for a proper kiss goodbye.

He held her close for a few moments before saying, "I will be thinking of you all day. And I cannot wait until our stump time tonight."

"Me too, *mi amor.* Safe trip and," she smiled as she stepped away, "don't let any mountain lions get you."

He mounted again and headed up toward the school. As he approached the bend in the road that would put him out of sight of the gate, he turned in his saddle. Maria Elena was still there watching him. He waved and she waved happily back.

He hobbled the horses in the *alerce* grotto and shuttled his tools and burlap bags to the clearing. On each return trip he cleared the path of fallen branches and other obstacles. Near the clearing, he cut down four pole-sized trees for corner posts. He situated the *ramada* a little back in the forest from the broad shelf so that he could dig holes for the posts. The open side of the *ramada* faced the shelf and all the beauty beyond.

He was lucky and the digging went quickly—he did not hit a single root or stone. After he had set the poles and tamped dirt around them, he looked at his watch. It was only a little after ten thirty and he figured he would finish in only a couple of hours more—three at the most. There would be no wasted steps. He had built so many of these structures—for the fiesta and now for the reception—that he knew what he was doing.

He was just about to start looking for saplings for the horizontal pieces when a large shadow passed over the clearing. He looked up and there, circling, was a condor. It had to be—nothing else could possibly have that wingspan. It was a hundred and fifty feet or so above him, and was gradually descending in wide circles. It looked as if it was coming down to the clearing.

In ultra-slow motion, he eased backwards, trying to melt into the edge of the forest. He did not want it to see him but he wanted to get a good look at it. It was silently and effortlessly gliding around and down. It did not flap its wings. Its circles were smaller and smaller, and gradually its shadow became more distinct. He could clearly see the up-tilted finger-like feathers at the ends of its tremendous wings, and its bald head. Its neck had white feathers around it like a collar. It swooped very low and seemed to be checking out the clearing. God, he wished Maria Elena could see this. She would never believe it.

It finally landed right in the center of the clearing on a thick mass of *copihue.* The vines sagged under its weight, but held. It settled those huge wings and tucked them in, and began to slowly turn its head as if it were looking for something. It must have been at least four feet tall. When the head was pointed in his direction, it stopped. It was eerie. Tomás could swear that it was looking right at him. It must have seen him, but it wasn't scared. It just stared. It did not move and neither did he. After what must have only been a minute or two—although it seemed much longer—the huge bird suddenly shook its head violently side to side—like it had tasted something bad—and began to unfold its wings and prepared to leave.

Tomás didn't dare breathe. He desperately wished he had a camera. A picture of the tall bird with its massive dark wings extended against the brilliant red backdrop of the *copihue* would have been priceless.

It pushed off, heading downhill, and flapped its wings mightily. After following the downward slope of the clearing, it slowly rose up in the air. As it gained altitude it turned to the east and made a beeline, he supposed, for the Andes. He watched it until it was only a small speck in the sky. But enough of this, he thought. He had better get a move on or he would lose out on some valuable stump time this evening. He picked up his axe and saw and went back into the woods.

After he finished the *ramada* and the tools were loaded, he went back to the clearing and carefully filled several burlap bags with *copihue* vines. He lashed the bags to Lobo who was a study in patience. Finally, he walked back to the clearing for one last look at his handiwork. The *ramada* fit right in and looked like it had been there for a hundred years. He went inside and looked out at the miraculous view. The next time he stood here, he would be saying his vows to Maria Elena. Hard to believe, he thought. He turned and walked quickly back to the horses. He could not wait to tell Maria Elena about the condor.

It was still light as he approached the schoolhouse in Caman. He saw several riders in the distance to his right, coming down the long hill from Casa Blanca. He thought that odd for so late in the day. He also noticed

that Hernán had not made a very big dent in his firewood pile behind the school. When he rounded the
last bend and saw the Montoya gate, he was surprised
that all of the bars had been pulled back. As he rode
up he could see horses hitched everywhere around the
house, and the porch was crowded with somber-look-
ing people. Oh my god, he thought, Juan has had an
accident! He quickly got off of Salton and found a
vacant section of fence to tie both horses. He hurried
over to the porch. From the way the people looked at
him with such sadness, he knew that something bad
had happened.

"What is it?" he asked. "Is Juan okay?"

He did not give them time to answer as he rushed
around the corner. He squeezed past some people and
went through the front door. The room was crowded
too. He saw Juan. He was weeping uncontrollably.
Standing next to him with his arm around his shoulder
was Ramon. Suddenly Tomás was very scared.

"What is it, Juan? What has happened?"

Juan tried to focus through his tears.

"Oh Tomás," he wailed, his chest heaving. "Maria
Elena!"

But he was racked by sobs and could say no more.
He shoved his head into Ramon's chest. Tomás panicked as he looked around furiously and did not see
her. He turned back to Ramon who was looking so
sadly at him.

Tears were streaming down his face too but he
was able to say, "There has been an accident, Tomás.
Hernán's truck lost its brakes on the highway, going
down the long hill to Valdivia. Everyone on the truck
was killed."

People rushed up to him, but he could not hear
what they were saying. It could not be true. He looked
back to Ramon, and from the overwhelming sadness

in his eyes, he could see that there was no doubt. Suddenly he fell down. He did not faint; he was still conscious, and he could see. He just collapsed as if he had been shot. He did not feel any pain. It was as if the life had gone out of his limbs and they could no longer support him. People crowded around him. They wanted to help. But he couldn't hear a word they were saying. Maria Elena. Oh my God. Maria Elena...

He woke up in the early morning in his sleeping bag. He had no idea how he had gotten there. He lay there all day. He felt no thirst or hunger. He felt nothing. That was the right word—nothing. Ramon checked on him several times. He urged him to eat or drink something, but Tomás did not respond. He did not care if he ever got up. His life had been taken away. He was dead, but his body was still here.

He remembered when he first saw her, when she threw him the ball at the tournament. She told him that she laughed with the others when he flailed at the ball in the opening seconds of that first game. But she also said that she could not help but feel his embarrassment, and she was happy for him when he scored the goal later. Then there was the *carrera* when she served him *empanadas* and they first called each other by name. She had seen his terrible loneliness that afternoon, and her heart had gone out to him. He never told her what he tried to do that night—he did not want her to know how weak he had been. He remembered how angry she had been when he spent the night with Lobo in Lote Once. She had begun caring for him way back then, but he hadn't had a clue. Ramon saw it before he did. He visited every time he was with her —returning to their happiest moments again and again. It was like wiggling a loose tooth. It hurt, but he could not stop doing it. He would never see her again except like this—in his memories. At least he had those. Whether or not that was good or bad, he didn't know.

Late in the afternoon of the second day he got out of bed and dressed. He may have gotten up before to pee, but he didn't remember. He drank some of the water that Ramon had left for him, and walked out into the kitchen. Ramon looked up. He was stirring a pot of soup.

He sat down at their little table and asked, "How did it happen?"

Ramon sighed and laid the long-handled wooden spoon across the pot.

"The brakes failed coming down the long hill to Valdivia. That old truck was way overloaded. There was a car behind Hernán, and the driver said that he could see smoke coming from the wheels and he could smell the brakes. He was about to pass the truck when all of a sudden it just took off. It went faster and faster and it caught up with a slower-moving bus. Hernán had to pull out to pass but it was at a curve in the road and he lost control. It looked to the people on the bus that the rear driver's-side wheels went onto the shoulder and the truck tipped. The firewood shifted and the truck rolled over and over and over. It finally struck a large boulder and stopped. There was firewood everywhere, including in the cab, where Hernán was crushed. Maria Elena was thrown out and was crushed by the truck as it rolled. She would have died very quickly, Tomás."

Tomás thought she must have been absolutely terrified.

Ramon added, "If the bus had not been there, they might have made it down."

"When will the service be?"

"Next Saturday." Ramon saw he was not quite sure when that was, and he added, "Three days from now. And there will be no viewing."

Indeed, Tomás thought. How did you put someone back together and make her look pretty after she had been crushed by a truck and pummeled by cordwood? A picture started to form in his mind, and he stood up abruptly to try to shake it. He walked over to the window and peered out through the only two panes that were intact.

"How is Juan?"

"Resting. Don Pedro's Señora gave him an injection. He has been so agitated that we could not leave him alone." Ramon hesitated and then added, "We feared that he might do something drastic."

Who could blame him, Tomás thought. His loss was indescribable. Ramon stood up.

"Will you be all right, Tomás, if I go over there? Pablo and Miriam are there now. The soup is ready if you get hungry."

"I'll be fine, Don Ramon."

"Tomás...You are family. Call me Ramon. Please."

Tomás made an attempt to smile and said, "Agreed, Ramon. Thank you. And thank you for the soup."

"Do you want to come over to see Juan with me?"

"No. I cannot. Not yet."

After Ramon left the house, he sat down weakly at the little table. The soup went untouched.

The weather fit the funeral procession—gray, raw, and dismal—but at least it was not raining. In southern Chile the casket of an adult was taken to the cemetery in a black shrouded carriage, drawn by black horses and followed on foot by the mourners. The driver was dressed in black tails and top-hat. If the funeral were for a child, everything would be white: the carriage, casket, and horses, as well as the clothes of the driver—symbolic of the purity and innocence of a child.

Tomás walked on one side of Juan. Ramon was on his other. They were directly behind the carriage. Miriam and Pablo were behind them. Tomás did not remember how long or where they walked. He only looked at the casket in front of him. They entered the cemetery and followed the carriage as far as it could go. Maria Elena would be placed in a crypt next to her parents. Strange that they too had died on that highway, he thought. The path to the crypt was narrow, and lined with tall cypress trees. Her casket was transferred to a small wagon which Ramon and Pablo pulled along the path. The rest of them followed until they stopped in front of the open crypt. A priest said some words which Tomás ignored. Then Juan, Ramon, Pablo, and he lifted her casket off of the wagon and slid it carefully into the crypt. Juan shut the little door, the mourners placed flowers on the ledge in front, and it was over. Handkerchiefs were put away and the crowd dispersed. There was to be a wake at Pablo's and Miriam's house afterwards.

Tomás remained. He sat down on someone's raised grave and stared at the crypt. Was that it? Was that all there was to it? Bam! Shut the door. Put some flowers in front of it and see you later. He sat there he did not know how long. They locked the gates at night, and at some point he was politely asked to leave by the custodian. As he walked away he thought this was the proper place for her to be buried—next to her parents. But he did not feel her here.

As the days passed, it became more and more obvious to Tomás that he could not stay in Chile. It was too painful; there were too many reminders of her every day. For the next six months he somehow made himself go through all the proper motions for his work, but it was by rote—all the excitement was gone. He took care of the inspections and deliveries. He requested that someone from SAG take over his program for the following year, and a young employee was selected. He seemed eager, and Tomás hoped it would work out. Tomás introduced him to Ramon, gave him his detailed map of Cufeo, and handed him a notebook full of ideas, observations, and suggestions. He introduced him to the bureaucrats in charge of the surplus food at the Municipality, and took him on all the deliveries. Other than hold his hand, Tomás felt that he could do no more. He had done his job adequately.

He visited Lilia a few times in Osorno. The first time he went with the Señora. Lilia had looked better and was going to try to enter school after the summer vacation. The family was hopeful. She was taller and thinner, and reminded him of a spring colt with her long legs. But she didn't smile anymore, and she held on to her mother's hand the entire time that he was there. The last time he went by himself. Lilia panicked when her *abuela* started to leave her alone with him in their living room, and made her stay while she politely talked to Tomás as if he were a stranger. She was scared of him. He rationalized that she was scared of all men now, and wondered what the future held for her. He couldn't help thinking about how he had opened his heart to her. And to Maria Elena. He wondered if he could ever open his heart again. He had been scorched by life and felt covered now by a hard, brittle glaze.

At night in Valdivia, he metamorphosed into someone else. He was the hard-working, responsible volunteer in the day, but night was a different story. He was decadent. Maybe he was developing a permanent problem, but he didn't care. When he had finished buying supplies and taking care of any other business he had, he would go have a beer. By dinnertime he would have had several beers, and then he would drink wine with his dinner. After dinner he would sit and drink and watch men play *cacho,* or walk around looking for new bars to drink in. When they closed he would go to a whorehouse. But it was only once, when he was really, really drunk, that he got laid. At least he thought he did because he woke up in bed with one of the girls. He felt guilty and never returned to that house. Sometimes when he was too drunk to leave, he would offer to pay the going rate for a woman and the room, even though he would sleep alone. Once or twice he was charged, but never after that. Valdivia was not that big of a town and the accident had been big news. The story and photos were all over the front page. The newspaper had said Maria Elena was to have been married in only a few days and that she was to marry a young man from the United States of America who was living in her community and working in reforestation for SAG. It did not take the girls long to figure out he was that person and they felt sorry for him. Mostly, though he spent his time in the whorehouses watching others as they danced, laughed, and enjoyed themselves, hoping that he might vicariously experience some of their frivolity. But that never happened.

Usually once a week, regardless of the weather, he rode up to the *copihue* clearing. He kept up the *ramada* and would sit in it for hours. He felt close to her there. The first time he went, he sat looking out at the *copihue.* Suddenly he remembered the condor. In his grief he had forgotten all about it. He looked down to where it had landed and an odd thought occurred to him. He became excited and decided to go to Valdivia the next day. He went in on the early bus. At the main *carabinero* headquarters, he asked if the time of the accident had been noted in their report. It took them a half hour to find the report. They told him that the watch Hernán had been wearing had stopped at ten twenty-eight. He thanked them and left. He walked to the center of town which was a long way. But he was thinking hard and did not notice.

Maybe it was just a huge coincidence. But maybe not. Psychics and others believed in this sort of thing. Think about it, Tomás. A condor in terrain totally foreign to it. Maria Elena told him that she had never seen one in Cufeo. And it had landed smack dab in the middle of the clearing and looked straight at him—at him!—for the longest time. And he remembered that he had looked at his watch just before he saw its shadow. It had been right around ten thirty. Of course he would never know, it was impossible to know. But he thought that Maria Elena had somehow been in that bird. She had hitched a ride in that condor—a bird that she knew he had so much wanted to see. And she had returned to see him one last time; to say goodbye. He thought about it some more. She had said the *copihue* clearing was like a little piece of heaven on earth to her. Maybe that was it. She had chosen the clearing and the grotto as her heaven. Her spirit was there.

As he walked towards the main plaza, he thought again how much Maria Elena had loved the clearing and her *alerce* trees. It was where they had married, for Christ's sake. He pictured her there, framed by the *copihue.* Oh God. Stop, Tomás! He caught himself. Easy, easy. Don't think about that or you'll lose it—you'll be crying again. Whew. That was close. God, he was such a mess.

He arrived at the Plaza and sat down on a vacant bench in the shade. He was sure of it now: that was where her spirit lived. It certainly was not hanging out in the confinement of that crypt. Her spirit would never have tolerated that—she would have busted out of there in no time. And she had...No! She had never been there. She went straight to the clearing. The beginnings of an idea slowly formed in his mind. He wanted to do something in her memory but hadn't been able to figure out what. But the clearing and the *alerce* had been so special to her. What could be more important or more fitting than to protect those trees and the clearing that she loved so much, forever?

Maybe he could buy that land. He still had his father's check. But how would he go about it? Someone sat down on the bench. He looked over and nodded at an old man. The man smiled back. He had a small bag of cracked corn. The Plaza had beautiful wrought-iron street lamps where the pigeons perched, waiting to be fed—there and on top of the round gazebo. They flew down and landed in front of the bench and the old man tossed them corn. Tomás was soon lost in thought again.

What was the first step? Who could he ask? Someone knowledgeable and capable. Someone he could trust. He sat there thinking for a long time. Finally it came to him. Of course. If he could not help him in this, no one could.

"Kurt," he said out loud and clapped his hands, startling the old man and scaring the pigeons away.

The old man gave him a dirty look. He didn't care. He rushed over to the INDAP office building. He asked the secretary if Kurt was in. He didn't even have time to sit before Kurt was out of his office and standing in front of him.

Kurt had walked with the others in the funeral procession and, before he left the cemetery, he had given Tomás a hug of support. Now, he put an arm around his shoulders and directed him towards his office.

"Come on, let's talk, my friend."

They entered and sat down. Kurt asked how he was doing.

"So-so, Kurt…I…I just miss her so much. I ache for her. Oh God!…"

Tomás started crying. He couldn't help it. Kurt quickly came over and put his hands on his shoulders.

"I know, *hombre*, I know…"

Tomás wiped his eyes.

"I am sorry Kurt. I didn't come here to cry."

When he was under control again, Kurt said, "Don't apologize. It's probably the best thing for you to do… Now, just why are you here?"

Tomás gave his eyes a final wipe with a sleeve.

"Kurt, I want to do something in her memory. I have this idea to buy some land that was very special to her—to us—and protect it forever."

"Forever is a long time, Tomás."

Tomás smiled thinly.

"So is death, Kurt."

Kurt folded his hands on his desk. Tomás continued.

"I think it is owned by the Government, but I am not sure. Is it ever possible to buy land from the Government?"

"Sure, it's done all the time, but not in small parcels. I take it the land is in Cufeo…"

Tomás nodded.

"Come on," he said, pushing himself up from his desk. "Let's go to the map room and see if we can get aerial photos and you can show me exactly where it is. Then we can get the maps and see which parcel it falls in and track down the owner. I know plenty of people whom I can call on for help. And if it is indeed government land, then, unless there is some high-up official who is interested in your particular piece—which I seriously doubt considering it is in Cufeo—I think we can probably find a way to do this."

Kurt was right—it was possible. It was not easy, but through his connections he found a way to pull it off. It took almost five months and would have taken a lot longer if not for a few well-placed bribes. Because it was so remote, the price of the land was cheap—the bribes cost almost as much. The parcel contained two hundred and fifty hectares. After signing the papers, Tomás set up an account, to be administered by Kurt, which would pay the taxes each year. Tomás would be leaving Chile shortly. He had no compunctions about cashing the wedding check in Santiago to pay for all this. He took those dollars down to Valdivia and exchanged them on the black market for as many escudos as he needed for the bribes, the land, and the future taxes. He would use the left over money from his father's check—plus what he had saved—for his travels.

He had quite an itinerary planned. After checking out of the Peace Corps in Santiago, he would return to Valdivia to say his goodbyes. From there he would take the bus-boat trip from Petrohue through the lakes over to Bariloche, Argentina. Then on to Buenos Aires, Uruguay, and to visit Oso in Paraguay. His wire informing Oso of the accident had reached him just in time to cancel his flight. Oso had wired back—he could not believe it—he was devastated—please forgive him, but he would not come to the service—he could no way handle that—he hoped Tomás was okay—please come and see him whenever he could.

From Paraguay he would travel up the coast of Brazil, and then inland, up the Amazon. From there he would go to Columbia and finally to Panama, where he hoped to buy a motorcycle. He planned to ride the motorcycle through Central America and back to the States. It was something he had dreamed of doing ever since he learned he was going to South America. Now, though, he found it difficult to get excited about it. He kept thinking that maybe once he started traveling it would change. He was excited, though, about visiting Oso. Maybe that was because he had known her—who she was and what they had....and what they had lost.

He walked up the road with Ramon. He would be leaving in a few days, and they were returning from a *despedida* dinner at Pablo and Miriam's. It was sad, but thank God no one had cried. They gave him a framed picture of Pablo on horseback in a *huaso* outfit. The frame was made out of leather, and it was the only framed picture in their house. It was a prized photo and a special gift. Pablo did not want to hear his apology for not having something for him. Tomás would miss him and Miriam and the boys. They were family.

They walked up the road where it had been so steep and severely eroded. It was well graded now, and the drainage ditches and culverts had held up well through the winter rain. He thought how ironic it was that Maria Elena had so tirelessly worked for this new road and it was this new road that had enabled Hernán to come up to Caman. If he had not come, she would have taken the bus and....Stop, he told himself. Stop! This was exactly why he had to leave. Everything and everybody reminded him of her, and it just would not let go. He did not know if he would ever get over it, but he knew he couldn't while he was here.

They stopped by Juan's and found him repairing a fence around his pine plantation. He had cobbled up some sort of system so he could stretch and nail the wire taut by himself. It would have gone at least twice as fast with another set of hands. How deeply he must miss his sister. Ramon and Tomás helped him until he finished that section. He still had a lot to do. As the three of them walked up to his house for *onces*, Tomás volunteered to help him during his last few days here. Juan accepted. Said he was a good brother.

They knew he had to leave and so did not try to talk him out of it anymore. He had given Salton and his saddle to Ramon, and Lobo to Juan. Today, the three of them would ride up to the *copihue* clearing, carrying his pack with them. They would leave him there. He was going to camp for the night and then walk down the back side of Lote Once to the tiny town of Reumen, where he would start his trip. He would take a bus to Paillaco and then on to Petrohue.

Flor was going to check on both farms until Juan and Ramon returned in the afternoon. She was at the farm while Ramon and Tomás saddled Lobo and Salton. Juan was already on his horse, waiting for them. Tomás saw him look at Flor more than once. As he tightened Lobo's cinch, he smiled. Now that would be an interesting development.

They mounted and rode out through the gate. They were silent for most of the ride, thinking whatever they were thinking. Juan occasionally joked about this or that, but his heart was not in it. They arrived at the grotto and walked out to the *ramada*. Tomás told them about the condor and they too thought that something extraordinary had taken place. Juan agreed that, if spirits do exist, then hers would be here. Earlier Tomás had told him that he and his sister had made love at the clearing. Juan was glad. Tomás thanked them when they said they would keep an eye on the property as much as possible. They had been very surprised when he told them that he had bought the two hundred and fifty hectares.

It was time to say good-bye. Juan and Ramon had their chores and, besides, it was hard to stand there, wait-

ing for the inevitable. Tomás walked back to the grotto
with them and patted Lobo, telling him not to be too *lobo*
for Juan. He also patted Salton and told him that he was a
great champion and now he had a real *huaso* to ride him.

He turned to his two friends. This was about as
tough as anything he ever had to do—saying goodbye
to these two men. He loved them. All of them were
emotional, but they got through it somehow. After the
abrazos, they mounted. Juan asked him if he thought
he would ever return. He said he didn't know. As Juan
and Ramon rode out of the grotto, he fastened his pack
back onto its frame and carried it to the clearing. He
worked a little on the *ramada*. He wanted it in perfect
shape when he left. He set his sleeping bag out and sat
on it for a very long time, looking at where the condor
had landed. He laid out a simple dinner of *empanadas,*
fresh bread, and Ramon's rubbery white cheese that he
liked so much. He drank some water. Much better for
you, Tomás, than all that beer and wine, he thought.
After dinner he walked back to the grotto and admired
the grandfather *alerces* one last time. He turned in just
before dark, wondering if Maria Elena would be angry
with him for camping out here alone.

The next morning he was up early and quickly
organized his pack. He was not hungry. He sat for
awhile, watching the sunlight gradually bring everything to life. He had never seen Puntiagudo like this at
sunrise. It was breathtaking. The early morning light
softened the stark, rugged volcano and gave its snowy
sharp peak a golden tinge. The *copihue* went from dull
to vivid red as the sun hit it. He almost expected the
condor to come out of the east and land on the *copihue* to say good-bye—but of course it didn't. If Maria
Elena's spirit were here, he knew she could not be happier—she was in heaven. He stood up and took one
long last look around.

Finally, he said softly, "Maria Elena, *mi querida*, if you can hear me... please, please forgive me for leaving. With all my heart I do not want to go. But I am not strong enough to stay."

He shouldered his pack, turned, and left the clearing.

ABOUT THE AUTHOR

David Mather served in Peace Corps Chile from 1968-1970. His experiences there provided the background for *One For The Road.* He and his wife now split their time between their homes in the woods of New Hampshire and in a small fishing village on Florida's gulf coast.

CPSIA information can be obtained
at www.ICGtesting.com
Printed in the USA
LVOW04s0231171215
466948LV00020B/672/P